Dawson: Blond and handsome, he has it all— and doesn't know it. His passion is to be a film director, but somehow real life just won't follow the script.

Joey: Slender and dark-haired, she's shared everything a best friend can share with her buddy Dawson—sleepovers, jokes, and the story of her life. But she's not a kid anymore and neither is he.

Pacey: He talks big and he's burning to grow up fast. Now someone's in town who could teach him everything he wants to know.

Jen: She's sweet and mature and Dawson's crazy about her. But she's running from a big secret back in the city. Maybe this new girl in town is too much for Dawson to handle.

DAWSON'S CREEK™

Dawson's Creek™

Omnibus 1

The Beginning of Everything Else, *Long Hot Summer* and
Shifting Into Overdrive were first published 1998 by Pocket Books,
a division of Simon & Schuster Inc.,
1230 Avenue of the Americas, New York, NY 10020

This omnibus edition published 2000 by Channel 4 Books
an imprint of Macmillan Publishers Ltd
25 Eccleston Place, London SW1W 9NF
Basingstoke and Oxford

www.macmillan.co.uk

Associated companies throughout the world

ISBN 0 7522 7149 0

5 7 9 8 6 4

A CIP catalogue record for this book is available from
the British Library.

Printed by Mackays of Chatham PLC

Dawson's Creek™
Omnibus 1

The Beginning of Everything Else
By Jennifer Baker

Long Hot Summer
By K. S. Rodriguez

Shifting Into Overdrive
By C. J. Anders

Based on the television series "Dawson's Creek"™ created by Kevin Williamson

4 BOOKS

The Beginning of Everything Else

Chapter 1

Outside the window of the big rambling white house, the water shimmered silver in the hazy moonlight. Inside, the TV cast its own glow in Dawson Leery's bedroom.

"I'll be ri-ight he-ere," E.T. promised on the large television screen.

Joey Potter stared at the TV, stretched out on her stomach on the big bed next to Dawson amid the sea of pillows and half-empty bags of Doritos and Oreo Double Stufs.

"I love this movie," Joey gushed. "This won the Oscar, didn't it?" She'd watched it a bunch of times, but she still hated to see it end.

"*Gandhi* won," Dawson corrected her. "Spielberg was robbed," he added with absolute conviction. "This was before he outgrew his Peter Pan syndrome." As the credits rolled, Dawson leveled the remote at the screen and hit the rewind. The local news anchors appeared on the screen, a his-and-hers set of pearly whites and lots of perfectly coiffed hair.

"But *Gandhi*?" Joey said. "Why give an Oscar to a movie you can't even sit through?" She didn't wait for Dawson to answer. She knew he agreed with her. "New do?" she asked, checking out the anchorwoman. It was weird, seeing *her* on TV every night. After all these years, Joey still hadn't quite gotten over it.

"Yeah. She likes big hair," Dawson said.

Joey turned her gaze away from the TV and foraged for her sneakers. The woman wore a Colgate smile. "Back to you, Bob," she told her co-anchor.

"Her hair must weigh a lot." Joey located one sneaker. Then the other. "How does she walk upright?"

Dawson laughed. Joey stuffed her feet into the sneakers and stood up.

"Where ya going?" Dawson asked.

"Home."

"Spend the night," Dawson said matter-of-factly.

"Can't," Joey answered, hoping she sounded just as matter-of-fact. She turned her face away from Dawson, not quite able to look at him.

"You always spend the night." Dawson's words had an edge of surprise.

"Not tonight."

"Why not?"

Joey moved toward the open window. She could

2

feel the warm late-summer breeze that toyed with the parted blue-and-gray curtains. Didn't Dawson get it? Didn't he see?

She whirled back around to face him—his strong face, his thick, wavy blond hair, his full mouth and deep-set, intelligent hazel eyes—intelligent about movies and stories and drama, at least. But this was *real* life. Dawson had always been able to read her like a script. And she him. So why did she have to spell this one out for him?

"I just don't think it's a good idea for me to sleep over anymore, you know?"

Dawson's solid, square jaw tightened. "No, I don't know! You've been sleeping over since we were seven. It's Saturday night, come on!"

"Things change, Dawson—evolve." Joey stressed this last word, hoping to make her point. "Go with it."

"What are you talking about?"

He was hopeless.

"Sleeping in the same bed was fine when we were kids," Joey began. "But we're fifteen now."

Dawson arched an eyebrow. "Yeah."

"We start high school on Monday."

"Yeah . . ."

Okay, she was going to have to cut to the chase. There just wasn't any other choice. "And I have breasts."

Joey's words hung in the humid air for a second. "What?" Dawson gave a startled laugh.

"And you have genitalia," Joey went on.

3

"I've always had genitalia." Dawson didn't miss a beat this time.

"But there's more of it now," Joey insisted.

She saw Dawson swallow. Okay. Maybe he was hearing her now.

"How do you know?" he asked.

In too deep. It was time for this little conversation to end. "Long fingers," Joey tossed out as she grabbed the window frame and slid one leg out the window. If Dawson didn't get it, she did. And it was time for her to leave.

"Whoa, Joe. Don't hit and run. Explain yourself," Dawson insisted.

Did she have to hit him over the head? Joey reeled herself back inside but stayed near the window. "I just think our emerging hormones are destined to alter our relationship and I'm trying to limit the fallout."

Joey watched her message finally get through. Dawson's eyes opened just a little. He pressed his lips together, but he recovered fast. "Your 'emerging hormones' aren't starting to get a thang for me, are they?"

Well, no. Couldn't be. It was just that she lived in the real world—unlike some people. And she could admit it—she noticed the cut of his jaw in a way she never had before. Noticed his . . . well, his long fingers. Noticed that she noticed. Even though this was Dawson. Same old same old from time immemorial. Or at least from second grade.

"A 'thang'?" Joey volleyed back. "Oh, so typical. No, I'm not getting a thang for you, Dawson. I've known you too long. I've seen you burp, barf, pick your nose, scratch your butt. I'm not getting a thang for you."

"Then what's the problem?"

Joey felt an electric trill of annoyance. "We're changing, and we have to adjust or the male-female thing will get in the way."

Dawson's irritation mirrored hers. "What is with the When Harry Met the Eighties crap? It doesn't apply to us. We transcend it."

"And how do we do that?"

"By going to sleep. I'm tired," Dawson said.

Right. Close your eyes to it, and it will go away. "That's avoidance," Joey told him, turning back to the window.

"No, it's proof. Proof that we can still remain friends despite any mounting sexual theoretics," Dawson said.

Go to sleep. Lie down together and go right to sleep. Nothing more. In the same bed, but separate. Proof. Well, maybe that *was* one way of showing they were friends and friends only. Maybe Dawson actually had a point there. Or maybe Joey just didn't really want to go home all that awfully. Things were better at Dawson's house than at hers. Better with Dawson. Had been ever since . . .

"I don't think it works that way Dawson," Joey said uncertainly. She felt the breeze blowing off the creek and through the window.

Dawson did an exaggerated back-flop onto his bed. "C'mon, don't get female on me, Joey. I don't wanna have to start calling you Josephine."

The sound of that name on Dawson's lips—it went straight to Joey's gut. Do not process through the brain. Do not pass go. "Josephine this," she said, taking a flying dive at Dawson. She landed smack on top of him and slugged him in the shoulder.

"Hey!" He seized her arms, his hands circling her slender forearms.

Joey shook them off.

Dawson moved in again, grabbing her in a bear hug and rolling her underneath him.

Joey struggled, her laugh slightly breathless. Dawson had her pinned down. His face was inches away from hers. Joey stopped struggling and looked up at him. "Okay, I give." Dawson grew suddenly still as well.

He flopped back down next to her. "We're friends, okay? No matter how much body hair we acquire. Deal?"

"Deal," Joey agreed. Of course they were friends. This was Dawson. She pushed her sneakers off and heard them fall to the floor with a soft thud.

"And we don't talk about this again, deal?" Dawson said.

"You got it," Joey said, staring up at the white ceiling. She certainly didn't want to do this one over again.

"Cool," Dawson said.

"Cool," Joey echoed with a note of uncertainty. She turned onto her side, away from Dawson, but she wasn't comfortable. She curled up, then stretched out again. Dawson was also squirming around next to her. She felt him moving around, pulling at the sheet.

"Good night, Joey," he said. He hit the light switch. The room went shadowy, but the moonlight filtering in through the curtains seemed to grow brighter.

"Night, Dawson," Joey answered.

She still couldn't get comfortable, but she willed herself to lie still. As her body finally started to relax, Dawson broke the silence.

"Why did you have to bring this up, anyway?" he asked.

Chapter 2

Joey was stretched out on the dock in a deck chair, her long, slim, gently bronzed body in white shorts, a light shirt open over her plaid bikini top, her long, dark hair loose in the breeze. The last sun of summer warmed her bare skin. The air smelled of salt water and the warm wood of the dock at the edge of the creek. A couple of guys raced by on Sunfishes, their sails bright against the blue sky.

It was a picture-perfect afternoon. A picture-perfect setting. One of the loveliest parts of a lovely town—a salty inlet winding in from the ocean and widening at this point into a gentle lagoon complete with sea grasses and a gray heron spreading its majestic wings and rising up off the water.

Joey was lying near Dawson's oversize but unpretentious house, but her eyes were closed to it as she took in the sun.

Suddenly the dock shook. Joey's eyes flew open as a slimy slate-green mega-huge sea monster split the surface of the water and rose up to grab her!

She let out a terrified scream. It was trying to pull her into the water! She struggled, straining every muscle in her body. She tucked her arm in close to her side and then let rip with a sharp elbow to the creature's belly.

The sea creature let out a yelp and sank back into the muddy depths but managed to take Joey along, chair and all.

"No! No! Cut!" Dawson yelled, pulling back from the camera mounted on its tripod. "Cut! Wait a second. You gotta wait three counts for that."

Out in the water, Joey shot a furious look at the sea creature as it pulled itself up onto the dock. She pushed him away and got out before he did.

"If you attack her before the scene is established, it's not scary," Dawson yelled. Now he'd never get that shot.

"He did it again. He grabbed my ass!" Joey yelled.

"Like you even have one," the sea creature shot back. He peeled his mask off—the mask Dawson had spent all week working on. Pacey's face appeared—his mouth open, as slack and gangly as the rest of him, his short, dark brown hair wet.

Dawson took a few quick steps toward them. "Guys, guys, you're killing me. We're way behind schedule. I'm never going to make the festival. I've got two months." These were supposed to be his best friends. "Hel-*lo!* Cooperation!"

"I'm not playing the victim," Joey mumbled.

Pacey pointed a green-gray rubber claw at her. "It's Meryl Streep's fault," he said, nonplussed. "I'm doing the best I can."

Joey spat out her annoyance. "Bite me!" she told Pacey disgustedly.

Dawson heard a car pulling up behind him, tires on the gravel driveway of his neighbors' house. He glanced over his shoulder as a yellow cab pulled to a stop.

He turned back to his camera for a moment, took a fresh video cartridge from the camera bag at his feet, and began to reload. His fingers worked as quickly as possible.

"Guys, from the top," he said, firmly. "And make me believe it. I want the truth."

He shot them a stern look, but Pacey was staring right past him. "Well, well . . . my mouth drops," Pacey said.

Dawson looked back at the taxi, then turned his whole body. A girl had stepped out. Her short, cream-colored sundress revealed her great curves. A light sea breeze blew her shoulder-length, honey-blond hair away from her delicate round face, and Dawson could see that she was way pretty. Beautiful. He felt his breath catch.

She smiled at them and came right over—no timid ready-to-fade flower, either. She made her way down the dock. A locket on a dainty gold chain around her neck winked in the sun.

Dawson took a quick look back at Pacey and Joey. Pacey was staring at the beautiful girl, as dumbstruck as—a sea creature. But Joey was looking right at Dawson. He arched an eyebrow at her and turned back toward the girl.

"Hey, you guys!" The girl's greeting was open and friendly.

Pacey jumped right in without a breath. "How's it going? I'm Pacey." He grabbed her hand and shook it.

Dawson followed. "I'm—"

"Dawson. I know. We've met before," the girl said. They shook, too. Her hand was warm. "I'm Jen."

Jen. The house next door. Whoa! "Okay, you're the granddaughter from New York," Dawson said. "You look so . . . different." Reluctantly he released her hand.

Dawson felt Joey step up beside him. "Puberty," she deadpanned. Dawson didn't know if he was supposed to feel embarrassed. "Hi, I'm Joey," she continued. "I live down the creek, and we've never met. Ever." Whatever.

"So are you just visiting?" Dawson asked Jen. He noticed the cabdriver unloading a couple of large suitcases. They looked as if they could hold a lot of sundresses.

"My grandfather's aorta collapsed, and they had to replace it with a plastic tube," Jen recited. "My parents sent me to help out for a while."

Yeah, Dawson had heard about the old guy next

door. Pretty serious stuff. So Jen might be around for some time. "So you'll be going to school here?"

"Yeah," Jen confirmed. "Tenth grade." She had a nice easygoing smile.

"Cool!" Pacey jumped in, overeager. "Us, too."

Jen nodded. A flock of seagulls passed overhead, screaming noisily as they wheeled and darted. "Well . . . Grams must be waiting," Jen said. "I should go. It was nice to meet you, guys. See ya at school."

"If not sooner," Dawson heard himself saying.

Jen smiled again. At him. Her eyes stayed on him for an extra beat. Dawson felt a wave of pleasurable embarrassment. Man, the girl was cute. She turned around and headed for the gate in the neat low fence that separated her grandparents' yard from Dawson's.

He watched her move toward the porch of the elegant white house with the blue trim. She looked back once and gave a last little wave before going inside.

Dawson continued to stare at the deserted porch.

"If not sooner," he heard Joey mimic before she brushed past him and took off in the other direction.

"Nice," Pacey commented, also still staring at the house next door.

"All right," Dawson agreed.

Pacey draped the wet monster suit over the slender wood railing of Dawson's back porch. It glistened in the sun like the wet suit of some demented diver.

Well, thought Dawson distractedly, Pacey can be pretty demented, sometimes. We got that much right. His mind was half on a bunch of things—his movie, Joey's weirdness lately—but at the same time it was totally on one thing: his new neighbor.

"Think she's a virgin?" Pacey asked. "You gonna nail her?"

Dawson was used to Pacey's bluntness. Its shock value was lost on him. He let himself in through the screen door and stashed his camera equipment in a corner of the mudroom. "We just met," he told Pacey evenly as his friend followed him inside.

"And a wasted moment it was." Pacey didn't let up. "Greater men would be nailing right now."

"Tact," Dawson said. "Look it up."

Before Pacey could parry, an impressive crash sounded from deep inside the house—some heavy object meeting its death as it struck a hard floor. Dawson and Pacey exchanged a quick glance and took off in the direction of the noise. Through the green-walled foyer, down the hall, and into the open, sun-drenched heart of the house. At the far end, the all-new kitchen gleamed in stainless steel and bright tile. The spacious living area rose two stories to the dark rough-hewn rafters that crossed the solid plaster-white ceiling at intervals. Another staircase led from a corner up to the second-floor landing that overlooked the room.

In front of the brick fireplace a man and a woman

were pressed together atop the coffee table, kissing passionately. Dawson froze, Pacey by his side.

"Oh, no," Dawson moaned. "Mom . . ." he protested.

His parents pulled apart quickly and looked up at him, and his mother rolled off the table and onto the floor. Busted!

Between her and the big-screen TV, a Mexican water jug lay broken, shards of terra-cotta littering the smoothly finished wide-plank floors.

Next to him, Dawson knew Pacey was staring, agape. Dawson could feel himself turning three shades of cooked lobster.

"Oh, hi, son," his father said sheepishly.

"Whoops," his mother said, sitting up and looking at him. The face of the local news, Mrs. Leery—otherwise known as dear old mom. She straightened her blouse and made a pass at patting her hair into place—the new do Joey had noticed the other night on TV.

"Your mom and I," said his father, "were . . ."

". . . just discussing whether or not . . ." his mother continued, groping to ad lib.

". . . we needed a new coffee table," Mr. Leery finished, as if he might even believe it.

Mrs. Leery gave an embarrassed laugh.

Mr. Leery stood up. "Hi, Pacey."

"Hi, Mr. Leery. Mrs. Leery," Pacey said brightly. Dawson sneaked a look at him. He was grinning from ear to ear, loving every minute of Dawson's shame. Toast. That's what he was if he said a word about this later.

"Hi, Pacey," Dawson's mother said from the floor. "Don't look so red, Dawson. It could be worse."

Right. Good morning to you, too, Mom. At least their clothes were still on. Maybe that was what his mom meant.

"I really love your new hairdo, Mrs. Leery," said Pacey.

"Oh, thank you, Pacey." Mom was recovering fast. And Pacey—the guy couldn't stop staring. And smirking.

"I thought you guys had to work today," Dawson's dad said.

"We're running late," Dawson replied. As if he was the one who needed to explain.

"Me too," his mother said. "I should get going." She stood up and straightened her skirt. Then she glanced over at Dawson's father. She gave him a private smile. "Okay, Mr. Man Meat, I'll see you later." She bent down and gave him a kiss. Really getting into it.

Dawson was aghast. He wished he could blast the swamp-licking grin right off Pacey's face.

"Oh, Mom . . ."

Joey pulled twice on one oar, then straightened out a little with a light pull on the other. She expertly steered the little rowboat up the creek toward her dock. You couldn't help noticing the difference between her house and Dawson's. At least she couldn't, even though she didn't want to.

It wasn't so much that her house was smaller—

though it was, a little. And the view of the creek here in the marshes was just as pretty, all blue-green water and waving grasses and the coveted privacy of a spot with not a single other house in sight. But the gray shingles of the low ranch-style house were worn, and the paint was peeling off the trim. You could see that the roof needed work, too. True, Bess and Bodie had brightened up the yard with lots of plants and flowers and homemade touches, but the place needed some professional care.

Joey tried to ignore the way the house looked as she hopped out of the boat and tied it to the dock. She made her way toward the wide front porch just as the door flew open.

Out stepped a tall, fit black man, in his early twenties. Handsome, an open smile on his face. He had on a crisp white T-shirt and carried a heavy cooking pot carefully in one hand, a wooden spoon in the other. "Just the victim I'm looking for," he said, coming toward Joey with the spoon pointed at her.

"No, Bodie!" Joey put a hand up. "Not again."

"I'm being tested on this one," he pleaded. "Just a taste."

Actually, it smelled good. Some garlic-rich, toma-toey potion. Joey obliged him. It was delicious. A smooth, velvety puree with bits of some pillowy pastalike thing that melted in her mouth.

"Orgasmic," she said. "Where's Bess?"

"Right here." Her sister's voice preceded her. Bess moved out onto the porch with slow steps, a hand on the small of her back, her belly hugely swollen with pregnancy. Somehow she still managed to come off looking good in her simple but elegant long dress, and necklace of tiny freshwater pearl beads. Ever the beautiful older sister.

The look on her face, however, was another story. And in her hand was a rumpled blue T-shirt—the one Joey had borrowed out of her sister's drawer the other day. Oops.

"If you want to wear my things, fine," Bess said harshly. "They're fairly useless to me at this point. But that means you put them back where you found them. Got it?"

"Got it," Joey said flatly. Okay, she knew Bess was tired. Scared, probably. You could see it in her eyes, and it made the seven-year difference between them seem bigger than ever. But Bess had no excuse for taking everything out on Joey. This had to be the longest pregnancy on human record.

"I am way too pregnant to be digging underneath your bed," Bess chastised.

"So stay out of my room," Joey shot back. "Got it?" She pushed past her sister and headed toward the door.

"I'm gonna knock her silly, I swear it," she heard Bess tell Bodie. She turned to shoot her sister a look. But Bodie was approaching Bess with the spoon now.

"Here, try this," he said easily, soothingly.

As Bess bent down to take a taste, Bodie leaned in and lingeringly kissed the curve of her neck.

"Orgasmic," Joey thought she heard her sister say.

Chapter 3

It was starting to quiet down in town. Finally. Some leftover tourists were still browsing in the shops, purchasing T-shirts with oysters printed on them and toy plastic sharks at an end-of-season discount, but there was a little more breathing room, and more of the faces were familiar. The S.S. Icehouse wasn't quite empty, but the waitresses were taking it easy, finding smiles that had been buried in the sand all through August. For a town whose unspoiled, undiscovered charm was its draw, an awful lot of people managed to discover it during the summer months. Now the postcard-pretty town of Capeside belonged to the Capesiders again.

Inside the video store Pacey stood behind the counter logging in the returns—all the big summer hits. Next to him, in a matching blue Screenplay

Video vest, Dawson was doing the same. A customer wandered around the new releases.

"Hey." Pacey couldn't resist razzing Dawson. "If your dad is Mr. Man Meat, does that make you Man Meat Junior or Man Meat the Second?" That scene in Dawson's living room had been great, Pacey gloated. Just great. Dawson couldn't have done it any better in one of his movies.

"They're gonna have to drag the creek to find your body," Dawson threatened.

Suddenly Nellie appeared in the comedy aisle, waving a video. Bad timing. Pacey was just getting started on Dawson. Of course, Nellie was always bad timing, no matter what was going down. A self-styled starlet with unnaturally blond ringlets and lips as red as a stop sign, Nellie was a nightmare caricature of Courtney Love meets Marilyn Monroe meets Shirley Temple with a little Cyndi Lauper dredged up from the eighties, just in case. Pacey was glad the vests looked better on him and Dawson.

"Does *Forrest Gump* go in the comedy or drama section?" she asked.

"How many times you gonna ask that?" Pacey answered her question with a question.

"It goes in the drama section," Dawson supplied the answer.

"Thank you, Dawson," Nellie said pointedly, looking hard at Pacey. Then she whirled and headed for drama.

"Can you say wet brain?" Pacey mumbled under his breath.

Nellie whirled back, her face livid. "I'm sorry,"

she said, her tone distinctly belying her words. "What did you say? Did you toss a disparaging remark my way? Because if you did, and correct me if I'm wrong, I'd like to remind you who you are."

Pacey gave an unruffled shrug. "I know. I know. Your dad owns this store."

"No, I'm talking about in the huge rotating world of life," Nellie spat out dramatically, as heated as Pacey was placid.

"And who am I, Nellie?" he asked, not caring much what she answered.

"Nobody. That's the point. You're not there. You don't even exist. 'Cause if you did, I might have to respond to your pathetic little under-your-breath one-liners, but instead I take comfort knowing you're vapor. *Pphhhhtt!*" Nellie did her mist-out-of-a-spray-can imitation. "*Pphhhhtt!*" She waved her hands around in front of her to signal that Pacey had disappeared into thin air. "Nonexistent nothing. *Pphhhhtt!*" She was clearly pleased with the way she was playing this scene.

Oooh. Pacey watched her walk off. Wet brain.

The jingle of bells over the door announced the arrival of another customer. Pacey looked toward the door and felt his face flush. The woman was gorgeous, wearing a short dress, her dark blond hair curving just past her shoulders, high cheekbones—the whole nine yards. Okay, she wasn't exactly Pacey's age. But she was curvy in all the right places, and she walked it, and her face was still at least a 9. Or a 9.5.

"Oh, my God. Look at her," Pacey said softly.

Dawson looked up, too. "Show some respect," he said. "She's somebody's mother."

Yes, Dawson had just set himself up. "I have it on good authority that mothers have great sex lives," Pacey said, waggling his eyebrows.

The woman moved toward the counter. She smiled. At Pacey. He went warm.

"Good afternoon," Pacey heard Dawson say. "Can we help you?"

"Yes, you can," she said, her voice smooth. "This is my first time here, and I'd like to rent a video."

Pacey grabbed a Screenplay Video membership application and stepped in front of Dawson. "Excellent. Just fill this out and shoot me a credit card." He edged Dawson out of the way.

Dawson obliged, grabbing a stack of videos and heading for the shelves. The woman started filling out the card, long, slender fingers holding the pen.

"So are you new in town?" Pacey asked. "I haven't seen you around." The good ones were always from somewhere else.

She looked right into his eyes. Hazel eyes, long lashes. A few delicate lines around the eyes, but they were sexy. Experienced. "Yes, I am. My name's Tamara." There was a sexy lilt to her words. "What's yours?"

"Pacey." He gulped. "Nice to meet you."

Tamara slid the application back across the counter along with her credit card. She continued to hold Pacey's gaze.

He looked right back at her. Couldn't look away. "Can I help you locate a video this afternoon?"

"Maybe. I'm in the mood for romance." He'd heard it. Straight from her luscious lips. She smiled at him.

He was hers. Her slave. "Uh . . . well, the new releases are—"

"No," Tamara interjected. "I'm vintage. All the way," she added.

Right on that one. The woman was severely hot. Pacey could barely move his mouth. "Uh . . . uh . . . the classics are—"

"Where would I find *The Graduate*?" she asked.

He wasn't imagining this. "*The Graduate*? Let's see . . . that was the one—"

"Where older woman Anne Bancroft seduces younger man Dustin Hoffman."

Pacey swallowed, his throat dry. "Uh, let me check."

Dawson appeared like a meddlesome big brother, video in hand. He held it out to Tamara. "It's right here, actually. Anything else we can help you with this afternoon?" he asked easily.

Back in the bottle, Dawson.

"No. That should do it," Tamara said. "How much?"

Too late. Dawson had spoiled the party.

"Pay when you return," Dawson said. "Don't forget your credit card." He slid it back toward her. "Enjoy the film."

"I will," Tamara said. She turned to leave. But she looked back over her shoulder and gave Pacey one more slow smile. "It was nice to meet you, Pacey."

"Uh, yeah . . . uh-huh," Pacey agreed, unable to find his tongue. He watched her walk toward the door—the gentle roll of her hips, the curve of her calves. The bells jingled as she left the store.

"Wipe the drool, dude," Dawson said.

"She was flirting with me," Pacey marveled.

"She was laughing at you."

"No way." Pacey was sure. He'd felt it. He'd heard the way she talked, felt her eyes holding him. "She wanted me," he said, feeling an expansion of his ego.

"She wanted Dustin Hoffman." Dawson took another stack of videos and went back to shelving them with Nellie. Pacey stared at the door, his last glimpse of Tamara burned into his mind.

Dawson appeared from around the corner of his house, balancing a pile of videos under one arm. The sun was low, swollen, and red over the far end of the creek and the gently rolling landscape. The sky around the sun was shot with pink and yellow, the bellies of the wispy clouds reflecting the fiery colors in a deepening blue sky overhead. Out toward the ocean, a sliver of moon had already risen.

Dawson saw her right away. Felt her even before he saw her. Jen was sitting on the dock, her feet dangling in the water. She was silhouetted against the setting sun. Perfect profile. He hesitated. Should he go over? She looked pretty peaceful. He took an uncertain step toward her, then stopped.

She turned toward him. Spotted him. "Hey!" she gave a little wave.

Dawson felt a breeze of relief. "Hey." He felt a little out of breath. "How's your granddad?" He sat down next to her. Close. But not too.

"Well . . . he's breathing—good sign," Jen said with a tentative laugh. "Grams, however, presents a challenge. She has this praying mentality. Always saying grace, which is really uncomfortable, since I don't do the God thing."

Jen glanced at the stack of videos Dawson was holding.

"Let's see what you've got here." Jen reached for his videotapes, moving on to an easier subject. *Swamp Thing. Humanoids from the Deep? Creature from the Black Lagoon?*"

"Research," he told her. "I'm making a movie."

"You're really young to be so ambitious." Jen sounded impressed.

Dawson felt a shudder of pride. But he didn't want to come on too puffed up. "I'm fifteen. Spielberg started on eight millimeter when he was thirteen."

"And why the movies?" Jen asked. "What's the attraction there?"

Easy one. He'd been over this footage before. "I reject reality."

"Oh!" Jen laughed.

"Would you like to see my studio?" Dawson asked, taking a chance.

Jen smiled right away.

*   *   *

24

Dawson's room was a shrine to Steven Spielberg. Posters lined every wall; a stuffed E.T. doll sat on a shelf next to a miniature great white shark, the famous jaws tamed in hard plastic. Toy dinosaurs, big and small—Jurassic era only—stalked across the floor. A framed photo of the man himself occupied a place of honor on Dawson's desk.

Dawson watched Jen take it all in. "Long shot. Spielberg fan?" she noted.

"I pretty much worship the man," Dawson admitted.

"Revealing," Jen said. Did that mean good or bad?

"I've chronicled his career on these walls," Dawson said, making fun of himself a little. "You'll notice everything is arranged in receding box-office order, starting with the blockbusters. *Jurassic Park*, *E.T.*, *Jaws*, the Indiana Jones series." He pointed around the room. "And you follow them around to the critically acclaimed wall." Jen eyed the posters that lined the walls of Dawson's room.

"Are you familiar with obsessive reality disorders?" Jen joked.

"It's beyond that," Dawson said, playing at a touch of vanity. "I firmly believe that the mysteries of the universe, the answers to all of life's questions, can be found in a Spielberg film. It's a theory I've been working on. Whenever I have a problem, all I have to do is look to the right Spielberg movie and the answer is revealed."

Jen arched a blond eyebrow. "Have you considered a twelve-step program?"

"Wit. We like that around here," Dawson said. Man, she thought as sharp as she looked.

"So that was your own movie you were shooting this morning, out on the dock?"

"Yeah. The Boston film critics offer this program for junior filmmakers. Heavy competition. The deadline's in two months. I'm really under the gun."

"Jennifer!" He heard a woman's voice outside calling. It was far away, but he didn't miss the edge.

Jen went over to the window. Dawson moved next to her and looked out. He could see the shadowy outline of the lady next door, standing on her porch. Jen's grandmother.

"I'd better go," Jen said. I don't want her to erupt." She took a few steps toward the door. "Later."

"See ya at school," Dawson said. As Jen raced out, he let the smile stretch across his face. He turned to the Spielberg photo. "Nice, huh?"

Joey got a sour taste in her mouth. She balanced precariously at the top of the ladder up to the second floor of Dawson's home.

She watched Jen run across the grass toward her grandparents' house. The new girl worked fast. First day here and she'd already had the tour of Dawson's bedroom.

Joey climbed onto the porch roof and looked through Dawson's window. She saw him grab two remotes. He clicked one of them and the TV popped on. He clicked the other and the VCR did its stuff.

A tape of his mother's news show came into focus. What was he doing?

Joey climbed in through the window.

Dawson looked up. "Hey, Joe, where have you been? Watch this."

As Joey settled down in front of the television, Dawson hit the Rewind button, then Play. His mother appeared, big hair, dishing out the news. "Call 555-5982," she announced. The camera pulled back to reveal her co-anchor next to her. "Back to you, Bob."

"Do you think my mom's sleeping with him?" Dawson asked.

Joey stared at Dawson. "Where did that come from?" Dawson had succeeded in distracting her from thoughts of that Jen person. At least a little.

"Watch," Dawson instructed. He rewound a few seconds of the tape, then pressed Play again.

On the TV screen, his mother looked over at her co-anchor. "Back to you, Bob," she said again, just as she always did.

"Something about her *b*'s," Dawson insisted. "They're too soft. 'Bbback to you, Bbbobb.' See?" He worked the remote and played it again.

"You're reaching," Joey said. "Why would your mom be sleeping with her co-anchor? Your dad's the perfect male specimen." Dawson looked kind of like him, actually.

"I don't know, but I think they are," Dawson said.

"You're just looking for conflict. Everything's a potential script to you. Accept your perfect life,

Dawson. It's a reality." Everyone should have it so good. Joey felt more annoyed than usual by Dawson's attitude. He had everything. Everything.

Joey glanced out the window, letting out a breath. Across the way, she could see Jen stepping onto her porch. The new girl. The bright, sunny new girl. And now it looked as if Dawson wanted her in addition to everything else. Joey turned back to Dawson. Passing on a reply to her outburst, he continued to watch his mother broadcasting the news.

Joey watched him watch. The face she knew so well. They'd agreed they were friends. Always friends. They wanted it that way. Joey had been his number one pal forever. The one he hung with. The one he told stuff to. Even if they were just being friends. Especially because they were just about being friends. Dawson insisted that didn't have to change. Ever. But Dawson didn't do reality that well. He'd never had to.

Chapter 4

The sun was hot already. It was still low in the morning sky, but it glinted powerfully off the creek. Jen could see it out her window—the window of her new bedroom in her grandparents' house. Not exactly the steel and brick and glass towers she was used to seeing when she got out of bed. Jen could feel the humid warmth rising off the water and filling her room as she dressed for the first day of her new school.

Short white denim skirt, pale blue short-sleeved cardigan. She glanced in the mirror over her dresser. Lower key than she would have chosen back in New York. Fine. It wasn't a fashion show around these parts. That was for sure. And just as well, probably. She grabbed her big canvas bag, a new notebook inside, and slung it over her shoulder.

She stepped out of her room and started down the hall.

Her grandfather's door was partly open. She stopped. She peered in, nudging it open farther with her arm. She could see her grandfather sleeping in his big bed in the center of the room. There wasn't a whole lot else in there. A chair. A bureau. A nightstand—with a pharmacopoeia of prescription bottles on top of it. Drugs. Jen felt a tremor of worry.

Quietly she entered the room. She got up close to her grandfather and watched him sleep. He looked pretty good, considering . . .

"G'morning, Grindeddy," she said gently.

One arm was outside the covers, his hand as fragile as a little bird, the skin papery thin and translucent, the delicate network of blood vessels clearly visible. His life was flowing through those veins and arteries. Jen reached out hesitantly. She let one finger touch his hand, lightly tracing a line of purplish blue. His hand felt more solid than it looked. She glanced at his face, but there was no reaction to her touch.

She took his whole hand in hers. Squeezed gently but firmly. Still nothing. Her eyes moved to his chest, rising and falling almost imperceptibly. His pajama shirt was open at the top. She focused on the bare, hairless skin. She felt a wave of curiosity. And tenderness. They'd opened him up like a cleaved chicken. Seen inside him. Held his heart in their hands. His life in their hands.

She let go of his hand and parted his pajama top

farther. She sucked in her breath sharply. A huge dark scar appeared. The massive cut had been stitched meticulously, and shiny new skin had grown over it, but it was still gruesomely impressive.

"What are you doing?"

Jen's pulse skipped a beat. She spun around to face her grandmother. "Uh . . . I was just . . . saying good morning."

Grams had a faintly distrusting shine in her pale eyes. "Your breakfast is ready," she said rather stiffly.

Grams looked younger than most of Jen's friends' grandparents, or at least she would have without that old-lady apron over her prim skirt and blouse, her hair pulled back severely, brown shot with gray. But the reserved, slightly starched way she held herself made her seem far older.

She and Jen looked at each other guardedly. What did Grams think? She'd just been spending time with her grandfather. Jen felt the silence between them. How had she let herself wind up here? Then she glanced at her grandfather, sleeping, and she felt the tension drain out of her.

"I'm glad I'm here, Grams." And as she said it, she knew she meant it. This was Grams, whom she'd spent summers with as a little girl. Grams and Gramps, whom she loved. It was going to be better here. Jen was going to make sure of that.

Grams kept Jen in check with her gaze for another moment. Then she seemed to give in a little. "You'd better hurry. You don't want to be late your first day."

First day. New school. Jen felt a trill of nerves. She wasn't exactly dying to get there, except maybe to get it over with.

A few minutes later she was seated at the heavy oak table in her grandmother's big old kitchen. Small pots of herbs grew on the sunny windowsill. Grams bustled around at the vintage stove, adjusting the flame on the gas burners and stirring and flipping the contents of two black cast-iron skillets. The smell of bacon and coffee filled the air.

"You know, I usually don't eat in the morning," Jen informed her grandmother as she set a huge plate of bacon and eggs in front of her. "I appreciate the fuss, though." She didn't want Grams to frost over again. "But my eyes don't even open till noon. A coffee fix and I'm set."

Grams poured a mug of java. "I'll remember that in the future," she said, not betraying any emotion. She put a cup of coffee down at Jen's place and poured herself a cup, too.

Jen took a sip. Strong. Black. Good. That much Grams had down. "So tell me about this Dawson-guy next door. He looks so different. He used to be short and compact." She thought about how Dawson looked now. And allowed herself a smile.

She felt Grams eyeing her. "You stay away. The boy's trouble."

"Aren't they all," Jen said more lightly than she felt. "And that girl from down the creek—Joey, I think her name is?"

Grams definitely did not like the way this was going. "That girl from down the creek has been crawling into the bedroom window of that boy next door for the past ten years."

Yeah? Jen felt a pinch of surprise. And disappointment. She didn't think she'd read Dawson wrong.

"And neither one of them goes to church," Grams added. "I believe they're what you call the wrong element."

Wrong. "Right," Jen said.

Her grandmother carried her own plate of breakfast to the table. She sat down next to Jen and pressed her hands together in prayer. "Say grace, dear."

Jen looked into her coffee mug. "That's okay. You can say it," she said quietly.

"It would be nice if you would say grace."

Now what? "I don't think so, Grams. Thanks, though," Jen said politely.

Her grandmother's face grew tight. "Is there some reason you don't want to thank our Lord this morning?"

Jen passed her hand through her hair. She was trying, but Grams was pushing it. "Oh, Grams, I didn't really want to get into this, since I just got here and I'm kind of prone to headaches," she threw in, "but I don't do well with prayer and church and that Bible stuff."

The fragile truce with Grams was over. "I beg your pardon?"

There was only one way to tell it—straight out. "I don't believe in a religious god. I'm an atheist," Jen said as honestly and gently as she could. There.

33

She'd told it. Her grandmother stared at her, too shocked to muster up a response. Her praying hands dropped to the table.

Dawson lay in bed, half watching the morning news. "A maritime disaster leaves forty-three dead in India," the newscaster announced. "And we'll have a bright, sunny day today. More when we get back."

Outside, a door slammed. The door of the house across the way. Dawson sat right up in bed, looking out his window. Jen! All long, shapely arms and legs in a sky-blue top and a short white skirt, her hair shining in the daylight. She headed down her grandparents' walkway, a vision of high school loveliness toting a book bag.

Dawson was out of bed. His bare feet hit the floor. This boy had places to go.

It looked like a school. Any school. Every school. The perfect school. The perfect small-town school, set back on a green lawn, a three-story red-brown brick building with wide steps leading up to the main doors, a clock with Roman numerals above the entrance, showing another quarter of an hour before anyone really had to be anywhere. Kids all over the place, heading into the building, spilling over the lawn, trading high fives, low fives, news of the summer. Music poured out across the grass, a rap rhythm blasting from someone's boom box. Two guys passed a football. A girl with long red hair tossed a Frisbee to her friend. A couple kissed under a tree.

Actually, it looked like what school was supposed to look like. At least in the movies. At least to Jen. Her school at home was a trio of brownstones on a city block.

Jen made her way across the grass, the ground soft under her mules. She couldn't quite shake the feeling that she was on a stage set. A set where everything and everyone was new to her. She felt vaguely removed. The whole fact of her being here seemed unreal. She climbed the steps up to the main door and blinked as she went from the bright sunshine to the fluorescently lit entranceway of Capeside High.

The bank of lockers was at the end of a crowded corridor. Jen made her way down it, searching for a familiar face. That meant Dawson. Or Joey. Or that Pacey character. But she didn't spot any of them. She located her locker, number 167, top row. Spinning the dial, she worked the combination. Opened the locker. Not that she had anything to put in it yet.

She found her schedule in her bag, pulled it out, and studied it nervously: bio, English, study hall.

"Hi!" A girl with blond curls and bright lipstick came right up to her. "I'm Nellie Olson."

Jen did a double take. "Nellie Olson? As in . . ."

"I know. I know," Nellie Olson said. *"Little House on the Prairie* was, like, my mom and dad's favorite show. But no preconceptions, okay? I'm not like her at all."

Whatever. "Hi, I'm Jen."

"From New York City. I know. How's your grandfather? He has us all worried," Nellie said with overwrought concern. "We've still got him on the prayer list at church. You party?"

"Excuse me?" From church prayer to partying without a breath?

"Par-ty," Nellie enunciated.

Yeah, Jen had heard her right. She tried to play it cool. "As in Do I enjoy a good time? Or party as in drink-and-use-drugs party?"

"It's subjective." Nellie sounded pleased by her own observation.

"I like to have a good time, substance-free," Jen added. That was as far as she needed to go.

Nellie looked disappointed. "Maybe we should call *you* Nellie. See ya." She took off down the hall, just as Dawson was pulling up. Jen looked after her with a little frown.

"Hey, how's it going?" Dawson asked.

"I need a cigarette," Jen said without thinking.

"Do you smoke?" Dawson sounded surprised.

"I quit," Jen said quickly. "Just a little tense."

"You're hiding it well." Dawson smiled at her.

"I have a great denial system," Jen said honestly, though hooking up with somebody she knew was making her feel much less like a stray.

"It's the first day," Dawson said. "We're all tense. It'll get easier."

The guy was sweet, whatever was going on between him and Joey.

"How's your schedule?" he asked. "They screwed mine up. Who do you have first period?"

Jen glanced at the paper in her hand, though she'd already looked at it often enough to know it by heart. Dawson came around and looked with her. A couple of guys racing past jostled him, and he moved closer to her.

"Brinson—biology," Jen said, feeling Dawson next to her.

"I was just heading that way," Dawson said.

Jen shut her locker. "Were you?" She looked up at him and smiled. She was glad to have company as she headed down the hall.

Pacey was goofing around at the front of the classroom. The seats were about half full, and more kids were streaming in. Most of them didn't pay much attention as Pacey selected the biggest book he could find, and balanced it on his head.

All of a sudden, *she* was walking through the classroom door. No way. He had to be seeing things. Tamara! In school! But if she was a hallucination, a fantasy, she was a degree or two more buttoned up than she'd been the day before. He blinked. She was still there, in a satiny white blouse and camel-colored skirt that almost reached her knees, her curves visible, but not quite so much bare skin.

Pacey felt the *Webster's* slip. It hit the floor loudly. "Tamara?" he managed.

She smiled at him. Also a couple of degrees more proper. And then she was heading for the big desk at the front of the room, putting a stack of books down on it. "Hello, Pacey. I'll tell you what. Why don't you call me Miss Jacobs during school hours?"

Jacobs? Pacey was sure his jaw was down on the floor next to that dictionary. First period English—Miss Jacobs. "Yeah, sure . . . of course," he said.

He wasn't sure how he got to his seat. He held Tamara—Miss Jacobs—in his gaze. She was it. Even in her camel-colored skirt. Just more to imagine taking off.

Taking off? Hit that Pause button. This Mrs. Robinson was his English teacher! Pacey watched her shuffle some papers and get ready for class. Unbelievable. This wasn't happening.

Well, he'd get to see her every morning. First thing to start the day right. And she was looking for romance. She'd said it. To him.

Joey sat at her desk, doodling in her notebook and waiting for Brinson to show. High school. Not so different. School was school, basically. Lots of the same faces. Capeside's living version of Barbie and Ken sitting next to each other up front there. Joey had gone to school with both of them for years. Destined to marry and have a bunch of kids and get divorced, all by age thirty. And Marla Adams had just come through the door. And . . . Jen. Miss Neighbor. Right behind Marla.

Joey slumped down in her chair, but it was too late. Jen was smiling at her. Coming over.

"Hi. I was hoping we'd have a class together," Jen said sweetly, sliding into the seat next to Joey.

"Here we are," Joey said tonelessly. She wished the second bell would ring.

Chapter 5

Quietly, Dawson let himself into Mr. Gold's class-room. The teacher was up at the front of the room, sitting alone at a large video monitor, the rows of tables and chairs in back of him unoccupied.

On the screen, in vintage black-and-white, a woman was letting herself into a room, too. Vera Miles. Dawson recognized the scene instantly. Cut to a withered, dead-still figure seated in an arm-chair, white hair in a bun.

"Mrs. Bates?" Vera Miles asked, with hushed worry.

Dawson came up behind Mr. Gold. *"Psycho."*

Mr. Gold spun around, startled.

On the monitor, Vera Miles spun Mrs. Bates around to reveal a decomposing skull.

Mr. Gold looked at Dawson. "You know the film?"

Did he know the film? "Please. Anthony Perkins. Janet Leigh. 1960." Who could not know? "One of Hitchcock's most celebrated works. Little known fact: in the shower scene, Hitchcock surprised Janet Leigh with freezing cold water in order to get her to scream so effectively."

Mr. Gold arched an eyebrow. "Did you know that the fake blood used was actually—"

"Chocolate syrup," Dawson finished.

Mr. Gold took a good look at him. "Who are you?"

"Dawson Leery. Film auteur."

Mr. Gold gave a little smile. "So I take it you'll be in my fifth period film lab?"

"Actually, that's why I'm here. There seems to have been some confusion about my schedule. I was denied admittance to your class." Dawson felt irritated all over again. Most important thing on his schedule, and they'd managed to mess it up.

"Then you must be a sophomore," Mr. Gold stated.

"And that's not a good thing?" On the monitor, Vera Miles was giving a silent scream of bloody murder.

"This is a very popular class," Mr. Gold explained. "Seating is limited. There's a waiting list. Priority goes to upperclassmen."

The irritation swelled. "That's stupid," Dawson blurted.

"Excuse me?" Mr. Gold was irritated too.

"Who made that rule?" Dawson demanded.

"I did. It was the only fair way to do it."

Oops. "Oh . . ." Dawson said. But he wasn't about to give up. He'd heard that Ben Gold was a fair and decent guy. Maybe a little buttoned up—shirt and tie, chinos, glasses around his neck on a chain, shiny loafers—but, hey, he was part of the brotherhood of film. "Well, have you ever considered a screening process—an audition of sorts—thereby guaranteeing the best possible candidates?"

"Why are you so insistent?" Mr. Gold asked mildly.

"Passion, Mr. Gold. Pure, mad, driven passion. Movies are my life."

"Oh, I see." Mr. Gold eyed the death's-head on the screen.

"Sorry, I'm not coming across well at all here," Dawson said, changing tacks. "The point is, I'm going to be a filmmaker. It's my life's ambition. It always has been. How many students in your class can say that?"

Well, maybe that wasn't such a great question. Didn't everyone want to make movies? Dawson forged ahead quickly. "This is a small town. There's not a lot of opportunity for me. You have the power. You can easily override this bizarre rule that denies students their education."

Ben Gold leaned back in his chair. "You're very convincing, Dawson Leery, but I'm afraid the class is maxed out. I wish I could make case-by-case exceptions, but that would be unfair and problematic. I'm sorry, but no is my definitive answer."

Dawson wasn't hearing this. "But—"

Mr. Gold gave a small frown. "No—period. It's a complete sentence."

Dawson felt a stab of anger. Hurt. Brotherhood of film? Under those shiny loafers lay the feet of a despot.

Jen again. Joey walked down the hallway briskly, but Jen caught up with her and fell into stride. Joey didn't look at her, but this didn't seem to discourage Jen.

"Hey!" she said lightly.

"Hey!" Joey tossed back without as much enthusiasm.

"Joey? Can I ask you something important?"

Did she have a choice? "Sure." Joey kept walking, and Jen kept walking with her.

"Are you and Dawson a thing?" Jen asked.

Thing? Thang? Of course that was Jen's question. Joey was tempted to lie. Keep Jen away. But of course she and Dawson weren't a thang. Or rather they were, in a different way, but not the kind of way Jen was asking about.

"No. Not at all," Joey said, as if it was a silly idea. "We're just friends."

"Like you and I are going to be, I hope," Jen said earnestly.

Joey was silent. Why was the girl trying so hard?

But Jen was tenacious. "You know, Grams warned me about you," she said lightly. "She says you're severely troubled."

Grams. That brittle relic who seemed to get a real high out of watching Joey climb the ladder into

Dawson's room. She must have given Jen an earful. "Well, no offense, but your grams is cracked," Joey said.

"Why does she rag on you?" Jen wanted to know.

"Pick a topic. There's my dad, the imprisoned convict, and there's my sister, impregnated by her black boyfriend . . ." Joey started ticking off the facts of her life.

"Your father's in prison?" Jen sounded genuinely startled.

"Conspiracy to traffic marijuana in excess of ten thousand pounds," Joey recited.

"Wow," Jen said nonjudgmentally. "And where's your mom?"

Joey felt a tug of emotion. She resisted it. She wasn't going to let it rip her open. Not here. Not with Jen. "She had this cancer thing," Joey said flippantly. "It got her."

And that got Jen. Joey could tell. Jen didn't say anything for a few seconds. Fine. Then she asked, "So you live with your sister?"

"And her black boyfriend. He likes you, you know."

"Who, the black boyfriend?"

Enough of this. "Dawson," Joey said. She stopped walking and turned to Jen. "Don't abuse his feelings," she ordered.

She turned and walked away. She could feel Jen staring after her. The girl had better listen. This time Jen didn't follow her.

Chapter 6

The lunchroom was packed. First day of school and you could already see how things were divided up around Capeside High. Jocks over on one side, major food fight under way; prom queens nearby, doing carrots and celery sticks they'd brought from home; burnouts slipping out the side door.

Joey picked at her franks and beans. Boiled and steamed to death. Listening to the Dawson and Jen show didn't help. Dawson was pointing people out and commenting on them. He stabbed his plastic fork at a short, hair-impaired teacher who was walking by.

"The bald man is Mr. Herman—teaches a timid calculus but packs a forty-five magnum. Opened fire last year, took out two students and a custodian."

"Pleaded justifiable homicide. They didn't have a hall pass." Jen was quick with a comeback.

"See that girl in the funky black dress?" Dawson picked out his next victim. "Periodic drinker. Blacks out after two glasses of cheap wine and runs through town with her dress over her head—"

"Singing Neil Diamond songs," Jen finished.

Back to you, Dawson, Joey thought sourly.

"You're good," Dawson told Jen. "I should bring you in to punch up my dialogue."

Joey picked up the script that lay in front of her on the table. "We're supposed to be working, Dawson?"

Dawson flashed her a "whatever" face. "Yeah, sure." He plucked the script out of her hand. Then he turned right back to Jen. "Hey, Jen, will you take a look at my third act? I'm having a climax issue."

Climax issue. Nothing like having a way with words. Joey's face burned. So much for lunch.

Pacey found her in her classroom by herself, finishing a yogurt and a bowl of fruit salad.

"Hi, Tamara—whoops—Miss Jacobs," he said obviously.

Tamara stifled a little laugh. "Hello, Pacey."

He felt himself go weak. But not too weak to quit. "How was *The Graduate*?"

"Just as I remembered it," Tamara said.

"Looking for romance tonight?" Pacey asked smoothly. Tamara's eyes seemed to widen just a bit. Nicely done. Pacey had practiced the line in his head, but he was a little surprised at how silkenly it had slipped out.

"Why?" Tamara was looking at him—that way. "Do you have any suggestions?" she said teasingly.

Down, boy. *"Summer of '42?"* he said, trying to stay cool.

"Refresh my memory." She leaned back in her chair and gave Pacey her full attention.

"It's about this beautiful woman who seduces a young boy on the verge of manhood."

Tamara stared at him. She raised one perfectly arched eyebrow. "It's a favorite," she said in a low voice.

I am your slave, Miss Jacobs. Pacey felt himself starting to sweat. "I can reserve it for you if you'd like," he said.

One of Tamara's students entered the room. A tall, skinny guy in a green watch cap. He was followed by a petite blond girl. Wet shower. Tamara sat upright in her chair. "Actually, tonight I'm going to see that new film playing at the Rialto." She took a last bite of yogurt.

"Yeah?" Pacey said, trying not to let the moment get away.

More students began to stream in. Some kids Pacey knew. That guy from the hockey team who'd just rented *Scream*. Pacey knew it was over.

"It's getting great reviews," Tamara commented— easily, suggestively.

"Oh yeah? Then I'll have to check it out," Pacey said. Maybe it *wasn't* over.

Pacey looked as if he'd done a couple of laps around the track in his street clothes, Dawson thought. He was breathing hard. His face was flushed. There was a line of moisture over his upper lip.

"Easy," Dawson said as Pacey caught up to him in the hall near the lockers.

"Check it out," Pacey commanded. "Video Woman is my new English teacher."

Video Woman? Dawson looked at Pacey's red cheeks. Wildman eyes. The woman from yesterday? An English teacher at Capeside High?

"Right, dude," Pacey confirmed, reading Dawson's expression. "So you and me—the movies. Tonight. We're stalking a faculty member."

"Negative," Dawson said immediately. He wasn't getting anywhere near Pacey's dream life. Anyway, he had his own.

Pacey jostled his arm. "Man, I actually have the possibility of losing my virginity in high-level fantasy fashion."

"Pacey, go home. Walk your dog. It's not gonna happen with the English teacher." Dawson stopped at the water fountain and took a drink.

"Not tonight," Pacey actually agreed. "That's not the plan."

Oh, no. Not a *plan*.

"I just wanna establish my presence," Pacey went on. "So she can start to become familiar with my smile, gaze, and other charming features."

"Don't do this to yourself," Dawson advised Pacey.

"It is a fact that a large percentage of older women are attracted to young boys on the verge of manhood. It keeps them feeling young. I read it in *Cosmopolitan*."

Cosmopolitan? Pacey was sicker than he'd thought. "What are you doing reading—"

"I have three menstrually diverse sisters. *Cosmo* is my salvation."

"So what do you need me for?" Dawson asked.

"Moral support. It'll be cool. You can invite Miss Teen New York," Pacey added. He looked down toward the bank of lockers. "Unless someone's beating you to it."

Dawson followed Pacey's gaze. Jen. Talking to Roger Fulford. Jen, her back against the lockers, kind of leaning into them with her shoulders and looking up at that swell-chested, towheaded slab of beef. Roger was standing just a little too close to her. The alligator Dawson knew was on Roger's shirt, under his letter jacket, was almost near enough to take a drink from her pale blue sweater. And he makes the pass.

Dawson felt Pacey give him a push toward Jen and Roger. "Get over there. Intercept, Dawson. Make it happen. Be assertive. Women like that. You should start reading *Cosmopolitan*. It'll build your female esteem," he coached, laughing.

Dawson ignored Pacey. Roger was moving away. Dawson moved in.

Jen looked over and saw him coming. "Hey, Dawson. How's it going?"

"I see you met Roger Fulford," Dawson noted.

"Nice guy," Jen said easily.

"Sure. Jock by day, schizophrenic transvestite by night," Dawson informed her.

"Really?" Jen laughed. They started walking down the hall together, leaving Pacey somewhere back in the Capeside High nebula.

"Has what you would call a Tori Spelling complex," Dawson went on, still describing Roger. "Partial to Victoria's Secret. Just so you know." Roger Fulford in a deep green satin push-up bra and matching panties.

"But can he run in pumps?" Jen winged back.

They were on a roll. No time like right now. "Hey, Pacey is cruise-directing a trip to the movies tonight," Dawson said. "Just a few of us. Nothing big. Would you like to come?" Easy. Casual.

Jen smiled at him just as easily and casually. "Sure," she said.

"Hey, I need a favor," Dawson called out to Joey as she walked home from school via the scenic route, along the harbor.

"Uh-oh." Joey looked at him and rolled her eyes.

"I have a semi-quasi date with Jen tonight. We're going to the movies with Pacey, and I need you to come with us."

"I'd rather go down in a plane crash."

"Come on! It'll be really weird, just two guys and Jen. You would even it out."

"So it would look like a double date?" Joey said, with a bad taste in her mouth.

"Sorta . . . but not really. Pacey's on this hormonal mission."

Pacey's hormones. This got better and better. Not. "Have you had an aneurysm?" Joey asked. "No way!"

"It's not a *date*-date," Dawson said pleadingly. "It's just so Jen won't be uncomfortable."

"We wouldn't want that," Joey said pointedly, letting the last word of her sentence rip like an arrow.

Dawson passed on that one. "Come on, Joe, please. Please, please, please, please, please."

Joey listened to him repeat the word until it dissolved into meaninglessness.

"Please, please, please . . ."

She stifled a small smile.

"Please, please, please, please . . ."

He wasn't going to stop. "Oh, whatever," she finally said. Dawson wanted her to do this for him. He was dying for her to do this. It was a couple of hours in her life.

He pounced on her and wrapped her in a hug. Not a tender, thang kind of hug. A friends, slap-on-the-back, guy kind of hug. "You're the best," he told her. "I mean it. I know you've been worried about our relationship and everything, but I told you nothing has to change. See? We can talk about anything."

Joey stared at him. Talk? Dawson had begged. She'd given in. When was he going to get his head out of the celluloid and grow up?

Chapter 7

Jen fastened the clasp on her locket chain as she came into the kitchen. Grams was preparing a bowl of egg salad, neatly chopping celery and onions to add to the eggs. As Jen entered the room, Grams paused, knife in midair as she fixed her gaze on her granddaughter. Jen saw her make a swift inventory of her outfit—blue floral-print dress, pale green sweater, sandals, a touch of makeup.

"Where exactly are you going?" her grandmother asked softly.

But under the softness was a demand. Jen felt a flicker of defensiveness. "Well . . . Dawson has a gun, and we thought we'd knock over a few liquor stores and then go for some tattoos," she said sweetly.

Her grandmother gave a distressed little laugh. "Why do you talk like that, dear?"

"I'm simply trying to establish a rapport with you, Grams, that's based on humor." It was the truth, more or less. That and she needed to let at least a little of her personality roam free. "I'm completely harmless," she added. "You'll see."

Grams didn't rise to the challenge. "Well, just be home by ten," she said.

"I can do that," Jen assured her. "Thanks for being so cool about this. I was a little worried you were going to chain me to a chair or something." She *was* relieved that Grams wasn't giving her a hard time about going out. "We're going to the movies," she added.

"Fine," her grandmother said. "You want to go to the movies, go. Have fun. As long as you come to church with me on Sunday."

Oh, that. "I should've known there was a catch. Look, Grams, I'm sorry, but you're gonna have to give up on that."

"I'm afraid I insist." There was forged steel under her pleasantness.

Jen took a deep breath. The face-off. This was about respect—Jen respecting herself. Expecting others to respect her, too. Grams included. "I'm firm about my beliefs, Grams. Please respect them."

Grams looked at Jen. "I know what happened in New York. *Church*"—she emphasized the word—"will do you good."

Go easy, Jen told herself. Easy but strong. She was ready to go forward without letting mistakes from the past pull her back. "Let me determine that, Grams. Church isn't the answer. Not for me. But I promise you I'll keep an open mind and respect and honor your beliefs as long as I'm here." Truth.

Her grandmother didn't budge. "The decision has been made. You're under my guard. You'll do what I say." Even the appearance of softness was gone from her voice now.

Jen felt her cheeks getting hot. "I'm really trying hard to keep my rebellious nature in check." She gave a forced laugh. "I'll tell you what, Grams. I'll go to church when you say the word 'penis.' "

Grams looked as though someone had dropped a bomb on her house. The knife fell to the table with a clatter. Jen actually felt a drop of pity for her. But she'd tried the considerate approach and it seemed as if her grandmother just couldn't hear her.

"You stop that talk," her grandmother ordered.

"It's just a word, Grams. Technical and clinical. 'Penis.' " And before Grams could muster a response, Jen leaned over and delivered a peremptory kiss to her cheek. "Grams, I really love you but you gotta lighten up." No lie.

Her grandmother looked as if she wondered what she'd gotten into. To that and only that, Jen related entirely.

"See ya later." She pushed open the rear screen door and sailed out into the mellow late afternoon.

Grams didn't make any move to stop her. But Jen knew that didn't mean she'd won.

When Dawson came downstairs to say good-bye, his dad was sweating over his restaurant model again. Across the room the TV was on. A tissue-thin, purple-inked architectural drawing was spread out over his desk. On top of it sat a miniature three-dimensional model of a building, all curved walls and undulating surfaces, rooms stuffed with dolls and tiny plastic fish, nautical decorations, and who knew what else. You could get seasick looking at it. Welcome to the dollhouse, Dad.

"I'm outta here," Dawson announced, pulling a light sweater over his head. "See ya, Dad."

His father held up one of the dolls. "What do you think?" She was wearing a scuba suit. "I thought all the waitresses should wear scuba gear."

"Completely impractical," Dawson said frankly. "You know, Dad, this whole aquatic-theme restaurant idea gets worse on a daily basis."

His father just craned his head as if to look past Dawson. "Shift," he said. "It's your mom. She's doing her oil spill exclusive."

Dawson turned toward the television. His mom was on screen with her serious face.

"Watching her work is the best foreplay," Dawson's father said.

"Thank you for sharing that with me, Dad. "I'm outta here," Dawson told him again, already halfway out of the room.

"Have fun," his father said. "Play safe."

Dawson stopped. He wished his dad would. "The condom chat is premature, Dad."

"It's never too early, son."

Dawson rolled his eyes. "What is up with the sex? That's all anybody thinks about anymore. Sex, sex,

sex. Why is our society so immersed in sex? What is the big deal?"

"Sex is a very big part of who we are as human beings," Mr. Leery lectured.

Thank you, Dr. Ruth. Dawson had heard more than enough. "Does that mean we have to roll all over the coffee table? C'mon, if sex is so important, how come Spielberg has never had a sex scene in one of his movies? Huh? He keeps it in its proper place in film. As we should in life."

The doorbell sounded throughout the house. Jen! Dawson was moving again. "I'll be home early."

He didn't like his father's superior smile.

As he left the room, he heard his mother's voice. "Back to you, Bob."

Ready for battle. Joey pulled on a tan work shirt over her T-shirt, brushed an imaginary speck of dirt off her white jeans, and pushed through the screen door. Bess was out on the porch, painting the wooden trim of their home. Smudges of rich oil paint streaked the smock she had on over a pretty cotton dress, and the scent of turpentine mingled with the salty-sulfur smell of low tide. Bodie lay on the porch couch next to Bess, studying some recipe in *Bon Appétit.* Jazz tunes floated out of the house. Ah, the perfect picture of tranquil domesticity. Yeah, right.

Joey raced past them. Tried to. But Bess caught her by her shirt. "Whoa. Where are you going?"

"I'm in a huge hurry," Joey said. The last thing she needed to start this fabulous evening off was an encounter with her sister.

"Your attitude has got to go," Bess said.

Joey felt her neck muscles clench. She strained to get free, but Bess grabbed her face in one hand and squeezed her cheeks together. Joey's mouth went into an involuntary pucker. Kiss of death. "Ouch!" she protested.

Bess plunged her free hand into her smock pocket and came up with a slender black-and-gold tube of lipstick. With her mouth, she managed to pop the top off and, with one hand, expertly swivel the deep red stick up. Joey felt her sister's hold ease. She aimed the lipstick at Joey's lips and carefully applied the color.

Joey was caught totally off guard. She'd been preparing for the usual war. She felt a queasy flutter of confusion.

Bodie glanced at them and smiled approvingly.

Bess let go of Joey's face. "Now blot 'em together like this." She pressed her own full, pretty lips together and moved them from side to side.

Joey obeyed automatically.

Bess swiveled the lipstick back down and closed it. She pressed it into Joey's hand. "You hold on to this, and every half hour to an hour you excuse yourself for a touch-up. Got it?"

For once, Joey had no snappy answer. Joey felt a funny little ache at her sister's tenderness, and she didn't know what to do about it. Stuffing the lipstick into a pocket of her work shirt, she took off across the front lawn. Then, without overthinking it, she stopped, turned, and gave Bess a genuine smile.

Bess smiled back, just as genuinely.

Chapter 8

Joey was stuck with Pacey, bringing up the rear of their little foursome. Dawson and Jen walked in front, weaving through the evening crowd. The weather was beautiful, and tonight there seemed to be a lot of people in town for September—doing a little late shopping before the stores closed, heading into one of the restaurants, taking the kids out for an ice-cream cone, or just enjoying an evening stroll on Main Street.

"So, do you plan on staying the whole school year?" Dawson was asking Jen.

Good question, Joey thought.

"Well, that all depends on my grandfather. And my mom and dad." There was a note of uncertainty in Jen's voice. "I don't know." She shrugged uncomfortably. Then she turned around toward Joey and gave a hesitant smile, as if to invite her into the conversation. "I love your lipstick, Joey. What shade is it?"

Joey started to smile without meaning to. Then she saw Dawson look at her mouth. She felt a wave of embarrassment. Thanks a lot, Jen. "Wicked Red. I like your hair color. What number is it?"

Dawson glared at her. "You'll have to excuse Joey. She was born in a barn."

And thank you, too, Dawson Leery.

"That's okay," Jen said quickly. "Joey, I only do highlights."

So sweet. So forthright. Didn't anything rattle Jen? "So, Jen, are you a virgin?" Joey asked.

Jen gave a strangled little sound halfway between a cough and a choke.

Got you.

Dawson's mouth dropped open. "That's mature," he said disgustedly.

Joey couldn't seem to stop. It was as if her words were taking on a life of their own. "Because Dawson is a virgin, and two virgins really makes for a clumsy first encounter. Don't you think?"

"You're gonna die," Dawson threatened. "Painfully."

"I just thought I'd help," Joey said extra sweetly. "You know, cut to the chase." The marquee of the Rialto was right in front of them, spelling out their movie: *Waiting for Guffman.*

"It's okay, Dawson." Jen saved the day again. "Yes, I'm a virgin. How about you, Joey? Are you?"

Joey wasn't ready for that one. Jen might be sweet

and unflappable, but she was also quick. "Please," Joey said, trying to come up with something fast. "Years ago. Trucker named Bubba." She moved toward the ticket window.

Dawson grabbed her arm. "What is up with you?" he whispered roughly.

They bought their tickets and headed in. Joey wasn't really sure she could have answered Dawson's question even if she'd wanted to. Jen was genuinely nice—and trying way harder than Joey deserved. But still . . .

Pacey led the way, finding four seats in a row about halfway back. Joey followed him in, Dawson behind her, but as she moved toward her seat, Dawson stopped in the aisle and let Jen go ahead of him. Well, chivalry was alive and well in Capeside. Which meant that Joey got stuck between Jen and Pacey.

She slumped down in her seat. All of a sudden Pacey shot to his feet again. "Back in a bit," he said cryptically, then hurried up toward one of the front rows.

And thank you, too, Pacey. Now it was just Dawson and Jen and Joey. Nothing quite like a trio. The lights dimmed. Joey sneaked a look over at Dawson. His hand hovered on the armrest between him and Jen. He drummed his fingers nervously. Jen's hand was on her leg—the one closest to Dawson, of course. Joey pursed her lips. Dawson shifted, leaning toward Jen. His hand started inching over. Stopped. Started again. Going, going . . .

"So, Jen," Joey found herself saying. "You a size queen?"

"Excuse me?" Jen asked.

"How important is the size to you?"

"Joey!" Dawson was shooting major bullets at her with his eyes.

Jen fixed Joey with a level gaze, as if considering what to say. "Being a virgin, I haven't given it much thought." Was that a note of weariness creeping in her voice? Was Miss Gung Ho Camper starting to get tired of their little game? But Jen kept playing stoically, turning Joey's question back at her. "How about you?" she asked Joey.

"I'm torn—" Joey managed to say, before Dawson yanked her out of her seat.

"You and me. Outside. Now."

"What do *you* think, Dawson?" Joey asked loudly.

"I'm gonna kill you," Dawson growled. "Kill you dead."

The opening credits were rolling. "Shhh," said someone in the next row.

Dawson was pulling Joey out into the aisle. She looked back over her shoulder at Jen and got in one last line. "Did you notice the long fingers?" she asked.

Dawson dragged Joey up the aisle and out of the theater.

Pacey plopped down in the empty seat next to Tamara. "Hi, Tamara."

She looked at him, and her face colored with surprise. "Pacey! What are you doing here?"

Well, she'd basically invited him. "I came to check out the movie, like you suggested," Pacey said. "I'm here with some friends."

Tamara's surprise melted into a smile. "Some friends? Oh, I'm glad."

"But I can sit with you, if you like. Milk Duds?" He held out the box.

"No," Tamara said. She shifted around in her seat. Hadn't her shirt been buttoned up one button farther in school, today?

"Oh, *Summer of '42* is officially reserved in your name," Pacey told her.

"Oh, Pacey, I don't think you understand."

"It was no problem," Pacey said quickly. He was trying to get up the nerve to suggest they watch it together, when some middle-aged guy entered their row—shirt and tie, chinos, glasses on a chain around his neck, shiny loafers. He carried a barrel-size tub of popcorn.

"Ah, Pacey, are you sure you don't want to sit with your friends?" Tamara asked. She looked from him to the popcorn dude.

Pacey gave him a second look too. Enough popcorn for two. At least. And then some. Heading right this way. Suddenly Pacey got a bad feeling. "Who's this guy?" he asked Tamara.

"Tammy, is this kid bothering you?" the man asked.

"Shhh!" said a guy behind them as the lights dimmed.

61

"No, Benji," Tamara said.

"*Benji?* Miss Jacobs invited me herself," Pacey clarified.

"Not exactly, Pacey, but I . . . can see how . . ." Tamara stumbled over her words.

Pacey felt a sudden flicker of insecurity.

"Why don't I help you find a seat?" the Benji character said. It was more of a statement than an offer. He reached for Pacey's arm.

"*Shh!*" the guy behind them hissed.

Pacey yanked his arm away. Benji staggered. The popcorn went flying. Suddenly the guy behind them was covered with it. Buried in the blizzard.

"What the—" He stood up menacingly.

He was huge. It was the last thing Pacey noticed, before a meaty fist came sailing toward his face.

Joey and Dawson stood in the lobby of the theater, arguing, their voices loud enough to provide a show for the refreshment vendors and ticket takers.

"Are you tweakin'?" Dawson shouted. "What is your problem?"

"My problem is that from the moment little Miss Highlights showed up you haven't said one word to me," Joey shouted back.

"Crap!" Dawson hurled the word. "That is pure crap and you know it."

"What I know is that all your blood is rushing downward and you can't acknowledge that another human being is present."

"I like her, okay? Sue me. I thought you were my

friend." Dawson frowned deeply. "Where's a little understanding?"

"I understand everything," Joey said. "I'm tired of understanding." And all of a sudden she *felt* tired. Really tired. "All I do is understand." She felt a tear settle in the corner of her eye.

Dawson took a long look at her. "Joey—"

"Nothing penetrates with you." Joey blinked hard against the tear. "You're so far removed from reality you don't see what's right in front of you."

"What are you talking about?" Dawson was yelling again.

"Your life, Dawson. It's a friggin' fairy tale, and you don't even know it. You just want conflict for that script you're writing in your head." Dawson's world. Joey was sick of it. "Stop living in the movies. Grow up!"

Chapter 9

The creek was bathed in moonlight. The Big Dipper sparkled crisply in the velvet sky. The first spicy-sweet note of fall rode a gentle breeze. Way in the distance, you could hear the surf.

Dawson and Jen headed slowly across her grandparents' front lawn.

"I'll walk you to your door," Dawson said.

Jen shook her head. "Not with Grams ready to pounce."

Dawson glanced toward her darkened porch. "Oh, that's right."

They stopped walking. "So . . ." he said.

She gave a soft laugh. "So . . ."

"It was . . ." Dawson groped for the right thing to say. "It was a really repulsive evening."

Jen's laugh opened up. "Yeah," she said. "Yeah, it was."

Dawson laughed too. There was a wordless moment. Wind through the trees. A bird chirping. They both stopped walking. Dawson looked at her. She was looking at him. Eyes bright. Hair shining, the color of moonlight. Dawson's heart was pounding. She was beautiful. And sweet. And smart. And fun to be with. He moved closer.

She tilted her face up toward his. He could smell the floral scent of her shampoo. He put his hand on her arm, felt an electricity go through him as he touched her. He leaned in toward her, his lips close to hers—

Suddenly she turned her face away. "This is all my fault," Jen said.

Dawson felt a jolt of disappointment. Her fault? A kiss?

"I know I don't possess much power in the universe, but I feel completely responsible for tonight," she explained.

She thought it was *her* fault? Joey goes ballistic. Pacey winds up on the floor of the theater. *His* two friends. And it's her fault?

"No, it's me," Dawson protested. "I pulled the pin. I tossed the grenade. I have this big *L* embedded right here." He made an *L* with his fingers and brought it to his forehead.

Jen shook her head. "No. You're not a loser, Dawson. I think you're very sweet and smart. And you have a great sense of humor."

Dawson felt an embarrassed grin starting to happen. But Jen wasn't finished.

"You're cool without being obnoxious about it. You're very, very talented."

"Yeah?" Dawson laughed softly. What had he done to deserve this?

"Yeah. And have clear skin. A big plus."

He laughed louder. The laugh faded, and he felt even more nervous than he'd been a few moments earlier. "Thank you," he said.

"No. Thank *you*. Things weren't so great for me in New York," Jen told him. "And, well . . . things are really scary for me right now, too." She glanced briefly at her grandparents' house.

Jen somehow seemed strong and fragile at the same time. Dawson pressed his palm against her face. Her skin was soft. Warm. They held each other's gaze. She didn't pull away. He leaned in for the kiss.

The porch lights snapped on. They both looked toward the house. Dawson could see Jen's grandmother standing just inside the door, peering out.

Jen took a step away from him. "I have to go," she said reluctantly. "Thanks for everything, Dawson."

"But—" he said to her back as she ran up the flagstone walkway. He felt his hope escaping with her.

Suddenly she turned back. "I'm just gonna pretend we kissed, Dawson, okay?"

Dawson grinned. Yeah. More than okay. He was going to pretend he'd kissed Jen, too.

* * *

Pacey could feel the dried blood, tight and brittle, on his face. One eye was swollen nearly shut, functional but throbbing. He wandered aimlessly down by the harbor, unable to bear the thought of going home, getting into bed, and being alone with his humiliation. Not that he was doing much of a job of getting away from it here. But at least he could delay having to explain his swollen eye to his parents or sisters or brother.

He ambled toward the area where the pleasure boats were docked. A half-dozen or so salt-darkened walkways were suspended over the water on solid wood piles. Yachts and elegant sailboats were berthed in neat rows. Many were dark, but there were signs of life on a few of them. A lamp burned in a sleek, well-appointed cabin. He saw the gray-purple glow of a television in another. A few people still sat up on deck here and there, enjoying the mild night.

Pacey picked a row at random and headed out toward the end of the boardwalk. He'd win the Fool of the Decade Award, for sure. Coming on all Romeo to some way seasoned Juliet. Except she wasn't Juliet. She was his English teacher. That's Miss Jacobs, to you. And he'd gotten so deep into fantasyland that he'd provided the dramatic high point of the week. Maybe the year. Pathos, violence, and comedy all rolled up in some stranger's fist on his face.

Of course it wasn't totally his fault. "I'm in the mood for romance," she'd said. "Where would I find *The Graduate*?" And how about *"Summer of*

'42 . . . ? It's a favorite." She had to know how that came off to a boy his age. And she'd said it anyway. Said it on purpose.

And suddenly there she was, like a mirage. Appearing in the moonlight and the lights from the harbor. Except he wasn't just imagining her this time. Tamara—Miss Jacobs—was standing at the end of the pier, looking out at the water with a troubled expression. The warm silver of the moon shone on her face, which was even more beautiful for her look of melancholy.

Pacey was hit with a mixture of fury and desire. He felt sick. And Tamara had spotted him. "Great. What are the chances?" he mumbled.

"Pacey, are you okay?" All full of concern.

"I'll live." Why was he talking to her? Hadn't tonight taught him anything? He turned to beat a retreat.

She caught up to him and reached for his arm. "Wait, Pacey. Talk to me a second."

Pacey felt her touch, all sensory input focused overtime on her hand. It just sharpened his anger. "About what? *The Graduate* or *Summer of '42*? Which would you rather discuss?"

"I'd like to clear up this misunderstanding," she said sincerely. Her hand was still on his arm.

Pacey shook it off. "I understand you perfectly well . . . Miss Jacobs," he added for emphasis.

"I'm so sorry," Tamara said simply.

"You should be, because you're a liar. How can you say you were only renting a movie?" Pacey felt his anger gathering momentum—a giant wave.

"Because it's the truth." Tamara actually sounded as if she believed that. And *Summer of '42*? The favorite? Just a casual comment?

"What a crock!" The wave of anger was rolling. "The truth is you're a well-put-together knockout of a woman who's feeling a little insecure about hitting forty. So when a young, virile boy such as myself flirts with you, you enjoy it. You encourage it. You even fantasize about what it would be like to be with that young boy on the verge of manhood." Pacey let it rip, and it felt good. "Because it helps you stay feeling attractive and makes the aging process a little more bearable. Well, let me tell you something. You blew it, lady. Because I'm the best sex you'll never have!"

Whoa! Pacey needed to catch his breath. That was totally unrehearsed. Totally what he wanted to say. Tamara looked stunned. Her gaze was frozen on him. She didn't say a word.

Now what? Pacey felt the surge of strength going out of him.

"You're wrong about one thing, Pacey," Tamara said softly.

Oh, really?

"You're not a boy." She grabbed his hands and drew him toward her. Their faces were only inches apart. They came together in a heated kiss.

Pacey wrapped her in his arms, feeling her body against his. Her lips were soft. He could taste their desire.

And then she was pulling away, staring at him, stunned. "I—I'm sorry," she whispered. "Oh, God!"

Regret and shock rang in her voice. She backed away from him.

Pacey watched her go. He could barely catch his breath.

She turned away from him and broke into an awkward jog. Hit and run. Into the night. Just renting a video. Gone.

"I'll see you in school," Pacey said to her back. "Miss Jacobs."

Dawson walked into his room and grabbed the remote. Power on. Gray snow morphed into the local weatherman. "There will be some fine weather in the next few days. . . ."

Dawson picked up a crumpled shirt from his bed, packed it into a ball, and yanked open his closet for the toss.

Joey was huddled on the floor, surrounded by dirty clothes.

"Joe! What are you doing in there?"

Joey stood up, holding the E.T. doll, looking sheepish. "Hanging with the clothes."

"What happened tonight, Joey?"

Joey took a perfectly aimed dive onto the bed. She landed on her stomach. "I wigged out."

That much he knew. Dawson let his sweater drop into the bottom of his closet. "*What* is going on between us?"

Joey shook her head, her long brown hair swirling around her. Her lipstick had rubbed off. "I have no idea," she said slowly.

Dawson felt the tension between them, joining

them but keeping them apart. There had always been this unspoken communication between him and Joey. Unspoken because each knew exactly what the other one was thinking. Now there was something unspoken, and Dawson didn't know what Joey was thinking. Feeling. Or what he was feeling, either. He couldn't get this vague, constant unease in him to crystallize, to form words, to shape itself into a script.

Joey was right. He was living a movie. "I know I have this incredibly perfect life and I completely underappreciate it," he said. He didn't want Joey to be angry. Especially not at him. And he didn't want to be angry, either.

"Yeah, you do," she said.

"And I'm sorry I'm such an insensitive male. I thought I was above it." Dawson pulled out his desk chair and sat down. "I don't want to lose you, Joey." As he said it, the weight of his words sank in even deeper. "What we have is the only thing that makes any sense to me."

Joey moved her head almost imperceptibly. Was that a nod of agreement or a shake of doubt, of having had enough? For a brief moment Dawson saw a confused, pretty girl lying on his bed. Not just his old pal. And that sent a jolt of surprise through him. Surprise and honesty. It wasn't the first time he'd felt this way. Even though he'd just realized it.

"You know, when I saw you tonight with lipstick on, I remember thinking how pretty you looked," he confessed. "I ignored it," he added with a quick laugh, "but I thought it."

"Yeah?" Joey asked. She smiled.

"But that was it, Joe," Dawson said with brutal sincerity. He'd never lied to Joey. "It didn't go further than that."

She shrugged. If he'd expected her to be crushed, she didn't look it. But her casual reaction didn't surprise him, either. "When I saw you going for Jen's hand tonight, it's not like I wanted to be the one holding your hand," Joey said with equal candor. "I just didn't want her holding it."

Dawson understood her completely. For a second the confusion between them vanished. But that didn't change the situation. "So where does that leave us?" Dawson asked.

Another shrug—this one less illuminating.

"It's all so complicated," Dawson said.

"We're growing up, Dawson. That's all." Suddenly Joey had an answer. "Even Spielberg outgrew his Peter Pan syndrome." And then she was up and moving toward the window.

"Where are you going?" Dawson asked, standing automatically. But he knew it was a lame question, even as he asked it.

"I can't sleep over anymore," Joey said. Again. "And we can't talk to each other the way we used to. There are things we can't say."

Every bit of Dawson's gut emotion rebelled against her words. Maybe things had gotten more complicated between them, but hadn't they both just admitted it? Hadn't they always, always told each other everything? Dawson couldn't bear to see Joey climb out that window. It was like his right leg, a piece of him, was going out, too. "That's just not true! I can tell you anything," he insisted.

Joey fixed him with a direct gaze. "How often do you walk your dog?"

"What?" Dawson looked puzzled.

"You know what I mean," said Joey. "What time of day? How many times a week?"

It took a second for her questions to sink in. Then Dawson felt the embarrassment of his most private moments laid right out there between them. What everyone knew but what you didn't talk about to anyone. Well, actually, he'd used that dog-walking line on Pacey the other day when he was getting all sweaty about that teacher lady. But it was guy talk. Code phrasing.

Dawson looked at Joey, poised to climb out the window. The look in her eyes challenged him to answer. Begged him to answer. "Good night." It was all he could say. Joey was right. He didn't want her to be right. And he could see she didn't want to be, either. She just was.

"See ya, Dawson," she said softly. She disappeared down the side of the house.

"See ya, Joey," Dawson said to himself. He stood there for a long time. He hurt. He didn't know what he felt. He wanted life to be simple again. He was so tired. He leaned his head against the closet door. He banged his head, hard, against the door. Again. As if he could bang out all his confusion and pain.

Joey struggled with the line to her rowboat. She wiped away her tears with the back of her hand, but more welled up in her eyes. The dock was blurry, and she couldn't see why the rope in her hands had snagged. She half stood in the little boat, gave a yank, and felt the boat wobble precariously. The tears made their way down her cheeks. Why fight them? No one could see her, anyway.

She finally got the boat unmoored and started rowing. She tugged on the oars angrily. Felt good, actually, to channel her anger into a purely physical activity. The rowboat glided out into the creek. It was a beautiful night. Moon, stars. The whole bit. Not too still, not too wild. In between summer and fall. Perfect. Unfair, really. Given the circumstances.

"Hey, Joey!" Dawson's voice carried across the water.

Startled, Joey looked up toward his room. Dawson was half out of the window, waving madly. She felt a funny little flutter inside—hope, anticipation.

"Usually in the morning, with Katie Couric!" Dawson yelled.

Huh? Katie Couric? And then it hit her. When do you walk your dog? Joey felt a huge grin stretch across her face. She waved back at Dawson just as athletically. Her spirit soared. She saw that Dawson was grinning too.

Whatever they were going through, at least they were going through it together. Dawson gave one last overdone wave and disappeared back inside. Joey began to row toward home.

Chapter 10

Joey's voice was emotional. "I know what I saw. It was big and ugly, and it attacked me. And it's still out there. Waiting."

As she sat on Dawson's bed, watching herself speak to Pacey in the dailies of Dawson's movie project, Joey was tempted to point the remote at the VCR and stop the film before she saw the next scene. She felt the corners of her mouth turn down with anticipated disgust.

"I may not believe you, Stephanie," Pacey was saying on the screen, "but I believe *in* you."

Here goes nothing. Joey watched as Pacey leaned over and kissed her movie alter ego on the mouth. As soon as his lips touched hers, she recoiled. On Dawson's bed, she felt herself pull back from thin air in horrified sympathy. On the screen, she saw herself cringe and make an exaggerated "gag me" face.

"Cut," Dawson could be heard saying on video.

"What? What?" Pacey asked defensively.

They were way off character, but the camera was still rolling.

"I'm sorry, Dawson," Joey heard her video self say, "but he's too repellent."

The picture shifted to snow.

"Joey, you're going to have to kiss him," Dawson said from the other side of the room. He sat in his desk chair, hunched over one of his latex masks, paintbrush in hand.

"I cannot and will not kiss that cretin," Joey stated.

Dawson clicked his tongue. "It's a movie. You're playing a character. It's not Pacey you're kissing."

If it looks like Pacey, if it tastes like Pacey . . .

"So he's a sea serpent from the deep. Cite the difference," Joey challenged.

"But you're not aware of his alter ego." Dawson did a quick, pointless plot summary. "You're in love with him."

"Forget it."

"The movie won't work without the kiss, Joey. It's a love story," Dawson said.

"It's a horror movie, Dawson."

"That's blasphemy! It's an homage with a heavy allegorical slant."

Just when you thought it was safe to go back to the movies.

Joey flopped onto her back on the bed, remembering the horror of Pacey's mouth diving down at her face. Eaten by the sea creature. "But he's so unkiss-worthy," Joey said.

"Do this for me," Dawson said.

"I don't want to regurgitate on camera. Why don't you kiss him, Dawson?"

"Because my lips are reserved for someone else." Dawson didn't miss a beat.

But Joey did. Suddenly it wasn't just a movie. She reached for a response. "What is up with that? Have you kissed Miss Someone Else yet?" Okay. Nicely tossed off. But she found herself waiting for the answer with just a little too much . . . well, interest.

"Almost," Dawson said. "The moment nears."

Wipe the smile, dude. "What's the delay?"

Dawson had to think for a moment too long. Two points to me, Joey thought. But so what?

"There's no need to rush fate," Dawson answered.

So now Jen was his fate? How dramatic. How classical. "Don't wait an eternity, Dawson. Your first date with her—such as it was—was days ago. She's from New York, where things tend to move faster."

"So how enchanting for her to meet a strapping young man who doesn't have sex on the brain." Dawson came back immediately with that one. Ooh, the pious hero.

"If it helps you sleep at night," Joey said. When was the guy going to stop living in a dream?

"You heard her yourself. By her own admission—she's a virgin."

"For another second."

"Jen happens to be a bright, intelligent young woman who is clearly in charge of her own body," Dawson said, walking on the defensive side.

Joey laughed. She hadn't meant to launch quite so direct an attack on the fantasy innocence of Dawson's daydreams. Or maybe she had. "I'm not suggesting leather straps and Crisco—just a kiss."

Dawson worked his paintbrush carefully. "Jen and I will definitely kiss. Don't you worry. The question is, will your lips ever find Pacey's?"

Oh, back to that. Back to you, Bob. "Rewrite," Joey demanded. "I vote for an extensive rewrite."

"That's too bad," Dawson said. "Because you definitely have kissable lips."

"What!" Joey sat up. She hadn't heard that.

Dawson held up the mask he was working on. A latex head, like the one Pacey wore as the sea creature. But it was definitely not a sea creature. It was her! It was Joey! How had she missed that one? And the scariest thing about this mask was how much it actually looked like her. Damn, Dawson was good.

"For the decapitation scene," Dawson said mildly. "Check out those lips. You give good lip."

Joey couldn't think of a single comeback. Did she have kissable lips? Did Dawson think so? Even though he really dreamed of kissing Miss Someone Else?

"You know, Joey, you could always just close your eyes and think of someone else." Think of Jen? Wait. He meant someone else. Not Someone Else, as in little Miss Someone Else. This was getting too confusing. All Joey knew was that she most decidedly did not want to kiss Pacey. Wasn't going to.

"You're full of solutions, Dawson." Joey flopped back down on the bed. So who was she supposed to pretend she was kissing? She glanced over at Dawson. He was studying the mask of her face, smiling, pleased with his work.

Suddenly he put it down. He looked at her. "Explain to me the Crisco?"

Joey laughed. She wasn't going to destroy Dawson's perfectly scripted innocence.

Chapter 11

Dawson slammed the door of his locker and threaded his way down the hall. "Hey, man," he greeted Keith Silves as they passed in the opposite directions. Hadn't seen him all summer. Probably out on his boat with his girlfriend, Marla. The hall was packed with kids racing to class before the second bell. Lots of familiar faces. Lots of new ones, too.

The loudspeaker crackled from somewhere up near the ceiling. Some kids kept going, ignoring the sound. Some stopped to listen to the disembodied voice blasting into the hall. "Good morning!"

Dawson kept walking, though for a second he thought he had been transported to Screenplay Video and that he was at work. That was Nellie's voice chasing him down the hall.

"Don't forget about the big dance on Saturday to celebrate our victory at the big game on Friday even if we don't know yet if we'll even win the big game, but the planning committee is really optimistic so get your tickets now. . . ."

Take a breath, Nell. Dawson made a right into Mr. Gold's room. The classroom was deserted, except for Ben Gold himself, fiddling with some camera equipment in the back of the room.

Dawson knocked on the inside of the door. "Mr. Gold. Got a sec?"

Ben Gold looked up, bringing his glasses to his eyes for a moment. "What is it, Dawson?" he asked briskly. He let his glasses fall back down around his neck.

"I was thinking about everything you said. And you were right not to let me into your class."

Mr. Gold lifted a skeptical eyebrow. "I'm glad you gave it some thought."

"I did. However, I'm in a jam. I have a study hall fifth period in the library, and it's really crowded in there—major overflow, really sweaty and unpleasant—and I talked to Mr. Givens about switching study halls, and he seemed to think, with your permission, I could spend study halls with you."

"Fifth period? That's exactly when film class is," Mr. Gold said dryly.

"Now, that's an uncanny coincidence," Dawson said. He could do dry, too.

"You would not be part of the class," Mr. Gold continued. You'd sit in the back and be quiet. You wouldn't participate or involve yourself in any way."

"Thanks, Mr. Gold. I really mean that. This is a big deal."

She walked toward him.

"Morning . . . Miss Jacobs," Pacey said. Softly tailored black skirt, low-cut white blouse. She looked beautiful. Sexy. There was no getting away from it.

"Good morning, Pacey," she said tightly, eyes compelling him to go, not to start.

"Can we talk?"

"This isn't your class, Pacey. I'll see you later."

Uh-uh. She wasn't getting off the hook. "No." Pacey stood his ground. "We really need to talk."

Tamara put her books down on her desk and looked away from him. "We have nothing to discuss, Pacey, except homework of which there is none, so you can run along." He thought he heard a note of desperation in her voice. But she had made her own bed. Did she think she could play with his head and then expect him to just go away?

"There's a lot to discuss." He felt his anger from the other night returning. "We can start with the open-mouthed kiss if you'd like."

More students were coming in. People were looking at them. Tamara glanced at her class, then back to Pacey, pleadingly. "I don't know what you're talking about. I'm going to have to insist you leave this classroom immediately." She put on her voice of authority, but it just wasn't working.

Pacey actually felt a little sorry for her. "Listen." His voice softened. "I'm just as confused as you are." Wicked understatement. Anger, desire, desperation . . . fear. Pacey was a battleground.

"Pacey, please!" Tamara's voice sounded as if it might break. "Nothing happened. There was no . . . kiss." She dropped the word in a whisper. "Please. Don't." Pacey saw that her hands were shaking. Unshed tears formed in the corners of her hazel eyes.

The bell shattered the silence between them. Her students were in their seats.

Pacey dropped his voice to a whisper too. But his anger was strong. "Your tongue was in my mouth. You're not being fair." He turned his back to her abruptly and stormed toward the door.

"Good morning, everyone," he heard her saying, her voice wavering on the brink of control.

Powwow in the lunchroom. Dawson was a hundred percent earnest, a hundred percent focused. And here they all were again—Joey, Pacey, Jen, and Dawson. Hadn't they learned a thing from their little adventure at the Rialto? Joey wondered.

"I can't count on the film class for support, as I was hoping," Dawson explained. "It means we'll have to work overtime to meet the festival deadline. We'll have to shoot all weekend. And, Joey, that means no lip about giving Pacey lip."

Joey shot a glance at Pacey's bum eye. His little souvenir from the other night was turning a rainbow of nasty colors. Pacey hardly needed a mask to play a monster from the deep. "I'm reaching my breaking point with this whole kiss thing," she announced.

"I'm not engorged with this, either," Pacey told

her. "It goes both ways, you know." He bit into his hot dog.

Dawson blew out an exasperated breath.

Dawson looked at Joey, then at Jen. He looked torn. Then suddenly he smiled. "Joey, major revelation!"

Joey felt herself go tight. Not another semi-quasi double-date idea.

"Joey, I think I've figured out how to make you the happiest actress in the world."

Back to the film, Bob. Phew. Joey relaxed.

"You know how you die at the end of the movie? How would you like it if you died sooner? Like tomorrow?"

"What do you mean?" Like Dawson murders Joey on Friday. Goes to the dance with Jen on Saturday?

"Your character, in a surprise attack, is killed violently," Dawson told Joey, a little too enthusiastically. He spun toward Jen. "And your beautiful and bright cousin from New York arrives just in time to discover your mutilated body."

"Dude, you're on to something," Pacey said approvingly.

Joey felt a chill that was altogether too real. New girl's here—you're out, Joe.

But it was Jen who rallied to her side. "Whoa!" Jen protested. "Wait a minute."

"No, it's perfect," Dawson insisted. "Isn't it, Joey?" He was smiling at her expectantly. Had Dawson lost it? "It nullifies the kiss issue and gets you back behind the camera with me, where you belong."

Huh. Sometimes you just couldn't see the forest for the trees. Or something like that. Joey liked the way it sounded—back with Dawson, where she belonged. Plus, she'd gotten out of the most repellent kiss in town. No small deal.

But Jen was a few steps behind this time. "But haven't you already filmed a lot with Joey's character?"

"Easy cover," Dawson said. "It's better this way. It's so unpredictable. The audience will never see it coming. It's like Janet Leigh in *Psycho.*"

"Or Drew Barrymore in *Scream,*" Pacey put in.

"A rip-off of a rip-off," Joey said, nodding.

"I really think it fits right in line with the tone of the piece. Don't you see?" Dawson asked.

Joey saw. She saw herself and Dawson on one side of the camera. Jen and Pacey on . . . Hold everything. Jen and Pacey. The kiss. Jen was the new romantic lead. The kiss with Pacey was her responsibility now. Joey looked from Jen to Pacey. Or rather Pacey's hideous eye. She smiled. "You're right, Dawson. It's perfect."

Chapter 12

Pacey was front and center, making sure Miss Jacobs felt his eyes on her every move. She wasn't getting off the hook so easily. He wasn't going to let her ignore him and pretend nothing had happened. Or that she'd played no role in that nothing.

The problem was that Pacey was supposed to be furious. He *was* furious. But he couldn't focus his rage on Tamara without looking at her and feeling something entirely different mixed in.

"Can someone explain to me the state of Catherine's mind as she drove Heathcliff away?" she was saying.

Pacey could barely concentrate on her words. As she studiously avoided looking at him, Pacey stared at the swell of her breasts under her white blouse, at her hips, at her perfect legs, her face, her lips. . . .

He tried to call up the sharpness of his anger, but he kept remembering how his lips had felt on her lips, the feel of her body pressed against his, the curve of her back under his hands. . . .

"Ooh, Miss Jacobs!" Nellie's voice brought him crashing back to planet high school. Hard to get romantic with Nellie's voice in his head.

"Yes? Ah, Nellie, is it?"

"The answer is that it was her tragic and dysfunctional way of letting him know she loved him," Nellie said dramatically.

"That's the obvious interpretation of the moment," Tamara said. She was straining with the effort to keep her eyes fixed on the back of the room. Pacey could see it. She was just as aware of him as he was of her. She couldn't hide from it. "However, I think it goes deeper than that. For some reason, this novel is regarded as a great love story," she went on. "But the reality is that Heathcliff and Catherine never should have been together."

Really? News to Emily Brontë, Pacey thought. Or was it Charlotte who'd written *Wuthering Heights*? One of those sisters. Definitely news to William Wyler and the 1939 movie version he'd directed with Merle Oberon and Laurence Olivier. Or Peter Kosminsky and his 1992 version starring Juliette Binoche and Ralph Fiennes. Pacey began to pay a little more attention to what Tamara was saying.

"They were all wrong for each other. Catherine was essentially a mess."

Pacey started getting a weird feeling.

"Heathcliff was basically a decent guy who had a

lot to learn about life and was inherently better off
without some whimpering, mentally unstable wet
rag following him around," Tamara said passionately. "The whole thing was wrong—never should
have happened."

Oh, my God. Pacey was getting a command
performance.

Tamara let her gaze wander to him for the briefest
second. Then it snapped back to that most fascinating of fascinating back walls. "Emily Brontë should
have saved her ink," she concluded.

Someone in the class gave a low whistle. People
were looking at her as if maybe she'd lost it. But
Pacey heard her loud and clear. What ever happened to letting your students make up their own
minds, Miss Jacobs?

"Enter Stephanie's cousin," Dawson noted in his
script as he started writing in the new role for Jen.
Mr. Gold may have banished him to the back of the
room and sentenced him to silence, but this was
fifth-period film class, and he was going to work on
his film like everyone else.

Up at the front, Mr. Gold was addressing a tall,
muscular boy with thick, dark hair and the chiseled
face of a Greek sculpture. "We'll have to move fast
if we're going to enter the film festival," the teacher
was saying to him.

The film festival? Dawson put down his script.

"We can make it," Mr. Perfect was saying. "The
script is done. The movie's boarded. We did a lot
of the work over the summer." Dawson felt a tug

of anguish. Wouldn't you know it? Gold's special student. The guy was a couple of grades ahead of him, but Dawson knew who he was. Everyone did. Cliff Elliot, a.k.a. Mr. Perfect, was the Capeside Wildcats quarterback—picture in the paper all the time, already being wooed by the college scouts. And if that wasn't enough, he was student council chairman, an A student, and the secret dream of more than a few Capeside girls. That stock character in every teen drama. You had to hate the guy on principle alone.

"I'll need a finalized budget before I can greenlight any shooting," Mr. Gold said to him.

Cliff turned to Nellie, sitting by his side. "The figures haven't changed," she said, giving Cliff a gooey smile. "We're still under budget."

Under budget. Dawson snorted to himself. Only Cliff. What film in the history of films had ever come in under budget? But even Mr. Gold was under the guy's spell.

"Then let's move to the story," the teacher said. Did you solve your third-act problem?"

Dawson couldn't believe this. Cliff Perfect's movie was going to the film festival. His would be the one official entry from Capeside High. Week one, and it was already decided. Dawson shot his hand up, waved it vigorously.

Mr. Gold lifted his glasses to his eyes and looked at him. "Yes, Dawson," he said, his voice heavy with indulgence.

"Would that be the Boston Film Festival?" Dawson asked.

"Yes, that's correct. They sponsor a junior-level video competition."

My film festival. Cliff's film is going to *my* film festival. Dawson got a sinking feeling as Cliff stood and addressed the class.

"Okay, I've just been injured in the big game with Tyler. My throwing arm has been crushed, the bone broken in three places. But I refuse to tell the coach because he won't let me play at homecoming if I do."

Dawson had heard this somewhere before.

"Remember," Cliff said, "we want the audience asking, 'Can he do it?' 'Will the team win the big game?'"

Correction. He'd heard this everywhere before— every B-rated sports flick that had ever been made.

"Remember, this is autobiographical, so if anybody has any questions, I was there, I lived it. Come talk to me, all right?" Cliff was saying.

Of course. Capeside's final game last year. Dawson made it a habit not to read the local sports section of the paper: "Mrs. Mason's Grandson Bats Fly Ball through Neighbor's Window." But even Dawson hadn't managed to miss this story. He'd even seen his mother report it on TV: Capeside victory, starring Cliff Perfect.

And now Cliff was going to replay it. In living color. At Dawson's festival. With Ben Gold's blessing.

Cute, Jen thought. More than cute, actually. The guy looked kind of like a living version of a Greek sculpture. Wonder what he looks like with just his fig leaf?

The guy must have felt her gaze. He shut his locker and looked over at her. Jen smiled. He smiled. And came over to her.

"Hi, I'm Cliff."

Oh. So he was the one. Nellie had mentioned him when she cornered Jen on the front steps of school a few mornings ago. No lie about the way he looked.

"Hi, I'm Jen."

"Short for Jennifer. I know. You're new."

"Is it that obvious? I was hoping to blend in," Jen joked.

"Sorry, but that's an impossibility on your part," Cliff tossed back flirtatiously.

Jen laughed. "I'll work on it."

"Well, I just wanted to introduce myself. I know that being the new kid can be traumatic, and if there's anything I can do to take the edge off, like show you around, introduce you to some cool people, take you out, maybe to dinner and a movie . . ."

"Subtle," Jen commented. The guy moved fast.

"It was meant to be assertive," Cliff said lightly.

"That's very nice of you." Jen had to admit she was enjoying the attention. But she'd left "fast" in New York. "Can I let you know? It's the first week. I'm still getting settled."

"Sure," Cliff said easily enough. "Absolutely, and I meant what I said about helping out. I know a lot of people around here. I can hook you up with some friends."

Cliff smiled.

"It was nice to meet you, Jen—short for Jennifer."

"You too, Cliff—short for Clifford."

Chapter 13

Dawson grabbed the latex version of Joey's head off his desk. "Morning, Joe," he said to the mask.

He bounded down the stairs and into the living room. His father was already up, huddled over his restaurant model, playing dollhouse. "Have you seen my camcorder, Dad?"

His father looked up. "You filming, today?"

Dawson held up Joey's rubber head. "Joey gets decapitated."

"Cool," Mitch Leery said. "Your camera's in my room. On the nightstand—your mother's side."

Dawson headed back up the stairs toward his parents' bedroom.

His father's voice followed him: "But you might want to take the tape out."

Dawson froze in midstep. Well, thank you for

sharing that with me, Dad. "You know, you can get arrested for that in some states," he said.

His father just grinned and went back to playing with his model.

"Um, Dad? While we're on the subject of . . . well . . ."

His father looked right at him. Full attention this time.

"I have a question. It's a girl-slash-relationship question," Dawson plunged in. He hadn't really meant to talk to his dad about this, but he hadn't really meant for his dad to bring the whole thing up, either. "I don't want it to go to your head like I'm soliciting fatherly advice or anything," he added quickly.

"What's the question?" his father asked.

"Because I clearly don't condone your perverse sex life—yours and Mom's—but I'm not too proud to admit that my inexperience is hindering my current female relations. . . ."

"And the question?" his father repeated, breaking into Dawson's rambling monologue.

Dawson shifted uncomfortably. He shouldn't have brought this up. His dad shouldn't have brought it up. "The question . . . The subject, actually." But he might as well finish what he'd started. "Mechanics of kissing."

His dad didn't try too hard to conceal a smile. "How can I help?"

"I'm interested in technique."

Mr. Leery laughed. "There is no technique, Dawson. You just put your lips together and go."

A no-answer answer. "But what makes a good kiss?" Dawson persevered.

"Performance anxiety?" his father asked.

Well, Dawson hadn't gotten to the performance yet. Only the rehearsal. In his head. Which was part of the problem. In his head, the kiss was climactic. Bogart. Brando. Leonardo DiCaprio. And what about the kiss in Jen's head? The one she'd said she was going to pretend had happened. What if it was equally awesome? And what if the performance didn't match up to the rehearsal? "I'm just a little confused about what distinguishes a good kiss from a superior kiss," he admitted.

"You'll know. In a big way," Mitch Leery added, passionately but vaguely.

"Could you expound?"

"You have to make it memorable. Something she can't forget."

Details, Dad. It's nothing without the details. "And how would you do that?" Dawson prodded.

"The first time I kissed your mother—"

"Don't get too detailed," Dawson interrupted. There were details and there were details.

"It was summer, and we were out on the boat," Mitch Leery continued. "And your mother's lips were chapped from the sun, and she asked to borrow my Chap Stick, so I took it out and put some on my lips, and then I leaned over and kissed her."

Okay. Dawson could see it. Well, with some other actors playing Mom's and Dad's roles.

"The Chap Stick was really smooth and just slid onto her lips. The sensation was amazing. The chemistry between us was already there, but it was one of those moments that cemented it. You know. It was unforgettable and, most important, romantic."

Dawson was surprised. "And here I thought you were all about sex."

"We still jumped each other. But you gotta have romance. It's all about romance . . . and Chap Stick," Mr. Leery added.

All right, good story. But what had Dawson learned? Besides row softly and carry a big Chap Stick? "But the kiss itself. What did you do?"

Mitch Leery thought for a moment. "Here's how it works. You clear your mind. Just think about her lips—nothing else."

Okay. Easy enough. Dawson had gotten that far already.

"Don't tense up. That destroys a kiss. And you gotta relax. Here . . ." Suddenly Dawson's dad grabbed the latex model of Joey's head. He held it up so that Dawson was staring her in the face. "Give it a try."

What! "Forget it," Dawson said. He backed away from the head.

His father stretched it out toward him. "C'mon. This is a big father-son moment. You asked for it."

No. His father had started it. With the camcorder. Of course, Dawson had asked for it. He wanted to know. Needed to know. He looked at Joey's head. This was too weird. Her lips. "Just think about her lips—nothing else," his dad had said. Dawson looked at the lips. Okay, they were nice lips. He'd told Joey that himself.

"Now, moisten your lips," his father was instructing.

Dawson followed instructions. The lips. Nothing but the lips . . .

"Now go for it. The trick is to relax your bottom lip. You want to let it have a mind of its own. You want it to dance with hers." His father moved the head into position.

The lips. Her lips. Dawson pressed his lips against Joey's.

Joey couldn't believe she was seeing this. She couldn't believe she was watching Dawson kiss her. Up at the top of the stairs, she peered through the railing, like a little girl spying on the grown-ups downstairs.

She'd come in the usual way—up the ladder and into Dawson's room—but she'd heard his voice downstairs. She hadn't meant to spy. She'd been on her way down when she saw them. Saw them and froze, incredulous. Mr. Leery was giving a kissing lesson to Dawson, using her head.

Now she studied Dawson as he pressed his mouth to the mask. Dawson was kissing her! She pictured herself—her real self—down there instead. His lips on her lips—yes, dancing, warm, moist. . . .

"Close your eyes," Mr. Leery was saying.

Joey let her eyes close. Dawson's arms around her, their mouths searching, tentative, then deeper, with intensity. . . .

"That's it," Dawson's father said.

Joey's eyes flew open. Dawson and his dad were

smiling at each other—Dawson sheepishly, his dad simply, proudly. A bonding moment. Between father and son. Not between her and Dawson. Joey gave her head a hard shake.

"That was good," Mr. Leery was saying downstairs.

"Yeah? Cool," Dawson responded. "Now forget this ever happened." He grabbed the Joey head roughly and headed toward the back door.

Joey felt a little shaky as she got to her feet. Best to go back down the ladder and forget she was ever here. Like she could really forget watching Dawson kiss that rubber mask with her face on it.

She backtracked to his room. But before she went through his door, she heard a giggle. She looked around. No one. But there it was again. A giggle and a whisper—coming from the hall closet. And then Joey saw the telephone cord snaking from the hall extension under the closet door.

"Okay, I promise," said the voice. The voice of the local news. The voice of Mrs. Leery. "Bye."

The closet door flew open. Dawson's mother, phone in hand, stifled a little shriek. "Joey! What are you doing here?"

"I was looking for Dawson. We're filming today," Joey explained. And what are you doing? she wanted to ask. Mrs. Leery's face was flushed. She definitely looked as if she'd been caught in the act. Whatever act it was.

"Filming?" Mrs. Leery echoed, flustered. "That's nice."

"I get killed today," Joey said.

"That's nice," Mrs. Leery repeated.

Guilty. Absolutely guilty. Joey faced Dawson's mother. Back to you, Bob. My God, Dawson was right.

Mrs. Leery shut the closet door and put the telephone on the little table in the hall. She turned back to Joey. "Secret anniversary present for Mitch," she said. "I'm making plans, and I don't want him to hear. Twenty years, it'll be."

Yeah?

"Don't say anything."

"Of course not," Joey said.

"Twenty years," Mrs. Leery repeated. "First time he kissed me was in a little rowboat." She got a faraway look in her eyes. "Like the one you use to come over here."

Joey was suddenly irritated with herself. What kind of script was she writing here? Twenty years was a long time, and Mr. and Mrs. Leery were still all over each other.

"Well, be careful out in the sun," Mrs. Leery said. "It's hot today. Use sunblock."

"Thanks, Mrs. Leery. See ya," Joey said.

"You too, Joey."

Joey turned to leave. This was Dawson's fault. His film fantasy conflict bug was catching. As if life didn't present enough conflicts. Like seeing your best friend kiss a rubber model of your face.

Chapter 14

Joey moved down the dock toward her rowboat. The sun was shining. The water was calm. A few birds chirped cheerfully. But you could see that something was wrong.

"Steven? Steven?" she called out.

Her glance fell on something lying at the edge of the dock. A towel? A piece of clothing? She walked over for a closer look. Leaned down toward it. A shirt. She began to pick it up.

"Aah!" She sucked her breath in, fear on her face. The shirt was torn and splattered with blood. "Steven!" her voice rang out, panicked.

She peered into the water. Suddenly the sea creature was upon her. Somehow more real, more nasty-looking than last time. She screamed, lashing out at the creature and bashing it on the head.

The creature fell away back into the water. Joey raced back up the dock, but the creature was pulling himself up on one of the solid wood piles. He clawed his way out of the water, and rose up to his full height on the dock, blocking her way back to the creek bank.

She spun around and ran for the other end of the dock. The creature lumbered after her. She jumped into her rowboat, grabbed the oars, and started to make a getaway, but the creature took a flying dive and landed in the water right next to the boat.

She screamed, struggling with the oars, but the creature latched on to the side of the rowboat with one taloned green claw. With the other one, he slashed at her face. Tore a raw, dripping wound right down her cheek.

Joey screamed bloody murder. The creature slashed his talons across her neck. Her head fell back as he sliced her neck open. Blood sprayed into the air like a geyser. He slashed again. Her head went flying off. More blood sprayed into the blue sky.

Joey's head fell into the bottom of the boat. Her body slumped nearby.

Dawson focused the camera in on the head, lying in a rich pool of blood. The head he'd kissed this morning . . . Uh-uh. He wasn't going there. "And . . . cut! Beautiful. Perfect."

At his side, Jen began to applaud. The real Joey stood up and emerged from the mess in the boat. She was covered, head to toe, with fake blood.

"That couldn't have gone better," Dawson said as she climbed onto the dock.

Pacey came onto shore, too, stripping off his creature costume. "Joey, you die so well," he said. "Dawson, can we do it again? Please? I so liked the image."

"No. Moving on," Dawson said, leaving no room for discussion. "We're behind schedule."

He saw Joey flash Pacey a victorious smile.

Joey was dripping fake blood all over Dawson's front porch. Jen carried out a bowl of soapy water and a towel from the kitchen. She put the bowl down on the porch table and dipped the edge of the towel in it.

"Here, Joey. Let me help you," she said.

Joey shied away. "It's okay. I can do it."

"I don't mind." Jen approached with the towel.

Joey felt a wave of discomfort. She didn't need a cleanup crew. She tugged at her button-front blouse. Ugh. The fake blood had started to dry in the sun, and her shirt stuck to her skin as if the blood were real.

"Ouch," Jen said sympathetically. "Looks like it's really stuck on you."

Before Joey could stop her, Jen took hold of the open neck of the shirt and gently pried it away from Joey's body. She reached for the top button and started to undo it.

Joey felt every muscle in her body clench up. What did Jen think she was doing? She looked into Jen's face, just inches from her own. Met her gaze.

Jen's hands went still, immobilized on Joey's blouse. Joey began to protest, then stopped. Was she being squeamish? Uptight? Jen was just going for the Miss Friendship Award, right? Like she'd been trying to do since she came on the scene.

Jen gingerly undid Joey's top button and wiped at her neckline with the towel. Carefully. Softly. Joey's discomfort swelled. Jen went for the next button down.

Joey abruptly pulled away. "I can do it," she said. She felt her cheeks grow pink. Turning slightly away from Jen, she unbuttoned her shirt and peeled it off her skin. Jen took the shirt from her and handed her the towel. Hot with self-consciousness, Joey began cleaning herself off.

"You have nice breasts," Jen said.

Joey froze. Deer in headlights. Well, Joey's headlights. Jen's eyes on them.

"Don't get the wrong idea," Jen said quickly. "I'm completely hetero. I'm just commenting girl to girl. You have a really nice body."

Joey rapidly finished cleaning herself up and pulled on a clean T-shirt she had set out on the porch rocker earlier. Just girl talk? Jen sounded sincere. She was just so unflappably friendly to Joey. Why? If Joey was nasty, Jen was nice. If Joey was nice, Jen was nice. Not bimbo nice, though. The girl had wit. Sharp wit. Joey was sure she could be nasty if she chose to.

It was too hard to figure out a strategy. "I'm too tall," Joey said, resorting to what she really felt.

Jen shook her head. "No, you're not at all . . . you're commanding."

She was? Joey was silent.

"I wish I had your stature," Jen said.

Uh-oh, thought Joey. She'd let a little honesty in, and now they were playing True Confessions. Best buds suddenly.

"And your long legs," Jen continued. "My body's a mess. I'm short. My hips do this weird thing, my face is shaped like a duck's, and I hate my breasts."

Despite herself, Joey felt empathy—and astonishment. "Are you serious?" Jen had to know how beautiful she was. That when she'd come down the dock that first day, Dawson and Pacey had been stupid with awe.

Jen shrugged. "It's normal, isn't it? To hate the way you look?"

Well, maybe Joey wouldn't have minded looking a little more like Bess—even though people told her there was a strong family resemblance—or a little more like, well . . . someone like Jen.

"You don't look like a duck."

Jen looked at her for a long moment. And smiled. "You know, that's the nicest thing you've said to me since we met." She grabbed the dirty towel and shirt and headed for the door. "I'm going to take these in and clean them up."

Joey felt a breath of relief. Enough of all this sweetness. She licked a streak of fake blood off her finger. She couldn't handle much more of this.

But Jen had one last remark as she went through

the door. "Joey? I plan to make it really hard for you not to like me," she said.

The sun was dropping quickly. Perfect. The darkening sky was just the right effect. Jen and Pacey stood at the end of the dock, talking. The creek glinted in the last light of the day. Dawson trained his camera on the spot where Joey had been decapitated, then focused in on Jen and Pacey.

"Don't worry," Pacey said. "I'll help you find your cousin."

"That's very sweet of you," Jen replied. Close-up on her, on the softness of her face. God, she was pretty. Then back just far enough for a full-body shot. Dawson let the camera follow the lines of her figure, caress them. Back a little more to see her and Pacey together.

"I can't thank you enough," she said with a smile. She looked into Pacey's eyes gratefully. Then she leaned closer to him and kissed him gently, simply.

In an instant Pacey's arms were around her, and he was going in for something more. His mouth pressed down. His lips were . . . dancing. Dawson experienced a moment of paralyzed shock. The kiss kept going. The camera kept capturing it.

"Cut!" Dawson yelled. "Pacey, what are you doing?"

Jen and Pacey broke apart. Dawson stormed over. Pacey's hand still rested on Jen's shoulder.

"What?" Pacey was an innocent. "I'm kissing. What does it look like I'm doing?"

"Snorkeling." Dawson gave Pacey a shove,

knocking his hand away from Jen. "And that's not the way it's scripted."

Jen gave a breezy laugh. Dawson looked at her. The laugh settled into a little smile. She didn't seem too much the worse for wear.

Behind him, Dawson heard Joey laughing too. She came down the dock to join the little party. "It was just a kiss, Dawson." Damn Joey. She was loving this.

"Yeah, and you know what? Honestly, I think we should have another," Pacey suggested.

"No." Dawson spun on Pacey. "I'm cutting the kiss. No kiss."

"Whoa. Wait a second," Joey protested. "You can't cut the kiss."

Dawson took a deep breath. Spielberg, he told himself. "Yes, I can," he said, regaining his composure. "And I just did. It's not working. It doesn't make sense for this new character to kiss her dead cousin's boyfriend. The kiss is officially cut."

Pacey shrugged and started walking up the dock. "Then that means it's a wrap, right? 'Cause I've got plans tonight."

Dawson had had enough of Pacey's hot plans already. "Yeah, that's a wrap. Get outta here."

Joey watched Dawson follow Jen across the lawn toward her grandparents' house. Back near the dock, Joey began packing up the camera equipment. Well, that had been fun, but as they said, all good things must come to an end. And there was Dawson tagging after Jen like a faithful puppy. And here she was, watching Pacey of the Rainbow Eye as he stripped out of his creeped-up wet suit, revealing only the skimpy bathing trunks he'd worn under his costume.

"And what are you up to this evening?" she asked with only mild curiosity.

"It just so happens that the woman of my dreams is attending the school dance tonight, and I plan on being there," Pacey said.

"Lucky her," Joey commented. She wasn't really that interested in who it was, but she did wonder if the woman of his dreams kissed as well as Jen.

Dawson and Jen walked toward her grandparents' house. He was fully aware that they were tracing the route to their pretend kiss, but he tried to keep things easier this time.

"So in honor of the school dance, I rented *Saturday Night Fever, Staying Alive*, and *Grease*," he said.

Jen looked at him questioningly. "In lieu of going?"

"Yeah, it'll be a John Travolta night of interpretive expression. This way we can dance, and our feet never have to move." He laughed. But he noticed Jen wasn't laughing along.

"I can't, Dawson." She looked away from him. "I'm sorry."

Dawson felt a punch of disappointment. But he tried not to let it show. "More enticing plans?" he asked.

"Actually, I'm going to go to the dance, Dawson."

To the dance? As in school spirit? As in "Rah-rah, Capeside"?

"I'm sorry. I didn't know you wanted to do the movie thing," she explained.

"Oh." Well, he hadn't told her. His fault. "That's okay," he said, unconvincingly. "You . . . going alone?"

Jen was quiet. Very quiet for a moment. Dawson felt a grip of dread. "No. Actually, Cliff Elliot asked me."

Dawson felt himself clench up inside. This was even worse than he'd expected.

"He thought it would be a good opportunity for me to meet some people," Jen went on hurriedly. As if her explanation made it all okay.

"Oh." Dawson didn't know what to say.

"C'mon, Dawson. Don't look so down. It's not like a date or anything. He just asked me if I wanted to go, and I said yes."

Dawson felt his defeat take on a bitter edge. "Call me confused. That's the definition of a date, Jen."

Jen looked right at him. Studied his face. "Yeah, you're right," she said softly. "I just wanted to go, you know. I'm new here in Capeside, and it sounded fun."

Dawson thought back to the other day in the lunchroom. Nellie inviting them all to the dance. Yeah, Jen had said she thought it sounded great. Okay, so Dawson didn't usually do dances, but why hadn't he listened a little harder?

"Hey," Jen said brightly, "why don't you show

up? We could dance," she said with a smile. A real smile. Dawson could see she meant it.

But what about Cliff Perfect? Cliff had asked Jen out. Jen had said yes. Was Dawson supposed to show up and hang with both of them? Maybe have a few dozen chances to hear about Cliff playing the homecoming game with his arm broken in three places?

"Nah, I've got a date with Travolta," Dawson said, way more casually than he felt. "I don't want to disappoint him."

"Yeah. Okay," Jen said guardedly. "See ya, Dawson."

She went inside. Dawson wandered back across to his house. He was miserable. Pure, unadulterated misery. What had happened to "I'm going to pretend we kissed, Dawson"?

He kind of wished some hideous sea creature would come up out of the depths and put him out of his misery.

Chapter 15

Dawson was out of his mind. Ranting, shell-shocked, a character in one of his own scripts. Joey stretched out in the middle of Dawson's bed and watched him pace back and forth. Window to wall, wall to window, again and again. It was a little like following a Ping-Pong match.

"Cliff!" Dawson spewed. "Cliff Elliot. What is *that* about? I don't get it. How could she be attracted to him? What's he got?"

"You could start with his chest measurement and work down," Joey suggested. Jen did seem to have a good eye.

"No, beyond the external," Dawson said, so worked up he answered her seriously. "There's nothing going on in here." He pointed to his head. "Head fumes. That's it. The guy's a lightweight.

You know what his film is called? You wanna know?"

"What's his film called, Dawson?"

"*Helmets of Glory*. It chronicles last year's football season. And get this—Mr. Cliff Perfect himself is writing, directing, and starring in it."

"A real Streisand," Joey commented.

Dawson stopped pacing just long enough to frown at her. "This is serious, Joey. Listen, that's this year's Capeside High entry in the film festival. *My* film festival."

"And it's a sports film," Joey egged him on.

"A thin and pedestrian sports film," Dawson concurred.

"The epitome of everything you're against. Could life be more cruel?"

"You're laughing at me, Joe. The point is that his script is ludicrous and his story sense is even worse." Dawson pounded his hand on the TV, as if *Helmets of Glory* might have made it to the small screen right in front of their eyes. "And this is my immediate competition."

"In more ways than one," Joey noted. "Dawson, I don't think his cinematic prowess is the attraction."

Dawson kept rolling, like a video that kept playing long after its viewer had fallen asleep in the armchair. "What kills me is she was so open about it. 'I'm going with Cliff Elliot.' Like it wouldn't bother me. I respect her candor, but it's a little on the thoughtless side, you know."

"Completely thoughtless," Joey echoed automatically. Where was the Stop button?

"At this very moment they're slow dancing. Her arms are wrapped around his waist and they're moving to some stupid, cheesy eighties song."

Well, Dawson was nothing if not good at setting the scene for his stories. Joey heard 'Eternal Flame' start to play in her head. Saw all those couples out on the dance floor, felt her interest starting to spark again.

"And he's whispering things in her ear that make her giggle and throw her hair to one side, and every once in a while their eyes meet and they shift awkwardly and uncomfortably because they both know that it's all leading to that one moment at night's end when he leans over and tells her what a great time he had."

Okay. Joey could see it. Teen love. Party of two.

"He asks if they can do it again, and she just smiles in that sexy, teasing way that doesn't seem teasing at all—just sexy—and she says, 'I'd like that,' and then their lips meet, their mouths come together, their tongues find each other . . . Aaahhh! I can't take it!"

Dawson flung himself onto the bed and collapsed next to Joey. The soliloquy was over.

"You are so dramatic," Joey said.

Dawson rolled over on his side and looked at her. "What did he do that I didn't?"

Joey was incredulous. "He. Asked. Her. Out," she said, measuring the space between words for the extra emphasis Dawson sorely needed.

Dawson's eyes opened wider. Joey could see the light of recognition pop on. This was a new and mind-bending thought to him. Joey couldn't believe it. Their voices dropped, they got a little body hair— and something happened to their brains.

Suddenly Dawson was leaping off the bed. "I'm going to the dance," he announced with determination.

"What!" Dawson didn't do dances. Dawson had never been to a dance in his life.

"I'm going. It's my only recourse."

"Why?" John Travolta was still waiting for them.

Dawson yanked open his closet and began searching the rack for something. "Because Jen is there," he answered.

"In the arms of another man," Joey reminded him. "Why torture yourself?"

Dawson pulled a blue, button-down shirt off a hanger and started changing. "I'm an artist. 'Tortured' is a prerequisite. Are you coming, or not?"

Joey wasn't very happy about giving up their triple feature. They hadn't hung out and watched movies all night since Jen had arrived. And besides, beneath the glib words she and Dawson liked to toss back and forth, she was actually worried about him. "Think it through, Dawson. This little movie plot you've got going may not end the way you want it to."

She was mad at Dawson. Okay, she had to admit it. Not to anyone else and certainly not to him, but she didn't like sharing him with Jen. Still, she didn't want to see Jen break his heart, either.

But Dawson was already playing the romantic lead. "I should be the one kissing her, Joey. Not some J. Crew ad. I can make my bottom lip dance. I know it!"

Joey had a flash of their kiss—Dawson and hers, or rather her head's. He'd been working that dancing lip just the way his father had told him to. At least in her mind.

"Tonight it will happen," Dawson decreed. "This plot will have a happy ending, Joey. You'll see. Tonight I'm going to kiss the girl."

And he didn't mean a latex mask, either. Joey sighed and got to her feet. She couldn't get into watching all those videos alone and having to imagine what was going on at the dance. Better to see it live. To face the pitiful truth.

"This is so pathetic, Dawson. But I am not above witnessing your hormonal suicide. Count me in."

Dawson smiled for the first time all night. Not the happiest smile, but it was something. "I'll meet you downstairs. Give me two seconds. Let me check my hair."

He raced into the bathroom as Joey made her way to the stairs. She pulled on her sweater, and halfway down the stairs she stopped to tie one sneaker. Mrs. Leery's voice floated up the stairs.

"We probably won't discuss the telethon until after dinner, so it could be late."

Joey glanced down. Dawson's mother was leaning over his father. She lowered her mouth onto his. "Mmm . . ." They kissed. And kissed. And kissed.

Finally Mrs. Leery broke away. "I'll shoot for midnight," she told her husband.

Joey was almost out of breath just watching that

kiss. Man, Mr. and Mrs. Leery were lucky. Joey thought about her own parents. The way her dad had run around on her mom forever. And how it had torn her mom apart. Destroyed her. Literally. The cancer came on the heels of her father's most sordid little fling. No matter how you did the math, he had put her six feet under.

Joey swallowed back the lump in her throat. She didn't want to think about it. She wasn't going to think about it. She just wished Dawson would understand how lucky he was. His parents had everything. And he had everything too. So why shouldn't he get the girl?

"Ready?" He came down the stairs behind her.

Joey turned and looked up at him.

"Joe? You okay?"

"Yeah. Sure," Joey said. "Dawson?"

"Uh-huh?"

"You know, I was thinking maybe your movie *will* have a happy ending."

Chapter 16

Jen and Cliff sipped aqua-blue drinks with little plastic fish floating around in them. The gym looked like the inside of an aquarium, nets and huge pieces of papier-mâché coral everywhere, sea life painted on the walls and hanging from the ceiling like mobiles. Vintage Beach Boys was a favorite with the DJ—in between Madonna and the Bangles' "Eternal Flame." The dance floor was crowded with kids.

"Fortunately, this is a victory dance," Cliff said over the music.

Jen took a sip of her blue punch. "And did you make the winning play?"

Cliff smiled at her. The Greek-sculpture smile. "You're here, aren't you?" he said smoothly.

Jen smiled back. "That could have been my exit cue, but somehow you pulled it off." She liked Cliff.

More than she'd expected to. He wasn't Dawson. But Dawson wasn't here, was he? And then there was Joey. It was probably better this way. Cliff was easy to be with. And certainly easy on the eyes.

"I sold it?" Cliff asked lightly.

"Oh, yes. You're smooth yet unassuming. It's endearing," Jen teased back. "Is there anything you're not good at?"

"Dancing," Cliff admitted. "I'm rhythmically challenged."

Jen hoped he was being modest. She loved to dance. "Prove it," she said.

Cliff nodded. He took their drinks and set them down on a nearby table. Then he led her onto the dance floor.

Pacey nodded to the girls he passed. Smiled. Cool. Suave. Bond. James Bond. The strawberry blonde over there looked good in her little black dress. Cute friend in forest-green velvet. Shaken, not stirred, ladies.

All of a sudden he spotted her. And the game was over. Tamara. Over by the punch bowl with that Benji guy—revealed on that humiliating night at the movies as Ben Gold, Dawson's film teacher. Cool melted into nervous and hot. Suave into unsteady.

Mr. Gold moved away, and Tamara was left standing by herself. Pacey felt even more uncertain. Now what? She was wearing a simple midnight-blue dress, nothing as revealing as what she'd had on that first time in the video store, but she looked incredibly sexy. Incredibly desirable. And Pacey knew what it felt like to hold her in his arms. To taste her lips.

He walked over. "Evening . . . Miss Jacobs."

She smiled awkwardly. "Hello, Pacey. How are you this evening?"

"Confused," Pacey answered honestly. "Bewildered. Perplexed. Mystified. A thesaurus of emotion."

The corners of Tamara's mouth turned down. "You know, I'm the chaperon, Pacey. I should make the rounds." She took one step.

Pacey moved in front of her. Close to her. Close enough to feel the electricity between them. "Would you like to dance, Tamara?" he asked softly.

He could see that she was as torn apart as he was. Her hazel eyes gleamed with pent-up emotion. She let her gaze drop. "That's not a good idea, Pacey."

"Of course it's not a good idea. But if things were different, would you?"

"I have to go," Tamara whispered. She side-stepped him and took off across the gym.

"Prepare to descend, Captain," Dawson said uneasily as he checked out the gym and the aquarium decor. Kinda like a full-scale version of his dad's restaurant. A cool band was pumping out their alterna-pop latest, and people were going wild on the dance floor. Go, Capeside.

He and Joey moved to the edge of the dance floor. Dawson scanned the room. It didn't take very long to spot her. Short black crocheted dress, baby T, bare legs, and black platform sandals. Or to spot him. To spot them.

Dawson watched Jen and Cliff moving to the beat. Cliff did a rolling wave kind of thing with his arms. Jen borrowed the gesture and turned it into something new. Cliff took the new movement and riffed on that. They were good.

"They make such a cute couple," Joey offered.

"Shut up," Dawson said.

"What exactly is your plan?"

Dawson felt a rush of desperation. "I didn't get that far."

"Well, you'd better write something quick," Joey said. "Because in some moral sectors what they're doing is known as foreplay."

Dawson grimaced. He was supposed to step into center stage now. But how? Jen and Cliff were swept up in their happy, shining world. The world that did school dances. The world that played football. The world that fit in. He was losing ground every second he stood here. He looked at Joey.

"Do you dance?" He knew the answer.

"Never."

"Now you do," Dawson corrected her. He grabbed her arm and pulled her onto the dance floor.

"Dawson, this is certifiable!" she protested.

"It'll be okay. Just jump around and shake your butt back and forth," Dawson said, as much to himself as to Joey.

He led her into the mass of writhing bodies, toward where Cliff and Jen were dancing. He let go of her arm and faced her, shifting tentatively from one foot to the other and nodding his head to the music. Joey shot him a skeptical look and worked her hands in a modified swimming motion.

And then it was over before it had started. The last notes of the song stretched out into a final chord. The lights in the gym dimmed even further, and the sound of softly lapping surf floated out of the loudspeakers, followed by the gentle, bluesy guitar notes of a slow song. Some of the dancers took it as a cue to move off the floor. The rest moved closer together, ready to glide silkenly and romantically to the music.

Dawson felt a ripple of panic. He looked at Joey. She looked at him. Advance or retreat? Dawson took Joey in his arms, simultaneously looking around for Jen.

"We lost her," he said in Joey's ear.

"Maybe she's with your brain," Joey retorted. But she put her arms around him.

It was surprisingly natural to start swaying to the tune. Dawson was dimly aware that this wasn't too unpleasant, even as he searched for Jen. He spun Joey around so he could get a glimpse of the other side of the room. Joey followed his lead, smoothly, gracefully. Dawson felt a little rush.

"Hey, you're pretty good at this," he whispered.

Joey didn't have an answer handy. But it was okay, because they filled in the wordlessness with the movement of their bodies to the music. Dawson felt himself relax into it. Not unpleasant at all.

"Hey, you guys." That caffeine feeling came rushing back at the sound of Jen's voice.

He and Joey turned in sync, to see Jen and Cliff right beside them. Twirling together as one.

"Hi," Dawson said cautiously.

"You made it," Jen noted brightly.

"Yeah."

"Guys, do you know Cliff?"

"Hi," Joey said. Dawson saw her start at the chest measurement and work down. Dawson gave Cliff a little nod.

"We have film class together, right?" Cliff asked him, easily spinning himself and Jen, so he and Dawson could hear each other.

"Not exactly. It's my study hall base."

"But Dawson is a very talented filmmaker," Jen put in quickly. Dawson would have appreciated it more if she hadn't been dancing in Cliff's arms.

"Oh, yeah?" Cliff asked. "You into movies?"

This was not going the way it was supposed to. The last thing Dawson had come here for was to have a cozy chat about film with Mr. *Helmets of Glory*. "I dabble," Dawson said dismissively.

"Cool," Cliff said.

Dawson felt his frustration building. Sometimes you had to know when to yell "cut."

"See ya," he said to Cliff and Jen. He spun Joey around and moved away. By the time the music ended Jen and Cliff were lost again.

Dawson and Joey let go of each other. "That went brilliantly," Joey said as they moved off the dance floor.

*   *   *

From the sidelines, Pacey watched Tamara studiously watching the dancers. Eyes straight ahead, determined, diligent, intent. Totally focused on avoiding his gaze. She knew he was looking at her. Knew exactly where he was standing.

Pacey dropped his gaze, disgusted, beaten. Tamara knew he was hers for the asking, and she wasn't asking. Then there was the other approach. Make her think about what she was missing. Pacey frowned. A tired plot device, for sure. Especially when she was missing exactly nothing. It wasn't like he was seeing much action these days. Okay, any days, to be honest. But he was desperate. Desperate enough to grab Nellie when he saw her walking by.

"Hi, Nellie." Smile, he coached himself.

"Uh-huh," Nellie said distrustfully.

"Nice dance. I really like what you've done with the place."

Nellie gave him a hard look. "You almost seem pleasant, Pacey. Have you been drinking?"

Pacey glanced over at Tamara. Yes indeed. She was unmistakably watching him talk to Nellie. The smile he bestowed on Nellie grew all the more genuine.

"Drinking? No, not at all. I was just noticing the detail in your neon tetras."

"Your compliments are suspect."

"There's no ulterior motive here." Pacey did his best Boy Scout. "It's just that all this glorious underwater sea life has put my contempt for you in perspective, and I thought maybe you would like to . . . I don't know . . . dance with me . . . maybe." Shy.

Uncertain. Way to go. And Tamara was absolutely checking them out.

"That's very sweet of you," Nellie said. "To ask me. Me. Of all mankind."

Pacey took a step toward her, ready to lead her onto the dance floor. He could stomach it for Tamara's sake.

"Me, who really wouldn't mind if you dropped, on the spot, dead—right at this moment. And I wish I could take this moment to laugh in your face, but I'm getting slightly nauseated just standing next to you, so excuse me." Nellie wriggled the fingers of one hand in an overdone ta-ta. Then she was off.

Pacey quickly looked over at Tamara. But Tamara was chatting away with a couple of her students. She wasn't looking Pacey's way at all. So much for the other approach.

Chapter 17

Hey!" Dawson caught up with Jen in the hallway, where the music and voices from the gym were muted.

Jen whirled around, surprise showing on her face. Then a smile. "I was looking for you. Where did you go?"

Dawson's felt his mood surge, but he played it easy. "I'm here. I'm there."

"I was hoping we could dance."

"What about Cliff?" Dawson reminded her.

"If you'd rather dance with him . . ." Jen teased.

"You know what I mean."

Jen sighed and continued walking down the hall. "It's a song. A three-minute distraction from life."

Jen really didn't seem to see that there was any-thing wrong with this picture, did she? Dawson

124

walked beside her. "But he might not like it. You being his date and all." He spit out the word "date" like a rotten fruit.

Jen paused in front of the door to the rest room. "Forget I asked, Dawson," she said, shaking her head.

"But . . ." But what? Jen had asked him to dance. All he'd had to do was say yes. She pushed open the door to the bathroom and went in.

Loser, man. You're a capital *L*, Dawson told himself. He followed her through the door.

Screams bounced off all the tiles and metal and hard, shiny surfaces. A trio of girls lined up at the mirrors over the sinks were all looking at Dawson and shrieking as if Freddy Krueger had just entered the girls' bathroom.

Dawson beat a hasty retreat. What did he think he was doing? Way to go, Leery, he congratulated himself.

"This is embarrassing," Joey said. She and Dawson were sitting at a table. Sitting with the rejects, the wallflowers, the assorted misfits. Watching Jen and Cliff mingle. A bunch of them down there, talking, laughing, kings and queens of the sock hop. Hard to believe she and Dawson had lived in Capeside forever and Jen was only working on week one. "Let's blow this Popsicle stand."

"No. I'm enjoying my misery," Dawson said self-pityingly.

"The ship has sailed, Dawson. And while you sit here on the dock pontificating, the USS *Jennie* is sailing farther and farther out to sea. Haven't you had enough?" Joey asked.

"No, I'm still breathing."

"You hardly know this girl, Dawson."

"That's the magic of it, Joey. True, Jen stepped into my life not more than two seconds ago, but already I feel that connection. That bond that says we're meant to be together. And you can call it wish fulfillment or delusion of the highest adolescent order, but something primal exists between us."

It was just the kind of dramatic speech Dawson liked to deliver. But beneath it, Joey couldn't miss the real hurt in his voice. Or the real yearning. It wasn't something she was used to hearing. "Dawson, you're scaring me. You're doing this Frankenstein-slash-Hyde thing. One minute you're Dawson, and the next you're his psycho alter ego. You've become the sea creature from your own movie."

"So be it," Dawson said. "I can't explain it any more clearly, Joe. The girl is a mystery, but I feel as if I've known her my whole life. It's like the way I feel about you."

Oh? Joey felt her breath catch.

"She challenges me the way you do. She could be you. Only she's Jen."

Joey was on her feet in a flash. What was *that* supposed to be about? She could be you. Only what? She's better than you? Cuter than you? Bigger bra size, for sure. "Well, just let me remind you how your little allegorical horror movie–slash–love story ends. The creature doesn't get the girl. It dies a violent, bloody, horrible death. Rest in peace,

Dawson. It was nice knowing you." Joey pushed her chair back.

"Where are you going?" Dawson asked mildly.

"I'm dead already. Remember?" Joey said. She stormed across the gym floor.

She didn't get far enough fast enough. Suddenly Pacey was grabbing her arm. "Dance with me, Joey," he commanded.

"What!" Had everyone in here gone crazy? Had someone slipped something into the tropical-fish punch?

"Please, you gotta," Pacey said. "I'm trying to make this girl jealous. Please, Joey, put aside all your disgust for one moment in time and dance with me. I beg you."

Joey's mouth tugged down in repulsion. Dawson might have turned into his own sea creature, but Pacey was, after all, the original monster from the deep. And typecast. "I'd rather slide down a razor blade into a huge Jacuzzi full of lemon juice."

But Pacey got his arms around her and started pushing her onto the dance floor.

Joey tried the elbow maneuver that she'd used on Pacey in the film. But this wasn't playacting. The guy was determined. He held her tight and started moving to the slow music. "I'm gonna kill you," Joey said through gritted teeth.

Pacey didn't ease up. "Please. I have cash."

"Let me go before I whip your ass all over this court," Joey threatened.

But Pacey was looking off to the side of the gym.

Joey saw a small, satisfied smile appear on his face. He looked back down at her. "Kiss me," he said.

"You've lost it." Joey yanked away from him. Hard.

Pacey pulled her back in just before she'd fully broken away. "You can hate me forever, Joey, but right now just close your eyes and think of someone else."

She didn't know what hit her. Pacey grabbed her face in his hands, and his mouth was on her mouth. She felt his lips moving over hers with surprising skill. Her eyes closed. Pacey vanished, and it was someone else. His lips. Just think about his lips— nothing else. She felt herself give in, her mouth melt open, their tongues meet. . . .

And then he was pulling away, and her eyes flew open and—Pacey! The horror of it crashed over her. She brought her hand up and slapped him across the face. Violently, her palm striking his cheek with a loud clap.

"You stagnant sewer filth!" she snarled.

"Time to rewrite," Dawson said to himself. He headed onto the dance floor, where Cliff and Jen were slow dancing in each other's arms. Taking a deep, courageous breath, he tapped Cliff on one massive, muscular shoulder.

"Excuse me. I'd like to cut in."

Cliff and Jen both looked up, startled. "What are you doing, Dawson?" Jen asked.

"Actually, I don't want to cut in. I'd like to take over. I'd like to thank you, Cliff, for showing Jen such a great time for the earlier part of the evening, but I'm here now, of sound mind and body, and can take it from here."

"What are you talking about?" Cliff asked.

Dawson looked at Jen expectantly.

"Yeah, what are you talking about?" Jen echoed.

Dawson was rattled. It wasn't the response he'd anticipated. But he'd let her slip away twice tonight already. Three times and you're out. Even if you're not into baseball, dude.

"I'm talking about you and me," he told Jen earnestly. He turned to Cliff. "Me and her. You see, it's all a little confusing, but all you really need to know, Cliff, is that Jen and I have something going on, and it's still a little raw and undefined, and this is my attempt to clarify the situation." Cliff and Jen had stopped dancing. "So I ask you to do the manly thing and step aside so that I may have a moment with the object of my desire."

Cliff took a step away from Jen and shot her a quizzical look. "Who is this guy?"

Jen looked at Dawson. He looked at her. She didn't look happy. "Dawson, what are you doing?" she asked in a low voice.

"Hey, you're going to have to leave now," Cliff said. "This is too weird."

Around them, people were beginning to stare. Well, it had to be uphill from here, didn't it? "No, you're going to have to leave," Dawson said with a show of bravado. "I'm staying."

Cliff turned to Jen. "What's going on, Jen? Do you want to be with this guy?"

Jen's round, pretty face was drawn. She looked from Dawson to Cliff and back to Dawson.

"Why don't you just leave?" Cliff said threateningly.

"No." Dawson stood his ground. "Why don't you?"

Cliff positioned himself between Dawson and Jen. "And if I don't?" He was looking down at Dawson. He was big. He could win football games with his arm broken in three places.

"Actually, I didn't think it through that far," Dawson said prudently.

But Jen was putting some distance between herself and both of them. "Tell you what," she said, disgust and anger ringing in her voice. "I'll make it easy for both of you. *I'll* go."

And she went.

Dawson and Cliff stood dumbly in the crowd of gently swaying couples. Good rewrite, dude, Dawson told himself. You just lost the girl.

Chapter 18

This could easily be the single most horrific night of my life," Dawson said.

Joey stayed safely on one side of him, far away from Pacey. If that sea creature came anywhere near her again, she was going to think about taking out a restraining order. Of course, with Pacey's father and brother making up fully one quarter of the year-round Capeside police force, it might be hard to get it enforced. But Dawson was oblivious to any extra tension between his best buds. Who, after all, could have any dramas that compared to his? The three of them walked home along the harbor as most of the restaurants were closing up for the night.

"I'm a simp," Dawson continued. "Joey, how could you let me do that?"

The moon slid behind a cloud and then out again.

"See? I knew this would turn against me somehow. It would all be my fault."

"And Pacey. My nonexistent friend," Dawson scolded him.

"Sorry man, I was otherwise engaged," Pacey said. He flashed Joey a lewd, secret little grin.

Joey refused to acknowledge him. "At least I didn't desert you," she told Dawson. "I came back."

Dawson whirled on Pacey. "And who is this mystery woman you keep alluding to?"

Pacey sighed. "Unfortunately, the mystery woman remains a mystery even to me," he said.

Dawson didn't pursue it. Not with *Helmets of Glory II* in the making. "I'll bet Jen's lips are pressing against Cliff's at this very moment."

"Don't go there," Joey advised.

They reached the road where Pacey turned off. "Okay, my friends, this is my stop. I'll see you mañana."

"Bye," Dawson said distractedly.

Joey let out a little breath of relief as Pacey detoured. Weird night. She and Dawson walked quietly for a few moments.

"Okay, Joe, let's assess," Dawson finally said. "What have we learned from tonight's 90210 evening?"

That was easy. "We should always stay home on Saturday night and watch movies, because the rewind on the remote of life does not work," Joey answered.

Dawson let out a long breath. "That will not be

a problem now that I've ruined it with Jen. It is officially over."

"It never began, Dawson," Joey corrected him.

Dawson was too dejected to bother with a snappy comeback. "I do feel like the monster from my movie," he said. "There's something going on inside of me I can't control. It's like I have no balance. Everything is a high or a low. It's either hot or cold. Black or white. There's no middle ground anymore. I mean, nothing is just okay."

"I'm too tired to philosophize, Dawson." And she was. They had covered an awful lot of ground in one week.

Dawson studied her and nodded slowly. Joey could see that she'd gotten through. "Do me a favor, when I start to get like this again, " he said, "and I'm sure I will—until this whole adolescent growth process is over—will you simply chain me to my bed and wait for my moment of clarity to come?"

"Can I use leather straps?"

"Not until you explain the Crisco," Dawson said, giving her a shove.

Joey laughed. A real, uncomplicated laugh. "Dawson, you are such a sphincter. You really are. I don't understand how someone can be so self-aware and yet utterly clueless. It escapes me."

"It's my charm," Dawson said.

Joey smiled to herself. Yeah. He was right about that. It *was* his charm. Suddenly she saw a shadow cross Dawson's face.

"Oh, no," he moaned, staring at something in the distance.

Joey followed his gaze. Not something. Someone. As in Miss Someone Else. Standing on the pier at the edge of the harbor, gazing out at the water. She looked beautiful in the shifting moonlight. Even Joey saw that.

"What do I do?" Dawson asked. He sounded genuinely afraid.

"It's your call." Joey couldn't have helped him out on this one even if she'd wanted to.

"I've pretty much ruined the evening. I may as well complete it."

"Until no one is left standing," Joey said with resignation.

"Can I bag on you, Joey?"

"Yeah, you can bag."

Dawson sucked in a breath of sea air. "Wish me luck."

Joey looked at him, then out at Jen, then back at Dawson. She ached. But she knew Dawson hurt, too, and that made her ache even more. "Good luck, Dawson. I hope you get your kiss."

And in some weird way she meant it. With all her heart.

"This cannot be happening." Pacey had been here before. Tamara in the very same spot, looking moody but beautiful in the soft, twinkling lights of the harbor. Pacey walking toward her. Just like last time.

"Miss Jacobs."

She turned. But this time she looked as if she had been expecting him. "Hi, Pacey."

"I feel a strange familiarity creeping over me."

"I thought I might find you here." So she *had* been waiting.

Pacey was instantly flattered. And instantly wary. "Are you here to reiterate what didn't happen—again?" he asked, keeping his distance.

"I thought talking to you might be appropriate."

"Give us a chance to do it all again."

"Only change the ending," Tamara said. "I'm sorry about my behavior, Pacey. I didn't mean to dismiss you, but this whole ordeal has completely thrown me."

Ordeal. Thanks a lot, Miss Jacobs.

"When I saw you at school," she said, "I didn't know what to say. This is without question the most absurd thing I've ever done in my life. Not to mention punishable in a court of law."

"It was just a kiss." Okay, it was some kiss. Still . . .

"No, it was more than that," Tamara said.

Pacey's pulse took off like a speedboat. What was Tamara trying to say?

"It was dead wrong of me, and I can stand here and explain to you my hopelessly troubled state of mind, because you do deserve an explanation for my behavior. But instead of feeding you ten years' worth of therapy, I thought maybe I could get away with a simple apology. Pacey, I'm sorry."

Oh. Sorry, as in sorry it ever happened. The speedboat sputtered to a halt.

"And I hope this hasn't left you with any permanent scars. What I did was wrong . . . and I'm sorry."

Scars? From a kiss? Maybe Tamara wanted to erase the moment, but Pacey didn't. If nothing else, he had the memory of it. The moment when it wasn't about how many years there were between them or which side of the teacher's desk they sat on. The moment when all that existed was the feel of her lips, her body, the desire pulling them together.

"Where do you get off taking all the responsibility for this?" he asked. "I may just be fifteen, but I'm long past the age of accountability." He stopped, realizing how pompous that sounded. "Okay, maybe not within the confines of the judicial system." He gave a short laugh. "But for me. I kissed back. My lips kissed you back."

"Fair enough," Tamara conceded.

"And I don't regret that at all. And you shouldn't, either."

Tamara gave a funny, bittersweet smile. "But it can't happen again, Pacey. From this moment on, our relationship is strictly that of teacher and student. I want that clear."

Too late for that, Pacey thought. "And if I were to object?" He took a step toward her.

"The subject is not up for discussion. You know it has to be this way. For all of the obvious and not so obvious reasons."

Pacey knew she was right. Knew it in his head. Knew it with every logical, rational part of him. But every other part of him knew she was dead wrong.

They stood together, locked in each other's gaze, holding each other without touching. The fire between them burned as white-hot as the scattering of stars overhead.

"This is so unfair," Pacey said softly. "I'm not good with girls, and now I finally meet someone and . . ." His words trailed off. Nothing he could say was going to change the situation.

Tamara reached a tentative hand out to him, then seemed to think better of it and pulled her hand back. "Don't worry, Pacey. That will change. Trust me." Her voice was brimming with tender feelings. Too tender. Pacey could feel himself breaking.

"Yeah, well . . ."

"Good night, Pacey."

"Good night, Tamara."

Pacey tore himself away. Turned and started walking. He could feel her behind him, feel her just standing there. No! It shouldn't be like this! Pacey spun around, closed the gap between them in a few strides, and took her in his arms.

They came together in a fiery kiss. The moment stretched out, potent and intense, obliterating everything else around them. They kissed again. And again.

Chapter 19

Dawson studied Jen from a few yards away. She was gazing out over the harbor at a small yacht docked nearby. But Dawson doubted she really saw it. On deck a couple drew close together. Jen pulled her light sweater around herself. Drawing into herself. Maybe she *was* watching the couple. Or maybe it was the cool fall air that you could feel riding in on the end of summer.

Dawson fought a silent tug-of-war. Leave bad enough alone? Or keep trying and risk making things worse? Though he wasn't sure that was possible.

"I'm starting to feel like your TV set," Jen said, without shifting her gaze.

Exposed. She'd known he was there all along. "I didn't know what to say," Dawson managed.

"A first?" Jen said flatly. She turned her face toward him.

Dawson stood motionless. Wordless. A first, a second . . . He didn't know what he could say to take back what he'd done.

"I am really angry, Dawson."

"I know." He felt her anger radiating from her like a force field, protecting her, holding him away.

She looked back at the water. "What do you want from me, Dawson?"

"I want to know what's going on between us." No script. Nothing clever. This was real.

"And does that question have to be answered tonight?"

"I'm sorry about tonight, Jen. I got a little scared. Scared I was becoming the 'friend.' "

Jen faced him full on. "Oh. The friend. How awful." There was a bitterness in her voice that he'd never heard before.

"It *is* awful," Dawson said. "I feel as if I'm becoming that friend who lives next door, the one you come and tell all your boy adventures to. And I don't want that to be the case, Jen. I want to be your boy adventure."

"Can't you be both?"

Dawson thought about it. In a strange, backward way, he'd had this conversation before. The first night Joey hadn't slept over. "No," he answered. "Not at fifteen you can't. It's too complicated."

"I see." Jen didn't try to hide her disappointment. Dawson felt his mood dive even lower. Her next words caught him by surprise. "So . . . I'm interested."

"In what?"

She laughed softly. "An adventure. What do I have to do?"

Dawson just stared at her. The smile in her deep-set eyes, the lure of her full mouth, something vaguely mysterious in the way she held herself—she'd never looked quite as beautiful as she did right this second.

"You could kiss me," Dawson dared.

Jen lowered her gaze. Dawson could see the breath go out of her. Feel it go out of him. "You know, I really am a cliché, Dawson. In New York, I was moving really, really fast. So fast, in fact, that I kept stumbling and falling."

Dawson heard the anguish behind her words. For the first time since she'd stepped out of that taxi, he paused to wonder where she'd come from. What place in her mind. If he felt as if he'd known her forever, he suddenly felt he also didn't know her at all. But Jen didn't leave space for questions.

"Here I feel like I'm walking at a steady pace for the first time in a long time," she went on. "And I'm scared that if I kiss you, my knees may buckle and I may stumble, and I don't think I could deal with that right now."

Dawson nodded. Scared of what their kiss could bring? That part he understood just fine. Out on the boat the music changed to Jann Arden singing "You Don't Know Me." The couple on deck moved to the music. Fluidly, intimately.

"Would you like to dance?" Jen asked.

"What? Here?" Dawson looked around as if they were about to get caught out in public with their pajamas on. By whom? And so what? A few cars went by on Bayview Drive. A handful of people, alone or in couples, were strolling on the docks and the beach that curved along the harbor.

"I've been wanting to dance with you all night, Dawson."

Here it was. Another chance. The fresh chance he'd come looking for. Dawson and Jen didn't need any more words. They came together slowly, rhythmically, the music and their feelings taking hold of both of them in unison.

Time slipped away like sand through the cracks in the boardwalk under their feet. There was only now. Only here. Only the cool light of the moon gliding in and out of the clouds, a few stars in the unveiled patches of sky. Jen's perfume mingled with the fresh scent of autumn's arrival. Their breathing—Jen's and Dawson's together—rose and fell like the water lapping at the shore.

They looked into each other's eyes as they danced. "You see, Dawson, the kiss is the end result," Jen whispered. "It's not really important. It's all about desire, and wanting . . ."

"And romance," Dawson whispered.

"Yes." He could feel Jen's breath on his cheek. "Romance . . ."

Well, it wasn't the USS *Jennie* sailing off, after all, Joey thought. It was the USS *Joey*. She climbed into her rowboat and just sat for a while, looking up at Dawson's darkened window.

It seemed like days ago that she'd rowed over for their triple feature. In a different life. Although maybe it had been a different life for longer than she or Dawson really wanted to admit.

It was strange being here without him. Being here and being alone. But the strangest thing was that the ache was gone. For now, at least. She just felt . . . accepting? Empty? Both? She felt as if her little boat had found the calm at the eye of the storm. She'd been swept up by these raging winds, raging feelings, and found a funny little stretch of tranquillity.

Of course, sooner or later she was bound to come crashing down hard. But for now there was only this moment.

Lazily, Joey untied the boat from the dock. It was easy to forget what a pretty place they lived in. Easy not to see what you saw every day. But when you really looked, really stopped to feel it, the world out there could be breathtaking. Awesome enough to dwarf all their little day-to-day problems. Big enough to make the dramas of a handful of people seem pretty insignificant. What was that line from *Casablanca*? "A few people's problems don't add up to a hill of beans in this world." Joey smiled and began rowing.

Close by, a car door slammed. She looked over to see someone parked under a tree by the creek bank, partially hidden. She dipped her oars silently a few times and glided forward for a clearer view.

Mrs. Leery was getting out of the car, coming around to the driver's side. She leaned down to the open window. Kissed the driver good night. It was a deep, long, passionate kiss. Wasn't Mr. Leery getting out too?

It hit Joey all at once. That wasn't Dawson's parents' car. His mother had said she'd be out until midnight. Without his father. As Mrs. Leery straightened up and took a step toward the house, Joey got a good look at the driver's face. Mrs. Leery's co-anchor's face.

Joey felt as if she'd been punched in the gut. Back to you, Bob. So it was true. This wasn't one of Dawson's made-up film fantasy conflicts. Not some carefully crafted drama to play counterpoint to Dawson's perfect life. Except that Dawson's life wasn't so perfect. Joey sat thunderstruck. Frozen with the knowledge.

And the knowledge that Dawson still didn't know.

**Meet the Stars
of the hit
television show produced by
Columbia TriStar Television**

DAWSON'S CREEK™

DAWSON

James Van Der Beek

*M*uch like the experience of the character he portrays, James Van Der Beek's dedication and talent surfaced at an early age. A mild concussion sidelined his school football career and instead Van Der Beek found himself playing the lead role in a local children's theater production of *Grease*. He fell in love with the theater and continued to perform locally.

"Dawson reminds me of myself when I was 15," say Van Der Beek. "I grew up in a small New England town and vacationed on Cape Cod, where the show takes place, and we both come from loving, supportive homes. We also look alike," jokes the 20-year-old actor.

"Dawson and I were both very impassioned at an early age," explains Van Der Beek. "Dawson is a burgeoning filmmaker, whose overactive imagination and idealism sometimes make him oblivious. He's prone to rejecting reality for a more romantic scenario. He's a bit of an innocent and is frequently off in his own little world, all of which I can definitely relate to."

When Van Der Beek was 16, his mother, noting his intense interest in performing, offered to support his aspirations by accompanying him on daily six-hour round trips into New York City, to test the waters. In spite of landing an agent and manager on their first trip into the city, Van Der Beek spent a year auditioning for commercials without much success.

At 17, Van Der Beek was cast in the off-Broadway play written and directed by Edward Albee, *Finding the Sun*. Juggling the long commute for rehearsals and performances during the play's limited three-month run while attending high school, Van Der Beek credits the play as the defining experience for him as an actor and still managed to finish the school year second in his class.

After his off-Broadway debut, he went on to star in *Shenandoah* at the Goodspeed Opera House. His first screen performance occurred in the 1995 feature film *Angus* as an arrogant jock. Van Der Beek also appeared in the Miramax film *I Love You . . . I Love You Not* with Claire Danes, and most recently in the independent feature film *Harvest*.

An excellent student, Van Der Beek received an academic scholarship to attend Drew University in Madison, New Jersey, where he majored in English and sociology and made the dean's list. He is currently on a leave of absence while shooting DAWSON'S CREEK in Wilmington, North Carolina.

JOEY

Katie Holmes

*E*ighteen-year-old Katie Holmes possesses an exceptional maturity much like Joey Potter, the character she portrays on DAWSON'S CREEK.

Born and raised in Toledo, Ohio, Holmes began acting in high school theater productions in spite of a personal belief that acting careers couldn't be sustained living in the Midwest. "Toledo is a bit bigger than Capeside (the fictional location of DAWSON'S CREEK), but there are similarities," she says. "I'm a small-town girl just like Joey. I wasn't the one that had the boys in high school. I was a little bit of a tomboy and also the youngest in my family, so I thought I knew everything. Like Joey, I made a lot of mistakes, but fortunately I haven't had the tragedy that she's experienced in her life."

Her character, Joey Potter, is something of a tomboy. As Holmes explains, "Joey is a 15-year-old girl that uses a tough attitude as a guard because she's been through so much. She's been hurt so many times that she doesn't want to be vulnerable and put herself out there for everyone. She has to be tough. She lost her mom [to cancer] and her dad's in prison. She lives with her unwed and pregnant sister and her sister's boyfriend. Her relationship with Dawson has been the only stable thing in her life and now it's beginning to change."

The stability and importance of friends played a

significant role in Holmes's life as well when she chose to honor her commitment to friends and classmates by performing in the school production of *Damn Yankees* instead of going to Los Angeles on a callback from the producers and casting agents for DAWSON'S CREEK. Fortunately, the producers were able to reschedule the audition and Holmes won the role of Joey Potter.

A captivating newcomer to the entertainment world, Holmes has experienced incredible success, landing major roles in both feature films and television projects while participating in only a handful of auditions. Her very first professional audition resulted in a plum role in the award-winning film *The Ice Storm*, directed by Ang Lee (*Sense and Sensibility*). The film, which recently won the screenplay award from the Cannes Film Festival, stars Kevin Kline, Sigourney Weaver, Elijah Wood, and Joan Allen and depicts the sexual revolution of the 1970s.

Having graduated from high school, Holmes is now living in Wilmington, North Carolina, while working on DAWSON'S CREEK.

PACEY

Joshua Jackson

*B*orn in Vancouver, 19-year-old Joshua Jackson spent his formative years in California, moving with his family back to Vancouver at the age of eight. It was there that he launched his professional career, appearing in a series of television commercials promoting tourism in British Columbia. While his family shuttled between Vancouver and California, Jackson also sang with the San Francisco Boys' Chorus.

In describing his character, Pacey, Jackson admits, "Four years ago, I had similar issues to what Pacey is dealing with. We both grew up in a community-based atmosphere. He grew up in a much smaller town, which has its own limitations and benefits, but I grew up in a community where I knew everybody in the neighborhood, went to school with all the same kids and spent a decade of my life with the same people. Like Pacey, I also have an offbeat sense of humor and I enjoy laughing, having a good time, and often get myself in trouble for it. But neither of us is mischievous for mischief's sake. Pacey's in his own world, doing his own thing, which unfortunately seems to offend a lot of people."

Jackson continues, "Pacey's basically an outsider at school who also feels disconnected from his family. He's always been told he's a screwup and isn't going to succeed, so he feels he can do anything he likes and has nothing to lose. He finds a group of friends that take him for what he is and both understand and appreciate his oddball quality. Pacey's also the odd man out in his family. His father is the sheriff of Capeside and his brother is a deputy. He is closer to his mother and sisters, but his sisters are off at school. Because of this family dynamic, Pacey is much more comfortable with women. I was raised among females; it was just me, my mom, and my sister, and I'm more comfortable being around women because of that too."

Unlike his DAWSON'S CREEK character, however, Jackson excelled at an early age. Landing his first feature-film role in Michael Bortman's *Crooked Hearts* for MGM/Pathe, Jackson's stage debut followed in 1991, when he played the lead role of Charlie in the Seattle production of *Willy Wonka and the Chocolate Factory*. Since then, Jackson has appeared in such films as *Andre the Seal*, *Tombstone*, *Digger*, and *Magic in the Water*, as well as all three of Disney's *The Mighty Ducks* features, portraying the coach's prodigy and the team's voice of reason, Charlie. Jackson has also recently completed principal photography for Bryan Singer's latest film, *Apt Pupil*, starring Ian McKellen and produced by Mike Medavoy.

His recent television projects include two Showtime Contemporary Classics, *Robin of Locksley*, based on the Robin Hood legend, and *Ronnie and Julie*, an updated version of Shakespeare's *Romeo and Juliet*. Jackson has also appeared in *Champs*, the DreamWorks/ABC series created and produced by *Family Ties* producer Gary David Goldberg.

As a regular on DAWSON'S CREEK, Jackson now lives in Wilmington, North Carolina, during production.

JEN

Michelle Williams

Michelle Williams, like her character Jennifer Lindley on DAWSON'S CREEK, is making the transition from big city to small-town life. The 17-year-old actress moved from Los Angeles to Wilmington, North Carolina, the production location for the series. As Williams recounts, "It's quite a change from Los Angeles. It's beautiful and a nice pace for a while, but at first it was a strange switch from the city and traffic. Having the experience of moving from a big city to a small town does make it easier to relate to Jen, however."

Williams explains that her character "is an outsider coming to Capeside from a fast-paced New York lifestyle. Ostensibly she's come to help her strict grandmother care for her seriously ailing grandfather, but she's hiding a troubled past. More sophisticated and worldly than the other three teen characters, she's an old soul, having done a lot and grown up fast. I think a part of Jen is really looking to regain her innocence and lead the quintessential teenage life, and she wants to fit in with these more carefree kids. But there's another part of her that still longs for the city lights, taxi rides, bars, and clubs. She made some mistakes, and got sent to Capeside by her parents in hopes that she'd begin to realize she should slow down and change her ways."

While Williams may be a bit homesick for big city

life herself, she is no stranger to the country, having grown up in an idyllic spot in Montana. After her family moved to San Diego, she took advantage of the proximity of Hollywood to explore an acting career, which quickly took off. At 16, after obtaining an accelerated high school degree, she moved to Los Angeles full time to pursue her craft. Most recently, she portrayed Michelle Pfeiffer's daughter in Propaganda Films' *A Thousand Acres*, starring Jessica Lange, Michelle Pfeiffer, and Jason Robards. Williams has also appeared in numerous theater productions. On television, she has won guest appearances on series including *Step by Step* and *Home Improvement*, as well as roles in the television movies *A Mother's Justice* and *Killing Mr. Griffin*. Her additional feature film credits include *Species*, *Lassie*, and *Time Master*.

While living in Wilmington to shoot DAWSON'S CREEK, Williams enjoys reading as many books as she can in her spare time.

"Meet the Stars" material provided courtesy of Columbia TriStar Interactive.

About the Author

Jennifer Baker is the author of over thirty novels for young readers and a creator of Web-based entertainment and dramas. She lives in New York City with her husband and son.

Long Hot Summer

Dawson's Creek™

Long Hot Summer

Based on the television series "Dawson's Creek™"
created by Kevin Williamson

Written by K. S. Rodriguez

For Arthur Termott and Alexandra Peredo,
my favorite teenagers.

Chapter 1

The girl races toward the dock, her expression turning from anguish to fear. A dead end. How would she escape? The hit man's urgent footsteps are pounding behind her, growing louder, coming closer and closer. . . .

She is the only living witness. The pretty, innocent teenager could blow the Capeside Connection wide open. If she doesn't get away and get help—fast—the mob will rub her out.

There is only one avenue of escape. Quickly she unties the rowboat attached to the dock. She scans the area—no other boats around. Perfect. If she can just find the oars, she'll be out of harm's way.

She spies the oars lying on the grass at the far end of the dock. But the hit man is in view now. He wears a wide-brimmed hat, pulled low over his dark and deadly eyes.

1

The girl anxiously looks from the oars to the hit man. He stretches an arm out and fires his first shot. Pow! She has no choice. She rushes to the paddles, risking her life with every second of delay.

Pow! Pow! She dodges the bullets. Luckily, the hit man misses, and she retrieves the oars. Tucking them under her arm, she races back down the dock, her long brown hair flying in the breeze.

Thump! *She lands in the center of the rowboat. It wobbles and wavers, but the girl takes immediate control.*

Pow! Plop! Pow! Plop! Gunshots sound, and bullets drop into the water around her. The girl doesn't hesitate. She doesn't flinch, and she doesn't look back. Dipping the oars into the water, she steadies the boat and glides quickly to a safe distance, taunting the hit man: "Does the Godfather know you're such a bad shot?"

The gunman throws down his weapon and curses in disgust. The girl, wearing a satisfied smile, continues to row. She knew joining the crew team would come in handy one day. Next year, she muses, maybe the skeet squad. "Target practice," she hollers triumphantly. "Look it up!"

"And it's a wrap!" Dawson Leery called out, still peering through the camera viewfinder at Joey Potter in the rowboat. He took a step closer to Joey as he faded out. "That was grea—"

Before he could finish his sentence, Dawson teetered off the end of the dock and plunked into the creek with a huge splash.

He surfaced and dunked his head backward into

the water so his hair slicked back like that of an old-time movie star. Hysterical laughter rang out around him. He saw Pacey Witter standing at the end of the dock, twirling the prop pistol. Joey still sat in the rowboat in the creek, a few feet away from Dawson.

"Smooth move, Baryshnikov," Pacey shouted.

Joey abruptly stopped laughing. "Hey!" she yelled from the boat. "Does this mean that all of that footage is ruined and we have to shoot this again?"

Dawson swam to the dock and handed Pacey the camera. "Nope—it's waterproof. I'm happy to say that *The Capeside Connection* is in the can."

Pacey whooped in celebration. He shed his hitman hat and overcoat, and cannonballed over Dawson's head into the creek.

"Now summer is really here!" Joey said happily.

Dawson looked toward her. She looked so nice and happy and dry in that rowboat. . . .

He locked eyes with Pacey. The good thing about having a friend like Pacey, Dawson thought, was that he always seemed to know exactly what Dawson was thinking. The second good thing was that he had the sickest and most mischievous sense of humor of anyone Dawson had ever met.

Dawson and Pacey swam over to the rowboat as Joey chattered on. "Can we lay off the filming for a while, now?" she was saying. "You've been working us like mules all year long, Dawson. I mean, I think your movies are good and everything, but they *are* a lot of work."

"Then stop complaining and join a union," Dawson said as he placed his hands on one side of the

3

boat, while Pacey grabbed on to the other. They exchanged a roguish glance, but this time it didn't escape Joey.

She picked up an oar and poked it at Dawson as he playfully started to rock the boat. "Don't!" she cried. "Please—I don't want to get wet again! I'm finally dry from the last take! And I have to go to work," she pleaded.

Dawson stopped rocking the boat and gave Joey his best sincere stare. "Okay," he said, "if you say so."

The two boys suddenly gave the rowboat a mighty shove.

The boat tipped.

Joey screamed.

Into the creek she went.

This time Dawson got to laugh with Pacey at Joey.

"They're two exhibits short in the immaturity museum," Joey sputtered when she emerged. "You guys should really get over there."

Pacey gave Joey a splash. "But we took the day off for your induction into the premenstrual hall of fame," he retorted. "We wouldn't miss that for the world."

Dawson laughed so hard he nearly swallowed a mouthful of water. He spit it out, straight at Joey.

"This is war," Joey declared, then splashed both boys with all of her might.

Dawson and Pacey retaliated, while Joey sank into the water to escape the attack.

A familiar voice called them from the end of the dock.

"I thought you guys were going to finish that film today. No one told me anything about having fun!"

Dawson grinned. It was Jen Lindley. Though she was making an all-out effort to be friends again after their breakup, Dawson still felt a small pang in his heart that their romance had died.

Joey popped her head out of the water and regarded Jen's pale arm moving in a friendly wave. "Captain Ahab arrives" she murmured, then felt guilty. Somehow she just couldn't seem to stop herself from making comments about Jen, even though they were friends now, after a rocky start. Joey always felt so gawky around cool, sophisticated Jen.

Dawson shot Joey a look and splashed her in the face. Even though he told himself he was totally over Jen, he still didn't like it when Joey gave her a hard time. He still felt protective of Jen.

He admired how the sun glistened off Jen's golden hair as she dangled a delicate foot off the dock. His breath caught in his throat again. He thought she was so beautiful. Every time he saw her he felt something between wanting her to disappear and wanting her back.

Jen smiled. "How'd it go today, Dawson?" she asked, her voice amiable.

Dawson called back, "Great, great!" trying to sound casual.

But he didn't feel casual. Trying to be all buddy-buddy with Jen was hard. Harder than he had ever imagined.

Pacey's voice cut through Dawson's thoughts and lightened his mood. "Hey, Jen, if you want to join us, you have to take off your clothes," he joked, grabbing the overturned rowboat as Joey and Dawson treaded water. "You can't see, but we're all skinny-dipping."

Jen laughed and made circles in the water with her foot. "Nice try, Pacey. I think I'll keep my clothes on and stay dry."

Pacey didn't give up. "If you want to stay dry, you can sunbathe naked. Nude sunbathing is legal in Capeside, you know. It was one of America's first settled nudist colonies. Townspeople here pay homage to the nude settlers every summer by shedding their clothing at the drop of a hat."

"I'll pass on that, too, but thanks for the history lesson," she answered.

Joey mumbled, "That's funny. Nothing's ever stopped her from taking off her clothes before."

"Oooh—meow," Pacey said.

Dawson put a giant hand on top of Joey's head and dunked her for that comment. Joey was his closest friend—even closer than Pacey—but sometimes she could really tick him off.

Dawson sighed. He had so many conflicting feelings about Joey. Sometimes he wanted to strangle her. Other times he wanted to kiss her. It was weird. Weirder, if possible, than his relationship with Jen.

He thought about a time recently when he and Joey had kissed. It was strange, but since then he had started to think about her in a different way. In a—dared he say it?—sexual way. It was hard for him to reconcile the images of Joey, the girl who used to hide in his closet and play Jaws with him, and Joey, the girl with pretty, thick brown hair and incredibly soft lips. He tried to push both images out of his mind.

Joey came up sputtering from his dunk. "What's your problem, Dawson?" she sputtered, clearly annoyed.

Dawson didn't answer. He didn't know *what* his problem was.

Chapter 2

Dawson, Joey, Pacey, and Jen spent the rest of the afternoon lying on the dock. The warm summer sun soaking into Joey's skin felt great. She was so relaxed she almost felt as if she were floating. She wished she didn't have to go to work. She could lie on the dock for days, free from all responsibility, her body limp.

The foursome was mostly silent, listening to the cry of the gulls that circled overhead and enjoying the breeze that made the waves splash against the rocking rowboat.

Joey noted that Dawson was quiet. His mood had changed as soon as Jen arrived. That was typical, she thought. He'd been acting like some kind of psychology experiment lately. One minute he'd be fun. The next minute he'd act warm and fuzzy and thoughtful. Then in a flash he'd turn into a tortured, scowling, grunting, typical teenage male.

What had happened to the old Dawson? Joey wondered. She wished he would be his old self again—the guy who could finish her sentences or say what she was thinking before she even said it. She hoped they could actually have some fun this summer—if it was possible in between baby-sitting and working like a slave.

Work. "What time is it?" Joey asked, breaking the silence. She figured she'd have to get over to the Icehouse soon.

"Why?" Pacey asked lazily. "There was a big zoo break and you have a date?"

"No," Joey answered. "Unlike you three layabouts I have to go to work. So what time *is* it?"

"It's four o'clock," Dawson said, "and you forget the many grueling hours Pacey and I have ahead of us at Screenplay Video this summer."

"The many grueling hours *you* have ahead of you at Screenplay Video, my friend," Pacey spoke up. "I officially resigned yesterday."

Dawson sat upright. "What?" he asked incredulously. "Why did you quit?"

Pacey opened his eyes and shielded them from the late afternoon sun. "Because I have bigger and better opportunities."

"Like what?" Dawson scoffed. "Cleaning your dad's guns? Helping your mom garden? Watching the creek evaporate?"

"Opportunities like meeting women in bikinis," Pacey answered, slipping on his sunglasses. "Saving damsels in distress from shark attacks. Sitting in the sun all day and flexing my muscles—that kind of stuff. Like that Blotto song from the eighties, I wanna be a lifeguard. And I'm going to be a lifeguard. You heard it here first."

Jen laughed and uncrossed her legs from their yoga position.

"You think that's funny?" Pacey asked defensively, lowering his shades. He did his best mobster impersonation. "Do I amuse you?"

Jen shook her head. "No, of course not. It's just that—that's what I'm doing this summer, too. Are you going to start Lifesaving 101 at the town pool bright and early tomorrow?"

"Seven-thirty," Pacey confirmed. "Cool. I'm glad I'll know someone else there."

Jen smiled. "Yeah. Me too."

Joey smiled too. It was good to know that Jen would be busy this summer. Maybe then she'd stop hanging around and force-feeding her friendliness to everyone. That gave Joey an idea.

She stood up to leave, but she lingered for a moment. "Hey, Dawson," she said, jabbing him with her foot, "before these two start playing *Baywatch*, why don't we hit the beach while it's still safe? How about Friday? Early, though, because I have to work the late lunch shift."

Dawson seemed to come out of whatever dream world he was in and answered Joey with a startled and uncertain "Sure." Then he added, "I mean— sounds great. I'll pick you up."

"Don't forget the Frisbee," Joey added. "Bye, guys!" She jumped into her rowboat, grabbed the oars, and glided toward home, feeling warm inside, as if the heat from the sun were radiating through her chest.

She watched the three figures grow smaller with each pull of the oars. She decided right then and there that she was going to have a good summer if it killed her. Despite everything she had to do, she was determined to have fun and spend a lot of time with Dawson, like the old days.

Maybe then his head would come down from planet Jen and come back to Capeside.

And maybe he would even be her best friend again.

Chapter 3

"The sights and sounds of Capeside at night," Dawson said in his best narrative voice. Though he didn't know what he'd do with this tape, Dawson enjoyed filming bits and pieces of his favorite places.

Dawson zoomed in and out on the reflection of moonlight on the water. He stopped the tape and lowered his camera, then walked over and sat beneath the tall oak tree. He stretched out and took in a deep breath of the warm night air.

He loved to sit by the creek at night. It was all so quiet and still. This was the only place and evening was the only time when he could truly be alone with his thoughts. The events of the day played in his mind like a movie.

It was going to be weird working at the video store without Pacey. They were sure to be short-handed now, but it never was busy in the summer anyway. Who would he talk to all day?

He'd spend the day at the beach with Joey on Friday, as he had promised. But after that, he'd cool off until he got his feelings sorted out. Or until he met someone else.

But how and where would he meet someone new? Capeside was so small, and unfortunately most of the girls didn't hold his interest. He had to find something else to do this summer—something that would keep him busy, out of trouble, and away from girls whose names began with *J*.

Male-female relationships were just too complicated, Dawson thought. He never had to go through any of that with Pacey. It was like that movie, *When Harry Met Sally*. In that movie, Harry says that men and women can't be friends because "the sex part always gets in the way." Too true, Dawson thought.

Dawson lifted his camera and restarted the tape. He panned the shoreline across the way. Orange lights twinkled like out-of-focus fireflies in the distance. A cricket perched on a nearby bush chirped a high-pitched chant. Boats rocked softly on the dark water.

Then it hit him: he could make a documentary. He'd never tried that before. But a documentary about what? Capeside?

He had lived in Capeside all his life, and though he thought it was a pretty ordinary place, he loved many things about it. He especially liked it in the fall, when the tourists went home, the beaches grew quiet, and it returned to being a low-key seaside town. But as much as he liked the quaint town, he didn't think it would make for a very interesting documentary.

Dawson groaned. He could make a documentary about his own sorrowful life. It would be called *Dawson Leery: Inside Every Loser Is an Even Bigger Dork.* "You're pathetic," he said to himself.

He hoped a better idea would come to him eventually. As a cloud passed over the moon and the cricket's chirps grew louder, Dawson stole a sideways glance at his wristwatch: nine o'clock.

He aimed the camera toward the houses along the shore, deciding to speculate on what other people were up to at that time of night.

Next to Jen's house was the Backmans' place. They were probably having a family fight, Dawson guessed. Sometimes they screamed so loud at one another that people on the other side of the creek claimed they could hear them.

Next to the Backmans were the Barclays. He focused on their gray Cape Cod home. They were a nice young yuppie couple. Dawson's mother had told him they'd just had twins. They were probably holding hands by the cribside, watching the babies sleep peacefully.

He zoomed in closer when he saw a figure come out the back door of the Barclay's house. Dawson stood up. It was a young woman. He'd never seen *her* before.

She leaned against the wooden porch railing and stared across the creek. Dawson could see that she was beautiful. She looked about his age, but it was hard to tell from that distance.

"This calls for some investigation, Geraldo," Dawson said softly to himself.

Quietly he crept along the grass, careful not to let the girl see him. He stopped when he had a full-face close-up of her.

The camera didn't lie. She *was* beautiful. Seventeen, eighteen, nineteen, maybe, Dawson thought. Intrigued, he raised his eyebrows. An older woman. Cool.

The moonlight danced down the girl's long sandy-colored hair—the longest hair Dawson had ever seen, even longer than Joey's. Her profile was soft and fragile, her expression dreamy.

Who was this mysterious new girl? "Enquiring minds want to know," Dawson whispered.

The girl turned back toward the house, as if someone had called her inside. She walked quickly across the porch and disappeared. Dawson could hear the screen door shut.

Dawson stopped the tape. "Cut," he said thoughtfully.

He lowered the camera and jogged back to his own yard, a big grin on his face. Well, well, a new girl in town. Tomorrow he'd make it his business to find out who she was.

Chapter 4

Jen regarded herself in the full-length mirror in her bedroom. The new hot pink bikini fit perfectly, but she wasn't sure she should wear it on the first day of lifesaving class. Maybe she should wear a one-piece—something more modest.

A soft tap at her door interrupted her decision. "Come in, Grams," she said.

Jen's grandmother quietly opened the door and poked her head in. "Don't forget to wear sunblock," she said. Then her eyes widened when she noticed what her granddaughter was wearing. "Certainly you're not going to class in *that*," she said sternly.

That made up Jen's mind. Forget the one-piece. The hot pink bikini it was. Though she knew what Grams' beef was, Jen feigned ignorance. "What's wrong with this suit, Grams? Does it reveal that I am a young woman?" She put on an expression of

16

mock horror. "Do you think people are going to notice my *breasts*?" she whispered in a fake shocked tone.

Jen could tell that Grams was trying her best not to show her embarrassment. She had to give her credit—with Jen's training, Grams was growing more and more flappable every day.

"You're going to train to be a lifesaver. You're going to be learning valuable skills like CPR," Grams said. "That class is not a fashion show, and it is certainly not a place to flaunt your anatomy."

Jen stifled a laugh, but before she could respond, a loud knock sounded on the front door downstairs. "Who could that be at this hour?" Grams asked, then charged downstairs in a huff.

Jen walked to her bedroom window and drew aside the curtain. Pacey, clutching a paper bag, was peering into the window next to the front door. After checking herself out in the mirror once more, Jen tugged a pair of shorts and a tank top on over her suit, stepped into her sandals, and ran down the stairs.

"I'll get it," Jen offered. "It's only Pacey. He's taking the class with me." She walked past her grandmother to the front door. "And don't worry," she said over her shoulder as she swung open the front door, "I think he's already aware of my breasts."

Pacey flinched at the last sentence, then laughed. For once, Jen thought, she had caught him off guard and he didn't have a clever comeback. "Morning," Pacey said. "Ready for the big day?"

"Let me just grab my bag," Jen said.

Through the screen door, Jen's grandmother

glared at Pacey disapprovingly. "Good morning to you, too, ma'am," he said.

Grams harrumphed, then scowled and disappeared into the kitchen.

"Have a nice day, Grams," Jen called, then followed Pacey into the yard, laughing.

"What's so funny?" Pacey asked.

"It's nothing," Jen said, pausing to pull her hair back into a ponytail. "It's just that I don't know when she last had a nice day. Or if she ever had a nice day!"

Pacey laughed along with her, then opened the paper bag he was carrying. "She's probably grouchy because she hasn't had her morning coffee." He offered Jen a large white cup with a lid. "Latte?"

Jen drew in a deep breath and eagerly grabbed the cup. "I'm an addict. Thanks! How did you know?"

Pacey smiled mysteriously. "I have my ways."

Jen arched an eyebrow at him.

"Okay," Pacey admitted. "Dawson might have mentioned it once. Or twice. Or three or four times. Along with every other detail about your likes and dislikes, thoughts, feelings, et cetera."

Jen punched Pacey in the arm playfully. "Give Dawson a break, Pace. I know he's kind of obsessive compulsive. But I messed everything up—"

"Hey," Pacey interrupted. "I promise not to talk about that dead horse of a relationship if you don't." He stuck out a hand. "Deal?"

Jen smiled. "Deal," she agreed, pumping Pacey's hand eagerly. She didn't want to rehash Dawson stuff anymore. She wanted to move on. Right now she just wanted to be on her own. No boyfriends. No worries.

She and Pacey didn't talk much more as they walked to the town pool, where they would begin their training. But she felt comfortable, knowing she didn't have to force conversation. Jen just strolled down the street, sipping her coffee and enjoying the warm, gentle morning breeze caressing her face.

At this very moment she finally felt that she belonged to Capeside. She had grown used to the little town, and she liked it. Life was less complicated here than in New York, she thought, though Capeside did have its share of mini-dramas.

Jen had managed to avoid personal catastrophes in Capeside—so far. She wanted to keep it that way. She wanted to live a plain, simple, ordinary life, moving at her own pace.

Now here she was, with a comfortable friend, on her way to her summer job, finally living like a normal kid in Anytown, U.S.A. She took a final gulp of her coffee. She just hoped the peace would last.

Joey sat numbly at the kitchen table, only half absorbing her sister's seemingly endless list of things for her to remember while she watched the baby today.

"And throw in a load of wash, if you can. Okay, Joey?" Bess was saying. "Earth to Joey?"

"I hear you!" Joey snapped impatiently. "It's not like I've never baby-sat before." Then she added under her breath, "It's like *all* I do."

Bess turned sharply on Joey. "What did you say?"

Joey looked her sister right in the eye. "I said, 'I

know what I'm doing.' " She knew Bess didn't have the time to challenge her.

"Look," Bess said. "This would be a lot easier if you lost the attitude. I know it's hard on you, but we have to do our best until we can afford to hire a permanent sitter. If you'll watch him until eleven, Bodie will relieve you so you can make it to the restaurant in time for the lunch shift."

"Happy, happy, joy, joy," Joey muttered. Then to deflect her sister's angry stare she quickly added, "You're going to be late." She took Alexander from her sister's arms. "Bye," she said.

Bess gave her son a kiss on the forehead. "Contrary to popular belief, I do appreciate this," she told Joey before she hurried out the door.

Joey looked down into Alexander's sweet face. He was adorable—red-apple cheeks, wondrous blue eyes, and teeny, tiny nose. When he smiled, he looked just like Joey's mother. God, how Joey missed her. If Mom were around, things would be different, she thought.

Why did she have to go and die on them? If Mom were around, she'd be able to pitch in and watch the baby. If Mom were around, who knows, maybe Bess wouldn't have even gotten pregnant. If Mom were around, Joey wouldn't have to break her back working at the Icehouse, scurrying around to feed the demanding and hungry tourists.

If Mom were around, maybe Joey would have a normal carefree summer. She cradled the baby in her arms and sighed wistfully. What did she have to look forward to this summer besides baby-sitting and working?

Well, she was going to the beach with Dawson tomorrow. That was something.

Sunlight streamed through the kitchen window. It looked like a beautiful day out there, and Joey figured there was no reason for her to stay cooped up in the house. "C'mon, kid, we're going outside," she announced to Alexander.

As Joey sat on the front porch, cradling Alexander, she heard a familiar voice singing jump-rope rhymes. It was her eight-year-old neighbor, Clarissa Cummings. Joey waved at the sweet little girl.

Clarissa dropped her jump rope and ran over to Joey, who smiled at her. Clarissa idolized her.

"Hi, Joey," Clarissa said. "Guess how many times I counted on the jump rope today?"

"Hmm," Joey answered, her face a mask of deep concentration. They played this game all the time. Joey always lowballed her first. "One hundred?"

"More," Clarissa said proudly.

Joey guessed again. "Two hundred?"

"Nope," Clarissa said, shaking her head. "Even more."

"Not five hundred!" Joey said. "That's humanly impossible!"

Clarissa laughed. "Six hundred. But I stopped to say hi and to ask you for a favor."

"Anything," Joey said. And she would do anything for Clarissa. If her nephew turned out to be half as nice, she'd be thrilled. Clarissa was the sweetest kid she knew.

"My family is going on vacation tomorrow for two weeks, and I was wondering if you would watch Howard for me," Clarissa asked.

"Howard?" Joey repeated.

"My pet," Clarissa explained.

Joey didn't recall Clarissa having a pet. That was all she needed—to be stuck with a baby, and a job, and a pet for the summer. "I'm sorry, Clarissa, I can't watch your pet," she said. When she saw the disappointment creep onto Clarissa's face, she thought of an excuse. "I'm allergic."

"Allergic? To plastic?" Clarissa asked.

Joey gave Clarissa a puzzled look. "Your pet is plastic? Is it a toy horse or something? In that case—"

"No, it's Howard, my virtual pet," Clarissa explained. "We're going to Europe, and my parents won't let me bring him. They say I'll pay too much attention to Howard and not enough to the sights, whatever that means."

Joey laughed. A virtual pet! She saw a lot of little kids carrying them around. They were key chain fobs that resembled video games. What a relief! "Sure, then! I'll be happy to watch Howard."

Clarissa gave Joey a jug. Thanks. You're the only person I would trust with Howard, anyway. He's been alive for a record 643 years. If you take care of him, I know he'll still be alive when I come back."

"No problem," Joey said. "If I can take care of my nephew, I'm sure Howard will be fine."

Clarissa excitedly darted off. "I'll go get him—and his manual—for you," she called back.

Manual? Joey thought. How complicated could that little piece of plastic be? Alexander squirmed in her arms and let out a whimper. He was hungry again. Joey stood up and carried him inside so she could give him his bottle.

When Joey had calmed Alexander, she put him in his portable seat on the porch. Clarissa came running over with the pet.

"Hey there, Howard," Joey said when Clarissa ceremoniously handed him over. It was a bright pink egg on a key chain, just as she had expected. But she didn't expect the length of the manual Clarissa gave her next. Joey laughed. "This is a joke, right—this manual?"

"No," Clarissa said seriously. "Joey, it's very important that you read it and follow every rule." Her eyes grew earnest. "If you don't, Howard will die! Please don't kill my pet, Joey! He's my best friend!"

"Okay, okay," Joey said hastily. She didn't want two crying kids on her hands! "I'll read it carefully."

"Thank you, Joey," Clarissa said. She stared at Joey with big liquid eyes. "Howard and you are my best friends."

Alexander started to gurgle and cry again. This time his sounds were more than whimpers. They were earsplitting shrieks.

"Have a great vacation," Joey said to Clarissa, as she carried the infant back into the house. Inside, as the baby screamed, she added, "God knows mine is already shot."

Chapter 5

Pacey scoped the crowd gathered outside at the pool, careful to hide behind his dark sunglasses so he didn't appear to be checking anyone out. Not bad, he thought. Of the ten people who were all together, six were girls. He recognized two kids from school, one girl and one guy, but that was all, and they didn't seem to recognize him. He figured that a good portion of these people just spent their summers in Capeside and this was their parents' way of making sure they had something to do all day. The others probably went to private schools.

There were more than a few cute girls. In fact, all of them were hookup material. The one he recognized from school was a petite redhead named Angela something. Then there were two older-looking girls, probably coeds, he guessed. One was a tall, sophisticated-looking brunette. The other seemed to have been born to be a lifeguard: sandy-haired, athletic, tanned, healthy.

That was when Pacey noticed the crowning glory. Twins. Blond twins. They were the only ones who weren't wearing cover-ups or shirts over their bathing suits. And what a shame it would be, Pacey thought, if they covered up those babacious bods. They looked like movie stars or quintessential California girls, except they were in Massachusetts.

"Dawson, you have no idea what you're missing," Pacey said softly.

He sized up the guys—his competition—quickly. Only three others besides him. He recognized one guy, Todd, from school. He was pasty, frail, and wimpy—definitely not a threat. The other guys looked pretty normal. One was nondescript, nothing special, Pacey thought. The other guy looked cool, but Pacey thought he had girlfriend written all over him. He hoped he was right.

A tall, tanned, muscular older man strolled into the crowd and blew a whistle. Great. Pacey grimaced. He could see the girls swooning already.

"I'm Tim," the man said. "I'll be your lifeguard instructor. I want to welcome you all here." He paused, then took off his sunglasses and regarded the students seriously. "I hope you all will be with me by the end of the course. But unfortunately we lose many students along the way."

Lose them? Pacey wondered what that was supposed to mean. Did people actually drop dead from lifeguard training? This guy Tim was obviously joking. Pacey laughed out loud.

Bad move. The instructor stopped and stared right

at him. Silently he marched over. He stopped right in front of Pacey and assumed a stiff military stance.

"What's your name, young man?" he snapped.

"Pacey,' he answered. "Pacey Witter."

"It's not funny, Witter," Tim said. Little droplets of spittle escaped his mouth and flew right into Pacey's face. "Not everyone graduates. In fact, a third of you will fail this course. Some of you won't even make it past today."

"O-okay," Pacey stammered. "When you said 'lose,' I thought you meant that people died from the intense training or something—that's all."

The class erupted into laughter. Tim, though, remained serious. "Practically," he said. "Some students can't hack it and wish they were dead." He turned away from Pacey and spoke out to the quiet crowd. "Let's get this straight right away. If you're here to get a tan, leave now. If you're here to pick up girls or boys, leave now. If you are here because you enjoy *Baywatch*, leave now."

No one moved. "If you are here for any reason," Tim went on, "other than to protect the safety of the Community of Capeside, leave now." Pacey shrank under Tim's withering stare, but he didn't move a muscle or utter another word.

"Good," Tim said. "Today I will give you a pre-test. You must pass this in order to continue with training. Is anyone here under fifteen years of age?" Tim again scanned the crowd. No one raised a hand. "Good. Let's get started. Sink or swim!" he bellowed, then laughed at his own joke.

The rest of the morning was spent mostly waiting and watching. Pacey took the opportunity to break the ice with some of the girls, smiling and helping them out, but many of them were afraid to talk, lest they be reprimanded by Tim.

The pretest consisted of swimming 500 yards, first with a breast stroke, then with a crawl, then with a sidestroke. The trainees also had to tread water with their legs only for at least two minutes, which was harder than Pacey thought it would be. Then they had to dive to the bottom of the deep end of the pool, retrieve a heavy brick, and bring it to the surface.

It was fairly easy stuff. Pacey and Jen passed the test without a problem, but one of the boys—Todd, the guy Pacey recognized from school—failed. He could barely swim, even. Pacey wondered why he was there in the first place.

It was a short day, and they were dismissed before lunch. But Tim made a point of letting everyone know that the days of real training would be longer and much more grueling.

He also passed out manuals and informed the trainees that they would be quizzed the next day on the first chapter.

Pacey took his book, feeling secure. No matter how harsh a picture Tough Tim wanted to paint, lifeguarding was going to be a piece of cake. The harder task would be to bag a babe without getting in trouble.

But Pacey had a feeling he could pass that test with flying colors, too.

Dawson fidgeted behind the counter at Screenplay Video. He had cataloged all the returns, straightened and dusted the shelves, and put out all of the new merchandise. Now he had absolutely nothing to do.

Summer at the store was going to be murder. No one rented movies in the summer, especially during the day. Normal people were outside, enjoying the beach and the nice weather. And here he was, pasty white, wearing a dumb black vest, with three hours to go, and absolutely, positively nothing to do except watch a movie. Suddenly that option seemed unappealing to Dawson.

The bells at the front door rang. Great, he thought. Either this person has the wrong store or it's some vampire wanna-be type, some psycho who holes up all day and watches videos. Dawson glanced toward the door.

It was her! The girl he had spotted last night. And here she was struggling to get a double baby carriage through the door. And here he was, Dawson realized, standing behind the counter like a jerk.

He immediately rushed to the door and held it open. "Wait! Allow me," he said gallantly.

The girl pulled in the carriage and smiled. She wore her shiny sandy-colored hair in a long braid that cascaded down her back. "Thank you. It's hard to get through doors with this thing," she said, laughing. "It's the Cadillac of baby carriages—in size only, of course."

Dawson's heart melted at her smile, but he especially liked her adorable accent. He couldn't quite place it. It sounded almost British but not quite. He was dying to know where she was from.

Dawson cooed over the tiny sleeping babies, who

offered the perfect opening for an introduction. "Are these the Barclay twins?" he asked softly, so not to wake them.

"Yes!" the girl answered cheerfully, tossing her braid over her shoulder. "You know the Barclays, then?"

"They live a few doors down from us," Dawson explained. He stuck out a hand. "Hi, I'm Dawson Leery."

The girl shook Dawson's hand eagerly. "And I'm Sheila Billingsley. I'm the Barclay's nanny."

"Welcome to Capeside," Dawson said. He liked her down-to-earth, friendly manner. And he also liked the comfortable but cool way she dressed: a long, flowing printed skirt, a baggy blue T-shirt, and several unique silver rings and bracelets.

"Where are you from?" Dawson asked.

"A little bit of everywhere, actually," the girl answered. "But mainly from Australia."

Australia. It sounded far away and romantic and fun, and Dawson bet that Sheila Billingsley was, too. "I love Australia," Dawson blurted out.

"Have you been there?" Sheila asked, surprised.

Dawson blushed. "No, actually. What I meant was that I love Australian films, like *Strictly Ballroom* and *Muriel's Wedding*."

"I'm impressed," Sheila said, grinning even wider. "Most Americans' knowledge of Australian films doesn't go beyond '*Crocodile Dundee*.'"

"Well, Dawson admitted. "I'm kind of film-obsessed. I mean, I work here and everything. I make my own films, too."

"That's grand," Sheila said. "Then you would be the perfect person to help me today."

"At your service," Dawson said.

Sheila started to describe the type of movie she was looking for. "Something fun, upbeat, for when I'm sitting tonight. Nothing scary," she warned. "I'll be home alone—except for these two guys, of course." She nodded, indicating the twins.

Dawson noticed her lovely green eyes, which had little flecks of gold in them. She had adorable dimples, too. Definite knockout, but in a wholesome way, Dawson noticed. "I can come up with more than enough suggestions," he assured her, but was drowned out by one baby's wail.

"Oh, dear," Sheila said, picking the baby up. She patted and soothed the infant, but then the other started to shriek, too. "I'm afraid they're getting colicky," she said. Balancing one baby in one arm, she lifted the other. She drew both of them to her breast, then rocked and twirled while singing softly and sweetly.

Dawson watched her calming the infants. She seemed so in control, so self-assured. Not the least bit flustered. Her voice didn't even waver as she sang. "You have a nice voice," he commented.

"I hope you don't mind," she told Dawson. "But this is the only way to quiet them."

"Don't be shy," Dawson said. "It's not like you're going to drive any customers away." After a minute the babies were quiet. He was amazed at how she was able to calm them so quickly and easily. When Joey's nephew started to cry, sometimes half a day seemed to pass before he stopped.

The twins seemed to be under Sheila's spell. They weren't the only ones, Dawson thought.

"I better go," Sheila whispered, when she put the twins back into the carriage. "I can come back for a movie another time. Sorry I have to run, but I should really be getting them home now. It was nice meeting you."

"Wait," Dawson said before she turned to go. "Why don't you let me pick out a tape for you. I can drop it by on my way home from work tonight," he offered hopefully. "It would be no trouble at all."

Sheila beamed. "That would be lovely! Thank you. It would make my life so much easier." She gave Dawson another winning smile. "I'll see you tonight, then, Dawson."

"Bye," Dawson said, then ran over to open the door for her.

When the door closed, Dawson pumped a fist into the air. He usually wasn't so forward with girls, but he had liked Sheila instantly. Now he would spend the next few slow hours picking out the perfect video and dreaming of when he'd see Sheila Billingsley's striking face again.

He could tell right away that Sheila was the answer to his problems. Her name did not start with a *J*. And she was different. She seemed mature and responsible, not cranky like Joey or fickle like Jen.

No doubt about it. Sheila Billingsley was definitely going to be the cure for his summertime blues.

Chapter 6

Pacey sat on the living room couch at home flipping through the lifesaving manual. He chuckled at the cheesy drawings and out-of-date photos as he turned the pages. But the book was thick. It seemed there was a lot to learn.

Crash! The book was suddenly knocked out of his hands by a basketball. His brother, Doug, had thrown it. Now he loomed over Pacey challengingly.

"Shouldn't you be out disco dancing to Abba or something? Or does your date have to spend the night with his wife and kids?" Pacey cracked, never one to miss an opportunity to accuse his older brother of being a closet case.

"Har-de-har," Doug said. "C'mon, I'm bored. Shoot hoops with me. I'm in the mood to whup your butt."

"Look," Pacey said. "I don't care what you're

into. But do me a favor and keep *my* butt out of it." He retrieved the manual, which had flown to the other side of the room. "Besides, I can't. I've got to study for a lifeguarding quiz tomorrow."

Doug let out a peal of laughter. "Lifeguarding? You? Now *that's* a funny joke. I don't know what's worse, drowning or having you, with your rancid breath, perform mouth-to-mouth on me."

Pacey didn't answer him. He cracked open the manual and started reading.

"Come on," Doug prodded. "That stuff is cake anyway, although I know that you're a little, shall we say, slow?"

Pacey closed the book. The only way to get Doug off his back was to shoot a few with him. Anyway, Pacey thought, the first chapter did look like cake—it was all about the history of life-guarding and being professional. Nothing too essential, he figured.

"All right," Pacey said, then followed Doug out to the driveway.

It was the same old story. Doug whooped and yelled and cheered for every basket he made. When he won, which Pacey always let him do, because he was all too familiar with the consequences if Doug lost, he strutted around like he was Muhammad Ali or something.

"What a surprise," Doug said, patting Pacey on the back way too hard. "You're a loser once again." He laughed, then ran inside to shower.

Pacey shook his head. He knew there was no way he was ever going to shed the loser label in his fam-

ily. But it would be a different story at the pool
tomorrow.

Pacey Witter the lifeguard was no loser.

When the clock hit the stroke of six, Dawson
ripped off his vest. Nellie, the owner's daughter, had
shown up on time to relieve him, thank God. Usually she was late. She had tried to engage Dawson
in a boring, gossipy conversation, but he cut her
short, telling her he had to go.

"Don't tell me you're finally growing a social life,
Dawson," Nellie said bitterly.

"I'm not the one working tonight; you are. Now,
that's not very sociable, is it?" Dawson answered as
he grabbed the three videos for Sheila. He enjoyed
watching Nellie's expression sour. "I guess schedul-
ing you at night is Daddy's way of making sure his
little girl isn't *too* social, huh?"

"I guess I'm wrong. You're renting videos again I
see," Nellie retorted. "Have a blast. Hope you don't
get too wild and crazy."

Dawson didn't even answer her as he raced out
the door. He hoped Sheila liked the videos he'd
chosen. He'd tell her they were a "welcome to
Capeside" gift, courtesy of the store. That was partially true: Dawson had paid for them with the
money he earned there.

When he stepped outside into the summer night,
he felt magic in the air, as if something special was
going to happen tonight. A new girl—just when he
needed her. He couldn't believe his luck.

Dawson stopped in his tracks on the sidewalk.
Calm down, he told himself. He was just dropping

videos off for the most beautiful girl he'd ever seen in his life. There was no call for him to get carried away with delusions of romance. For all he knew, she had a boyfriend. For all he knew, she wasn't the slightest bit interested in him.

But this just had to work out! Dawson thought. She was his only hope of moving on with his life.

As he approached the Barclays' house, his heart pounded with excitement. He couldn't help but get his hopes up about her. She seemed so cool.

When Dawson tapped on the front door, Mr. Barclay answered. He invited Dawson in, giving him a hearty handshake. The hall was full of luggage, and Mr. Barclay explained that he and his wife were going on a week-long trip. "I didn't know that Screenplay Video delivered," he said.

Dawson laughed. "We don't, but Sheila here had her hands full today, so I figured I'd help her out and drop these by on my way home."

Mr. Barclay ushered Dawson into the family room, where he found Sheila feeding one of the twins. "Dawson!" she said cheerfully. "I really appreciate this."

"It was no problem at all," Dawson said. "I hope you like what I've chosen." He laid the three videos on the coffee table.

Sheila immediately pointed out one box. "I've been dying to see that one," she said.

"Me too," Mr. Barclay added, "but every time I try to rent it, it's out!"

"Well, you know," Dawson said with mock pride, "I have pull at the video store."

Mr. Barclay laughed then excused himself. "We

have to get going. But stay as long as you'd like, Dawson. I'm glad Sheila's already made a friend."

"Thanks. Have a great trip." Dawson rose and shook his hand once again. "Cute babies!" he called after him.

Sheila finished feeding the twins and smiled at Dawson. "Hey, if you're not busy, would you like to watch the movie with me?"

Dawson smiled so broadly he thought his face might split in half. Just what he had hoped. "Sure," he said, trying to sound casual.

"I'll make popcorn," Sheila offered.

"I'll help," Dawson countered.

He followed her into the kitchen and they talked as they prepared their snack. Dawson asked her a lot of questions; he wanted to know everything about her. He found out that she was eighteen—not so much older than he was. He learned that she had come to live with the Barclays the week before. He discovered that she liked to sing, play the piano, paint, and read biographies of great women.

"What brought you to Capeside?" Dawson asked her as they walked back to the family room.

"The job," Sheila said. "It sounded too good to pass up."

Dawson nodded. "Capeside may be small and kind of corny, but it has everything you need in a small town—a movie theater, video store, good restaurants."

"I think it's wonderful," Sheila said. "I hope to stay for a while."

Dawson's heart leaped at her last statement. He hoped she stayed, too. "So where were you before

Capeside?" he asked. "Or did you come here straight from the Land of Oz."

"Boston," Sheila answered quickly. "I was there briefly."

"Cool!" Dawson said. "Did you hang out at the Commons a lot? I hear there's this great section for good restaurants, called the North End. Was Boston a fun city?"

"Yes," Sheila said vaguely. Then she picked up a video. "Let's slip this in, shall we?"

They watched the movie, mostly in silence, and they both enjoyed it. By the time the movie ended, Sheila had to put the twins to bed. Dawson helped her, and they chatted a little. Sheila wanted to know all about Dawson's films. He was more than happy to fill her in. She even invited him to bring his own films the next night.

After the twins were asleep, Dawson reluctantly said good-bye. He felt really comfortable with Sheila, and he thought she was an amazing person: smart, talented, beautiful, easy to talk to, and startlingly terrific with newborn twins.

He couldn't wait to get to know her better.

Chapter 7

Joey sat on the beach reading a magazine the next morning. She sighed discontentedly. She wished the hot summer sun would burn Dawson up into a tiny little prune. She didn't know what his problem was, but he was acting like a total stranger today. Almost as if he didn't want to be there. Or maybe as if he didn't want to be there with *her*.

Earlier, when Dawson had come to pick her up, he had walked into the house and immediately fussed over the baby. It seemed as if fifteen minutes had gone by before he even noticed that Joey was there. Then, when the baby started crying and Joey tried to calm him, Dawson had said, "You should sing to him. That's what professional nannies do"— like he was some kind of baby expert or something!

When they finally got going, Joey had asked, "Did you bring the Frisbee?"

"Oh, sorry, I forgot," was Dawson's response.

Joey had specifically asked him to bring it, so what was Dawson's problem? But Dawson was so deep into another galaxy that he claimed she had said no such thing.

To top it all off, on the walk to the beach, Dawson had blathered about this Australian girl he'd met. "Her name is Sheila, and she's from Australia. You should hear her accent—it would sound great on film. She's really photogenic, and she's doing a great job of taking care of the Barclay twins. Maybe she could give you some pointers." And on and on and on.

He had finally stopped talking about Sheila, and now Joey and Dawson sat silently on the beach, Dawson catching some rays, Joey pretending to be engrossed in her magazine, grateful for the silence.

Joey saw Dawson notice the virtual pet hanging from her beach bag. He lifted the little pink egg. "Why do you have one of these things?" he asked.

"That's Howard," Joey responded, looking up from her magazine. "You know Clarissa, my next-door neighbor?"

Dawson nodded.

"She's away in Europe with her family, and she asked me to watch it for her. I said okay, but this thing is kind of a pain. I had no idea until I read the instructions that it had to be constantly monitored. I'm not even sure how to work it."

Dawson laughed again. "Hey, you might learn something from it. It would be good practice for caring for your nephew."

That ticked Joey off. "I get more than enough

'practice,' Dawson, from the real-life baby. It seems like all I do is baby-sit."

"I was just saying—" Dawson began.

Joey threw her magazine down in frustration and cut him off. "You know, it's not my fault that Bess got pregnant. I don't know why I'm the one saddled with all the responsibility."

Dawson held his hands up in defense. "Whoa! I was just making an inane comment. Touchy subject, huh?"

"Like you wouldn't believe," Joey answered. She noticed that a group had started a pick-up volleyball game over at the net. She tried to tune Dawson out by watching the game, but he was being so annoying that it was impossible.

"But it must be hard for Bess," Dawson was saying. "I'm sure it's not easy being a mom and working and looking after her sullen teenage little sister." He lifted his eyebrows.

Joey could tell that Dawson was in lecture mode.

"You should cut her a break and help out a little more," he added.

Joey was furious. Dawson was being such a jerk! "When is someone going to cut *me* a break? That's what I want to know!"

But Dawson didn't stop. He went right on with his unsolicited oration. "You know Sheila, the Australian girl I was telling you about?"

How could I not know her? Joey thought. This was the sixth or seventh time he'd brought her up in the past hour.

Dawson went on. "She has to care for newborn twins. *Twins,* Joey. And she makes it seem like it's no sweat. And she's only two years older than we are. It's mind-blowing."

Your mind is blown! Joey thought. She'd had it with Dawson. She didn't feel like listening to him anymore. She didn't even like looking at him. She stood up. "Look, Dr. Spock," she sneered. "I'm going to watch the volleyball game. Keep an eye on Howard, would ya?" She gave him a phony smile and stomped away to the game in progress.

Joey found a grassy spot on a dune to sit and watch the game. She fumed inwardly as she watched the two teams dive, lunge, and scramble for the ball. She tried to follow the game, but she couldn't get Dawson and his stupid lecture out of her mind.

Maybe she *should* help her sister a little more. At the very least, she guessed she could try to "lose the attitude," as Bess had said. But no one seemed to care that Joey was growing up and had no sign of a social life, outside of an occasional video in Dawson's bedroom.

"You want to step in for me?" a panting girl asked Joey.

"Sure," Joey said. Maybe a good hard workout was just what she needed.

In no time it was her turn to whack the volleyball across the net. She slammed it as if it were Dawson Leery's head. Power shot! She looked across the net to see where it was going. Oh, my God! She thought. He's gorgeous! On the other side of the net was a total dream guy—blue eyes, brown hair, and a tanned chest to die for! And he was looking at her. Joey quickly looked away, then back again.

He wore blue bathing trunks with Day-Glo Hawaiian flowers down the sides. They were off-beat for Capeside, but Joey liked that. She especially liked the hair stuck up a little on top. He was gorgeous but a little disheveled, almost like he didn't know how incredibly hot he was. He was smiling at her again. Joey nervously smiled back. What if he was smiling at the girl behind her?

After the game was over, Joey jogged back to her blanket. Her frustrations were at bay after playing volleyball, and she felt a lot better.

Dawson wasn't at the blanket. Joey spied him walking toward the water to take a swim. Hadn't she asked him to watch her stuff? What a space case!

Joey was pretty tired from the game, so she stretched out on the blanket and closed her eyes. The sun felt great, beating down on her. Soon she'd have to leave and get ready for work. What a bummer. She didn't want to move.

She nearly drifted into a nap. The sounds of the waves beating against the beach, the gulls squawking overhead, the . . . beeping? She sat bolt upright. Where was that annoying sound coming from?

Howard. Howard was beeping. She took the egg and peered at the screen. It didn't tell her anything. There was a splotch on one corner of the screen, and in another corner a figure that looked like a duck was flashing.

What in the world did that mean? What kind of genius could decipher these bizarre symbols, anyway? As she dug through her bag for her instruction manual, she noticed that the cute guy from the volleyball game was staring at her.

Joey was ready to die. How was she going to shut this thing up? She wanted to dig a huge hole in the sand and disappear. The guy in the Hawaiian shorts probably thought she was a total dork! Not to mention that everyone else in the immediate area was glaring at her.

She continued to grope for the manual. She knew it was in her bag somewhere, under the extra towel, the water bottle, the sunscreen, and her magazine. Her fingers found the booklet, and she frantically leafed through it as Howard continued to beep.

"It's easier if someone shows you," she heard a voice say. Joey looked up to see Mr. Hawaiian Shorts standing right over her, a pearly white smile on his face.

Before Joey could say anything, he crouched down next to her. "May I?" he asked, gently touching her hand.

"Please," Joey said, maybe a little too eagerly. Up close, Joey noticed what great biceps he had. She handed the virtual pet to him.

"When you see this duck flashing, it means the pet pooped," he said, laughing. "So you have to press this button here to clean it up. Then the flashing stops." The annoying beeping finally ceased, too.

Joey smiled shyly. "Thanks," she said. "I hope it didn't disturb you too much."

"Not at all," he said, handing the pet back to her. "I'm Jeremy, by the way. Jeremy Fields."

"Joey Potter." She laughed. "Why on earth do you know so much about virtual pets, Jeremy Fields?" she asked with another smile.

"I don't get out much," he answered, sitting down in the sand.

Joey laughed again. Looking closely, Joey noticed a dusting of freckles beneath the tan on his smooth, well defined chest. She thought they were adorable.

"The truth is, my younger brother has like five or six of those things," he admitted. "Half the time I get stuck caring for them."

"This belongs to my next-door neighbor," Joey offered. "And it's the first—and last—time I'm going to do this for her. Where are you from?" Joey asked, figuring he was a summer tourist.

"New Hampshire," Jeremy answered. "And you?"

"Capeside—born and bred," Joey said.

Jeremy leaned on an elbow. "I like it here. It's my first time. I'm here on vacation with my parents, my brother, *and* cyberpets of all shapes, sizes, colors, and sounds. I think I could get used to this place." His voice trailed off. "And I guess I'd better take off—looks like your boyfriend is coming back," he said, sitting up.

Joey turned her head to see a dripping wet Dawson approach the blanket. "Him?" she said, laughing. "He's not my boyfriend. I don't have a boyfriend—right now, that is," she added hastily, in case he thought she was a total loser. Oh, God, she was making it worse.

"Well, in that case, are you free for a movie tonight?" Jeremy asked as he stood.

"Sure," Joey said. "I have to work, but I get off at nine, if that's okay," she said as Dawson sat down on the blanket. Jeremy introduced himself to Dawson, but Dawson was ice-cold.

"So," Jeremy said, breaking the tension. "Where should I pick you up?"

Joey gave Jeremy directions to the Icehouse as Dawson sat there glaring.

"See you later, Joey. Nice to meet you Dawson," Jeremy said, before walking back to his blanket.

"Nice shorts," Dawson mumbled. Then he shot Joey a cross look. "Who was that guy?"

Joey, her mood transformed, explained. "He was playing volleyball. Really nice—helped me with this stupid pet."

Dawson stared at Joey in amazement. "You mean you're going to go out with him, just like that?"

"Why not?" Joey challenged. What had gotten into Dawson? First he acted like he'd rather be anywhere in the world but at the beach with her, then he copped an attitude when she made a date with another guy. Could he possibly be jealous? Good! Joey thought with glee.

"I guess you're not coming to movie night, then," Dawson said.

Joey chuckled. Did Dawson actually think she would pass up a date to sit in his bedroom and watch *E.T.* for the five hundredth time? "No. I guess not."

"That's okay, because I had to cancel anyway," Dawson said. "I made plans with Sheila tonight."

"Good," Joey said. "For you."

"Fine," Dawson stated. "Have fun. I just hope this guy isn't some psycho or anything. I mean, he's a perfect stranger."

Joey laughed. " 'Perfect' is right," she quipped. "I hope he won't be a stranger for long."

Chapter 8

Jen sat on the back porch waiting for Pacey. They had decided to walk to class together every day— make it a morning ritual.

It was a beautiful Friday. Once again Pacey brought her a latte. And once again Jen was grateful. "You don't have to do this every day," she said, taking the big white cup. "You'll spoil me."

"You're already rotten," Pacey joked. "I can't do much more harm."

Jen was eager to get to know Pacey better. She'd known him only through Dawson, and she was glad to make her own connection with him.

These days she needed friends. She knew that Dawson was having a hard time trying to be just friends with her. And Joey certainly wasn't making any friendly overtures. So it felt good to be making a bona fide friend.

46

As they walked to the pool, Pacey made Jen laugh with his "Tough Tim" imitation, complete with spittle. Pacey puffed out his chest. "If anyone here wants to go in the water, leave. If anyone here can't take a little spit in his face, leave. If anyone here is not a bullying macho ignoramus, leave!"

Jen laughed and nearly choked on her coffee. "I think he was probably a lifeguard in Nam or something," she said.

"Or maybe in Alcatraz," Pacey added. "Or maybe he was the Ty-D-Bol man, but he let the promotion go to his head."

They arrived at the pool just in time, luckily. One of the other trainees wasn't so fortunate. He arrived a minute late and was promptly chewed up and spit out by Sergeant Tim.

"I will not tolerate tardiness or absenteeism," Tim bellowed. "During training you are to show up promptly every day. That means Saturday and Sunday too." He ordered them all to sit, accentuating the point by blowing his whistle.

Jen stiffled a giggle. This guy was like something out of a bad television show. But she sat quietly and listened as Tim went through the bylaws of lifeguarding.

"Number one," he said as he marched through the crowd, sizing everyone up, "a lifeguard is humble. He or she does not revel in glory after a rescue."

Pacey and Jen exchanged smirks but grew serious again when Tim neared them. "Number two," Tim went on, twirling his whistle, "a lifeguard will do his best to prevent all dangers and accidents. Number three, a lifeguard is dignified and never abuses his authority."

Jen could hear Pacey choke on those. Tim was the antithesis of all of these statements. "Number four," Tim continued, "a lifeguard acts as a member of a team. He or she does not act for individual gain. He or she follows orders from superiors."

When Tim turned his back, Pacey muttered sarcastically, "Yes, sir," and several people giggled.

Tim whipped around, his steely eyes pinning the group. "Do we have a comedian in our midst?" he said, stomping over to the offending trainees. "If you think you are here to crack jokes, leave now. I will not tolerate humor. Of any kind. At any time. You are training to save *lives*, here. It is no laughing matter. Is that clear?"

The class remained silent. Pacey was grateful that Tim hadn't realized he had cracked that joke.

"I said, is that clear?" Tim repeated.

"Yes," the class chorused.

"Good," Tim said. He went on. "Number five, a lifeguard has a clean and neat appearance. Number six, a lifeguard has a cool head and uses good judgment. Number seven, a lifeguard is prompt and always alert."

Tim stopped pacing and sat down in a plastic chair to finish barking out the bylaws. "Number eight, a lifeguard is always prepared. Number nine, a lifeguard is responsible. And Number ten, a lifeguard is always honing his or her skills."

Tim paused and stared at the uncertain faces before him. "Any questions?"

One of the twins raised her hand. "Yes," Tim said,

picking up a clipboard and looking at a chart. "Mallory or Mindy?"

"I'm Mallory," the girl answered. "Is this going to be on a test?" she asked.

Jen looked at her. What a dumb question. She hated when people were only concerned about learning because of the possibility of tests.

"As a matter of fact," Tim answered, "if you remember, you're going to have a quiz today on chapter one. You will be tested on everything, and I mean everything you learn in this course. You must know all of the information inside out. You will have written tests and performance tests. You will be tested on lifeguarding philosophy and on rescue skills, including artificial respiration." Tim paused dramatically. "I will give you every test imaginable.

"After a few weeks of this class, you will need to take a separate course in CPR," Tim continued. "Then and only then will you get your lifesaving certification. *If* you pass."

"But the summer will be almost over by then!" Pacey protested.

"Right," Tim said. "Then you will assist a lifeguard for the remainder of the season. You will not become a full-fledged lifeguard until next summer."

Pacey felt incredibly let down. Tim had burst his aquatic bubble. His visions of performing mouth-to-mouth on bikini-clad women dissolved. Ideas of heroic acts, such as saving a child or fighting off a man-eating shark, fizzled. Notions of sitting in an elevated chair, being adored and idolized by teenage girls faded away. All images of attaining the perfect savage tan were kaput. If I'd wanted to go to summer school, Pacey thought, I wouldn't have worked so hard for that D in geometry. But his eyes moved from the petite redhead to the twins to the college girls, and he decided that the lifesaving class did have some saving graces after all.

The class spent the rest of the morning listening to Tim's lectures, then taking the quiz. Jen felt fidgety and hot and sweaty, but she had to admit that the information, despite its militaristic presentation, was interesting and valuable. She thought the quiz was a breeze, but she noticed that Pacey didn't seem to be having an easy time with it. She knew he wasn't much of a student, but the chapter had taken a mere twenty minutes to read.

When they were dismissed for lunch, the entire class seemed to breathe a collective sigh of relief.

Jen turned to Pacey, who a minute before had been sitting next to her. But he was gone. She looked around and saw him talking with the twins. Some of the other kids were pairing off and walking to the food stand. She walked toward Pacey and lingered, not wanting to interrupt his conversation.

"Yeah, I would have brought my motorcycle, but it's in the shop. So I guess we're stuck here for lunch. Want to join me?" Pacey was saying.

Motorcycle? What a line, Jen thought. But she noted that the twins seemed more than happy to join him. "Uh, you guys getting something to eat?" Jen asked them timidly. But Pacey and the twins walked off, apparently not having heard her.

Jen couldn't help feeling hurt.

* * *

"You certainly have an extra spring in your step today," Bodie teased Joey at the Icehouse later that day.

Joey laughed. "I had a good day at the beach today. I think I'll make a habit of relaxing before I come here."

"Miss!" someone shouted from a nearby table. Joey rolled her eyes and rushed over.

Funny, she thought, as she wiped up a messy spill that a customer had made. Usually, this type of thing would ruin her day. But since she'd met that Jeremy guy, nothing could kill her good mood.

Except maybe Bess. She called Joey over. "Are you going straight home after work tonight?" she asked.

Joey cut her off before Bess could elaborate. "I can't baby-sit tonight. I have a date," she said impatiently.

Bess arched her eyebrows in surprise. "A date? That's terrific. Who's the lucky guy?"

Joey softened when she saw that her sister was truly interested and happy. "Someone I met at the beach today. A total hunk."

"Great," Bess said, patting her little sister on the back. "Have a terrific time."

"I'm sorry I can't help out tonight," Joey added apologetically.

Bess waved the worry away. "I don't need you to baby-sit. I was just going to give you money to give to the sitter before I got home. She can wait."

"Oh," Joey said. She felt bad for snapping the minute her sister asked her a question. "Well, you'll probably meet Jeremy, then. He's going to pick me up here tonight."

"Good, then I can warn him before he gets in too deep," Bodie cracked as he passed by. Joey flicked a wet towel at him and laughed.

Sometimes, she thought, this poor excuse for a family was okay.

Jen munched on her burger. Alone. Two tables away from Pacey. She thought about getting up and moving to another table because she didn't know how much longer she could listen to him and his harem of fans. Even though she wasn't right next to him, she could hear every last detail of his conversation—actually, monologue was more like it.

She felt as if she'd been dumped. Jen knew that was ridiculous, but she couldn't help it. Dumped by Pacey, just when she thought they might be good friends. She understood that he wanted to meet new girls, and she didn't want to ruin his rap. But did he have to totally ignore her? And did he have to act like such a jerk?

"Well, after the shark attack, that's when I decided I wanted to train to be a lifeguard," he was saying.

Jen shook her head. He was making up all these preposterous stories to impress the girls. And they were falling for it, egging him on with oohs and aahs and questions. Even the guys at that table were looking at him and nodding with respect. What was with Pacey's Jekyll and Hyde act? Jen wondered. How could someone so sweet turn into such an imbecile in just one day?

She finished her burger and carried her tray over to the trash bin. When she walked past Pacey's table, his audience was roaring with laughter. Jen couldn't resist. She had to go over.

"Hey," she said, pleasantly enough. "What's so funny?"

Pacey looked like a deer caught in headlights. Mallory—or was it Mindy?—said, "Pacey was just telling us about the time that he met that famous DJ and told him off." She giggled.

Pacey's look acknowledged that Jen was the only person who could bust him. But she didn't want to do that. She just wanted to see him squirm a little.

Jen gave Pacey a meaningful glance and then laughed. "Oh, yeah," she said. "That was a good one. I should know—I was there," she lied. Instantly she saw the relief and gratitude in Pacey's eyes.

Jen grabbed a seat at the table and looked at her watch. They still had ten minutes to kill before they had to report back to class. "So tell me, when is that motorcycle of yours getting out of the shop?"

Pacey shrugged and mumbled something about the difficulty of finding a good mechanic these days.

Jen didn't challenge him. She'd saved him this time, she thought. But she wouldn't be so gallant in the future. No way.

Chapter 9

Dawson checked himself out in the mirror. He looked okay—no zits, at least. He slapped on a dab of cologne, afraid to put on too much like his dad's friend Ed. His family liked to joke that they could always smell Ed coming.

Then Dawson gathered his tapes and his camera and ran down the stairs, in a hurry to get to Sheila's house. He nearly bowled his father over on his way out the door.

"Whoa!" Mr. Leery said, putting his hands out before him. "Where's the fire, kiddo?"

"Only in my heart, Dad," Dawson answered poetically. "I'm going over to the Barclays'."

Mr. Leery threw Dawson a funny look. "What's at the Barclays'?"

"Only the most beautiful, amazing, stupendous, incredible woman I've ever met," he said.

Mr. Leery shifted uncomfortably. He looked around awkwardly, his face growing serious. "Isn't she a little old for you, son?" he asked quietly.

Dawson stared at his dad, surprised. Usually he was so supportive. Sheila was only a little older, for God's sake. "She's not that much older, Dad," he said defensively, then added, "What difference does age make, anyway, in a great romance?"

Dawson wanted to bolt, but his father put a hand on his shoulder, then cleared his throat and scratched his chin. "Well, let me put it this way, then." He hesitated. "Isn't she a little *married* for you, son?"

Dawson stared at his father, stunned for a second. Then he broke into laughter. His dad obviously thought he meant Mrs. Barclay. As Mr. Leery watched Dawson, perplexed, Dawson tried to catch his breath. "Dad, you've got it wrong," he was able to get out, finally. "I'm not going to see Mrs. Barclay. I'm going to see Sheila, their new nanny."

"Oh, huh, huh," Mr. Leery said, half laughing, half embarrassed. "I wasn't aware of the new boarder in the Barclay household. Give me the details!"

Dawson usually loved to sit and chat with his dad, but right now he just wanted to get to Sheila's. Tonight he was going to show her his movies. He didn't want to be a minute later than he had to. "Listen, Dad," he said politely, "I'll give you details another time, okay?"

Mr. Leery good-naturedly punched his son in the arm. " 'Kay. Have a good time."

When Dawson stepped outside, he noticed that

the moon was full. Its brightness was startling, throwing a magical glow upon the creek. It reminded him of that romantic movie, *Moonstruck*. Coincidence? Dawson thought. Not likely. But hopefully Sheila would be the Cher to his Nicholas Cage before long.

Dawson quickened his pace. He couldn't get to Sheila's fast enough. It had been a long day, and he needed to get his mind off things. Things like Joey.

What was with her today? With that guy at the beach, a total stranger, she had acted all goofy and giddy and flirty, whereas she had chastised Dawson for forgetting the Frisbee, and she'd thrown a tantrum when he mentioned Bess and the baby.

Which reminded him—she was going out with that guy tonight. A knot twisted in his stomach at the thought. He hoped the guy wasn't some kind of psycho. Though he did seem all right at the beach—despite his shorts, Dawson mused.

But still, something didn't feel right about it. Something didn't feel right about Joey *dating*.

When he arrived at the Barclays', Dawson decided to leave all thoughts of Joey and her date at the door. Thanks to Sheila, however, that was nearly impossible.

"Hello, Dawson," Sheila said.

At the first sight of Sheila's smiling face, Dawson felt better about everything. She seemed so genuinely pleased to see him—unlike Joey today at the beach.

And Sheila showed a genuine interest in Dawson's films. It felt nice to have a new and interested audience. All of Dawson's friends seemed indifferent to his projects and efforts. When he tried to talk to them about new ideas or techniques, they all seemed to be stifling mammoth yawns. Sheila, on the other hand, was attentive and inquisitive and, best of all, impressed.

Dawson felt comfortable and relaxed for the first time in days, was he popped a tape into the VCR and sat on the couch. He was fine—until Sheila asked a disturbing question. In the middle of the monster film she pointed to Joey and asked, "Is she your girlfriend?"

Dawson laughed uncomfortably. "No! That's Joey. She's just a friend. We've known each other since we were little," he explained.

"She's pretty," Sheila added.

"I guess," Dawson hedged. "I mean, if that's your type. There's a really good scene coming up," he added, trying to change the subject.

But Sheila wouldn't let it go. "Is Joey *your* type? Do you like her?"

Dawson didn't understand why she was prodding. He didn't want to talk about Joey, of all people, when he was trying to get to know someone new. Was Sheila feeling out his romantic status? If so, he was going to make it perfectly clear that he was unattached and looking.

Sheila watched Dawson expectantly. He realized he hadn't answered her question. "My type? We're just friends. I've never thought about it," he lied.

"It's just that I thought I saw something there," Sheila went on.

Though Dawson desperately wanted to change

the subject, he couldn't resist asking, "What do you mean?"

"The way you project her—the roles you write for her. She's always a smart and capable heroine, at least in the movies you've shown me. It's like you respect her—put her on a pedestal, almost. And the way she looks at the camera, at you . . ." Her voice trailed off. "I guess I'm just being silly," she conceded.

"Yeah, I guess," Dawson answered, embarrassed.

There was an awkward pause, but they both relaxed as they continued watching the film.

Sheila spoke when the film was over. "Does Joey star in all of your films?" she asked playfully. "Many directors fall in love with their lead actresses, you know."

"Yeah, yeah," Dawson said. "Woody and Mia. Cassavetes and Rowlands. The list goes on." He waved an impatient hand at her. "But that's not the case here at all. Joey and I are just friends."

"Okay," Sheila said, then added teasingly, "If you say so."

Dawson popped in another tape. He wondered as they sat on the couch, nearly touching, if he should lean over and kiss Sheila—show her that his mind wasn't on his leading lady after all.

He turned and admired her pretty profile, her smooth, healthy complexion. But oddly, something held him back: he didn't *want* to kiss her.

Dawson couldn't believe it. Something felt weird. Something was missing.

Why? he wondered desperately. Why was this happening to him now?

"How do you keep the camera steady during those action scenes?" Sheila asked, breaking through Dawson's thoughts. "How do you zoom so fast?"

Dawson picked up his camera, happy that she was talking about something else. "Here," he offered. "I'll show you how."

Dawson's mood lightened when he demonstrated some of his favorite camera techniques. They took turns filming each other.

Sheila filmed Dawson from different angles. She giggled when Dawson made funny faces to the camera. He enjoyed filming Sheila just as much: Sheila holding the babies. Sheila singing. Sheila doing a cartwheel outside in the moonlight. Sheila playing the piano.

Fooling around with the camera on Sheila gave Dawson an idea: the documentary—he could practice documentary technique on Sheila. Why not? He thought. He could shadow her, filming her with the babies, adding a few snippets about an Australian living abroad. The story angle would be great practice.

It would also give him an opportunity to get to know her better. If he spent more time with her, he was bound to feel a spark. Once he felt more comfortable around her, he wouldn't feel so awkward if he wanted to steal a kiss.

"How about if I shadow you for a day?" Dawson asked, excited about the idea.

"Shadow me?" Sheila repeated. "I don't know what you mean."

"Don't worry, it doesn't mean 'stalk,'" Dawson

explained. "I would just film you as you work. It would be great practice for my next project—a documentary. I could practice with *A Day in the Life of a Young Australian Nanny.*"

Sheila hesitated a bit. "I'm pretty camera shy, but if it would help you . . . It's just for practice, right?" she confirmed.

"Yes," Dawson said. "Practice."

"Okay, then," Sheila agreed. "Why don't you come on Sunday? Early. These two get up at the crack of dawn."

"Great!" Dawson said. "Maybe we can take them to the beach or something, get a few scenery changes."

"Sounds marvelous," Sheila said in her Australian lilt. She looked at her watch. "Right now I'm afraid I have to get these two peanuts to bed."

Dawson took the cue and gathered up his tapes and camera. "Okay, then. Sunday." He paused at the front door. "Thanks for inviting me over. I had a great time tonight," he told her.

Sheila grinned. "Ditto. You feel like an old friend, Dawson Leery."

An old friend. More like a comfortable old shoe. That was exactly what Dawson had been afraid she would think.

Chapter 10

The last few customers lingered in the Icehouse on the warm, breezy Capeside night. As Joey bussed a table, she thought her stomach would burst with excitement by the time nine o'clock rolled around.

Bess walked over and helped Joey clear the table. "Why don't you knock off a little early?" she said. "Get pretty for your hot date."

Joey happily untied the strings of her apron. "Thanks, Bess," she said. "I'll put in some extra time tomorrow."

She walked to the back room and unzipped a duffel bag. She pulled out a change of clothes and a small makeup case. Joey didn't usually wear a lot of makeup. In fact, she had nice coloring from her time at the beach that day. But she did want to brush her hair, put on a bit of lipstick, and maybe borrow a dab of perfume from her sister.

She pulled off her food-stained jeans and changed into her outfit for the night: black pants and a silvery halter top. She dressed the ensemble up with a silver chain, then regarded herself in the mirror, pleased at what she saw. She hoped Jeremy would like her style.

Precisely at nine, Joey perched on a stool at the bar. She grabbed some menus to stuff with flyers announcing house specialties for the next day so she wouldn't seem to be waiting with bated breath, which she was.

After a minute, Bodie approached her and whistled. "Hello, foxy lady. Have you seen Josephine?" he asked. "There's someone here to see her," he said.

Joey whirled around and saw Jeremy, clutching a dozen roses, scanning the Icehouse. Joey smiled and waved him over.

As he walked toward her, Bess stopped him and introduced herself. They chatted for a minute, and Joey was pleased to see her sister's approving smile.

Jeremy looked neater than he had at the beach. His hair was combed, and his clothes were neatly pressed. He wore a casual, colorful bright blue shirt with comfortable light tan pants.

Jeremy smiled as he strolled over. He stopped before Joey and thrust out the roses. "Hi," he said. "Uh, these are for you."

Was that a hint of nervousness she heard in his voice? She liked that, too. She was starting to think she liked everything about Jeremy Fields.

"Thanks," Joey said shyly as she took the bouquet

from him. No boy had ever given her roses before. "They're pretty," she said.

"Like you," Jeremy said. "You look really pretty tonight."

Joey blushed. She wasn't used to being complimented in that way. But she didn't want to seem like a flattery-flustered airhead. "Plastic surgery pays off," she said. "Everyone says it's a major improvement from before the kitchen fire."

Jeremy laughed. "Well, then, I feel more comfortable telling you about my artificial baboon heart, then," he said.

Quick comeback, Joey thought. He thinks on his feet. Another great quality. "We should get going," she told him, "if we want to make the movie on time. Just let me put these in water—"

"Taken care of," Bess said, popping up behind Joey and grabbing the roses from her hand.

Joey felt a twinge of guilt. Bess always seemed to be there when she needed her. Was Joey there for Bess as much? Yes, Joey thought. She did more than her share to help Bess—at home and at the restaurant. It was nice to know, though, that Bess returned the favors.

They walked to the theater, which was just down the road from the Icehouse. "So do your parents own the restaurant?" Jeremy asked to make conversation.

Joey froze up inside. She knew it was an innocent question, but he had no idea what a can of worms he was opening up when he mentioned her parents.

"Um, well, my Mom died, and my Dad left," Joey

said, fibbing slightly. She figured that Jeremy didn't have to know that her dad was in jail.

Jeremy looked concerned. "I'm sorry," he said.

Joey shrugged. "So Bess and I own the restaurant, I guess," she said. "We're the sad excuse for the Potter family: me, my sister, her live-in boyfriend, and their child." Joey watched Jeremy's face carefully for a reaction.

He didn't seem the least bit fazed. "So you're not the Brady Bunch," Jeremy said. "Your sister and her boyfriend seem pretty cool. They've got to be more tolerable than my mom and dad."

"Which rerun TV family did you always wish was yours?" Joey asked. "I always wanted to be one of the Keatons on *Family Ties.*"

Jeremy laughed. "Why? They were so corny!"

"But they seemed so happy," Joey countered. "The Keatons seemed so normal." She felt comfortable with Jeremy, making easy conversation. But at the same time, being near him sent tiny shivers up and down her arms.

Jeremy thought about Joey's question. "I always wanted to be one of the Munsters," he said.

Joey laughed. "You're not serious," she said.

"I am," Jeremy insisted. "I always wanted to be in *The Munsters* because I had a crush on Marilyn, the normal cousin."

That put Joey in stitches. She liked his sense of humor.

"I've been looking forward to seeing this movie," Joey said as they approached the ticket window. "I hope you're into it. Dinky little Capeside only has one theater, so we don't have much choice."

"Sounds like my town in New Hampshire," Jeremy said. "One movie theater. One grocery store. One school. Hundreds of people dying to get out."

They hurried into the theater when Joey noticed the time.

"I know you'll think this is weird," Jeremy said. "But I like to sit in the front row. No one ever sits there and it has the most leg room."

Joey giggled. She'd never thought of it that way. She was game for the front row. They walked toward the screen just as the previews started to roll.

But as soon as they sat down, Jeremy raced out to get some snacks. "I'll be back," he told her, doing his best Terminator impression.

After a couple of minutes, Jeremy returned with a big bucket of popcorn. When he offered her some, Joey declined. She was a little hungry, but movie-theater popcorn always gave her a stomachache. But Jeremy had no way of knowing that. It was the thought that counted, she told herself.

Jeremy cocked an eyebrow when Joey passed up the popcorn. "I suppose you'd be interested in some of these, then," he said, slowly sliding a box of Sno-Caps out of his shirt pocket. He gave her a knowing smile and chuckled.

Sno-Caps were Joey's favorite. "How did you know?" she asked, making a grab for them.

"Your sister tipped me off," Jeremy confessed.

Sno-Caps, a good movie, and a cute guy, Joey thought. What more could a girl ask?

*　　*　　*

Dawson quietly opened the door and walked into the living room. His parents were snuggled up on the couch, watching a movie. "What are you watching?" Dawson asked.

Dawson's mother hit the pause button. *"When Harry Met Sally,"* she answered. "Do you want to watch it with us?"

"No," Dawson answered abruptly. "I've seen it." I *live* it, he thought.

He abruptly wished his parents good night and climbed the stairs to his bedroom. What a night, he thought as he plopped onto his bed. He'd had a great time with Sheila, but why had they spent so much time talking about Joey? And why had he spent most of the night thinking about Joey? He turned his TV on, not ready to go to sleep. He thought he might dream about Joey if he did.

Dawson took the tape he'd made tonight and popped it in the VCR. Sheila's smiling face came up on the screen. Now *that's* who you should be dreaming about, he told himself.

He stopped the tape when there was a tap at his door. "Come in," Dawson called.

His mother opened the door a crack. "We're done watching the movie," she said. "Are you okay?" she asked tenderly.

"Yeah," Dawson answered.

"You seemed to run up here so quickly," his mother explained. "That's not like you."

Leave it to his parents to notice every emotion he had. Sometimes he thought they had X-ray vision that pierced right into his psyche. "I just made this tape, and I was anxious to watch it," Dawson said. "That's all."

"Oh." His mom sat on the corner of his bed. "Not soft porn, I hope," she joked.

Dawson laughed. "Just hard-core goofing around with the Barclays' new nanny." He played part of the tape for her.

"She's pretty—and charming," Mrs. Leery noted. "And look how good she is with those twins." She cocked her head, as if she were struck by an idea. "How old is she, Dawson?"

"Eighteen," he answered.

"Is this her summer job?" she asked.

"I suppose," Dawson said. "She just started." He didn't understand her sudden interest.

"Perfect!" Mrs. Leery said happily. "I'm doing a TV series on teens and their summer jobs for the station. Do you think Sheila would be interested in being one of my subjects? Her story would give my series the international flair it needs."

Dawson quickly thought it over. Sheila would be perfect. She was beautiful, photogenic, and an all-around amazing person. "I don't see why not," he said. "She would be perfect." In fact, Dawson saw a perfect opportunity. Maybe he could do the piece for his mother. He told her how he planned to shadow Sheila on Sunday.

Dawson's mother balked a bit. "I don't know. Isn't that nepotism?"

"I've got great equipment, and I need the experience," he pleaded. "Plus I am extremely cheap," he added for effect.

Dawson's mother laughed. "You have a great

point there." She considered the idea for another moment. "If my producers approve, you're in," she conceded.

"All right!" Dawson cheered.

Mrs. Leery rose to leave. "But first I need Sheila's written permission to use her as a subject."

"No problem, Mom," Dawson said confidently. "I'll take care of it Sunday."

Dawson's mother kissed him on the forehead and wished him good night. When she closed the door behind her, Dawson turned off the VCR, undressed, and crawled under the covers.

He couldn't wait to tell Sheila about the project. He was sure she would flip. This could be the perfect thing to bring them together.

Dawson shut his eyes, eager to get to sleep. Tonight Dawson was sure to have sweet dreams—very sweet dreams about *The Life and Times of Sheila Billingsley*.

Chapter 11

On the screen a policeman ran down a dank, dark alley. He could barely see. He held his gun out in front of him, ready for anything.

The alley came to a dead end. The criminal had to be in there somewhere. At any minute he could jump, shoot, or—

Beep. The familiar high-pitched sound sent Joey scrambling in her purse.

Howard. He was back.

Beep.

"Hey! Shut that thing off!" someone shouted at her.

Joey retrieved the pink egg and swiftly silenced it.

She breathed a sigh of relief. But then she heard a stifled snort of laughter from Jeremy.

Joey could tell that Jeremy was trying his best to hold it in. But he was sputtering through a mouthful of popcorn. Before she could control it, she was laughing, too.

"Shh!" came from all over the theater. But the harder Joey tried not to laugh, the more she wanted to. She couldn't help it.

She and Jeremy were in the midst of an all-out laughing fit.

Jeremy took Joey's hand and, clasping a hand over his mouth, stood up and raced for the exit.

He pushed open the door, and when they emerged outside, they both let loose.

"What timing!" Jeremy said between guffaws. "That thing needs discipline! I think that little girl spoils it."

Joey wiped tears from her eyes. "Shh! Turn that thing off!" she said in imitation of the annoyed people behind her.

Jeremy took a deep breath and sighed. "I didn't mean to make you miss the movie," he said. "We can go back in."

"No," Joey said. "I wasn't into it anyway. The acting wasn't very good." Even though she hadn't enjoyed the movie, she was having a great time. "I— I haven't laughed like that in a long time," she confessed. And it was true. With Mom gone, and Dad in jail, and with her and Bess and Bodie trying to make ends meet, there wasn't a lot for Joey to laugh about these days. But for a few beautiful moments Jeremy had made her forget.

"If *you* want to go back, though . . ." she said, thinking that Jeremy might want to catch the ending.

Jeremy's expression grew sheepish. "Don't worry

about it," he said casually, then let out a rueful laugh. "I am such a dork," he muttered.

"What?" Joey pressed.

"I've seen the movie already," he blurted. "And I can tell you that it doesn't get any better. I know you're going to think I'm a big loser, but you seemed to really want to see it, so . . ."

Joey grinned delightedly. She thought that was the sweetest thing she'd ever heard. No one ever wanted to see the movies she wanted to see. Dawson—Mr. Film—always seemed to dictate what they would see and when. It was so nice of Jeremy to sit through it a second time for her. "Thanks," she said tenderly.

"What for?" Jeremy asked.

"For sitting through a bad movie again. And especially for making me laugh," Joey told him. She wanted him to know what his kindness had meant to her. "I needed it. Too much."

Before she could say anything more, Jeremy took her hand.

Joey could feel his strength. His sleeve brushed against her bare arm, and her skin tingled. There, right in the middle of the parking lot, his lips brushed hers.

"C'mon. I'll walk you home," he said after a trancelike moment. "Then I'll give you a real goodnight kiss."

And he did.

When they approached her house, Jeremy pulled Joey close and gave her an incredibly sweet, soft, and tender kiss.

Chapter 12

"Morning," Pacey greeted Jen. He strolled up to the back porch, coffee in hand as usual.

"Morning," Jen answered. She accepted her latte and took a sip. She needed to wake up this morning—she felt a little slow and sleepy. But the coffee, along with the chilly New England air, perked her up instantly.

As they walked slowly and silently toward the pool, Jen noticed that Pacey seemed preoccupied. He looked as if he had something important to say, something that might escape his lips at any moment, but he was searching for the right words.

Jen was right. Suddenly Pacey blurted, "Thanks for yesterday." He gave her an uncomfortable nod and shrug.

Jen knew what he was talking about, but she wasn't going to let him off the hook so easily.

"Thanks for what?" she asked, a little too nonchalantly.

Pacey sighed. "You know, at lunch. Helping with my story."

Jen feigned enlightenment. "Oh, you mean thanks for helping you with your big *lies* yesterday."

Pacey grew irritable. He stopped walking. "I knew you'd cop an attitude about this."

Jen opened her mouth, outraged. He should be grateful to her! She could have made him look like a fool in front of the whole class. But she didn't.

She wanted to shake Pacey. Instead she said quietly, "You know, Pacey, you could meet girls by being yourself, too. It's easier. It's hard to keep up a false image. And it will be hell when the lies are peeled away."

Pacey scoffed. "Obviously you're not familiar with my track record as Pacey Witter, major-league mess-up."

"If you don't have faith in who you are, no one else will," Jen insisted. She knew Pacey was insecure. But he was fooling himself. He was a likable guy. Why wouldn't anyone like that?"

Jen could see color rising in Pacey's face. "It's easy for you to say, Miss I'm-So-Self-Assured-and-Beautiful-That-Men-Fight-Over-Me-and-Sulk-About-Me-All-Day," he said quietly. "You have no idea what it's like to be rejected."

Now Jen was getting mad. "You're *wrong*, Pacey," she answered, her voice angry. "I do know. You don't know about my past."

"Right! Exactly!" Pacey said heatedly. "Because you ran away from New York and reinvented yourself here in Capeside. Not everyone gets a second chance. Not everyone gets to move away." He paused, his eyes entreating. "I have a label everywhere I go. At home I'm a disappointment, a failure. At school I'm a joke. Let me have my clean slate. Let me be who I want to be."

"Who do you want to be, Pacey?" Jen asked. She felt a little sorry for Pacey, but she still didn't agree with him.

"Anyone but me," he told her. "Anyone but me."

Pacey looked at the corrected quiz that Tim shoved into his hand. He'd gotten an F. Pacey figured that he shouldn't be surprised. He hadn't read that first chapter the other night. But it was only a quiz, after all. It didn't mean anything in the grand scheme of things, he reasoned.

Pacey saw Jen notice his grade and shoot him a look.

He just didn't get her. Did she think that he wanted to have to lie about who he was? Didn't she get it? No girl who really knew him would like him.

After Tim handed out the quizzes, he turned and faced the class. "Everyone into the pool," he ordered. "Let's see twenty laps—pronto." The class jumped into the water. Then Tim strode out of the area. "I'll be back," he said over his shoulder.

"Probably has to use the john," Pacey muttered.

The minute Tim left, Pacey pulled himself out of the pool. While everyone else was swimming, he decided to entertain the class.

He strutted around the edge of the pool, puffing out his chest in his best Tim imitation. "I am living proof," he shouted, "that size *does* matter. If I didn't have my—shall we say, *shortcomings?*—I wouldn't be the beefed-up bully I am now!"

The students in the pool slowed their laps and laughed, except for Jen. "You should get in the pool, Pace, before he comes back," she warned.

"Why don't you dislodge the life preserver from your butt, young lady?" he barked, again in Tim mode. The crowd lost it, and Pacey basked in the laughter and approval of the class.

He smirked at Jen. She shot him a wounded look.

He had to admit. He felt bad.

He stood at the edge of the pool, frozen, wondering what he should do. Suddenly he felt a hand push him from behind.

A big strong hand.

Tim's hand.

Pacey splashed into the water. When he emerged, coughing, he was staring into Tim's icy eyes.

"I thought I told you to swim twenty laps."

"Yes, sir." Pacey didn't see any way out of this. He treaded water, silently praying that Tim hadn't overheard the mimic show he had put on.

"Then what are you waiting for?" Tim growled.

"Nothing, sir," Pacey answered.

Tim blew his whistle. "Everybody out!" he ordered.

When Pacey started to climb out of the pool, Tim pushed him back in. "Except for you. You swim one hundred laps. Starting now."

Joey felt as if she were floating when she woke that morning. Had the evening before been a dream? It sure seemed like one. But it had been real.

She stretched and yawned, a little tired. It had taken her a long time to fall asleep last night. Between replaying the evening in her mind and being disturbed by her nephew's bawling, Joey was surprised she slept at all.

She had to work today. But tomorrow she would be off, and she was going to spend the day with Jeremy at the beach. Today he was going on a boating trip with his family. She couldn't believe she had to wait a whole day until she saw him again.

It would be torture.

Joey got out of bed and slowly made her way to the kitchen. She found Bess sitting at the table with some orange juice. Joey flinched when she saw the dark circles under her sister's eyes. Bess looked like she hadn't slept in days.

"Little one keep you up?" Joey asked.

Bess nodded. "I'm exhausted."

No kidding, Joey thought. But Bess looked worse than tired. She looked pale. In the summertime, she used to be glued to the beach. Now she looked as if she'd never seen the sun. And her hair, once long and shiny, was dull and frazzled.

"Did you have a good time last night?" she asked wearily.

"Yeah," Joey answered, distracted by how worn-out Bess looked. Was this her sister? Suddenly she seemed twenty years older. And Bess was young, Joey realized. She and Bodie should be going out at night and having fun, like other people their age.

They should be going to the beach, eating at chic restaurants, and checking out local bands.

"I'm going to shower," Joey said abruptly. The sight of Bess had freaked her out. She felt bad that Bess was saddled with this kind of responsibility so young. But then she got mad. It was one thing for Bess to have to take care of Joey—that wasn't her fault. But why did she have to go and get pregnant? She didn't even have time for Joey anymore. Everything revolved around Alexander.

Joey hurried to the bathroom and closed the door behind her. In the shower she closed her eyes and pretended she was somewhere else.

Someplace where there were no worn-out older sisters, no babies who cried in the night, no feelings of guilt bombarding her.

A faraway place where she could hide away with Jeremy Fields.

Chapter 13

Pacey missed lunch. He was busy swimming laps. By the time class ended, in the late afternoon, he was starving. He told Jen to go ahead without him, and he stopped at a pay phone to call Dawson.

He hadn't seen Dawson since he started this dumb class. Maybe Dawson would grab a bite with him.

He put a quarter in the pay phone and dialed. Dawson answered, and Pacey asked him to meet him at the Icehouse. Dawson was more than happy to agree.

By the time Pacey arrived at the Icehouse, Dawson was already there. They grabbed a table, and Joey gave them menus.

"What's up?" Joey asked happily when she saw them.

"*Nada,*" Pacey answered.

Joey rushed off to pick up a food order.

"How's lifesaving class going?" Dawson asked as he scanned the menu.

Pacey sighed. "Not what I expected," he admitted. "Screenplay Video is looking better and better."

Dawson laughed. "At least you're outside all day. It stinks being cooped up in that tiny store."

"Yes," Pacey agreed, "but you don't have some neo-Nazi spitting in your face and barking orders at you. And you're not subjected to boring lectures or Jen glowering at you the whole time just because you want to meet some girls."

Dawson put down his menu and gave Pacey his full attention. "Glowering? Jen? Why would she care?"

"Good question," Pacey said. He'd never thought about that. Why *would* Jen care? He paused thoughtfully. "I don't know, man. Maybe she's jealous."

Dawson's face tightened. "Why would she be jealous of *you*?"

Pacey shrugged. "Maybe she has the hots for me?" He laughed, but still, he thought about it. Maybe that was her problem. That would make sense of all those touchy-feely conversations she was having with him about being himself.

"Yeah, right," Dawson said, giving Pacey a dirty look.

"No," Pacey said. "It makes sense. She digs my scene. That's why she doesn't want me to meet other girls!" Pacey shook his head in bewilderment. Why had it taken him so long to notice that Jen Lindley had the hots for him?

Just then he saw Jen walk into the Icehouse. "Whoa, here's my woman now," he said. He waved her over as Dawson shot him a dirty look.

"Hey, guys. Okay if I join you while I wait for my take-out?" Jen asked. She was wearing a short fluttery skirt that showed off her tanned legs.

Pacey gave her a wide smile. "Sure," he said, and gallantly stood and pulled out a chair for her. She did look good. Very good.

"Hi, Jen," Dawson said.

"Hey, Dawson," she answered pleasantly.

Joey came by with some water. She greeted Jen cheerily. "Long time no see!"

Jen appeared surprised at Joey's friendliness. She grabbed a glass and took a sip of water. "Hi Joey," she said. "Yeah, long time no see."

Pacey thought about what he should do. He liked Jen, but he wanted to meet someone new. He figured he ought to let Jen down easy and cut things short before they got started.

"I'm sorry about the life-preserver comment today in class," Pacey said.

"Don't worry about it," Jen said. "I've kinda been acting like a stick-in-the-mud."

Pacey gently patted her hand. "I didn't understand why before, but I get it now."

"I'm glad," Jen answered, taking another sip of water. "I mean, I had no idea what had gotten in to you."

Pacey smiled and nodded. "I didn't mean to—" He stopped. How was he going to put this? "I know you're used to guys making a big fuss over you and stuff. But . . . can we just be friends?"

Jen swallowed another sip of water and gave Pacey a curious look. "What are you talking about?" she asked. "Of course we're friends."

Pacey noticed Dawson's face just then. His expression was a combination of dismay and disgust. Right then it occurred to him that Dawson might not be comfortable with this conversation. Pacey knew he had not completely recovered from his breakup with Jen.

Trying to be tactful, Pacey leaned over confidentially, tipping his head toward Dawson. "Maybe we should have this conversation another time," he said.

"Don't stop on account of me," Dawson said bitterly.

Jen glanced from Dawson back to Pacey. She looked as if she had no idea what was going on. "Here and now is as good a place as any. What's up with you guys, anyway? Am I in the dark about something?"

Pacey went on, "I didn't realize you were jealous, that's all. Forgive me for being so clueless," he said warmly, looking Jen in the eye, "but I'm afraid I think of you only as a friend."

"Jealous?" Jen's eyes widened. "Jealous!" Then she started to laugh hysterically. "That's the stupidest thing I've ever heard! Why would I be jealous?"

"Don't be embarrassed," said Pacey. "I know you're jealous because you have the hots for me. It's okay. But I'm a healthy, young guy. I can't commit myself to one girl right now."

Jen stopped laughing. Her mouth dropped open.

She stood up, grabbed Dawson's glass of water, and threw it in Pacey's face. "You're an arrogant jerk and a pig, Pacey," she said before she stormed off.

Pacey sat there in shocked silence, but that was soon broken by Dawson's laughter. Pacey couldn't believe what Jen had just done—right there in the restaurant for everyone to see!

He glared at Dawson. Why was he laughing?

"Guess you were on the wrong track there," Dawson said, smiling. "Don't drown now! You haven't finished the lifesaving class yet!" He laughed some more at his own joke as Pacey took a napkin and dried his face.

Pacey crumpled the napkin and stood up to leave. He tossed the napkin in Dawson's laughing face, then noisily shoved his chair in. "Good to see you, pal," he spat. "Not!"

He didn't care that he was still hungry and hadn't ordered. Now that Jen had made a fool out of him, he didn't want to hang around the Icehouse for another minute.

"You're popular today," Joey said to Dawson as she wiped up the table.

Dawson brushed the last tears of laughter from his eyes. "Yeah, well, maybe the heat's getting to everyone," he said. He hadn't meant to laugh at Pacey, but it was preposterous of him to think that Jen liked him. Completely preposterous. Right?

"It's not that hot out," Joey countered. She pulled out her order pad. "What are you going to have?"

"With all the excitement, I haven't decided yet," Dawson said.

"Take your time," Joey said cheerfully.

Dawson eyed her curiously. "Why are you in such a good mood today?"

Joey eagerly sat down. "I had the most amazing date last night," she said excitedly.

"Oh, that's right," Dawson said flatly. "I hope he didn't wear those Hawaiian shorts."

Joey looked at Dawson in surprise. "I can share these things with you, can't I?"

"Sure," Dawson said without much enthusiasm. "Go right ahead."

"I mean," Joey said, "how many hours of Jen interactions did I have to sit through?"

Dawson gave her a sheepish grin. "You're right," he admitted. "How was your date?" he asked, giving her his full attention.

"It was phenomenal," Joey said. Dawson could see Bodie eyeing her from the other side of the restaurant. "Three-minute break!" Joey called to him.

"First, Jeremy picked me up and gave me a dozen roses," she began. "Then we went to see *The Cop Who Couldn't Cry.*"

"Ick," Dawson interrupted.

"I wanted to see it," Joey continued. "But it *was* terrible. Anyway, he had asked Bess what my favorite snack was."

"Milk Duds," Dawson stated.

"No!" Joey said, wounded. "Sno-Caps."

"Oh, right," Dawson said. "Continue."

"So he surprised me with the Sno-Caps."

Dawson suddenly decided that he didn't want to hear this. Picturing Joey on a date was starting to upset his stomach. "Sounds like fun. You know, I don't think I'm going to order anything. I'm not hungry anymore." He stood up to go.

"But I'm not finished!" Joey protested.

Dawson sat back down. He hoped she would hurry up and finish this story.

"So the funny thing was that Clarissa's pet started to beep in the middle of the movie, and we started having a laughing fit because it was right in the middle of the most dramatic scene. So we left."

Dawson stood up again. "That's funny."

Joey pushed him back down in his seat. "I'm still not done. It turned out that Jeremy had already seen the movie anyway, but he sat through it again because I really wanted to see it."

Dawson laughed. This guy sounded like a sap case. "That's so corny! What a dork!"

"Hey!" Joey yelled, hurt. "He is not a dork! He is charming, funny, and adorable, and he's a great date. The best date I've ever had in my life!" She ripped the menu out of Dawson's hand. "If you're not going to order, you can't sit at a table," she snapped, then stomped over to the bar.

Dawson put his head in his hands. Great. Just great. Pacey was mad at him. Jen could barely say a sentence to him. And now Joey would probably never talk to him again.

Chapter 14

Joey couldn't decide which bathing suit to wear. She only had two that she felt were decent. The others were old and ragged, and she had quickly grown out of them.

She'd been wearing the red one when Jeremy met her, but it was her favorite, and the newest. Her other option wasn't nearly as exciting: it was navy blue and not cut as high on the legs.

She decided she had no choice but to go with the red one. She pulled on the suit, then put on shorts and a T-shirt. Glancing out the window, Joey could see that the sky was clear, and it looked like this was going to be a beautiful day.

She jumped when she heard a knock at the front door. She glanced at the clock. That was probably Jeremy! Bess and Bodie were at the Icehouse with the baby, so she had to answer the door herself.

After checking her appearance in the mirror, she calmly walked to the door. Though she was bursting with excitement, she knew it wouldn't be cool to appear too eager. But when she pulled the door open, all serenity left her.

"Hey!" Jeremy said, smiling his huge smile. Joey loved the way the corners of his mouth curved up and the way his eyes crinkled when he smiled. She wondered if he noticed little things like that about her, too.

"Hi." Joey returned his greeting and wide smile. "I'm ready," she said, grabbing her bag and stepping out the front door. She noticed that he was wearing the same Hawaiian shorts he'd had on the day before. That made her feel better about wearing the red bathing suit. But today Jeremy also wore a bright red retro bowling shirt. The word "Bird" was stitched over the pocket.

"Is that your nickname?" Joey asked, playfully pointing at his chest.

"No," Jeremy answered, shaking his head. "It's the nickname of my favorite jazz musician, Charlie Parker. I saw this shirt in an antique clothing store and I just had to have it. It called out to me."

"That's cool," Joey said. "That you like jazz. I don't know much about it, but my mother used to listen to jazz all the time. She had all these Ella Fitzgerald and Louis Armstrong records."

"The true greats," Jeremy said. "Next time I come to Capeside, I'll bring my sax."

So he plays the saxophone, Joey thought. She was looking forward to finding out more about him. At the movies the other night, they hadn't had a chance to talk too much, and there was so much she wanted to know about him.

Jeremy was carrying a cooler and a duffel bag. He held up the cooler for Joey to see. "I packed us some lunch—stopped at the deli. Today's menu features chicken salad or roast beef sandwiches and potato chips."

"No Sno-Caps?" Joey teased.

"Ah, yes," Jeremy said, smiling. "The roast beef is actually encrusted with Sno-Caps, making for a delicate blend of flavors."

"Yum!" Joey exclaimed.

Jeremy threw the strap of the duffel bag over his shoulder, so he would have a free hand. He reached for Joey's hand and took it in his. Joey liked the way his hand felt around hers. It was warm and cozy and strong. Not sweaty and clammy like some boys' hands.

Walking down the street with Jeremy, Joey felt special. He made her feel interesting and beautiful and fun.

When they reached the beach, they spread out a blanket. Jeremy pulled a Frisbee and a paddleball set out of the duffel bag. "So we won't get bored staring into each other's eyes," he said.

Joey laughed, but she thought that she would be content to stare at him all day.

"How's Howard?" Jeremy asked as he sat down.

"Still alive and kicking," Joey answered, as she sank down on the blanket. "Thanks to you," she added.

They stretched out side by side on the blanket and began to talk. Joey was struck by how easy the conversation was. She never had to rack her brain to think of something to say. There was never an awkward pause or dull lull.

They talked about their schools and their families. Joey told him the truth about her dad, and she was relieved that Jeremy didn't seem at all fazed.

"My family is far from perfect, too," he assured her. He told her that he liked to play soccer and that he loved to travel. He said it was his dream to visit all seven continents.

Joey imagined jetting off to Paris with Jeremy. Or going on safari in Africa to photograph beautiful and unusual animals. Or holding him close on a secluded iceberg somewhere near Antarctica. Or just sitting on the beach in Capeside for many summers to come.

Joey felt the heat beat down on her. Today was already a scorcher, but she couldn't tell if it was the sun or being close to Jeremy that made her feel hot. She decided to go for a swim before she started to sweat. She didn't think perspiration would be very appealing, so she challenged Jeremy to race her to the water.

It was a perfect day for a swim. The sun was bright. The water was calm. The beach was quiet, for a Sunday. She laughed all the way to the cooling blue water. And right then she was happier than she'd ever been before in her life.

Dawson slowly circled the beach blanket, ending with a close-up of Sheila. "Tell me about Australia," he said.

He sat down next to her on the blanket under the

huge beach umbrella. Dawson preferred to sit right under the scorching summer sun, but the umbrella had to be there to protect the babies.

Sheila adjusted the strap on her blue tie-dyed bikini. "What do you want to know?" she asked.

"I don't know," Dawson said, carefully steadying the camera, slightly distracted by her beautiful figure. Since Sheila had said she was camera-shy, Dawson hadn't told her about his news story opportunity. He figured he'd wait until the end of the day to inform her. That way she'd be more natural in front of the camera as he filmed her. Dawson's heart started to beat a little faster. He was happy that he felt something for her. "Tell me about your life there," Dawson probed. "Do you miss it?"

Sheila's expression grew sad. "I miss some things," she answered vaguely, "but other things I don't miss at all."

How mysterious, Dawson thought. She must have some deep, dark secrets. But he could tell she didn't want to be pressed about the things she didn't miss. "Tell me about the things you miss," he encouraged.

Sheila's expression grew wistful. "I miss my friends. I miss meat pies. I miss scuba diving at the reef, seeing all the colorful amazing fish." Her expression grew tender at the memories.

"Did you come to the States alone?" he asked.

Sheila nodded.

"Wow," Dawson said. "That's amazing."

Sheila shrugged. "Aussies are big travelers. Sometimes we go away just to think. We call that a walkabout. I guess I'm kind of on a walkabout for a while."

"What about Boston?" Dawson continued.

"Boston?" Sheila repeated, puzzled.

"Do you miss Boston? That's where you came first, right?"

"Oh, yeah, Boston," Sheila said vaguely. "Actually, I like it better here in Capeside."

Dawson could tell that Sheila wanted to change the subject. "I'll take some beach background shots," he told her, turning the camera away.

Things were going well so far, Dawson mused. He didn't want to screw it up by putting Sheila on the spot, asking her prying questions. But he couldn't help wondering how tough it must be for a teenager to go abroad alone. It sounded kind of cool, but kind of lonely, too.

Dawson pushed questions about Sheila's past out of his mind and concentrated on the setting. He had gotten some great shots already. He had arrived at the Barclays' just in time this morning. Sheila was awake, but the babies weren't. They had shared some juice until Sheila heard the first cry of the morning. After Sheila had changed and fed the twins, they came to the beach, and what a perfect day it was for it. Dawson panned the ocean, the sand, the sky, Joey . . . *Joey?* Dawson stopped panning his camera. A familiar brown-haired girl in a red bathing suit was running to a blanket, hand in hand with a boy. He would have recognized those Hawaiian shorts anywhere. It was Joey, with that guy, Jeremy.

Dawson zoomed in on Joey and Jeremy as they collapsed on the blanket, giggling. Then—Dawson couldn't believe his eyes—they kissed. *Really* kissed. Right there on the beach!

"Oh, my God!" Dawson said, his camera transfixed on the frolicking young couple. "I can't believe them! Right in the middle of a public beach!"

"Who? What?" Sheila asked excitedly.

Dawson pointed toward Joey and Jeremy. "Over there. It's disgusting!"

"Let me see." Sheila eagerly peered through Dawson's lens. "Aw, they're perfectly sweet! Wait—isn't that the girl who's in all your movies?"

"Yes," Dawson said, taking the camera back and focusing in on them. "I don't know about this guy. . . ."

Sheila started to laugh.

"What's so funny?" Dawson asked.

"It's so obvious, Dawson," Sheila said. "You're annoyed because you're completely into her. You're *jealous.*"

Dawson gasped. "I—I . . . That's not true!" He didn't know what to say. But he did feel a familiar pang in his chest.

But he had his sights on Sheila! Didn't she see that? How could she have noticed all this stuff between him and Joey without seeing that he was there, right in front of her, dying to get to know her?

There was only one way she'd get it, Dawson thought. He put down the camera, impulsively grabbed Sheila by the shoulders, and planted a huge kiss on her lips.

When he pulled back, Dawson sighed. Nothing. It was about as exciting as kissing Pacey, he thought. It wasn't like kissing Joey at all. He longed for that feeling again. Why wasn't that chemistry there with Sheila?

Sheila giggled. "Nice try, Dawson. But I still think you two make a darling couple."

Dawson started to think that maybe Sheila was right.

Chapter 15

On Sunday morning Pacey didn't show up to walk Jen to class. Not that she expected him to. After all, she had thrown a glass of water in his face. But even though Jen was mad at him, she felt that something was missing. No latte. No Pacey.

She sighed. Just when she thought she had a new friend, things had started to get ugly. Was it her fault? Had she overreacted?

When she arrived at class, Pacey was already there, chatting up a few girls. He glanced at Jen briefly, but coldly turned away when she came to join the group.

The class snapped to attention when Tim strode over. "Everyone into the pool for laps," he ordered.

Jen groaned inwardly. The laps were tiring, and this morning she hadn't had her coffee. But she understood the importance of becoming a strong swimmer to save lives. Apparently Pacey didn't feel the same way.

While the trainees dutifully swam their laps, Tim sat in a chair and leafed through a magazine. Thanks to Pacey, Jen figured he didn't want to leave the class alone anymore while they were swimming.

But leave it to Pacey to continue to goof off. While Tim flipped through his magazine, Pacey swam one lap to everyone else's two. Then, when people finished and climbed out of the pool, Pacey climbed out, too, after swimming only half as many laps as everyone else.

Jen shot him a dirty look. Pacey didn't belong in this class. Tim's approach might be harsh and comical, but he was right: lifesaving was an important skill, and there was no room for slacking off and goofing around. Tim was giving them essential job training, and his military manner was effective in making everyone pay attention and take the class seriously. Everyone except for Pacey.

After they finished their laps, Tim lectured them about rescue skills, such as how to hold and tow a drowning swimmer. Tim said that these were among the most important skills they would learn in class and that he would test them repeatedly.

But while Tim was lecturing and demonstrating, Jen could see that Pacey's eyes were closing behind his sunglasses. He wasn't paying attention to a bit of what Tim said.

"If a person is in distress," Tim explained, "he or she is in a panic. It is very important that you don't worsen the situation. The first thing you need to do when saving a person in distress is to calm the person down.

"Always, *always* take a life buoy or flotation device with you when saving someone," Tim continued emphatically. Tim couldn't stress the importance of these basics enough. Jen wrote everything down. She noticed that Pacey didn't even have a pen.

"Never, ever grab the person during a rescue," Tim went on.

One of the guys raised his hand. "But in movies and stuff, you always see the lifeguard swimming out, grabbing the victim, and towing him in. Is that wrong?" he asked uncertainly.

Tim chuckled. "One thing I want you all to know," Tim said, "is that lifeguarding on television and in the movies is entirely fake. Those people are actors and actresses. They are not in real-life situations."

Tim glanced at each class member. "Understand? Don't ever, ever use television or movies as your reference point for lifeguarding.

"When you approach a frightened victim, he may be thrashing around." Tim moved his arms wildly about to illustrate the point. "If you come too close to him, he can harm you, too, and all of your lifesaving efforts will be useless."

Tim's expression grew serious. "I have seen five- and six-year-olds, one-third the size of an adult nearly choke a lifesaver to death because the lifeguard acted in the wrong manner. And of course if a big guy like me was in a panic, he would drown you almost instantly."

Tim's voice grew urgent. "*Always* bring the victim

in with a life preserver. Hand him the buoy. Never try to grab him."

This sounded like serious stuff, Jen thought. She heard a light snore come from her right side. Half the class turned to look.

Pacey was dozing. The girl next to him elbowed him, and he snapped awake. He tried to act casual, but Jen could see that Tim had noticed.

Tim ignored Pacey for the moment, but Jen suspected that he was writing himself a mental note about Pacey. And he wasn't writing it in pencil. He was carving it in stone.

Pacey was back at the pool right after lunch, performing all sorts of stupid-human tricks and showing off in the water. He was doing dumb daredevil dives, too, in the shallow end of the pool The other girls seemed to be growing tired of his one-man show, and Jen simply couldn't take it anymore.

If he wanted to crack his head on the shallow end of the pool, that was his own problem, Jen thought. But if he didn't know what to do in a lifesaving situation because he hadn't paid attention in class, that was another case altogether. He could cause someone else to die.

But that was, of course, if Pacey actually became a lifeguard. At this point, Jen figured he would never pass the exam.

"You know, Pacey, you should stop goofing around and pay attention in class," Jen said, unable to hold her tongue any longer. "You're never going to pass the exam at this rate."

Pacey shot her a cold stare. "What is it with

you?" he asked angrily. "I think you made your point yesterday that you're not jealous. So what is your problem? Why are you always on my back?"

"Because I like you Pacey," Jen said, "and I don't want to see you make any more dumb mistakes."

"Well, thanks for your concern," Pacey said sarcastically. "But I already have one mother."

Then he took a running leap and turned a somersault into the pool, making a huge splash that drenched Jen.

How obnoxious can you get? Jen thought.

Where Pacey was concerned, it seemed there was no limit.

Dawson put his camera down and lay on the beach blanket that he had moved out of the umbrella's shadow. The sun shone down on him like a huge interrogation light. What did he feel for Joey? It was all too confusing.

She had been his best friend all his life. Earlier he'd never thought of her as a girlfriend.

Then things had changed. He and Joey had kissed a few times. At first he didn't think the kisses meant anything. But the memories had lingered. And then romantic thoughts of Joey had slowly crept into his mind.

Now he had seen another side of Joey. How attractive she was to other guys. How her chestnut-brown hair shone in the sun, how cute and shy her smile was, how just a touch of lipstick accentuated her lips. Dawson wanted to kiss them again.

But could friends be lovers? Wouldn't it make

sense, Dawson thought, for the love of your life to be your best friend?

And what about Sheila? Was there any hope of a spark developing there? Dawson knew the answer was no.

Sheila stirred and started to pack a bag. "I think the babies have gotten more than enough sun," she said.

That reminded Dawson—he hadn't told her about the news story yet. "Hey!" he said, sitting up excitedly. "I guess I'll tell you now."

· "Tell me what?"

"My mother is an anchorperson for the local news station. She happens to be doing a piece on teens and their summer jobs."

Sheila's eyes widened.

Dawson smiled at Sheila's expression of surprise. He went on. "So she thinks you would be the perfect candidate for the piece. She said it would give her series the international flair it needs. Isn't that great? You roll into Capeside as a nanny, and now you'll end up a television star!"

Sheila froze.

"I know," Dawson said. "Isn't it amazing? And she said I could do the piece. I could use the footage from today."

"But you said it was for practice only!" Sheila said. "You lied! How could you do this to me?"

"No!" Dawson assured her. "It *was* for practice. It's just a coincidence that my mom has this story going on. I just thought I could—"

"No," Sheila said abruptly, her face red. "No, you can't. I won't do it. This project is over as of *now*."

She quickly gathered her belongings, slung her tote-bag over her shoulder, and picked up the twin's.

"But—" Dawson protested.

Sheila hurried away across the sand.

He couldn't believe it. He started to chase after Sheila. "Wait!" he called. "There's nothing to be scared of! You looked great while I was taping you! You look terrific! You were completely natural!"

But Sheila didn't turn back.

Dawson stopped. He stood on the beach watching her retreating figure. "That's why I waited to tell you," he finished quietly.

He sank down onto the hot sand, defeated. Pacey was mad at him. Jen hadn't been able to have a conversation with him in weeks. He'd ruined any relationship he might have had with Joey. And now his only remaining friend was furious with him.

How had his life become such a mess?

Chapter 16

Dawson carried his equipment into his room and stretched out on his bed. How had today ended up such a disaster?

First he couldn't get his mind off seeing Joey kiss that guy. He was plagued by images of her, lip-locked with Mr. Loud Shorts.

Then Sheila had gone psycho on him. For the world of him, Dawson couldn't understand her reaction. Was she really *that* shy? Or was it something else?

Already his summer was turning out to be one enormous bummer, like some high-budget film disaster with an overpriced all-star cast. See how one teen single-handedly ticks off every woman in town! Watch with amazement at how he doesn't go on one single date for the rest of his life! Gasp in horror at the dark, disgusting boredom oozing out of every facet of his life. Coming to a theater near you. And hopelessly rated G.

Dawson heard the front door open and shut. That had to be his dad. Maybe he'd talk to him. His father always seemed to be able to make sense out of things.

Dawson walked down the stairs and into the kitchen, where he found his father grabbing a soda from the fridge. "Hey, Dad," Dawson said.

"Dawson," Mr. Leery answered. "I thought you'd be out enjoying this fabulous day."

"I was," Dawson answered. "And it's not that fabulous a day. More like the total opposite."

Dawson's dad regarded him curiously, and sat down at the kitchen table. "Something happen?"

Dawson pulled out a chair and sat across from his father. "Dad," he asked, "have you ever liked more than one girl at the same time?"

His father laughed. "When I was your age, it was more a question of did a girl exist that I *didn't* like."

Dawson let out a heavy breath. "I mean, I just can't get my feelings straight. If Jen wanted me, I'd take her back in a second. But then, I don't know, I think Joey and I could have something special. And then there's Sheila. . . . She's so wonderful, but it just doesn't feel right." He paused thoughtfully. "I guess it doesn't make any difference, though, because they all hate me."

Mr. Leery took a sip of soda, his expression one of fond remembrance. "It's called hormones. You're full of them now. They creep into your bloodstream and your brain and mix everything up."

Dawson was still unsettled. What bothered him

the most was that crazy kiss. The Joey kiss on the beach. With a total stranger. He wondered if Joey thought Mr. Fancy Pants kissed better than he did.

"Dad," Dawson asked carefully, "do you think it's possible for best friends to be lovers?"

"Absolutely," Mr. Leery answered unhaltingly. "Your mother is the best friend I've ever had. *Ever.*"

Dawson nodded thoughtfully.

Mr. Leery looked at him seriously. "Listen to your heart, Dawson. Then go for it."

"Thanks, Dad," Dawson said. He nodded, lost in thought. Then he rose and walked out the back door to stare out across the creek. He'd been acting like a jerk to Joey lately. And he didn't blame her if she was crazy about this new guy. But Dawson wouldn't step aside without a fight.

And what was he going to do about Sheila? Dawson realized that he'd been desperately trying to start a romance with her in a sad attempt to run away from his true feelings. But Sheila'd had it right all along. And he wanted to have her as a friend.

But first things first. He was going to call Joey and apologize for the way he'd acted at the Icehouse. Even if he had missed his chance with her, Dawson thought their friendship was too important to let go of. Maybe they could spend the day together tomorrow, like old times.

He walked back into the house to call her.

When Joey got home, she listened to the message tape on her answering machine: "Hey, Joey, it's Dawson. Sorry about what I said yesterday. I didn't mean it. I was wondering if you wanted to go on a bike ride or something tomorrow morning. Give me a call."

Dawson sounded pretty normal, Joey thought. She was happy that he'd apologized. She hadn't been able to spend any quality time with him in the past two days because she had been so busy with Jeremy. She liked the idea of getting together with Dawson and doing something fun.

She called him back and left a message: "See you at eight tomorrow morning. It's supposed to be good biking weather."

She'd had an amazing time at the beach with Jeremy that day. They hadn't even ended up playing Frisbee or paddleball. They swam and shared lunch and a few kisses, but they spent most of the day talking, and Joey discovered so many wonderful things about him.

Tonight Jeremy was going to take her to dinner at Romano's, a fancy restaurant where Joey had eaten only once before. She sat on the couch and closed her eyes, picturing his adorable smile and handsome face.

Bess came in the front door just then, holding a bawling Alexander.

All images of romance instantly dissolved. "Hey," Joey greeted her sister.

"Hey," Bess said back. "You looked as if you were in outer space."

Joey giggled. "Kind of."

Bodie strolled into the house, holding out the baby's formula. "You left this in the hot car," he said to Bess, sounding annoyed.

"Oh," Bess answered. "Thanks for bringing it in."

Bodie's face was hard. "Where is your head lately? You made a bazillion accounting errors at the restaurant today. You leave the baby's stuff all over town. I'm surprised we still have him, and that you haven't left him behind somewhere!"

Bess put the baby on the couch next to Joey. She turned on Bodie, hands planted defiantly on her hips. "Well, if you were the one getting up nights to feed him, you'd be forgetful, too. Sometimes you seem to forget *that*."

Joey could tell that they were gearing up for a big-league blowup. It was so depressing to watch them fight after she'd had such a great day.

Bodie slammed the baby's bottle down on the coffee table. "I've been working quadruple overtime to make sure that this child is provided for! Don't tell me I don't contribute!" Then he turned to Joey. "And look at this house! It's a mess! Joey, you were off today. Couldn't you at least have put the dishes in the dishwasher?"

Joey was angry that he put her in the middle of this. "Hey!" she said. "No one told you two to have a baby. Don't blame me if the responsibility is too much for you in your warped game of playing house!"

"You don't know anything about responsibility," Bess cut in. "You're conveniently never around to understand how hard it is! I'm bringing you up, too. You *could* help out more around here."

Joey couldn't believe it. They were ganging up on her. What had she done to deserve this? "You are not bringing me up!" Joey lashed out. *"Mom*

104

brought me up. Don't you dare take the credit! *You* will never be Mom."

The room fell silent. Bodie looked away. Bess stood as if she had been slapped in the face.

Then the baby started to cry again. Bess picked him up and cradled him in her arms, still looking hurt.

Joey got up and ran out the front door, slamming it hard behind her. She had to get out. She had to get away.

She ran hard and fast, as fast as she could, away from her family, past and present.

Tim marched into the pool area and announced, "No more lecturing for the rest of the day. This afternoon you will learn by example. This morning I talked about what to do in a rescue situation. Now we'll do some rescue practices in the pool."

Pacey was psyched. Finally they'd get to the good stuff and spend more time in the water and less time sitting on their butts.

"I'm going to play the victim each time," Tim said, pulling off his T-shirt and sunglasses but leaving his whistle around his neck. When I call you, I want you to follow all of the correct procedures to rescue me."

Tim jumped into the pool and sized up the group. "Witter," he said. "I will pretend to be a distressed swimmer. I want you to rescue me."

Pacey nodded. This should be easy enough, he thought.

Tim submerged himself. He swam a few laps.

Then he stopped and treaded water for a few seconds.

Pacey took that as his sign, and he leaped into the water.

Tim immediately blew his whistle. "What was wrong with that, folks?" he asked the class.

Pacey stood in the pool, confused. He hadn't even started to save Tim. How could he be doing something wrong already?

One of the twins—Pacey wasn't sure if it was Mindy or Mallory—raised her hand. "You didn't show any sign of distress," she pointed out, then giggled. "He went running in there for no reason."

"Exactly," Tim confirmed. "Pacey here just attacked a confident swimmer who was minding his own business."

The entire class laughed at him then. Pacey steamed up inside. He'd like to see any of these other clowns do better.

Tim looked Pacey right in the eye. "Okay, now," he said. "We're going to try this again. Are you ready this time?" he challenged.

"Yes," Pacey asserted. "I'm ready."

Tim wouldn't back off. "Are you sure?"

Pacey gritted his teeth and hopped out of the pool. "Yes, I'm sure," he responded.

"Then sit in the lifeguard chair," Tim said. "Don't hover at the edge of the pool. That's unrealistic."

Pacey walked over to the tall chair and started to climb the ladder. Just when he turned his back, he heard a thrashing in the water. He figured Tim was just swimming around, but when he sat in the chair, all eyes of the class were staring at him.

Tim blew the whistle again. "What are you, deaf?" he asked. "I'd be dead by now, if I waited for you."

"I—I had my back turned! That wasn't fair!" Pacey protested.

"That was more than fair," Tim corrected. He turned to the class. "Why was that fair?" he asked the group.

One guy raised his hand. "If he is the lifeguard on duty, he should never have his back turned. He should always be alert and scanning the area. Also, he should have acted as soon as he heard the splashing, but he didn't even turn around."

"Correct," Tim said. "Class, what lifeguard bylaw applies to what we have just seen?"

"A lifeguard is always prepared," the class chorused.

"Exactly," Tim said.

Pacey sat in the chair, turning a deep shade of red. Why was Tim picking on him? This was totally unfair.

"Now," Tim said to Pacey, "I'll give you one more chance. Are you ready?"

"Yeah," Pacey mumbled, embarrassed.

"I can't hear you!" Tim bellowed.

"Yes," Pacey said louder. He saw his classmates whispering and snickering. And Jen's sanctimonious glare seemed stuck on him. He'd show them all this time. They'd see a rescue that would make David Hasselhoff jealous.

"Okay, then," Tim said. He blew his whistle. "Let's go."

Tim swam a few lazy laps. Pacey didn't take his

eyes off him. Tim stopped and treaded water. Pacey sat stone-still in the chair. He wasn't falling for that again. Tim swam around a little bit more, and all eyes were glued to him as the trainees watched for signs of distress.

Finally Tim went under. Pacey watched him. He didn't panic. He saw him swimming underwater. When Tim came up, he seemed normal. He was.

Tim went under a second time, but this time he resurfaced quickly and began flailing his arms and kicking his legs in a panic.

Pacey acted immediately.

Instantly he climbed down from the lifeguard chair, dived into the water, swam right to Tim, and threw his arms around him.

Which tow should I use? Pacey searched his mind. There was the one where you dragged the victim from behind. But wasn't that for a swimmer with a spinal injury? Or not?

Pacey found it hard to concentrate with Tim thrashing around. He tried to pull him, but the next thing he knew, Tim had him in a stranglehold, and he wouldn't let go. Pacey went under because of the pressure of Tim grabbing on to him.

Then Pacey started to panic. Was Tim trying to drown him, right there in front of the class? He knew the instructor had it in for him, but was he crazy enough to kill him? Did he hate Pacey that much? Tim was obviously deranged! Why wasn't anyone trying to help?

Pacey started to yell, "Help me! Help!"

Finally Tim released his grip. Pacey kicked and splashed his way to the edge of the pool. Gasping and coughing, he pulled himself out of the water. Pacey glared at Tim, who was laughing. What kind of a maniac was this guy?

"Congratulations, Witter," Tim said. "You killed us both."

The entire class burst into laughter.

"*You* killed us both," Pacey said defensively. "You were strangling me!"

Tim waded over to the edge of the pool and propped his elbows on the concrete. "No, Pacey," he said quietly. "*You* killed us. You had no idea what you were doing, did you?"

Pacey stared at Tim in guilty silence. Without saying anything, he grabbed a towel and wrapped it around his shoulders. The whole class stared at him, and this time they weren't laughing.

Pacey wanted to dive into the water and never come up.

"If this had been a real situation," Tim said, "there would have been two victims."

Pacey swallowed hard and looked at the ground. When was this torture going to end?

"Ladies and gentlemen, I do want you to know that Pacey *did* do a good job," Tim said lightly. "He did a great job, as a matter of fact, of showing you all precisely how *not* to act in a lifesaving situation.

"Thank you, Pacey," Tim said.

Pacey didn't even look at him. He slunk over to the group and sat down on the hot concrete.

"Now who is going to show us how a real lifeguard should act?" Tim asked. "Who will be my next victim? Or savior?"

Tim scanned the worried faces in the crowd.

Pacey felt self-satisfied. No one else wanted to be made an example of.

Tim's eyes fell on Jen. "Miss Lindley? How about you?"

Jen stood up immediately. "Yes, sir," she answered.

Pacey felt even worse. That was all he needed now—to have Jen, of all people, show him up. He hoped she would fail. For once, Pacey thought, let someone else feel as embarrassed as I do.

Jen walked to the lifeguard chair and carefully watched Tim as he swam. She continued to keep her eye on him as she quickly climbed up the ladder.

She looks so smug in that chair, Pacey thought. Sitting there like she's the queen of lifesaving.

Tim reacted suddenly this time. Seconds after Jen planted herself in the chair, he started to thrash in the water.

Pacey watched as Jen responded immediately.

She grabbed the bright orange life buoy that hung next to her on the chair, then climbed down.

The life buoy! Pacey thought. I forgot about that!

Then Jen jumped into the water and swam rapidly toward Tim.

"Okay, take it easy," Jen said soothingly. "Grab the life buoy. Hold on to the life preserver and everything will be okay."

Tim advanced toward Jen in a panic, but Jen thrust the buoy toward him, while backing slightly away. Tim grabbed the buoy, and with the situation totally under control, Jen towed him to the edge of the pool.

Tim blew his whistle. "Excellent!" he said. "Class, I want you to give Jen a round of applause. She did everything perfectly."

Pacey clapped reluctantly along with the class. What a show-off she was, he thought. Little Miss Can't-Be-Wrong.

"Now, Jen," Tim said. "For bonus points: If I'd been unconscious, what would you have done when you got me on land?"

Jen wrinkled her forehead in concentration. Pacey smirked. He didn't think they had learned this yet. Or had they? He wanted to see Little Miss Can't-Be-Wrong get this one right.

"I would check the pulse, then check for breathing," Jen answered, nodding. "Then I would give you artificial respiration, or CPR, depending on what the situation called for."

"Perfect, once again," Tim said. "Class, I want you to remember Jen's actions today. She took absolutely correct lifesaving precautions."

She could use an absolutely correct enema, Pacey thought later that afternoon as he neared his house and tried to wipe the afternoon out of his mind. He was glad to be out of his misery, for today, at least. Tomorrow was sure to be another story.

He didn't know how much more he could take. Of lifesaving or of Jen.

Chapter 17

Joey went for a long, solitary walk on the beach and returned to the house only when she was sure that Bess and Bodie would be at the restaurant. She had to get ready for her date tonight and she wanted to dress in peace.

She had cooled down from the argument, but she was still mad at how Bess and Bodie always put her in the middle of their problems. They had never acted like that before the baby was born. Sure, her nephew was adorable, and they all loved him. But he had no idea how much trouble he caused in the family.

Joey felt that she needed a vacation. She needed to get away from Bess and Bodie and the baby. The house was too small for the four of them.

She also needed a vacation from boring old Cape-side. She wanted to go somewhere else—anywhere else. Somewhere far away where she had no family, no job, and no school.

Joey turned her thoughts away from her family strife and back to her date. Thank God for Jeremy, she thought. Without him the summer would be nothing but working, baby-sitting, and fighting.

When she was with Jeremy, all of that seemed far away and insignificant. She sure hoped the summer would pass slowly. She didn't know what she would do when it was over and Jeremy had to go back to New Hampshire. She didn't even want to think about it.

Maybe she could earn enough money this summer to pay him a few visits in New Hampshire in the fall. That would certainly be a worthwhile and well-deserved getaway vacation.

She wondered what life was like for Jeremy in New Hampshire. He had said his town wasn't that different from Capeside. Joey laughed at the thought. She couldn't imagine another place just as dull. It had to be more exciting. After all, Jeremy lived there.

Joey wanted to dress up for tonight. She looked in her closet and moved things aside until she found the perfect outfit—a short, lightweight powder-blue dress. It was from last summer, but it was still in style. It would be cool enough for a hot summer night and sexy enough for a romantic dinner at Romano's.

She sprayed a bit of perfume on her neck and winced as the cool spray hit her. She wasn't used to wearing perfume, but she wanted to smell nice. Then she rummaged in her jewelry box for the perfect baubles. She found them: tiny, elegant pearl earrings and a delicate pearl necklace.

She completed the outfit with strappy sandals. Looking at herself in the mirror, Joey smiled. She glanced at the clock. She was to meet Jeremy tonight at Romano's, but it was still too early to go.

She picked up Howard and played with him for a little while, just to kill time. She thought about how Jeremy had taught her everything she needed to know about caring for Howard: how to feed him, clean him, give him medicine, put him to bed, discipline him. She now knew what to do in any beeping situation.

Joey examined the pink egg and grinned. When Clarissa came back from her family vacation, Joey would have to thank her. Who would have thought that Howard would bring her Jeremy—and the romance of a lifetime!

The Leery household was quiet except for the clinking of silverware on china as Dawson and his parents sat around the kitchen table. Darkness had fallen, and moonlight peeked in through the windows.

"How's your documentary coming along?" Dawson's mother asked him as she passed the asparagus.

Dawson stopped chewing his chicken. "Um," he stalled with his mouth full. Should he tell his mother that the project was a bust? Or should he talk to Sheila and find out what the problem was?

The latter sounded like the better idea to Dawson. He didn't want to give up on the project just yet.

Before he let Mom down, he would see if he could calm Sheila down.

"It's going to be great," Dawson said. "I got some terrific shots at the Barclay house in this morning and at the beach this afternoon."

Mrs. Leery beamed. "That's great, Dawson. I'm so proud of you for pursuing this. With your enthusiasm and talent, I'm sure my producers will take your piece."

If there is a piece, Dawson thought glumly.

"Just remember to thank the Academy *and* us when you get your Oscar, son," Mr. Leery joked.

"Maybe one day we can work as a team," Mrs. Leery added. "A mother-and-son investigative reporting team!"

The more excited his mother became, the more uncomfortable Dawson grew. He didn't want to disappoint her. He had to find some way to get Sheila to change her mind.

Dawson speared another piece of chicken. Looking up at his mom, he was suddenly struck with an idea. Maybe, just maybe, if he used some of the professional editing equipment at the station, he could put together a brief clip to show to Sheila, to clarify for her what he was doing, and especially to reveal how wonderfully she came off on camera. With the high-tech stuff they used at the station, Dawson was sure he could put together a piece that would wow her.

"I was wondering," Dawson said between bites, "if I could use some of the station's editing equipment."

Mrs. Leery looked at Dawson in surprise. "Don't tell me you're finished already?"

"No," Dawson admitted, "but I want to put together a sample film to surprise Sheila—just to give her a teaser of what's to come."

Mrs. Leery nodded. "I don't see a problem with that," she said. "But it has to be early in the morning, before the editors get in. I wouldn't want you to interfere with their work."

"Okay," Dawson agreed. "I'll go with you to the station early tomorrow, then."

"Great," Mr. Leery added. "Tomorrow will be Bring Your Son to Work Day, honey."

Dawson breathed a sigh of relief. This might just work. With a few nifty editing tricks, he might be able to save the documentary—and his friendship with Sheila—after all.

Pacey dribbled the basketball, slamming it into the blacktop as he ran down the court and planted a layup right in the basket.

He stopped, peeled off his shirt, and wiped the sweat from his brow. He'd been at it since he came home from lifesaving class.

He walked over to the grass and collapsed. He always came to the school yard when he needed to think. In the summertime there was never a soul around, so it was quiet enough for him to sort things out.

Plus he could play basketball without his brother harassing him, reminding him he was a loser.

Pacey's head was spinning from the events of the

day. Class had been awful, and when he left the pool, he had been steaming mad.

He was mad at Tim. He was mad at Jen. He was mad at the world. He had been caught napping—literally.

But now that he had cooled off, Pacey was getting that sinking feeling. That feeling that maybe he should be angry with himself.

Once again he was the town screwup. No big surprise, Pacey thought. He wondered why he'd ever thought he could be anything but a big fat failure at everything he pursued. He had earned that loser label for a reason, he figured.

He had to face the facts. He had been goofing off in class. He hadn't been paying attention.

Maybe he wanted to be a lifeguard for the wrong reasons. Saving lives had never really crossed his mind when he pictured himself sitting up in the chair, surrounded by adoring babes.

And Jen was right. He had been acting like a jerk, telling outrageous lies to impress the girls. He had ignored Jen, refusing to see that she was trying to be his friend. Then he had insulted her when his inflated ego had led him to guess wrong about why she was angry.

Now she was furious with him. Everything felt all wrong.

Pacey got up and stepped onto the court once again. He took a foul shot.

Swoosh! He shoots, he scores, Pacey thought. Too bad life wasn't like a basketball court: a place where you could focus on one goal and, with enough practice, you could make the shot. The crowd was there to cheer you on. And if you missed, it didn't hurt so bad. There would always be other shots. Your chances would improve with each toss. You could make up for missing the last shot by sinking the next one.

He wanted another shot with Jen. He didn't want to lose her friendship. He wanted to make things right again.

But to do that, he knew what his first step had to be: he had to apologize.

Romano's wasn't too crowded, and it wasn't too empty. Candles flickered throughout the room, dripping just a touch of wax on the silver holders. Tuxedoed waiters bustled through the restaurant, making sure everything was just so. Joey and Jeremy had ordered lobster—her favorite.

Joey was pleased that her dress had received an approving glance and wide smile from Jeremy when she arrived at the restaurant. He looked great, too, Joey mused, in his clean white shirt and blue blazer. This time Jeremy had presented her with a single white rose. She loved his old-fashioned romantic gestures. They made her glow, and they made her feel beautiful and glamorous—less like a teenage girl, more like a woman.

The whole scene was perfect, Joey thought. The lights were just dim enough. A strolling violinist serenaded a couple in the corner for their anniversary. A full band was setting up for swing dancing. The whole place seemed to have a rosy glow.

Joey sat across from Jeremy, sipping a soda. Jeremy had an especially rosy glow—a sunburn. "You got a lot of sun today," she said, noticing the blush that covered his nose and cheeks.

"Yeah," Jeremy agreed, "but it will probably be all gone by the time I get home tomorrow."

Joey nearly choked on her soda. *"Tomorrow?"*

"Yeah," Jeremy said, his face falling when he noticed Joey's shocked expression. "I was only here for a long weekend. You didn't think—"

"I did," Joey said, half sad, half angry. Visions of a carefree, endless summer of love dissipated instantly. "I thought you were here for the whole season."

Jeremy shook his head sadly. "I don't know what to say. I thought you knew. I guess I assumed . . ." He threw up his hands in frustration. "I don't know what I'm trying to say. I suppose I should have made that more clear."

Yes, Joey thought. He should have made it clear before she got her hopes up about spending the rest of the summer with him. He should have made it clear so she could have been prepared to say goodbye. He should have made it clear before she let herself fall madly in love with him.

"I'm so sorry," Jeremy said. "But we'll keep in touch. I'll call and write, and if I can save enough money, I'll visit."

Joey nodded. "Sure," she said flatly. She knew all of this had to come to an end, but so soon? Had he looked at her as just a weekend romance? Was he the type of guy who had a girl in every port?

Their waiter came by with their lobsters, placing one in front of each of them. Joey glumly stared down at hers. She suddenly didn't feel much like eating.

Jeremy didn't look as if he had an appetite either. He ignored his food and reached across the table for Joey's hand. "I'm sorry for the misunderstanding," he said. "But I want you to know that these few days with you have been the best in my entire life. I've never met a girl like you before, Joey."

Joey thought that Jeremy sounded so earnest. She wanted to believe him. But she also didn't want him to know how deeply hurt she was. "It's no big deal," she said, casually waving a hand. She forced a smile. "About the misunderstanding. I mean, we were just having fun. It had to end sometime, right?"

Jeremy looked as if he was about to say something, but he hesitated. "Would you excuse me for a minute?" he asked. "I'll be right back, I promise," he assured her. "Don't go anywhere."

Joey wondered if she should take this chance to run out the door and never come back. But she thought better of it. She knew that would be immature and foolish. Even though she was upset that he was leaving so soon, she wanted to spend the few last valuable moments with him.

Anyway, she should have known better than to think he'd stay all summer. Life just wasn't supposed to go her way. Some overwhelming higher power was watching her, making sure that every situation would be as difficult for her as possible. Why did she even bother having hopes and dreams?

Joey stared at the flickering candle flame dancing in front of her. She couldn't believe her bad luck.

No sooner had she found her knight in shining armor than he went racing away, back to New Hampshire. How would she ever get through the rest of the summer? How was she going to get through the rest of her life?

How could Jeremy just casually come to Capeside, take her heart, and then leave?

Joey suddenly heard a familiar voice boom through the restaurant. "May I have your attention, ladies and gentlemen."

It was Jeremy. He was standing at the microphone over where the band was setting up. The musicians had stepped aside, and Jeremy stood alone on the stage. Joey felt her face get hot with embarrassment. What was he doing?

"This is dedicated to the one I love," he said sweetly. He looked at Joey with intense eyes. "Joey, someday we'll be together. I'm sorry that it can't be now. But in the meantime, whenever I hear this song, I will think of you. I hope you will do the same. It's called 'Summertime.' " Then a band member handed Jeremy a saxophone. He strapped it on and started to play.

Joey recognized the tune from *Porgy and Bess*. She was touched by Jeremy's gesture, but she was touched for another reason, too. Her mother always played Ella Fitzgerald's jazzy version of the song when she was in a good mood. The memory brought tears to Joey's eyes.

Jeremy walked right over to their table as he wailed on the saxophone, the smooth notes blending into a swaying melody. He knelt in front of her, his face a mask of passion, his fingers magically moving up and down the instrument's golden throat.

Joey couldn't help but get caught up in the music. He sure was good. She smiled at him appreciatively. He certainly had the golden touch, in music and in romance. She appreciated his attentiveness and his sweet gestures, no matter how brief.

If he was going to leave so soon, at least he was giving her memories. Memories of a summer she would never forget.

Chapter 18

She stepped out of the car, and it sped away. The propellers of the plane whirred in the background. Fog crept up all around her. The mist was cool on her face; she pulled the brim of her hat down.

Jeremy pulled the brim of his hat down, too, and stubbed out the cigarette he'd been smoking. That's funny, Joey thought. I don't remember him smoking. Then again, I've know him for only a few days, Joey reminded herself.

Jeremy took her hand. "Come on," he said, pulling her along. "We're going to miss the plane."

She picked up the small bag sitting on the tarmac. Jeremy lifted his saxophone case. Hand in hand they walked toward the plane.

Finally they were leaving Capeside behind. My dream come true, Joey thought. Jeremy was going to whisk her away somewhere exotic. She couldn't wait.

But Joey stopped in her tracks when she heard a faint voice calling her back. She could barely make it out above the plane engines, but it was there. "Wait!" the voice called.

She turned toward the voice. Appearing out of the fog was Dawson Leery.

"Why are you here, Dawson?" Joey asked. "Don't ruin my departure! Don't ruin my dream! Who asked you to come here?"

Strangely, Dawson was smoking, too. He also wore a hat, its brim pulled down over his eyes. An overcoat hung loosely from his frame. "You expect to dream about one of the greatest movies of all time and not have me appear, sweetheart?" he asked, in a strange voice.

Joey looked frantically from Dawson to Jeremy. "Give me one second," she told Jeremy.

She stormed over to Dawson. "What are you doing here?" she asked. "And when did you start smoking?"

"Old habits die hard," Dawson answered. He drew on the cigarette, then dropped it on the tarmac and stubbed it out with his shoe. "Like you, schweetheart. Like you and me. We're an old habit."

Joey thought Dawson was talking funny. "Stop calling me sweetheart. And when did you pick up the speech impediment? Is that an old habit, too? Or another sign that you've completely lost your mind?"

"Look, sweetheart," Dawson said, unfazed. "All I'm saying is you can leave with him, that stranger who could still turn out to be a psychopath, and hope that the honeymoon won't end." He nodded toward Jeremy, still waiting in the shadows, the fog growing thicker around him. "Or you can stay here with me, the psychopath you know."

"Jeremy's not a psychopath," Joey spat. "But you, on the other hand—"

"Joey darling!" Jeremy's voice called from the fog. "We must go. The plane is leaving. This is our last chance."

Joey began to panic. Something told her she should listen to Dawson. Something told her she should give him a chance. She felt as if a huge invisible magnet was drawing her to him.

Dawson nodded knowingly, but he looked defeated. "He's right, you know. You should go with him. If you stay here, you'll regret it," he said. "Maybe not today, maybe not tomorrow, but soon, and for the rest of your life."

"What about us?" she asked, suddenly overcome with despair at the thought of leaving Dawson.

"We'll always have Capeside," Dawson said. He slowly raised a hand to her face and stroked her chin. "Here's looking at you, kid," he said, then turned and walked away.

Jeremy came over to her, his white suit and hat spotless despite the horrible rainy night. She turned and quickly walked with him to the plane, the engines whirring in the fog.

As her high heels clicked on the tarmac, the decision tore at her heart. A real life with Dawson? Or a fantasy life with Jeremy?

She stopped. She turned.

Impulsively she ran toward the one she knew she must be with.

Joey woke with a start. She sat bolt upright in bed. She had just had the worst nightmare. It was sort of like *Casablanca*. But she was Ilsa, Jeremy was Victor Laszlo, and Dawson was Rick.

In the dream she had to choose between the two boys. In the end, she couldn't believe what had happened: she had chosen Dawson. Thank God it was only a dream.

She thought about the dream as she stretched in her bed. What a dumb dream, she thought, as if she would choose Dawson if she ever had to make that choice in real life. Jeremy could have kicked Dawson's butt all the way from Capeside to Casablanca.

She and Jeremy had had a great farewell date last night. After he played the sax for her, she cheered up and was able to have a good time. The lobster ended up being delicious. They'd even had dessert, and they danced just one slow dance to the big band. It was fun—like nothing she'd ever done with any other boy.

Then Jeremy had walked her home, and once again they shared an earth-shattering kiss. They said their good-byes softly, and she stared after Jeremy as he disappeared into the night, and probably, from her life.

She was able to hold back her tears until she got to her room. She was going to miss him so much.

But still, she felt an uncomfortable tug at her heart from last night's dream. She'd had strong feelings about Dawson once. But when Jeremy came around, those feelings had disappeared.

She'd forgotten what it was like to pine for a boy who saw her as one of the guys. She had forgotten what it was like to get steamed when he chased some other girl. She had almost forgotten all about Dawson.

She threw the covers off. But now, with Jeremy gone, would all of those feelings for Dawson come rushing back?

She sure hoped not. She didn't know if she could stand the torture.

That was when she remembered that she was going to spend the morning with Dawson. Biking.

She figured she'd find out about those feelings soon enough. Right now she had to get going because she knew that Dawson had to work in the afternoon.

Joey threw on shorts and a T-shirt, figuring she'd shower after the bike ride. She pulled on her sneakers and hurried into the kitchen.

She found Bess—exhausted, as usual—feeding the baby. Joey grunted in response to her sister's "Good morning." She hadn't seen her since the big fight the day before. Joey was still a bit steamed about that.

Remembering the fight quickly turned Joey grouchy. Seeing Bess also reminded her of all of the fun times she *wasn't* going to have for the remainder of the summer.

Joey was glad she didn't have to work Mondays. Bodie took over the Icehouse on Mondays, so Bess and Alexander were sure to be sitting around the house all day.

"I'm sorry about yesterday," Bess said, reading Joey's mood. "We didn't mean to pick on you. It's just that sometimes the pressure is too much for us. We shouldn't have taken it out on you."

Joey gulped down a glass of milk, then rinsed the glass and pointedly put it in the drying rack, lest she be reprimanded again for leaving dishes in the sink. She didn't say anything. She didn't feel like talking. Bess could apologize all she wanted, but it wasn't going to change their warped family situation one bit.

"I thought the four of us could do something together today," Bess said tentatively. "You know, like have a family day."

Joey glared at her sister. "I can't play house today. I have plans."

Bess returned the glare.

Joey stomped out the front door, jumped on her bike, and fiercely started to pedal. If Bess and Bodie were going to chastise her for not helping out enough, then they were going to find out what it would be like if she didn't help out at all.

She pedaled around the creek to the Leery house. It was a breezy morning, and Joey started to feel better when she got her adrenaline up.

When she reached Dawson's house, she parked the bike and climbed the ladder into Dawson's room.

"Wake up, sleepyhead!" she called.

But there was no answer. Dawson wasn't there. She figured that he was probably in the shower.

"Hey, Dawson!" Joey peered around to the bathroom but it was deserted. "Dawson?" she called again.

"Joey?" Mr. Leery called from downstairs. "What brings you here so early in the morning?"

"Dawson," Joey stated. "We were supposed to go bike riding this morning. Where is he?"

An apologetic look crossed Mr. Leery's face. "He must have forgotten, Joey. He went down to the station early with his mom to use some of the editing equipment there. You know, for that piece he's doing about the Australian girl."

Joey nodded. What a morning this was turning out to be! Dawson had made her get up early and haul her butt over, and then he had blown her off. He hadn't even had the courtesy to call her to cancel.

To top it all off, he was with that Australian girl again. Even if Joey and Dawson did get together, he'd probably moon about Sheila the whole time, like he did at the beach the other day.

"Thanks, Mr. Leery," Joey said quietly.

"I'm heading out now, but when I come back, I'll tell him that he's a scatterbrain," Mr. Leery called. "Don't worry."

"Scatterbrain" was a polite way of putting it, Joey thought, as she climbed out the window and down the ladder. What a jerk Dawson was! How could she have chosen him in that dream? *Nightmare*, she corrected. If she ever found herself in that situation in real life, she would be sure not only to choose Jeremy but to run Dawson down with the plane.

Joey stared out over the creek, toward her house. Well, she certainly couldn't go home right now. Bess was sure to rip her head off. Maybe she'd just dangle her feet off the dock for a while, till she was sure that her sister was gone, off somewhere playing family with Bodie and Alexander.

She pulled off her sneakers and socks and dangled her feet in the water. She leaned back, letting the morning sun beat down on her face. She tried to wipe her mind clean of everything: Jeremy, Dawson, Bess, life in general.

Her meditation was interrupted by Howard. Joey pulled out the key chain and checked the virtual pet. The pink egg suddenly made her sad. She remembered the day on the beach when she and Jeremy met, when he gently showed her how to clean up after Howard.

She didn't want to think about Jeremy anymore. It made her too sad, too angry. She took the egg and threw it into the creek. "Good-bye," she said bitterly. "I'll call. I'll be in touch. Yeah, right."

She pulled on her sneakers and socks. She thought about what she'd do all day. Maybe she'd just ride around town all day long.

She walked over to her bike. As soon as she mounted it, her conscience pulled her off. She saw a vision of Clarissa Cummings's sweet face turning sad when Joey gave her the news that Howard was gone. She also envisioned Jeremy, dressed like Victor Laszlo in *Casablanca*, disappearing into the fog. Finally, she pictured Bess, dark circles under her eyes, feeding the baby. Bess couldn't throw Alexander away when he was too much trouble, and Alexander was much harder to care for than a virtual pet.

What had she been thinking? Joey couldn't leave Howard in the creek.

Rats! she thought. She couldn't do this to Clarissa. And she didn't want to throw away the memory of Jeremy, either. And maybe her sister really did need her, she realized as she whipped off her shoes and socks. She couldn't turn her back on her own family, no matter how frighteningly screwed up they were.

She had to find Howard. She hoped he was still alive.

Joey ran back out onto the dock and dived into the creek.

Pacey woke early on Monday and hurried to the specialty coffee shop. "Two lattes," he told the guy behind the register. He drummed his fingers on the counter impatiently as the server grappled with the milk-steaming machine. Pacey didn't want to be late. He wanted to catch Jen before she left for life-saving class.

He'd apologize to her and then take off. He certainly wasn't going to show his face in class anymore. It had been a joke for him to think he could actually be a lifeguard, anyway. Somehow he didn't fit the mold of the macho, heroic, babe-magnet rescue type.

Tim would get the hint that he wasn't coming back. Pacey doubted that Tim or anyone else would miss him anyway. Pacey certainly wouldn't miss the lectures, but he was going to miss the morning routine.

That didn't matter, he realized. Jen probably wanted nothing to do with him. But he had to try to make amends anyway. He owed it to her. He owed it to himself.

After what seemed like an eternity, Pacey was served his two coffees. He quickly paid and raced out the door.

He arrived at Jen's house just as she was walking out the door. Pacey caught her by surprise. "Good morning," he said awkwardly.

At first Pacey thought Jen might grab the hot coffee from his hand and dump it over his head. He would deserve it, he thought.

But instead, she answered him pleasantly. "Morning, Pacey," she said.

Pacey handed her the latte. "Peace offering," he said.

Jen accepted it, pulled the lid off, and sat down on the porch steps. "I haven't been able to function correctly without it," she said, taking a swallow.

Pacey sat down next to her and took a sip of his coffee. "Listen, I want to apologize," he said. "I've been acting like a mega-idiot this past week."

Jen was silent for a few seconds. Pacey uncomfortably turned away and spotted Joey climbing down Dawson's ladder in a huff. He waved, but she didn't see him. Joey looked like she was in her own world.

"It's okay," Jen said softly, drawing Pacey's attention away from Joey.

Pacey shook his head. He took another sip of

coffee and swallowed. "It's not okay," he said. "I was rude to you. And you were only trying to help—trying to be my friend. I don't know what gets into me sometimes. Now that I've been humiliated in class, I can say good-bye to any hope of starting over."

"That's not true," Jen said. "All you have to do is be yourself."

Pacey shook his head and sighed. "That won't work either. Girls my own age just don't find anything remotely attractive about me."

Jen put her coffee down and gave Pacey a tender look. "That's not true," she said.

Pacey knew Jen was just trying to be nice. "Nah," he said. "Unfortunately you are wrong."

"I'm right," Jen said. "I know a girl your age who does find you attractive. I know a girl your age who sees many things to like about you."

Pacey looked at Jen as if he thought she was crazy. "Like who?" he asked doubtfully.

"Like me," Jen said. "I think you're cute and sweet, and you have a great sense of humor." She laughed. "That is, when you're acting like the real you—not your evil twin. The real you is a catch."

Pacey couldn't believe what he was hearing.

Jen went on. "And maybe I was a little jealous the other day. Maybe I was developing the slightest bit of a crush on you."

For a moment Pacey didn't know what to say. But then his eyes widened. "So I was right? You want me! You have the hots for me!"

"I said a tiny crush," Jen said. "Before your ego blows up again, the key word there was 'was.' I liked the friendship we were developing. I want to keep it that way, okay?"

Pacey nodded. She was right. They were really just starting to get to know each other well. He wanted to have a friendship with Jen before he started ruining things.

"I think someday you're going to find a very lucky girl, a girl you can feel comfortable around—so comfortable that you can just be yourself," Jen added.

Now Pacey was getting embarrassed. He looked at his watch. "Hey, you're going to be late for class."

"Me?" Jen asked. "You mean 'we.'"

"No," Pacey said, shaking his head. "You. I've decided I'm not cut out to save lives. I'm better off shelving videotapes."

Jen looked disappointed. "You shouldn't give up, Pacey. You can do this if you'll just pay attention in class and take it seriously." She stopped and raised her eyebrows. "I can tutor you on the stuff you missed."

Pacey nodded. That didn't sound like such a bad proposition. "Okay," he said, standing up, "but only if you promise not to spit in my face when you lecture."

Jen giggled. "Deal," she said. She stuck out her hand. "Friends, though, okay?"

But before Pacey could shake it, they heard a loud splash and turned toward the creek.

Why in the world was Joey going for a swim so early in the morning?

"What's with her?" Pacey said. "She just plunged into the creek fully clothed."

Jen squinted curiously at Joey in the creek. Pacey could see Joey's head bob in and out of the water a few times. She almost seemed to be diving for something.

"What is she doing?" Jen asked.

"It's hard to tell with her," Pacey said. "She's been acting so weird lately, like in a good mood—" Pacey stopped.

He turned toward Jen. "Where is she?" he asked. "Did you see her come up that time?"

"No," Jen said.

Without another word, Pacey and Jen raced to the creek.

Dawson came in the front door. The house was quiet. No one was home.

He was so mad at himself. He'd forgotten one of the tapes he needed, and he didn't have much time left to use the equipment at the station before the editing crew got in.

He ran up the stairs and into his room. He had accomplished a lot this morning, however. When he finished the tape, Sheila was definitely going to be wowed. He'd call her and ask if he could bring by a surprise for her. He hoped she would say yes and they'd be friends again.

He rifled through his video rack and picked out the tape he'd forgotten. He perked up when he heard a commotion outside.

He moved to the window and saw Jen and Pacey dash toward the creek, shouting something. They must be practicing some lifesaving technique, he figured, but why were they yelling so loud and why so early in the morning?

He picked up his camera and zoomed out the window for a close-up. This way, he could really see what was going on.

He saw Jen, then Pacey, dive into the creek.

What in the world were they doing? They didn't seem to be practicing. They seemed anxious and panicked.

That's when he spotted it.

The bike.

Joey's bike.

He slapped himself on the forehead. He'd forgotten all about her! They were supposed to go biking this morning! How could he have been such an idiot?

Joey was probably furious. She'd never forgive him now. He wouldn't blame her if she didn't.

Wait—if Joey's bike was here, then where was Joey?

He got his answer when he saw Pacey pull her limp body out of the water, while Jen helped him lift her onto the dock.

Chapter 19

Pacey had hit the water right next to Jen. He had spotted Joey right away. She was unconscious. Jen figured she must have hit her head on Dawson's rowboat while surfacing.

"I got her," Pacey yelled as he towed Joey through the water. Jen reached them and helped lift Joey onto the dock. They laid her out flat.

Quickly Jen checked Joey's pulse while she mentally reviewed her CPR lessons.

"Is she breathing?" Pacey asked urgently.

"No," Jen said. Instantly she started to give her artificial respiration. Jen carefully tilted Joey's head back. Then, while holding her nose closed, she breathed into Joey's mouth.

She waited a few seconds, then repeated the procedure. She waited again, then repeated it once more.

Pacey watched. Jen could feel his nervous energy, but she knew she had to stay cool.

Jen repeated the respiration one last time.

"You can do it," Pacey encouraged. "You know what you're doing. Everything's going to be okay."

Finally Joey came to, coughing up water.

When Joey regained consciousness, she didn't know what was happening. All she did know was that Jen Lindley was cradling her, asking if she was all right, and Pacey was standing above her, staring at her as if he had seen a ghost.

Joey searched her memory for what had happened. She remembered diving into the creek. She remembered searching around for Howard. She remembered finally spotting him, retrieving him, and shoving him into her pocket while she was underwater.

Then she didn't remember anything else. But her head sure hurt.

"Are you okay," Jen asked again.

Joey realized she should answer or Jen would think she was brain-damaged. She sat up, wobbly. "I'm fine. I must have hit my head." As she looked at Jen, something occurred to her. "Did you—did you save my life?"

Jen didn't say anything.

But Pacey said, "Yes, she did, and, boy, are you ever lucky that the best lifesaver in the class was around. Jen had the situation totally under control. She knew exactly what to do."

Jen smiled at Pacey. "Pacey pulled you out of the creek."

Pacey ducked his head. For once he had no wise-crack ready. He grinned at Joey.

Joey regarded Jen and Pacey with awe, then embarrassment. "Thanks," she said. "I don't know what to say. Thank you so much."

"We should get you to a hospital to get your head checked out," Jen said. "Make sure you don't have a concussion."

"Okay," Joey said. "But I just need to sit here for a few seconds." She felt worn out, freaked out, and a little dizzy. This sure was weird.

And to make things even weirder, Dawson suddenly ran out of his house, camera in hand. When he got close to Joey, he tossed the camera aside, pushed Jen and Pacey out of the way, and took Joey in his arms.

"Are you okay?" Dawson said in a panic. "I—I'm sorry I forgot about this morning!" He seemed to be on the verge of tears. "I promise I'll never forget about you again. Ever."

Then an even weirder thing happened.

Out of nowhere, Dawson planted a huge wet kiss right on her lips. A warm, lingering, kiss.

When he pulled away, Joey looked at him in shock. Those feelings skittered through her all over again. Her expression then slowly changed from shock to tenderness.

"Don't ever leave me," Dawson said.

Joey giggled, thinking about Dawson in his Humphrey Bogart garb. "I won't," she answered.

And suddenly, though she had been daydreaming about leaving Capeside behind, right then and there, with her friends around her, Joey never wanted to leave. She never wanted to have any best friend except Dawson Leery. And she certainly wanted to stick around to kiss him again.

And she didn't want to leave her family—Bess, Bodie, and Alexander. Though they were as ragtag as a family could get, they were all she had. Joey didn't want to lose them ever.

She vowed to do her best, from then on, to help them stay a family. Forever.

When Pacey and Jen showed up late for class that day, Tim was not pleased. They and Dawson had taken Joey to the hospital. She was examined and released right away, since she had no injuries beyond the bump on her head, but Pacey and Jen didn't get to class until nearly lunchtime.

Tim stopped lecturing. "How nice of you two to show up!" he growled. "Ms. Lindley, I'm surprised at you. Don't tell me you spent the morning goofing off with Witter?"

"Quite the opposite," Pacey answered. "We actually spent the morning saving a friend from drowning."

Tim's eyes narrowed in a threatening squint. "I'm sick and tired of your excuses and your lame attempts at humor, Witter." Tim stared Pacey down, then turned to Jen. "I'll get a real answer from Ms. Lindley. Why are you two late?"

"Pacey is telling the truth," she said. "We had to pull a friend out of the creek this morning and take her to the hospital."

The class gasped and whispered and mumbled. Tim blew his whistle. Pacey was sure that he didn't believe them. "Tell us what happened," Tim said calmly.

As Pacey and Jen related the story, Pacey enjoyed the looks of awe and wonder he was getting from his classmates, both male and female. But he wasn't going to take the credit. He pointed out that Jen was the one who had really saved Joey's life.

But then Jen added that Pacey was the one who was alert and watching. He had noticed the swimmer in distress, and he had pulled Joey out of the creek. That made Pacey feel great. For once, he had done something right.

"You did the right things, though it was dangerous, as you are novice lifesavers," Tim said when they had finished. He smiled, then, for the first time ever in class. Pacey nearly winced at how unnatural a smile looked on his usually expressionless face. "I'm proud of you," he said. "Both of you."

Then class resumed as usual, and Pacey and Jen took their seats and listened to the lecture. This time, Pacey was attentive. Even if he never became a lifeguard, he wanted to know how to save lives. He was in awe of how capable Jen was and how she took calm control of the whole situation.

And even though Pacey knew he'd probably end up working at Screenplay Video again, wearing a dumb black vest, he would have skills that he could use for the rest of his life. Skills that could save a friend. Skills that could save a child. Or even, skills that could save a bikini-clad damsel in distress.

When Joey walked into the house with a bandage on her head that afternoon, Bess ran over to her. "What happened?" she asked, concerned.

Joey sat down and told Bess the whole story. She

told her how Pacey and Jen had saved her life. She told her about Dawson's kiss. And as she talked, she realized that she hadn't had a real conversation with her sister in days.

She then filled Bess in on the events of the past few days. She described her day at the beach and her last night with Jeremy. She told her about how he played the saxophone in the restaurant and dedicated the song to her. Bess's face grew sad when she told her it was one of Mom's favorite songs. Then they shared a laugh over her weird *Casablanca* dream, and they laughed even more about Howard, who was miraculously still alive after the whole ordeal.

"We're going to have to have a special celebration at the Icehouse tonight," Bess said. "I want to thank your friends for saving the life of my only sister." Her eyes grew a little watery. "I don't know what I'd do without you, kid," she whispered.

"Thanks, Bess," Joey said. "You can count on me from now on. I realize that I've been acting like a selfish brat lately."

When the baby started to cry, Joey was the first to move. "I'll change him," she offered.

"Thanks for the offer," Bess said, "but today I want you to rest up. Tomorrow, on the other hand," she said with a grin, "he's all yours."

As Bess changed Alexander, her face lit up. "Oh! I almost forgot to tell you! There's a message on the machine for you."

Joey pressed the play button on the answering machine. A familiar voice came out of the speaker: "Hi, Joey. This is Jeremy. We just stopped for a bite to eat on the road, and I wanted to call you and let you know that I haven't stopped thinking about you the whole time. I'll call you when I get home. I miss you. Bye."

Joey smiled, a warm feeling spreading from her heart all throughout her body as she looked back on the whirlwind week she'd just had. It felt good to have two men in her life: one her soul mate and friend for life; the other a mysterious romantic stranger who could appear at any time, stir things up, and make life interesting.

Life could be a lot worse, she thought.

Chapter 20

Dawson was shaken up all day after Joey nearly drowned. At Screenplay, he could barely concentrate. He just stared into space, but it didn't matter much, because he had only a few customers.

He did have one surprise customer, however. Sheila stopped by—without the babies.

"Where are your other two-thirds?" Dawson asked.

Sheila laughed lightly. "The Barclays are back from their trip. They've given me some time off," she explained. "It feels great."

There was an awkward pause, but Sheila broke it first. "I wanted to apologize for the way I reacted the other day. I didn't mean to be so harsh," she said. "It's just that . . . I can't really explain it." She paused.

Dawson stepped in. "Listen, I think I understand.

But I have a surprise for you," he said. "Can you come by my house tonight?"

"Okay," Sheila agreed. "What time?"

"I work until six," Dawson explained. "How about seven or so?"

"Sounds good," Sheila said. Then she smiled her dazzling smile, dimples lighting up her whole face. She gave Dawson a small wave and left.

Dawson was glad he would have an opportunity to fix things with Sheila. Though he'd decided that his heart belonged to Joey, he wanted to stay friends with Sheila. He was happy that she'd stopped by. He couldn't wait to show her the tape tonight.

When the doorbell rang at precisely seven o'clock, Dawson had everything ready. The tape was cued up, and he had even chosen some great music to go with his glowing piece on Sheila.

Mr. Leery answered the door. Dawson had instructed his parents not to say a word to Sheila. When his mom gave him a curious look, Dawson told her that the tape was a surprise.

Dawson came down to greet Sheila and he led her up to his room. He threw open the door with a grand gesture. "This is where it all happens," he said.

Sheila laughed when she saw all of the movie posters on the walls. "Just what I expected," she said. She picked up Dawson's E.T. doll. "I love E.T.!" she exclaimed. "I always wanted one. . . ." Her voice trailed off. She changed the subject and placed the doll back on Dawson's bed. "So what is the grand surprise?"

Dawson patted the edge of his bed. "Have a seat," he said, then shut off all the lights and pressed Play.

Sheila came on the screen. A voice-over described "a spunky young Australian who came to the U.S. and works as a nanny to newborn twins." A montage followed, with Sheila feeding, changing, and playing with the twins.

But while Dawson beamed at his work, Sheila looked as if she might cry. And eventually she did. She burst into tears and grabbed the remote off Dawson's bed. While Dawson flicked on the lights, she stopped the tape.

"What's wrong?" Dawson asked, rushing to her side. He put an arm around her.

Sheila pulled away. "You can't put this on the news," she said through her tears. "You simply can't. I beg you."

Dawson leaned closer to Sheila curiously. "Of course I won't if you don't want me to. I—I just thought that if you could see how great you looked, you'd change your mind. I know you said you were shy, but I guess I just didn't understand. I'm sorry."

Sheila took a deep breath and stopped crying. "I'm not shy, Dawson. I know you meant well." She took another deep breath. "I'll tell you the truth, because I trust you. Then you'll understand, and you'll see why you can't show this.

"I left Australia when I was seventeen. My parents had split up. My father disappeared. My mother took up with an awful man." She paused for breath. "So I left. I wanted to start over as far away as possible. I packed up everything I owned and came to Providence.

"I lied about Boston," she went on. "I never went there. Providence seemed just perfect—big enough to be anonymous, but cheap enough to live, and small enough so as not to be overwhelming."

Dawson hugged Sheila encouragingly. She went on. "When you're seventeen and a foreigner, and you haven't finished school, it's hard to find decent work to support yourself. I did find a job in a clothing store. . . ." Her voice faltered. "But I had a hard time making ends meet. Then I got into some trouble. I fell in with another girl who was stealing from the store and selling the clothes. The store owners didn't press charges, and the police let me go."

She stopped again. "So I scoured the newspapers, and I answered an ad for a live-in nanny."

"It's okay," Dawson consoled her. "It's okay."

She went on. "I figured the nanny job was perfect, because I love kids, I would have a roof over my head, and the money was good. I had a lot of baby-sitting experience in Australia—I was always taking care of the neighbors' kids. Though I didn't have any other credentials, I gave the Barclays my old neighbors' numbers. They had no idea I had run away. My mother doesn't live anywhere near there now. She probably doesn't even care."

She stopped short and started to cry again. Dawson hushed her and cradled her in his arms.

After a few minutes she composed herself and went on. "So you see," she continued, "if someone in Providence were to see your news story and tell the Barclays about my past, I would lose everything.

They are wonderful, loving people. Please, Dawson, I don't want to lose my job. And my home."

Dawson was stunned. It must have been rough for Sheila, running away at such a young age. And when she finally found her niche, Dawson had almost ruined her life. He couldn't believe how thoughtless he had been. He should have just let it go when she initially said no. "I don't know what to say," he said, "except that I'm really, really sorry."

But actions spoke louder than words, Dawson figured. He got up, took the tape from the VCR, and unspooled it, destroying it right before her eyes. "Your secret is safe with me. I'll destroy all the other tapes I have, too."

"Thank you, Dawson," Sheila said, a few last tears streaming down her face.

Dawson took a tissue from his night table and dabbed at her eyes. "You can trust me," Dawson assured her.

"I know," Sheila whispered. "I know I can."

By the time Dawson walked Sheila home, she had composed herself. She told Dawson she felt a lot better, and Dawson apologized again for everything.

He gave her a kiss on the cheek, and once again assured her that he would never again do anything to jeopardize her security.

As he walked back home through the cool summer afternoon, the breeze from the creek washed over him. He remembered the first night he'd spotted Sheila. He remembered wishing for an exciting summer.

If this first week was any indication, the summer would be full of twists and turns and surprises.

When he walked into the house, Dawson's mother said eagerly, "When do I get my story?"

"I'm sorry, Mom, I couldn't get Sheila's permission," Dawson explained. "I'm afraid that she's painfully camera-shy."

Mrs. Leery's face fell. "Oh, Dawson," she said, her voice full of disappointment, "I was looking forward to that piece!" She paused, thoughtfully. "But if we can't get her permission, then we're up against a legal wall."

"Don't worry, Mom," Dawson assured her with a jubilant grin. "I have an even better story for you. How about 'Teens Training as Lifeguards Save a Drowning Girl'—right on Leery property?"

"Is that for real?" his Mom asked, her eyes widening.

"I've got the exclusive," Dawson assured her. "Film at eleven."

Bess and Bodie opened the Icehouse that night for a special occasion: the celebration of Joey's rescue. Joey, Jen, Dawson, and Pacey sat around a wooden table, the whole restaurant to themselves. Bess came to take their orders.

"Everything's free," she said, giving Joey a quick hug. "For saving my baby sister's life."

Pacey and Dawson locked eyes. "In that case, we're going to chow down," Pacey said excitedly.

"Anything you want," Bess assured them, as Bodie came by with a full bottle of sparkling apple cider and six glasses.

"Heads up!" Bodie said, as he unscrewed the cap. Joey and Jen took cover from the foam that escaped from the bottle. He carefully poured a glass for each person.

"A toast!" Bess announced. "To heroic acts!"

They lifted their glasses, clinking them happily.

"I have a toast," Joey said between sips. "To family and friends," she said. "You guys are the best."

Pacey clanged his fork on his glass. "One more," he said. "To Jen's television debut and mine, courtesy of director extraordinaire Dawson Leery."

They all raised their glasses again. "I'm not finished yet," Pacey said. "And to Jen, who taught me to try to be myself, because my alter ego is even worse than I am."

They all laughed, but they grew quiet as dusk began to fall and the sunset threw an orange glow over the restaurant. It was a magical summer night, Joey thought. A summer night you could have only in Capeside.

About the Creator/Executive Producer

Born in New Bern, North Carolina, Kevin Williamson studied theater and film at East Carolina University before moving to New York to pursue an acting career. He relocated to Los Angeles and took a job as an assistant to a music video director. Eventually deciding to explore his gift for storytelling, Williamson took an extension course in screenwriting at UCLA (University of California, Los Angeles).

Kevin Williamson has experienced incredible success in the film medium. His first feature film was *Scream*, directed by Wes Craven and starring Drew Barrymore, Courteney Cox and Neve Campbell. He has also written other feature films including the psychological thriller *I Know What You Did Last Summer*, based on the Lois Duncan novel, and directed by Jim Gillespie. His first foray into television, *Dawson's Creek*™, has already received high praise from television critics for its honest portrayal of teen life.

About the Author

K. S. Rodriguez is an entertainment glutton who has written several books about television and movie personalities. She lives in New York City amid a clutter of magazines, newspapers, videos, and CDs with her husband, Ronnie.

Shifting Into Overdrive

Dawson's Creek™

Shifting Into Overdrive

Based on the television series "Dawson's Creek™"
created by Kevin Williamson

Written by C. J. Anders

—for Claire G., teen diva—

Chapter 1

Dawson Leery lay with his head against the pillows and frowned as he watched the end of *Thelma and Louise* on videotape, gazing at the TV against the wall.

"I ask you, Joey," he said, as the credits began to roll, "what point was the filmmaker trying to make with this cop-out ending? I mean, two women who've just pillaged their way across the country decide to run their car off a cliff with themselves in it? Which means . . . ?"

"No one but you cares what it means," his best friend, Josephine—better known as Joey—Potter stated, from her spot next to him on his bed. "And they didn't pillage, Dawson. They plundered. They plundered idiotic men who deserved to be plundered."

"And they murdered," Dawson added.

"Oh well, that," Joey said breezily.

"So why do girls love this movie?" Dawson asked. "It gives the illusion of depth when really it—"

"I hate to break this to you, Dawson, since I know how fragile your psyche is. But the reason we love this movie is not because of its quasi-feminist bent or nihilistic ending. I can sum it up for you in two words, Dawson, and those two words are: Brad Pitt."

Joey made a grab for the remote and reran the movie until she found the scene of Brad Pitt kissing Geena Davis. "Now *this* is art." She settled back against the pillows.

"But he's a drifter who rips her off!" Dawson protested. "What about romance?"

"What about those lips?" Joey replied.

A flush of irritation crept up the back of Dawson's neck. How did she expect him to feel when she talked like that? True, they'd been best friends forever and had only been a couple for, well, it had felt like minutes, until Joey had decided that being a couple wasn't what she really wanted at all.

Of course, that had happened just when Dawson finally decided that being a couple was exactly what *he* wanted. Why couldn't they ever both be in friendship mode or relationship mode at the same time?

"This part is great," Joey said, watching the screen. "This is where Brad—"

Dawson grabbed the remote from her.

"Hey!" Joey protested, lunging for it.

Dawson held it away from her. "Say 'Good night, Brad.' "

"Not until I *want* to say 'Good night, Brad.' " She scrambled over Dawson's stomach to get the remote. He began to tickle her, she punched him in the bicep, and he pushed her over until, before he knew it, he was lying on top of her, gazing down into those huge brown eyes of hers.

The fire was there. Incendiary. Not a "best friends" thing.

But did she feel it, too? "Joe?" he whispered.

Silence. She stared up at him.

So she *did* feel it! Slowly, his mouth came down, and—

"This is what is commonly called a compromising position," Joey said. "And best friends don't compromise."

He rolled off of her, beyond embarrassed.

"Well, was it good for you?" Joey quipped, trying to ease the tension. "If I smoked, I'd light a cigarette."

Dawson stared up at the ceiling. "The story arc of our movie is seriously flawed, Joe. Our act one was endless. Our act two lasted a nanosecond yet changed everything. And now there seems to be some confusion over whether we are to acknowledge that act two happened at all."

Joey pushed some hair away from her eyes. "It happened," she said. "We've just gone back to act one."

His eyes slid over to her. "In my admittedly limited experience, once you've experienced act two—

3

brief as it might have been—you can't go back to act one."

Joey sat up. "Sure you can. Just press rewind."

She knew exactly what Dawson meant, but at the moment, she didn't *want* to know. For so long it seemed as if all her time and energy had gone into wanting him. It wasn't that she didn't still have those feelings for him, because she did. But now . . . well, now she wanted the time and energy for something else. Maybe even *someone* else.

Dawson sat up, too. "I think it would benefit the everchanging nature of our relationship to discuss this."

"I think not," Joey replied. "Where's the remote?"

"I think so," Dawson insisted. He clicked off *Thelma and Louise*. "The delicate balance of us, whatever that may or may not be, dictates that—"

"We've talked it to death, Dawson," Joey said. "Let's give it a funeral and let it rest in peace."

Dawson shook his head. "That is not the most productive course of action. What would be helpful is—"

Joey made a noise of impatience under her breath. He could be so infuriating! "Let me ask you a question, Dawson, and feel free to answer it in twenty-five words or less because I'd hate to find myself experiencing middle-age spread with you still pondering this: Who made you writer, director, and star of this little drama?"

"We could share credit. I think the Directors Guild allows that," Dawson said. "Two equals who are—"

"Equals?" she interrupted. "All last year you called the shots. That is not what I call equal."

"I didn't mean to call the shots," Dawson said.

Joey shot him a dubious look.

"The salient point here is, I can change."

"No, you can't," Joey said. "I know you better than you know yourself, Dawson. It's easy for you to want me when I don't want you. No pressure there. But deep down your ambivalence about us is just as ambivalent as ever." She got up and grabbed her jacket.

"Where are you going?" he called to her.

"She gives him the big kiss off, fade to black." Joey headed for the window, her usual mode for entering and exiting Dawson's bedroom.

"You should stay. We can talk about this."

Joey whirled around. "You can sit in your bedroom forever and write pithy dialogue for us, Dawson, but it's meaning-free. Within these four walls you are utterly safe. No need to take any chances. No need to be bold. But out there, Dawson, is real life. And what I know about real life could fit into a thimble with room to spare. So you just stay in your room, Dawson, if that's what you want. But pardon me if I want to find out what's in that big, bad world besides Dawson Leery." She climbed through the open window.

"Joey, wait!" Dawson called.

But it was too late. She was already gone.

From next door, Jen Lindley saw Joey climb down the ladder from Dawson's room, small clouds of

Joey's breath forming in the cold New England night air.

Jen tried to feel detached. After all, she and Dawson had not been a couple for a long time. She was the one who had broken off their relationship. So there was really no reason for her to feel anything at all about Joey not spending the night with him.

Then why did she feel so relieved?

Because you're insane, she answered herself, as she saw Joey trot toward the edge of the creek—a lagoon, really—where she'd beached the rowboat that would take her home.

Jen turned away from the window and stared at her reflection in the dresser mirror. How could she look so okay on the outside and feel so *not* okay on the inside?

What she felt was lonely. And it was her own fault. After all, she was the one who had broken up with Dawson.

She tried to remember why she'd done it. Ever since she'd been old enough to realize that boys and girls were different, she'd had a boyfriend. But who was she, Jen, on her own? She'd have to fly solo to find out. So, good-bye Dawson. It had seemed to make sense at the time.

Beware of what you ask for and all that. Because now she was on her own, and frankly, it wasn't so terrific.

She'd been so hopeful when she'd left behind her life in New York—parents, friends, and, she hoped, her bad rep—to live with her grandparents in tiny, coastal Capeside. Here she could start fresh. But then her beloved Gramps had had a stroke and died. And Grams was more interested in her own relationship with the Lord than she was in a real relationship with her granddaughter.

The kids at Capeside High hadn't exactly welcomed her with open arms, either. But for a while, there had at least been Dawson. She plopped down on her bed and sighed. "Maybe I should have just stayed in New York."

"Lie down with pigs and you get up dirty," Grams said from the doorway.

Jen looked up. "Excuse me. Were we having a conversation?"

"Your door is open," Grams pointed out. "If you didn't want to be overheard, you should have closed it."

"I'll certainly keep that in mind," Jen replied coldly.

"Jennifer—" Grams began hesitantly, her voice softer.

"Jennifer, what? Please, don't hold back on my account."

Grams sighed. "You don't give me a chance, Jennifer. And that's a pity. You certainly came to Capeside hoping people would give you a chance."

Jen felt a stab of guilt. Her grandmother was right. Sort of.

"I'm sorry," Jen said. "I'm in a weird mood."

Grams nodded tersely. "You might consider praying on it, Jennifer." She disappeared down the hallway.

Jen went to her window again, and looked into Dawson's room. "Petitioning the Lord with prayer doesn't work, Grams," she said, though she was well aware her grandmother was out of earshot. She watched Dawson pull his T-shirt over his head. "If it did, Gramps would still be alive."

Dawson turned out his light.

A lump of loneliness came to her throat. Maybe coming to Capeside really had been a big mistake.

Maybe it was time for her parents to let her come home.

"Pacey?"

Busted!

Pacey Witter froze in the middle of the darkened living room. As his eyes adjusted to the lack of light, he saw his older brother, Doug, sitting on the couch. Doug was a cop. The good son. Which left Pacey only one obvious role to fill.

"Well, if it isn't Deputy Doug," Pacey said, trying for the jocular. "What're you doing, holding a séance for one? Trying to call up the spirit of Rock Hudson?"

"The gay jokes are tired and you know it," Doug said. "It's a school night. Your curfew was two hours ago."

Pacey's anger flared. "Excuse me, I was under the distinct impression I had a father. You're not him."

"I told Dad I'd wait up for you. Why should he lose any more sleep over your antics?" Doug asked.

"Oh, Deputy Doug, your maturity makes me weep!" Pacey sobbed. "I'm not worthy!"

"You're right, you're not."

Pacey sat down next to his brother. "Aw, come on. Lighten up! The thing is, I was with a girl. A great girl. And I lost track of the time. You've been there, right?"

Doug just stared at him.

"Okay, you haven't been there," Pacey allowed. "But you've been with a great guy sometime in your sordid past. Same difference!"

Doug shook his head. "I had this crazy idea you were growing up. But you're the same loser you always were."

The words were like a knife in Pacey's heart. He really thought he should be numb to it by now. It wasn't like he hadn't heard everyone in his family call him a loser every single day of his life.

Doug stood up. "Dad told me to report to him what time you came in. I plan to tell him the truth. There will be repercussions."

"Oh no, Deputy Doug! Not . . . repercussions!" Pacey cried in falsetto.

"Change your life, Pacey," Doug said over his shoulder, as he walked out of the room, "before it's too late."

It was everything Pacey could do not to slam his fist into the wall. At the moment he hated his father, his brother, and the whole stupid, provincial town of Capeside. Even his friendship with Dawson didn't seem like enough reason to hang around.

He banged out of the house, sat on the front porch steps, and fixed his gaze skyward, at the moon.

And all he could think was: Somehow, some way, I've got to get out of this town.

Chapter 2

Jen ran the brush through her hair and checked out her outfit one last time—black boot-cut pants, black cable-knit sweater over a white T-shirt—then grabbed her backpack and headed downstairs. Grams was already in the kitchen, a calico apron over her dress, putting breakfast on the table.

Jen rolled her eyes. As many times as she had told Grams that eating first thing in the morning made her gag, her grandmother still had not gotten the message.

"Toast and oatmeal are on the table," Grams said, going back to the stove to stir something or other.

"Thanks, Grams, but I'm late for school already." Jen poured herself a mug of coffee and sipped it gratefully.

"Sound nutrition is not optional," Grams said.

Jen grabbed a piece of toast. It beat doing the

same old song and dance. She took another long sip of her coffee, then kissed her grandmother's cheek. "Gotta run."

Without turning from the stove, Grams pulled a large, white envelope out of her apron pocket and handed it to Jen.

"What's this?" Jen asked, surprised. The envelope was addressed to her in delicate calligraphy. The return address was in New York City. Clearly it was some kind of invitation. She checked out the postmark.

"Grams, this is two weeks old!" Jen realized.

Her grandmother shrugged. "I just cleared up the pile of bills this morning and there it was. I can't be responsible for keeping track of your things, Jennifer."

"Yeah, right," Jen muttered. "It came from Sin City so you buried it and hoped for the best."

She tore open the envelope. Inside was an embossed invitation to her cousin Courtney's sweet sixteen party, to be held that Saturday night at the Plaza Hotel.

Jen could see Courtney in her mind's eye. Long blond hair, blue eyes, her cousin looked as if she had just stepped out of *Nauseating Female Perfection* magazine. Gorgeous in a completely ordinary way. Honor student. Choir soloist. And the most shallow, self-involved, judgmental witch Jen had ever met.

All Jen's life, she'd been asked why she couldn't be more like Courtney. When Jen pointed out how awful Courtney really was under that perfect exterior of hers, everyone in the family just said Jen was jealous.

"Perfect cousin Courtney is having a perfect sweet sixteen," Jen told Grams.

"Send your regrets in writing, Jennifer. She's very wellbred; it's the wellbred thing to do."

Jen's temper flared. "No point, Grams. Because ill-bred, wicked cousin Jennifer plans to attend." She stuck the invitation in her backpack and headed for the door.

"Jennifer, do you think that's wise?" Gram called.

Jen pushed the door open, then stopped.

"Grams, do you think I care?"

Dawson shoved some of his books into his locker as kids dodged around him, scurrying to class. Joey came up next to him, pointedly ignored him, and spun the combination lock on her own locker.

He had lain awake forever the night before, examining and reexamining, and *re*-reexamining, their relationship. He'd ended up right back where he'd started—wishing that Joey was there next to him. Wishing that *she* wished she was next to him. Like she used to be.

"So, it got cold last night, huh?" Dawson said.

"This is New England, Dawson," Joey said, as she opened her locker and stashed her jacket. "It's supposed to get cold."

"Okay, that was a lame opening line and not the one I had intended to use," Dawson admitted.

Joey shot him a dubious look. Dawson noticed the dark circles under her eyes and a wave of tenderness for her hit him. She lived with her older sister, Bessie, and her sister's baby, Alexander.

Joey's mom had died and her dad was in prison. There was no money. After school, she waitressed at the Ice House. On top of that there was studying, helping with the baby, and cleaning the house.

Compared to Joey's life, Dawson knew he was living in a smiley-faced TV sitcom.

"Did the baby keep you up last night?" Dawson asked, his script for this encounter flying out of his head.

"Just for six hours, the seventh hour I slept beautifully, thanks," Joey said.

"You should have slept at my house. We could have talked about things instead of—"

"This scene is definitely overwritten, Dawson," Joey said. "And I have a splitting headache. So—"

"Joey, Joey, Joey, the woman I adore," Pacey crooned, as he sidled over. He put his hand against her locker and leaned close to her. "You look ravishing today."

Joey shot him a sour look. "What do you want, Pacey?"

"The Marine Bio homework," Pacey admitted.

"Did the concept of studying ever cross your mind?" Dawson asked him.

Pacey put his hands over his heart. "You wound me. How could I study when I was with the bodacious Tia?"

Dawson was surprised. "Tia? As in Tia Swain? Pretty, nice, smart, what-was-she-doing-with-you Tia?"

"That would be her," Pacey agreed. He turned back to Joey. "About that homework—"

"No," Joey said.

13

"Pacey, you actually had a date with Tia Swain?" Dawson asked.

Pacey smiled smugly. "Not only was I with the aforementioned babe, she asked me to take her to the Nightshade concert in Albany on Saturday night."

"Get real," Joey scoffed.

"I am beyond real, Joey," Pacey said. "Picture it. Me. Tia. All alone in Albany for the weekend."

Joey snorted back a laugh. "Right, Pacey. Tia Swain is going away with you for the weekend. What will be your mode of transportation, your bicycle?"

"As the proud possessor of a Massachusetts driver's license—" Pacey began.

"*Finally,*" interrupted Joey.

"—I plan to use a truck, thank you very much," Pacey said, ignoring Joey's comment. "I am formulating final plans even as we speak."

"You're going to take your dad's truck?" Dawson asked. "He'll kill you."

"Details are still pending," Pacey admitted. He turned back to Joey. "Meanwhile, it would behoove me to pass the Marine Bio quiz. Flunking does not further the course of true love."

Joey rolled her eyes.

Pacey clasped his hands together in Joey's face. "Please-please-please," he begged. "I'd get on the floor and grovel but as I recall this is the exact spot where Roger Fulford lost his lunch last week."

"Actually, Pacey, before you interrupted us Joey and I were talking—"

"No," Joey said. "*You* were talking, Dawson."

She turned to Pacey. "Walk me to class. I'll talk you through the Cliffs Notes version so you can pass the quiz."

"You are saving my life," Pacey told her.

Dawson watched them walk away. Joey even looked beautiful from the back.

"Hey, Dawson," Jen said, walking up to him.

"Hi." He didn't look at her. Jen's eyes followed his, and she saw that he was zeroed in on the retreating Joey.

Jen leaned against Joey's closed locker. "So, I was thinking of running naked through the halls today. What do you think?"

Dawson tore his eyes from Joey and looked blankly at Jen. "Sorry. Did you say something?"

"Evidently not. Later." She headed for class. So much for Dawson. Clearly he belonged to Joey now. Even if Joey has cut him loose. Relationships were just so insane.

"Hey, Jen," Cliff Elliot said, falling in next to her as she walked down the hall. "You look great today."

With his perfectly chiseled face and tall, hunky body, so did Cliff. But though that thought registered on Jen's brain, no feeling accompanied it.

"Thanks," Jen said. They headed into the bio lab.

"Did I mention that I'm getting into photography?" Cliff asked. "It sort of accompanies my interest in film."

"Uh-huh," Jen replied diffidently, as she chose a seat in the back of the classroom. As far as she had seen, Cliff had absolutely no talent for film, whereas Dawson—

15

Forget Dawson, she ordered herself.

"I was thinking maybe you could pose for me sometime," Cliff said. He slid into the seat next to her.

"Maybe," Jen said vaguely.

From across the room, Nellie Olson, who Jen suspected was in love with Cliff, shot Jen a wicked look. With her bouncing curls, pink-lipsticked pouty mouth, and evil eyes, Nellie looked like a teen Shirley Temple on acid. She strolled over toward them and slid onto Cliff's desk.

"Well, if it isn't Jessica Rabbit," Nellie cooed nastily to Jen. "Nice outfit. It hides your thighs."

The bell rang shrilly.

"Miss Olson, I believe you have a seat?" Mr. Brinson called drolly from the front of the room. "Let's open our books to page sixty-two, the life cycle of spiders—arachnids."

Jen pulled out her biology book, and the invitation to Courtney's sweet sixteen fell out of it. She picked it up and looked at it. Was she really going, or had she just said that to tick Grams off?

"After the male spider impregnates the female," Mr. Brinson droned from the front of the room, "she no longer has any use for him, so she kills him."

Cliff caught Jen's eye. "Dangerous, huh?"

Jen shrugged.

Nah. Dangerous was going back to New York, even for the weekend. Back to all that temptation. Back to her old boyfriend, Billy.

Back to the scene of her crimes.

* * *

Joey yawned, leaned against the wall of the gym, and watched the girls practicing foul shots on the basketball court under the gung-ho supervision of Miss Gaglia, their estrogen-challenged gym teacher. Baby Alexander had been up all night, screaming from an ear infection, and sleep deprivation was taking its toll. Every time Gaglia blew her whistle, the shriek echoed off the walls and right through Joey's head.

"Let's hustle, ladies! Let's see you guys sink a few!" Miss Gaglia blew her whistle again.

Joey winced. "I'd like to take that whistle and—"

"Me, too," Jen said, as she came out of the girls' locker room in her gym uniform.

Joey looked over at her. Even though she knew it was stupid, she still felt insecure every time she was around Jen. Jen was sophisticated, beautiful, and rich. From day one, she had seen Dawson's IQ slump every time he looked at her. At the time, it had broken Joey's heart.

All that's over now, Joey thought. So why when I look at her do I still feel like I'm Janeane Garofalo and she's Uma Thurman?

Out on the court, Miss Gaglia blew her beloved whistle again. "Not like that, Olson!" Nellie had just taken a pathetic underhanded shot at the basket. "You throw like a girl!"

"*Quelle* surprise," Joey said. "Nellie reeks of girl."

"My guess is, she's overcompensating for a serious case of gender confusion," Jen said.

Joey laughed. "Meaning Nellie was formerly Nelson?"

"Exactly," Jen agreed.

"Not a pretty thought." Joey chuckled again. It was funny. It it hadn't been for all that angst last year with Dawson, maybe she and Jen would have been friends.

Yeah, right. Sexy, sophisticated New Yorker Jen and tomboy, small-town poor girl Joey, buds. Sure.

Gaglia blew her whistle again. "New group, on the court, let's hustle!" She looked pointedly over at Joey and Jen. "In this lifetime, ladies?"

"Next round," Jen called to her.

Miss Gaglia gave Jen and Joey a look of disgust and turned back to the court. Jen and Joey slid down the wall and sat on the wooden gym floor.

"So, how's life?" Jen asked carefully. She had vowed to herself that she wouldn't ask Joey anything about Dawson.

"If you mean 'How's Dawson?,' we're the same non-couple that we were yesterday."

Jen hugged her knees to her chest. "Is that good?"

"I'm too busy enjoying my carefree youth to have a relationship," Joey said blithely. "Haven't you heard? These are the best years of our lives."

"Now, that's a depressing thought," Jen said.

Cliff Elliot and a friend stuck their heads into the gym to check out the girls. As soon as Nellie saw him, she ran to him and threw her arms around his neck.

"Gee, how subtle," Joey remarked. "Maybe Dawson could make a movie about her and call it *Nellie or Nelson*?" Gaglia blew her stupid whistle again, which made Joey wince and rub her temples.

"Headache?" Jen asked, kindly.

"Lately, it's permanent," Joey said. "What I need is a vacation. From everyone and everything."

"Even from Dawson?" Jen asked. She just couldn't seem to help herself.

"Especially from Dawson," Joey replied. "But I might as well dream of winning the lottery, because the odds of my doing either are roughly equivalent."

Miss Gaglia, clearly addicted to the sound of it, blew her whistle yet again and yelled for everyone to hit the locker room. As Jen got up, a thought popped into her mind. About Courtney's sweet sixteen and her own fears about facing everyone in New York.

It wouldn't be so scary if I didn't go by myself, Jen thought. I could stand to have a human shield. And Joey needs a vacation.

Jen caught up with Joey in the locker room. "So, is your idea of a vacation big city, or small town?"

"I live in Capeside, USA," Joey said, untying her gym shoes. "What do you think?"

Bingo.

Jen grinned. "Well then, Miss Potter, I'd say you just won the lottery."

Chapter 3

Right after school, Jen headed for the Ice House. She looked around for Joey. The place was jammed—high school kids, stay-at-home moms on outings with their babies, some stray off-season tourists who found Capeside's late autumn chill a quaint experience.

"Hey, Miss, I ordered a veggie burger!" an irate, male voice called from behind her. Jen turned around to see Joey rushing over to the table. Two middle-aged guys with thinning gray ponytails were frowning into their food.

"That is a veggie burger," Joey told the irate guy, trying to keep her own voice calm.

"It looks like turkey," the guy said suspiciously. "I don't eat anything that ever had a face."

"Tofu does not smile, so you're safe," Joey assured him, as she hurried toward the next table.

20

Jen went to sit at the counter, and ordered a cup of coffee from Bessie, Joey's older sister.

"Joey, your order's up!" Bessie called to her sister.

"Miss, coffee?" a woman asked as Joey hurried by.

"Miss, my check? This is the third time I've asked you."

"Yeah, yeah," Joey hurried behind the counter and began to sling coleslaw into paper cups. "What are you doing here?" she asked Jen.

"Sipping coffee," Jen replied innocently.

"You know what I mean," Joey said. "I already told you I'm not going to New York with you."

It had totally shocked Joey when Jen had invited her. It seemed that Jen wanted to go to her cousin's sweet sixteen at some glitzy hotel in Manhattan, but didn't want to go alone. And Joey was desperate for a big-city vacation. So?

New York! How fantastic would that be? Joey could already picture herself there. Bright lights, big city.

Yeah. Right. Let's just call "Cut!" to that little fantasy, she'd told herself. You are not Audrey Hepburn and this is not *Breakfast at Tiffany's*. You have no clothes for New York. You have no money. You have nothing.

"Reconsider," Jen was saying now, as she stirred a little more Equal into her cup. "You'd really be doing me a favor. The idea of going back there alone doesn't warm my heart."

"And my heart bleeds," Joey said, filling salad bowls.

"Joey, table five says they've been waiting for fifteen minutes for you to take their order and Tom's not here yet," Bessie said irritably.

"How about if you take it," Joey snapped. "It's *supposed* to be dead in here. I'm *supposed* to be studying."

"Can I help it if everyone in Capeside got hungry this afternoon?" Bessie dropped pickles on the burger plates and loaded them onto a tray, which she handed to Joey. "Go."

"I live to serve," Joey mumbled, hoisting the tray.

Bessie sighed. "Why does she make everything my fault?"

"She needs a vacation," Jen said.

"Yeah, well, don't we all." Bessie hurried to the other end of the counter to take some orders.

Jen turned around and surveyed the noisy restaurant. Two women came in with a group of screaming preschoolers. Bessie had disappeared into the kitchen. Clearly it was more than Joey could handle.

Impetuously, Jen got up, grabbed an order pad from behind the counter, and went over to the table of kids.

"Can I help you?"

"Ten pieces of chocolate cake with chocolate frosting," one of the women ordered, "and ten glasses of milk, please. And two cups of coffee. Black."

"I hate chocolate frosting. Gross! It looks like doody!" one little girl yelled. "I want white frosting!"

"Sorry," Jen said sweetly. "We only have the doody frosting."

Across the restaurant, Joey watched Jen in amazement. They met up as they both put their orders in.

22

"Thanks for the helping hand, but I'm onto you," Joey said tersely. "You can't guilt-jerk me into going to New York with you."

"Look, I'm not exactly asking you to scrub out toilets with a toothbrush," Jen said irritably. "Some people might look *forward* to a weekend in New York."

"Some people might have the *money* to go, too," Joey shot back. "And the right clothes to wear while they mingle with the rich and ostentatious, but none of those people would be me."

Oh, so *that's* it, Jen thought. I'm an idiot.

"Listen," Jen said, "I'll pay for the train tickets. We'll stay at my parents, so if you don't mind some intentional infliction of emotional distress, that's a freebie, too. And I'll loan you a dress."

"Order up!" Bessie called.

Joey grabbed the food from the warmer and put it on a tray. "Look at this place—it's insane—and this is a weekday. I can't leave Bessie in the lurch for the weekend. So even if I wanted to go, I couldn't."

"Go where?" Bessie asked, overhearing her. She picked up the order slip Jen had taken for the pre-schoolers. "This isn't your handwriting, Joey."

"Jen took it," Joey explained.

"Yeah?" Bessie grinned at Jen. "Cool. So where is it you can't go, Joey?"

"To New York with Jen for the weekend, to some sweet sixteen thing," Joey explained. "I told her it's impossible."

"Go," Bessie said, as she sank the cake knife into

23

a freshly baked chocolate cake with chocolate frosting.

Joey's jaw hung open. "Excuse me? My hearing aid needs adjusting. I thought you just said 'Go.'"

"I did." Bessie deftly slid slices of cake onto plates.

"But what about—" Joey began.

"Read my lips, Joey. Go." Bessie licked chocolate frosting off her pinky. "You need a break."

Joey just stared at her, shocked.

Bessie gently touched Joey's hair. "I know you've cast me as the older sister from hell, but I really do remember what it's like to be a teenager."

"Thanks," Joey said softly. "Really."

"You're welcome, really. Now would you two please get these orders out before the customers mutiny?"

"I was a fool, Derrick. I only pretended not to want you because I was afraid of being hurt again."

"What is it that you do want, Joanne?"

"You. Now. Kiss me. Please, just kiss me."

From behind him, Dawson heard a noise. Joey, climbing through the window. Quickly, he put his computer into "hibernate" mode, blacking out the new dialogue he'd just added to his screenplay. If Joey saw it, she might think it was his fantasy conversation between Dawson and Joey, instead of a scene about Derrick and Joanne.

That would, of course, be a ridiculous assumption.

He was seriously happy to see her. They hadn't

24

talked since their aborted conversation that morning. Clearly she was avoiding him. But all day at school, after school while he did his homework, and all through dinner with his parents, he'd been thinking about her. Nothing in the world felt right when things weren't right between them. And now, here she was. So clearly, she felt the same way he did.

"Impeccable timing," Dawson said. "I'm starting revisions. I'm thinking of giving Joanne a black belt in karate."

"Derivative," Joey said. "Way too *Buffy*." She closed the window behind her and threw her jacket on his bed. "I didn't row across the frozen lagoon to talk movies."

Dawson smiled. Excellent. She wanted to talk about their relationship. It was about time. He picked up his E.T. doll, and playfully pointed it at her. "Relationship mediator."

"Dawson, your brain is experiencing a meltdown."

He put down E.T. "Fine. No mediation. No movies. Just us. You can go first."

"Big of you, Dawson, but I didn't come over for another fifteen rounds of 'Death By Talking,' either. Actually, I have news."

She told him about her weekend getaway with Jen. New York. The sweet sixteen party at the Plaza Hotel.

He sat on the bed, incredulous. "You and Jen? *Together?* In *New York?* At some rich girl's *sweet sixteen?*"

Joey folded her arms. "I just said that."

"So . . . would a sweet sixteen be a coed sort of an event?"

25

"No, Dawson," Joey replied evenly. "It's all girls. That is, until the male stripper jumps out of the cake."

"Pardon me if the logic eludes me," Dawson said. "You and Jen have never exactly been soul mates. And I picture Joey Potter at a rich girl's sweet sixteen at the Plaza Hotel about as easily as I picture her eloping with Cliff Elliot."

Joey's eyes blazed with fury. "You're just so sure that hick chick Joey would be the laughingstock of the party, aren't you? Well, it just so happens that—"

"That's not what I meant!" Dawson protested. "I meant that those don't seem like your kind of people."

She sat down next to him. "You've only ever seen me with the so-called human beings of stultifying Capeside. Which, by the by, would include you. So how would you know what my kind of people are?"

Her face was only inches from his. Her hair smelled like a meadow. A movie moment flew into his mind: Joey all dressed up in some sexy dress, dancing in the arms of some oh-so-hip New York type. His name was Stone. No, Brick. He drove a Ferrari. He pulled Joey closer, and—

"Dawson?"

He blinked. The movie moment was gone. Joey remained. Mad. He had hurt her feelings. He hadn't meant to.

"This conversation is not going at all well," Dawson said. "Would you consider take two?"

She nodded. "Consider it considered."

"You just told me you're going to New York with

Jen. My line is: 'While it seems odd that the two of you are going on a trip together, and while as your best friend I have some concerns about your welfare, I hope you have a nice time.' "

"Take two notes: overwritten per usual, but the sentiment was nice," Joey said softly. "Theoretically."

She was sitting so close.

"Theoretically?" Dawson verified

She nodded. "I suggest we go for take three. And Dawson, this time, when you tell me to have a nice time . . ."

"Yes?"

She smiled. "Try to mean it."

Chapter 4

Pacey pounded the basketball down the court, coming to a quick stop at the top of the key. School had let out a half hour ago, and he was killing some time while waiting for Dawson to finish some meeting with Mr. Gold, the film teacher. Then, the two of them would head over to Screenplay, the video store where they both worked.

Pacey head-faked to the left, whirled, and let fly with a jumper. "Yes! And the Celtics go up by a deuce!"

Behind him, someone applauded.

Pacey turned around. Tia Swain, the girl he had been with the night Doug had busted him, stood at the entrance to the gym, smiling. Well, "been with" was a slight exaggeration. Actually, they had run into each other in the library after he had gotten off work at the video store.

But they had talked. That counted. And she *had* mentioned how much she'd like to go to the Nightshade concert in Albany on Saturday, even if that was hours from Capeside. Pacey figured that if she was telling him, then theoretically she'd be willing to go with him. Now all he had to do was connect the dots from the theoretical to the actual.

Tia was a ray of light in the otherwise black doom known as Pacey's history class. Long auburn hair. Green eyes. A smattering of freckles. World's greatest smile.

Which was now aimed at him. Be still my heart.

Pacey sauntered over to her, basketball under his arm. "Please, please, no autographs."

She smiled. "Nice bucket." She cocked her head at him. "Did anyone ever tell you that you look a little like a young George Clooney?"

Clearly the girl was delusional. Cute girls his age *never* flirted with him. But this was definitely a flirting-type conversation. It was beginning to look like the Nightshade concert was not such a long shot after all. All he had to do was "borrow" his father's truck for the weekend. Find some extra money. And then there was the minor detail of actually inviting Tia.

Ease into it, Pacey, he told himself. Don't blow it.

He looked both ways, as if checking to make sure no one was listening. "Actually, I *am* George Clooney."

"Oh, really," she laughed.

Pacey nodded. "Yeah, I'm incognito in this crazy little burg."

"Well, I'm just so thrilled to meet you," Tia teased.

Thrilled. The girl had said *thrilled.* Albany was getting closer by the second.

"Actually, pretty lady," Pacey continued in his best George Clooney–type voice, "I'm here doing research for my next project. Very hot. Serious nudity. Wide angle lens. Screen might not be big enough."

"Is this big enough?"

A fist the size of Rhode Island appeared in front of Pacey's face. It belonged to Tom Reynolds, a senior pituitary case who was the starting left defensive end on Capeside's football team.

"Mighty manly meathook you got there, Tom!" Pacey said brightly.

"Who the hell are you, you little twerp?"

"Hey, that would be *Mister* Twerp to you," Pacey said.

Tom got right in Pacey's face. "You think talking dirty to Tia is funny, turd-brain?"

Whoa. Backpedal time. "You've got it all wrong." Pacey feigned astonishment. "Those are lines from a movie!"

A dubious look furrowed Tom's prehistoric-looking brow. At that moment, Dawson came into the gym.

"*His* movie," Pacey said, pointing at Dawson. "Title? *The Big Braggart.* I gotta tell you, the guy's mind is a cesspool."

Tia snorted back a laugh as Tom advanced on Dawson.

"What're you, some kinda sicko freak?" he demanded.

"Missing the beginning makes it so difficult to follow the dramatic thrust," Dawson said, pointedly staring at Pacey.

"Dramatic *thrust?*" Tom grabbed the collar of Dawson's flannel shirt. "That a line from your porno, twerp?"

This time Tia actually laughed out loud. "Come on, Tom," she said, reaching for his hand. "Time to go."

As they walked away, Tom looked over his shoulder and pointed at Dawson. "I've got my eye on you."

"Tom, you're beautiful when you're angry," Pacey called to him.

Dawson stared at Pacey. "Have you lost what little mind you might have at one time possessed?"

Pacey nodded. "Most likely. It seems The Terminator and Tia are an item. But I could swear she was sending me signals."

They left the gym and headed out of the building, taking the side door to assure that they wouldn't run into Big Tom, and cut across the lawn to the bike stand in the parking lot.

"I was *this close* to cinching my date with Tia to the Nightshade concert." Pacey held his thumb and forefinger a fraction of an inch apart. "I mean it. *This close.*"

"Too bad," Dawson sympathized, unlocking his bike.

Pacey sighed. "It's probably for the best. Look at it this way. If we'd gone away together for the weekend, I would have fallen madly in love with her. But eventually, I would have done something monumentally stupid to screw it up, she'd drop me, and my heart would be broken. This way I never have to go through any of that."

"There may be something to your bizarre logic," Dawson admitted, thinking about the sleepless night he'd just spent staring at the ceiling and thinking about Joey.

"Absolutely," Pacey said. "I mean, look at you, going crazy over this weekend in New York thing with Joey and Jen. A loser like me never has to deal with that."

Dawson had told Pacey about Joey and Jen's impending New York road trip during lunch. Pacey thought it was a hoot. He had titled it "The She-Devils Shift Into Overdrive."

They got on their bikes and headed for Screenplay. As they passed the Ice House, they saw Jen and Joey in front, talking and laughing. Dawson couldn't take his eyes off of them.

Honk! Ho-o-onk!

Dawson's eyes darted back to the road, as he barely swerved out of the way of an oncoming car.

"Dying young is highly overrated." Pacey said, as they locked their bikes in front of Screenplay.

"Isn't it strange to see them together?" Dawson asked, as they went inside and got their black Screenplay Video vests from underneath the counter.

"Together without you, you mean." Pacey slipped on his black vest. "Maybe they're bonding over war stories about love-'em-and-leave-'em Leery."

"The painful truth is, I didn't do anything," Dawson reminded Pacey. "They both broke up with me.

Besides, Joey and Jen are both much too evolved to discuss their relationship with me with each other."

Pacey laughed. "Yeah, dream on, my man."

"You're late," Nellie accused, advancing on them, a huge stack of videos in her arms. "My father pays you to be on time. And I hope you two don't think I plan to stock the returns by myself." She placed the videos on the counter, and a couple managed to fall to the floor.

"Never." Pacey bent over to pick up the fallen videos. "That requires alphabetical order. Which implies a working knowledge of the alphabet."

Nellie gave him a withering look. "Multiple choice: Who is practically flunking out of school? A—Nellie. B—Dawson. C—Pacey. Anyone? Bueller? I love no-brainers like that." She flounced back to the comedy section.

"The brain-free always do," Pacey called after her. He turned to Dawson. "I ask you, why isn't Tom Reynolds with Nellie instead of Tia? What could a gorgeous, smart, and did I mention gorgeous girl like Tia see in that mutant?"

"Maybe attraction takes place on some basic biological level over which we have no real control," Dawson mused, as he logged the recent video returns into the computer. "For the species to survive, it makes sense that females are attracted to the males who can best protect them."

The movie moment Dawson did not want to see flashed in his head again. Joey in New York, in the manly arms of some guy with Leonardo DiCaprio's face and Arnold Schwarzenegger's body. Brick Studly. Brick pulled her to him, and—

Cut. He forced the image away and looked at the next video title. *Carnal Knowledge*. Great.

Pacey eyed him and grinned. "I am so onto you, Dawson. You're thinking about Joey. Like what if she meets some genetically superior stud in New York."

"Biology is not destiny," Dawson insisted. He logged in the next film. "Besides, while Joey and I might not be, at this moment, a so-called couple, you underestimate her commitment to our past and future relationship."

Pacey laughed. "Get over yourself! The truth is, you're scared spitless that Joey will find some hunka burnin' love in New York who'll get her to cruise in the fast lane, while you're here in Capeside stuck in neutral."

"You miss the point, Pacey," Dawson insisted. "My concern is the best-friend variety. I'm worried about her."

"For the Jeep and the Tahiti vacation, who is Dawson Leery really worried about?" Pacey asked in his best game-show-host voice. "I'll need that answer, contestant number one—"

"Hey, we're missing a *Liar, Liar* back here!" Nellie called from the video racks.

"Yes!" Pacey yelled, pumping his fist in the air. "Vanna, show the girl with the wet brain what she's won!"

"I heard that," Nellie called. "You'll pay, Pacey."

"Oooh," Pacey called back. "Beat me with your curls."

Dawson leaned against the wall. "The truth, Pacey?"

Pacey grinned. "A delightful change of pace."

"I keep seeing this horror movie moment in my mind," Dawson admitted. "Joey's in New York with this guy, and—"

"Oh, I'm good," Pacey interrupted, as a look of devilish glee spread over his face.

"Does an explanation come with that statement?"

"A plot is forming," Pacey said slowly, "which will close your little horror flick before it opens. The beauty part is that it gets you what you want—Joey. And it gets me what I want—out of Capeside."

"Does logic play any part in this?" Dawson asked.

Pacey made a square with his fingers as if he was framing a shot. "Opening credits. Followed by us, two wild and crazy guys liberating my father's pick-up truck after work tomorrow. You tell your parents you're at my house, I say I'm at yours. Next stop, New York. You and Joey. And thank you, yes, I am a god."

"Flawed plot, Pacey. What if my parents call?"

"Flawed characterizations, Dawson. Your parents never check up on you because you are disgustingly trustworthy."

Dawson knew it was a bad idea. Joey was her own person and she made her own decisions. So if she wanted to be with some guy, she had every right to be with him, even if his name was Brick.

Or Buck.

Or Bulge.

Dawson felt sick.

He gave reason one last try. "Your father will miss his truck, Pacey."

"Wrong. Dad and Deputy Doug will be at a Juvenile Justice Convention in Hartford this weekend, plotting a future police state—that's how I knew I could get the truck for my fantasy weekend rendezvous with Tia."

"Which is the only reason you want to do this, Pacey. In your mind, you were already in that truck, on the road with Tia. But that doesn't make this a good idea."

"No, it doesn't," Pacey agreed. "Because this was already a good idea. We'll have the truck back on Sunday. Dad and Deputy Doug will never know it was gone." He hit Dawson in the bicep. "Or would you rather leave Joey in the arms of Studman?"

Dawson's jaw set. "Tomorrow night, we're outta here."

Joey handed her ticket to the conductor, and he handed her back the stub. She could hardly believe she was here, on a train bound for New York, with Jen Lindley of all people, former love of Dawson's life.

At least I hope it's former, popped into her mind. Whoa. Those were feelings best left unexamined.

She looked over at Jen, who was watching the countryside pass by out the window. Jen had on jeans and an expensive-looking black sweater. Over that she had on a leather jacket that must have cost more than Joey's entire wardrobe.

Joey looked down at her T-shirt, flannel shirt, and denim jacket combo. Swell.

"I can't believe I'm going back," Jen murmured.

"Is that a good 'I can't believe' or a bad 'I can't believe'?" Joey asked.

"Both," Jen admitted. "I miss the excitement. And my friends. But I don't miss the person I was back then. I did some seriously dumb stuff."

"Who hasn't?" Joey asked breezily.

"I had this really wild rep," Jen said slowly. "Some of it I earned. Some of it I didn't. So when I go back—"

"People have long memories," Joey filled in. "Got it."

"And then there are my parents. My father once asked my mother if I got the slut gene from her side of the family."

"Ouch."

Jen turned to her. "I probably should prepare you for the shocking family drama that is about to encompass you in Surround Sound."

"Please. You're talking to Miss Capeside-family-scandal-of-the-decade, here. I walk down the street and people part like the Red Sea."

"Maybe you'll understand, then," Jen said. "My father is . . ." She stopped herself and gave a short, bitter laugh. "I guess that's the problem. I have no earthly idea who my father is. A benevolent despot. Minus benevolence."

"What about your mom?"

Jen shrugged. "Never met a face-lift she didn't like. Majored in MasterCard." She hesitated. "The truth is, I don't know either one of them. And they don't know me."

"Well, I don't exactly know dear old dad, the

felon, either," Joey said. She fiddled with one earring. "It was different with my mom, though."

"You must really miss her," Jen said.

Joey got a faraway look in her eye. "She was one of those people who really listens, you know? Like, when she was with you, she was a hundred percent with you. Even if you were a little kid, she made you feel like what you thought and felt was important."

"That must have been great."

Joey nodded. "My mom was the most loving person I ever knew." She blinked. Her eyes focused again on Jen. "But then she got sick and died. How do you make sense of that?"

"I keep thinking that life should make sense, too," Jen told her gently, "but it never does."

For a long moment, they were quiet.

"S'funny," Joey finally said.

"What?"

"I always think the only thing we have in common is our mutually insane relationship with Dawson, but it isn't true. Both of our families belong in the Dysfunctional Family Hall of Fame. And people love to talk about both of us behind our backs."

Jen laughed. "Sisterhood has occurred over less."

A slight smile curled Joey's lips. "Yeah," she said. "Maybe it has."

Chapter 5

Jen paid the taxi driver while Joey stood on the sidewalk, staring up at Jen's modern high-rise apartment building. A uniformed doorman stood in front of the ornate doors. Through the glass, she could see a huge lobby decorated like some rich person's living room. Large burgundy leather couches. Gleaming mahogany tables. A huge vase of fresh flowers on a marble pedestal. Another uniformed doorman sitting behind a large desk.

So this was how the other half lived.

"Ready?" Jen asked, as the taxi took off.

Joey nodded. As nervous as she felt, she wasn't about to let on to Jen, sisterhood or no sisterhood.

"Good evening, Miss Lindley," the doorman said, opening the door for them. "How nice to see you."

"Hi, Sam," Jen said. "This is my friend, Joey Potter."

The doorman nodded his head deferentially. Jen waved to another doorman, and they headed for a bank of elevators.

"What floor do you live on?" Joey asked. Anything to cover her sudden attack of nerves.

Jen stabbed a button that read PH.

"P-H?"

"Penthouse."

"Ah, of course," Joey replied.

Jen used her keys to open the front door of her apartment. Inside, it was shadowy and silent. "Maybe they went out for an early dinner or something," Jen said.

She flipped a light switch, and Joey gasped. The living room was huge. Everything was shades of white—the carpet, the couches, the marble tables. Abstract paintings covered the walls.

"Anyone home?" Jen threw her suitcase on the couch. Jen's voice echoed throughout the place. There was no answer. "That's weird," she said. "They knew we were coming."

"Miss Lindley?"

Jennifer turned around. A very thin, sour-faced woman in her fifties was standing there, ramrod straight.

"Yes?" Jen said politely.

"I'm Mrs. Richardson, your parents' new household manager," she said. "They told me you were expected."

"Ah, yet another new household manager," Jen said. "Don't get too used to the job. There's heavy turnover."

Mrs. Richardson ignored Jen's remark. "Your parents asked that I tell you that they were called away on an unexpected business trip."

"Why, how unexpected," Jen said dryly. "And you would be here because . . . ?"

"Because they asked that I spend the weekend here in case you need assistance."

Jen laughed bitterly. "Right. You're supposed to keep me in my cage. Deter my wild behavior."

Mrs. Richardson was clearly not amused. "Your parents did inform me that you were not to have any male company in the apartment while they are away."

Jen turned to Joey. "Darn. I guess that orgy we had planned is out now, huh?"

"Is there anything you need?" Mrs. Richardson asked.

"World peace?" Jen ventured. Mrs. Richardson didn't crack a smile.

"I'm kidding," Jen told her. "You know. Deflecting a strange situation with humor?"

"I'll be in the manager's quarters if you need me," Mrs. Richardson replied, and walked away.

"It's so heartwarming to see what a priority my parents have made my homecoming," Jen said. She picked up her small suitcase. "Come on."

She led Joey down a hallway to her bedroom and opened the door. Joey was again in awe. Framed posters from rock concerts, some of them signed, lined the walls. The huge platform bed was covered with a velvet tapestry quilt and a dozen ornate velvet and tapestry pillows.

She walked over to take a look at the signed Smashing Pumpkins poster. Next to it was a photo of Jen and another girl with the band. "Friends of yours?"

"My friend's mom books for William Morris Agency," Jen said, as she pulled stuff out of her backpack. "She gets us backstage passes."

Backstage passes, Joey thought. I would kill for backstage passes. She says it like it's so been-there-done-that. Well, for her it probably is. Joey caught a glimpse of her reflection in the mirror over Jen's dresser. She just looked so, so . . . hick. Tall, dark, and hick.

"You can throw your stuff in the closet." Jen cocked her head toward the double closet doors.

Joey opened them and was assaulted by the scent of roses. The closet was as big as her entire bedroom in Capeside. There were already enough clothes in there to stock a small department store. Row after row of gorgeous clothes hung on pristine white quilted hangers.

What the heck am I doing here? Joey asked herself. She dropped her backpack and closed the door. She looked around for Jen. The room was empty.

"Out here!" Jen called.

Joey hadn't noticed the patio balcony off of Jen's room. She walked outside. And there it was—the night skyline of New York City. The skyscrapers glittered like towers of jewels that Joey knew she could never have.

"Wow," Joey breathed, the air cold on her face.

"Yeah," Jen said softly, leaning against the balcony. "I missed this."

"It's so . . . immense," Joey said.

"Not exactly Capeside, huh?" Jen asked with a chuckle.

"What's Capeside?" Joey murmured. Suddenly she got the most incredible, tingly feeling in the pit of her stomach. "It's like everything is possible here. Like you could be anyone. Reinvent yourself."

"Just watch your back," Jen advised. "All that glitters out there is definitely not gold."

"Who's talking gold?" Joey said softly. "Maybe I just want glitter for a while." Suddenly she didn't care if she belonged here or not. She *was* here. So New York could just deal with it.

Jen turned to her. "So, you up for it?"

"For what?"

"Checking out the glitter," Jen said. "You didn't really want to hang out here all night, did you?"

Joey grinned. "Definitely not."

"Tomorrow we can do the tourist stuff if you want—Statue of Liberty, Empire State Building—it's funny, when you live here you never go to those things. But tonight I thought we'd go down to Soho."

"Which is?"

"A neighborhood downtown," Jen explained. "Lots of clubs. Very happening."

"Works for me," Joey said. "Uh . . . what do you wear?"

Jen shrugged. "Whatever."

Joey tried to stifle her impatience. It was easy for Jen to say "whatever." Jen had a closet full of "whatevers" and the sophistication to match. But just as Joey was about to explain this to Jen, Mrs. Richardson knocked on the glass doors to the balcony.

"Excuse me, but I called from the hallway a number of times and you didn't hear me," the older woman said.

"What is it?" Jen asked.

"The doorman says a young man by the name of Billy is downstairs for you."

Billy. She had once thought he was the love of her life. Little did she know he was simply the *lust* of her life. At one time she would have done anything for him. She almost did. But moving to Capeside and getting far away from him had probably saved her life. Even if it hadn't been her idea.

Billy had shown up in Capeside once. He'd wanted her back. The person she had become in Capeside had told him to leave. But it was scary. Just being near him had brought back all those old feelings of wanting. And now here he was, waiting downstairs. As if he had read her mind.

Well, she could handle it. Joey was here. Everything was under control.

"You can tell him to come up," Jen said.

Mrs. Richardson hesitated. "Your parents said—"

"Put it in your bad girl report on me," Jen said. "Item one: had guy upstairs within first half hour—something like that."

"I suggest you go downstairs to see your friend," the older woman said.

Jen gave her a look and went into her bedroom, where she pressed a button on an intercom grid in the wall.

"Yes?" came a staticky male voice through the grid.

"Send Billy up," Jen said.

"Very good," the voice said.

Jen turned to Mrs. Richardson. "Look, I'm a big girl, okay? I don't need a baby-sitter."

The older woman walked stiffly out of the room, her body language reeking disapproval.

"Geez, she must take lessons from Grams," Jen said.

Joey watched the woman leave. Jen might not worry about the woman getting fired, because Jen didn't ever have to think about money. But Joey did.

"Will your parents be mad at her?"

"If you mean will they fire her, the answer is probably yes," Jen said. "But firing the help is my mother's main hobby." She went over to her dresser mirror, checked out her reflection, and sprayed some perfume in her hair.

"You want Billy back?" Joey asked. She had met him in Capeside. A serious hunk. Tall. Dark. Very hot.

"No," Jen said.

"Then why the perfume?"

"Simple," Jen said. "I want him to want me."

They went into the living room just as the doorbell rang. Jen took a deep breath and opened it. Billy, leaning against the door frame. He still made her knees weak. The problem was, he made her brain even weaker.

"Hi," he said softly.

"Come on in," Jen said. He did. "You remember Joey? From Capeside?"

"You're friends with that kid Dawson who was hot for Jen, right?" Billy asked.

"And you're the guy Jen dumped for that kid Dawson, right?" Joey shot back.

Billy grinned. "You've got a mouth. I like that."

"My thrill level knows no bounds," Joey said dryly.

Jen sat on the back of the sofa. "How did you know I was home, Billy?"

"When it comes to you, Jen, I have radar." He moved closer to her.

She moved away, pretending she needed to straighten the flowers on the coffee table.

Billy looked amused. He knew the effect he had on her. "Besides, word got around that you were coming back for Courtney's sweet sixteen. I figured you'd show up tonight."

Jen moved closer to Joey, as if she was seeking her protection. "So, we were thinking of hitting Soho. Joey's never been."

"That right, Joey?" Billy asked laconically. "Is the small-town girl ready to get wild in the big bad city?"

"Who writes your dialogue?" Joey asked. "It sucks."

Billy laughed. He turned to Jen. "Everyone's going to The Cellar later. They made me promise to get you to come, on pain of death."

"We might cruise by," Jen said casually.

"Good. I'll be waiting." Slowly he walked over to her, and touched her lips with one outstretched finger. Then he turned and sauntered to the door. "Ladies," he said, nodding his head slightly. Then he was gone.

"Is it my imagination, or did he just make your temperature rise and your IQ fall?" Joey asked.

"I hate that," Jen said, plopping down on the couch. She put her head in her hands. "And I hate that I'm so obvious about it. He just . . . he still *gets* to me."

Like Dawson gets to me, Joey thought. No. Forget Dawson. You are over him, so banish him from your mind, she instructed herself.

She sat down next to Jen. "The way I see it, there are lots of guys who can make your hormones dance."

Jen laughed. "Billy makes mine party way too hard."

And Dawson makes mine—Joey stopped herself. No. He *used* to make mine. Past tense. She jumped up from the couch, dragging Jen up, too.

"Listen, what we need here is a lot less brooding and a lot more playing."

Jen cocked her head at Joey. "You know, you're right. My brain is just about brooded out."

"Mine, too," Joey said. "The way I see it, I have forty-eight hours to be Cinderella. Then I turn back into the scullery maid. So I am up for anything."

Jen raised her eyebrows. "Anything?"

"Anything," Joey confirmed. "Let's go be bad."

Chapter 6

"I was thinking of something cheerful," the skinny, teenaged guy with the bad skin whined. "What's the most cheerful movie you can think of?"

"*Revenge of the Nerds?*" Pacey suggested.

The guy shook his head. "Too depressing. I used to be one."

Buddy, I hate to break it to you, Pacey thought, but it's ten-thirty on Friday night and you're in here by your lonesome. You still *are* one. He checked his watch. Only thirty minutes until Screenplay closed. And then it was bye-bye Capeside, hello New York.

So far the plan was rolling. Dawson's parents hadn't blinked when he'd told them he was spending the weekend at Pacey's. And when Pacey had told his dad, the Chief of Police, that he'd be hanging with Dawson, his father had barely grunted. The

Chief of Police was too jazzed about going to the Juvenile Justice Convention with Deputy Doug, the good son, to pay much attention to the bad seed, Pacey.

Which was exactly how the bad seed had planned it.

"How about an action movie?" Pacey asked.

"Butt Bongo Babes in Toyland?" the nerd smirked.

Pacey spotted Nellie in the action movie aisle. "See that blonde over there? With the curls? She is an expert on action, if you know what I mean." He winked meaningfully.

The guy looked over at Nellie. "Oh yeah?"

Pacey leaned close. "Between you and me, I saw her looking at you before. She wants you. Bad."

The nerd blew into his hand to check his breath, then headed for Nellie, action queen. Dawson rang a woman up at the register. "Due back on Tuesday," he told her.

"I can't wait to get out of here," Pacey said. He checked his watch again. "Twenty-eight minutes and counting."

"I have to tell you, Pacey, I still have some ambivalence about following Joey to New York," Dawson said. "Any good relationship by definition is based on mutual trust."

"Dawson?" Pacey asked.

"Yeah?"

"Stuff a sock in it." Pacey checked his watch again.

From the action aisle, Nellie screamed and

punched the nerd hard in his arm. "You cretin! Get away from me!"

Pacey sighed. "And I had so hoped it was a match made in heaven."

"Hello, Pacey. Dawson."

Abby Morgan, a girl in their class whom neither of them could stand, stood in front of them, a smug grin on her face.

"Abby," Dawson said, nodding. "How's life?"

"Fantastic, Dawson," Abby said. "When I think that it's Friday night and I'm totally free, while you two are slaving away in those dweeby black vests, I get this really happy feeling inside."

"Hey, Ab, your date is waiting for you in the action aisle," Pacey said, cocking his head toward the nerd, who was still hovering around Nellie, giving her lingering looks.

"Nah, he's more your type, Pacey," Abby said. "Actually, I'm here to meet Nellie. We're going to a party. To which neither of you were invited, boohoo."

"Not to worry, Ab. Say, is that short for 'abnormal'?" Pacey mused. "Anyway, we've made alternate plans."

"Wow, that's a relief," Abby said sarcastically. "Catch you later, Vest Boys." She sauntered over to Nellie.

"Somehow their friendship does not surprise me," Dawson said. He rang up an older woman renting a stack of exercise videos.

Pacey checked his watch yet again. "Twenty minutes and we are so outta here."

Dawson pulled a sheet of notebook paper out of his back pocket. "Let's review our checklist."

Pacey arched one eyebrow. "We have a checklist?"

"Number one," Dawson read, "pack video camera."

"It's in the truck graciously donated to us, albeit without his knowledge, by dear old dad. While he and Deputy Doug are in Hartford at the Juvenile Justice confab, we'll be using said truck for our great escape. There's a certain poetic justice in that, Dawson."

"Two, gas up truck," Dawson read.

"Done," Pacey said.

"Number three, pack clothes."

Pacey grabbed the list from Dawson. "At this rate we'll still be here Monday morning when it's time to go back to the mind-numbing hell laughingly known as school."

His eyes scanned the list. "Sleeping bags, junk food, stash of great tapes—check, check, and check." He handed the checklist back to Dawson.

"Hey, do either of you guys actually work here?"

They looked up. A pretty girl in a low-cut sweater stood there, holding a video. Neither of them had ever seen her before.

"Hel-lo," Pacey said, pushing in front of Dawson. "I definitely work here. And I'd be thrilled to assist you with anything at all."

"Just the video," the girl said, handing it to him.

Pacey looked at it—*Nightshade: Socrates' Cocktail.* It was a documentary about the band's last tour. Pacey grinned at the girl. "The moment I saw you I knew we had a lot in common. I'm a huge Nightshade fan."

"Really?" She looked amused.

Pacey nodded. "As a matter of fact, me and my bud here are doing a little road trip to Albany for the weekend. Catch their concert, hang with the band, you know." He leaned toward her on the counter. "Maybe you'd like to come along, we could hook you up."

"Sure," the girl said. "I'll just tell my husband. He's waiting in the car." She waggled her left hand in the air, showing him her wedding band.

Pacey straightened up. "On second thought, the truck is a two-seater. Some other time, though." He quickly rang up her rental, and she left.

"Do you consider it your moral duty to hit on anything with breasts?" Dawson asked him.

"Pretty much," Pacey said.

"What would you have done if she had said yes?"

"Sadly, there was very little chance of that," he admitted, checking his watch again. "On a brighter note, that little encounter brought us four minutes closer to the great escape."

Dawson took off his vest and stashed it under the counter. "I still have some concerns, Pacey. Call it what you will, basically you've stolen your father's truck. And we both lied to our parents. If they find out, we are grounded for life."

"Yeah," Pacey agreed. "So what's your point?"

Dawson sighed. Enumerating to Pacey the many things that could go wrong was an obvious waste of time. And dwelling on his guilt over lying to his parents would only make him feel worse.

"No point," Dawson admitted. "I am, for once, point-free."

"There you go," Pacey agreed. He threw his vest under the counter, too. "It's Nellie's turn to close, so we're bustin' outta this burg. I'm telling you, nothing can possibly go wrong."

From behind the foreign film rack, which was taller than she was, Abby smiled.

She had heard everything.

Something certainly can go wrong, she thought, grinning maliciously. And I'm just the girl to make it happen.

Joey looked down at herself and gulped hard. "This is possibly the worst idea in the history of bad ideas."

"Are you kidding?" Jen asked. "You look gorgeous. Look in the mirror!"

Joey did. Staring back was her, but not her. Her long brown hair had been set on large hot rollers. Parted on the side, it fell across her face like a forties movie star's. She, who rarely wore makeup, had on mascara, black eyeliner, and dark red lipstick. Her outfit, on loan from Jen, was all black: a long, skinny, Lycra skirt that began well below her navel, and a matching top that ended well above it.

"I look very bizarre," Joey decided.

"Very tasty, I mean it," Jen said. "I never even wore that skirt because I kept meaning to get it shortened—it puddles around my feet. But it's perfect on you."

Joey sighed. "You have clothes in your closet that

you've never worn, and I have clothes in my closet I've been wearing since I hit puberty."

"Keep the skirt," Jen said carelessly, as she put on some lipstick.

Joey's temper flared. "I don't need handouts from you. If you thought I was hinting—"

"No, no, I didn't," Jen insisted quickly. "I'm sorry if that's how it sounded. Really."

Joey nodded quickly. Get a grip, she told herself. Jen is being incredibly nice to you. She took in Jen's short dress and sexy, thigh-high black suede boots. "You never wear that stuff in Capeside," she noted.

"I want to fit in, not stand out," Jen said. She dropped her lipstick into her little red satin purse with the black Chinese dragon on it. Then she went into her closet and brought out a black motorcycle jacket. She handed it to Joey.

"What's this?"

"It's freezing out and it'll look great with that," Jen said. "Put it on."

She did. Yes. The motorcycle jacket she liked. Joey smiled at her reflection. "Well, I just decided."

"What?" Jen asked.

She tossed her head sexily at her reflection, then batted her eyelashes at Jen. "I'd go for me."

Laughing, the two of them turned out the lights and headed out of the apartment. Instead of going out for dinner, they had ordered in Chinese. Joey decided it was the best food she had ever eaten. Now they finally were on their way to The Cellar to meet Jen's friends. And Billy.

"So, what is this place, The Cellar?" Joey asked, as they got into a cab Jen had hailed. The taxi inched back into the center lane, then zoomed down the street.

"Coffeehouse," Jen said, over the music blaring from the driver's radio. "Excruciatingly hip. Friday is open mike night. You never know who you'll hear."

The driver pulled up in front of a dingy building that didn't look like any coffeehouse Joey had ever seen or imagined. They were in the middle of some warehouse district, it looked like.

"Keep the change," Jen told the driver as they got out.

"Thank you," the cabbie said, and pulled away.

She's paying for everything, Joey thought self-consciously. *And there's not a thing I can do about it.* She shivered in Jen's leather jacket. "You sure this is the place? There isn't even a sign."

Jen pointed to a silver plaque not much larger than a business card embedded in the gray stone of the building. THE CELLAR, it read.

"So, like, if you wear glasses you never find it, right?" Joey asked.

"You're supposed to just know," Jen explained. She started to open the door, then stopped. "I just had a big-time attack of nerves."

Joey comically wrapped her arm around Jen's shoulders, and lowered her voice to a bass level. "Don't worry, little lady. I'll protect you."

Jen laughed. "Right. Now I'm *really* worried!"

Chapter 7

At first, Joey couldn't see at all. But as her eyes adjusted, she saw that they were in a hallway. From the other end, she could hear a band playing, a girl singing.

They went down some steps into the dimly lit club. A band played on a tiny stage. The girl singer wore a bikini with a see-through plastic coat over it, and combat boots.

The place was packed with people, almost all young, sitting at round tables, standing four deep at the bar in the back, or lolling on mismatched couches. In the corner, up high, a huge hammock was strung between two floor-to-ceiling poles that glittered with tiny white Christmas lights. A bunch of people were in the hammock, Joey couldn't see exactly how many. One couple was kissing furiously.

I am *so* not in Capeside, Joey thought.

"Jen! Oh my god, it's Jen!" a girl screamed, jumping out of the hammock and running over to them. She had long red hair and wore hip-hugger jeans that showed off her navel ring. She hugged Jen hard. "I can't believe you're here!"

Jen hugged her back. "I'm here," she said. "This is my friend, Joey. Joey, this is Carson. We go to boarding school together. Well, I mean, we used to."

"Yeah, you got out of it, you lucky wench," Carson said, laughing. "Come on, everyone's back there. They all want to see you."

Carson grabbed Jen's hand and began to drag her through the crowd. "Come on, Joey," Jen called over her shoulder. Joey had no choice but to follow.

Carson led Jen to a crowd of people scrunched together on two couches in a dark corner. Everyone screamed when they saw Jen. Someone pulled her onto the couch, and she fell over her old friends, laughing, while everyone hugged her.

Joey just stood there. What else could she do? She felt out of place and horribly self-conscious, like a little girl playing dress-up who hadn't pulled it off very well.

She looked around. In the corner a gorgeous girl with long, straight hair leaned against the wall. She shook her hair out of her eyes and looked exquisitely bored.

That's the look, Joey decided. She shook her hair off her face, tried to look bored, and leaned one hand oh-so-casually against the nearest table.

It toppled over and crashed to the floor.

She was frozen with embarrassment. Until she realized that the music was so loud, and the place was so wild, that no one had even noticed.

A skinny guy wearing a black T-shirt that read THE CELLAR quickly righted the table. "Drink?" he asked her. "There's a minimum. Two."

Drink. This was a coffeehouse, but did the waiter mean alcohol when he said two-drink minimum? She didn't drink. Plus she had no idea how much a drink cost, and had all of twenty-five dollars in her purse. Ten of those dollars had been a gift from Bessie before she left Capeside.

"Uh . . . juice?" Joey asked tentatively.

"We have sixteen kinds of juice and thirty-two kinds of coffee," the guy said impatiently, "and I don't have all night."

"Orange?"

"Racy," the waiter said sarcastically before he took off for the bar.

Okay, so far so terrible, Joey thought. Jen was still in the midst of her friends, laughing and talking, so Joey looked around some more, her eyes sweeping the room. And there he was. The most gorgeous guy, looking straight at her. Tall. Dark hair. Absolutely perfect-looking.

Joey looked away and pretended to be watching the girl singer. When she glanced oh-so-casually in his direction again, the gorgeous guy was gone.

"Hey, Joey!" Jen called to her. Joey moved closer to Jen. "I want you to meet my friends. You guys, this is Joey Potter, a friend of mine from Capeside."

"Hi," Joey said.

Pointing at each of her friends in turn, Jen quickly rattled off their names. Joey tried to keep them straight—Carson with the red hair and the navel ring she had already met. Amy was a preppie type with dark curls. A huge crew-cut guy named Scott had his arm around her. Alexis looked like a model. She had a small tattoo just below her collarbone that Joey couldn't read. Her twin brother Tucker had a sweet face and puppy dog eyes.

"You will be tested on this later," Tucker told Joey from his seat on the couch.

Amy lit a cigarette. "You're so lucky, Joey. I'd love to get my butt out of the city." She exhaled a smoke ring.

"And live without Chinese food delivery?" Joey asked.

"I am so totally sick of Chinese," Alexis said. "I swear, it makes me hurl."

"Yeah, like you don't make yourself hurl, Alex," Carson said, laughing. "Two hurls a day keeps the poundage away."

"That's just a nasty rumor based on the truth," Alexis said airily. "So, what's Capetown like?"

"Cape*side*," Tucker corrected her. "Cape Town would be in South Africa."

"Whatever," Alexis said, annoyed. She turned back to Joey. "So, what's it like?"

"Quiet," Joey said. "Very quiet."

Up on stage, the band finished their number. A few people applauded. A fat guy with a ponytail came out to adjust the equipment for the next act.

"So, I thought Billy was going to be here," Jen said, trying to sound nonchalant.

"He is here," came a low, sexy voice from behind her.

Jen turned around.

Billy.

"I was in that crush at the bar," Billy said. "You look fantastic, Jen."

"Thanks." She looked up at him, and got that same old feeling. All the way down to her toes. Then she glanced over at Joey, who shrugged at her.

"Man, it's good to see you," Billy murmured. "Hey, you want a drink?"

"This is a coffeehouse with a juice bar," Jen said. "No alcohol."

Billy laughed. "Get real, Jen. We brought our own." He took an old-fashioned metal flask out of the pocket of his leather jacket. "Strictly high test."

"No thanks," Jen said lightly.

"Oh, come on," Billy said. "Where's my party girl?"

"*Ex*-party girl," Jen reminded him.

Amy laughed and took another hard drag on her cigarette. "Yeah, right, Jen. And I gave up smoking."

"Hey, cut the girl some slack," Billy said, putting his arm around Jen. He threw back a long hit from the flask and then put it in his pocket. "Come sit with me."

Jen looked over at Joey, a question in her eyes. Joey nodded that she was okay, so Jen's friends made room for her and Billy on the couch, while Joey continued to lean against the back of it, doing her best to look cool. The hair that dipped over one eye kept migrating to her mouth each time she moved, where it got stuck in her goopy red lipstick.

She pulled a strand of hair off her lips and looked around again for the beautiful guy she had seen earlier. Gone. A figment of my overheated imagination, Joey thought.

"Would you like a drink?" Tucker asked, craning his neck around from where he sat.

"I already ordered one, thanks."

"In this place, that's meaningless," Tucker said. "I'll go to the bar and get you one, if you want. The fresh papaya-peach juice is great."

No alcohol, he's paying. Perfect, Joey thought. "That would be nice. Thanks."

Tucker got up from the couch and stood eye to eye with her. Or rather, eye to shoulder. He was a good four inches shorter than she was.

Joey smiled down at him and bent her knees a little. If he noticed, he didn't say anything. "Be right back," he promised, and headed for the bar.

The fat guy on stage tapped the microphone. "Okay, our next singer is from Harlem, please welcome the blues styles of Shanda DeWayne."

A couple of people clapped, most people paid no attention. A beautiful black girl in a short white dress took the mike. She began to croon an old blues song into the mike.

"Dance?"

Joey turned around. Standing there, as if she had conjured him up from her dreams, was him.

The perfect guy from across the room.

And he was smiling right into her eyes.

Chapter 8

"*D*ance where?" Joey asked, looking around. There was no dance floor.

"Anywhere," the guy said. "I'm Danny Fields." He held out his hand.

Joey shook it. "Joey Potter."

Up close, he was even more fantastic-looking then he had seemed from far away. Taller than her. Broad shoulders. A cleft in his chin. One pierced ear. His eyes were electric blue.

"Trust Danny to zero in on the hot new girl," Alexis said, stumbling up from the couch. Apparently she had been drinking. A lot. "Do you have radar or something, Fields?"

"I have eyes," he replied, keeping his glued to Joey.

Alexis leaned in between them drunkenly. "He's got moves, too, Joey," Alexis slurred. "Consider

62

yourself warned. I have to pee so bad." She staggered toward the ladies' room.

Danny didn't take his eyes from Joey's face. It was as if she was the only girl in the universe. "What is Joey short for?"

She refused to say Josephine. *No one* was named Josephine. "Joelle," Joey invented, trying to flip her hair off her face with a casual gesture. It got stuck in her lipstick again, she pulled it free. "My mother is French."

"Beautiful name for a beautiful girl." He released her hand, but smiled into her eyes. "Really. You are really beautiful. You walked in with Jen and I couldn't take my eyes off of you."

Joey was thrilled, but she refused to let it show. She tossed her hair again. "Why do I have the feeling you've said that before?"

He smiled. "Okay, I have. The difference is, this time I mean it."

"And you've said that before, too," Joey said.

This time he didn't smile. "No. I haven't."

He was so hot. Like, movie-star hot. And there he was, flirting with her, tall tomboy Josephine Potter from Capeside, Massachusetts.

Easy, Joey, she told herself. You are not the kind of girl who falls for a guy just because he's hot.

I don't think.

Suddenly, Tucker was there. "Here you go," he said, handing her a frosted glass of juice. "Sorry it took so long, but it's a zoo at the bar."

"Thanks," Joey said. "Uh, do you two know each other?"

Tucker looked up at Danny and nodded tersely.

Danny was six inches taller than he was. "I've seen you around. You're a senior, right?"

"Right," Danny agreed. "Hey, thanks for getting my lady a drink." He put his arm around Joey and began to lead her away.

"Oh, sorry," Tucker said quickly, "I didn't realize you two were together."

"We're—" Joey began.

"Catch you later, my man," Danny said.

Joey just looked at him. "We're not together."

He smiled at her. "We're not?"

She looked over her shoulder, back at Tucker. He had already joined his friends again. "It's just that he bought me the drink . . ."

"Those deb manners," Danny said, shaking his head ruefully. "Finishing school finishes you girls off, I mean it. Listen, just because he bought you a glass of juice does not obligate you. Unless you want to be with him instead of me."

He looked into her eyes, and Joey felt as if an electric current was running between them. "No," she said faintly.

"So you want to tell me about yourself? Or would you rather be mysterious?" Danny asked her.

What would you like to know, Joey thought. *About my latest fun trip to visit Dad in prison? Or how about the time I sewed some old ribbons around the hem of my jeans when I outgrew them, because I couldn't afford new ones?*

I think not.

On the other hand, the time she'd tried to lie about her life to a rich guy she'd met who was on vacation in Capeside, she'd blown it completely. Better to be mysterious and keep her mouth shut.

"There's not much to tell," Joey said breezily. "I'm planning to be either a Victoria's Secret model or a brain surgeon."

Danny laughed. "I love a girl with big dreams."

"I don't want to talk about me," Joey said. I live with me on a daily basis, she added in her mind. And basically, I'm sick of me. "Tell me about you." She took a sip of her juice.

He folded his arms. "Let's see. I'm going to Duke next year—that is if I get in. I'll probably end up in my dad's brokerage firm. And next summer I'm going to bum around Europe with my friends."

Gee, I'll be waitressing at the Ice House, Joey thought. We have so much in common.

A bored-looking girl with two nose rings, carrying a basket overflowing with roses, wandered through the crowd. "Roses. Two dollars. Roses."

"How much for the whole basket?" Danny asked her.

"Got me," the girl said. "I'm not counting 'em all, either."

Danny took a hundred-dollar bill out of his bill-fold and handed it to her. It was the first hundred-dollar bill Joey had ever seen, outside of the Ice House.

"Cool," the flower girl said, and handed him the basket before she wandered away.

Joey searched her mind for something flip to say. "I think that is what is commonly known as conspicuous consumption."

"I know all about you old-money girls," Danny

said, putting the basket of roses on the nearest table. "You never even carry it with you. You think cash is tacky, right?"

"Right," Joey agreed. She had no idea in the world what he was talking about, except that he seemed to think she was rich—which was kind of hilarious.

Danny took one rose from the basket and broke the flower off the stem. Then he gently put the rose behind Joey's ear.

"Why did you do that?"

"Because, Joelle, you look like a girl who smells like roses." His arms slid around her waist. "And one other reason."

She stared up at him. "What's that?"

"So when I kiss you, I can find out if I was right."

The cold late autumn rain beat down on Pacey's truck like a barrage of shots from a BB gun. He had pulled off the road and into this truck stop an hour ago, when it had started pouring so hard that he couldn't see the highway. And it was still pouring.

"Are we having fun yet?" Dawson asked glumly.

"It has to stop raining soon," Pacey said. He reached into the bag of chips. Nothing left but crumbs.

"We could go into the truck stop and mingle with the outlaws," Pacey suggested. "Pick us up some chewing tobacco or something. Curse, cheat, and lie."

Dawson shot him a look. "We're still in Massachusetts, Pacey. This isn't *Deliverance*."

"Oh, lighten up, Dawson. Look on the bright

side. The rain will stop eventually—I watch the Weather Channel so I know these things—and we are not in Capeside."

"No, we're in a truck stop, in a stolen truck."

"Borrowed," Pacey corrected. "From my father. Which does not exactly warrant a manhunt for the one-armed man, okay?"

For a while they just sat there, listening to the rain. Pacey pushed a Counting Crows tape into the tape deck.

"What do you think Joey's doing right now?" Dawson asked over the music.

Pacey closed his eyes and put his hands on his forehead. "Let Pacey's Psychic Network divine it for you. I see . . . yes! I see Joey with—can it be?— four, no five guys. All of them tall, exceedingly buff specimens. Manly men. One is named Brick. One is named—"

"Your attempt at levity is not appreciated."

Pacey opened his eyes. "Relax, Dawson. It's late. Obviously Joey and Jen are at Jen's apartment."

"With Brick?" Dawson asked.

Pacey shook his head. "Earth to Dawson. You made Brick up. He is a figment of your heated little mind. There is no Brick."

"So Joey is solo."

"At the moment, Han Solo," Pacey agreed.

Dawson drummed his fingers on the dashboard. "It's not that I begrudge her spreading her wings, Pacey. Contrary to her wounding comments to me, I realize there is life outside of my room. I understand that Joey wants the opportunity to experience it. It's just that—"

"You don't want her to experience it with a guy," Pacey put in, "unless the guy is you."

"Joey is much more fragile than she looks or seems," Dawson said. "Her toughness is an act. Even if we aren't romantically involved right now, that doesn't mean my concern for her welfare is any less genuine."

Pacey rolled his eyes. "She's alone, Dawson. In bed. Asleep. Alone."

"You're positive?"

"Positive," Pacey said. "Joey might annoy the hell out of me, but this I know about her. She would not get it on with some guy she just met. I'm telling you, Dawson, you have totally, absolutely nothing to worry about."

Chapter 9

Joey knew that Danny was going to kiss her.

She felt flustered, flushed, dizzy. She took a step away from him. "Who says I want to be kissed?"

He didn't answer her, just took her hand, and led her through the crowd, up the steps, into the long, dark entranceway. From outside she heard a rumble of thunder.

Their eyes locked in the dim light. Another rumble of thunder. The singer's sultry voice wafted over them.

"When he's near me, my brain catches fire.
  And I can't hide my desire . . ."

Danny held out his hands. "May I have this dance?"

This is not a dream, Joey, she told herself. This is not a movie. It's real life. Your life.

She stepped into his arms.

Usually she felt self-conscious dancing. But this time, everything fit. They swayed to the music.

"I knew it," he murmured into her hair.

"What, that I'd smell like a hundred-dollar rose?"

"That you'd feel like a million-dollar rose, Joelle."

Joey closed her eyes and gave herself up to the moment. She wanted to feel, not think about the minutia of her sad little life. The scrambling for money. The whispers behind her back about her messed-up family. And the biggest fear of all—that somehow she'd get stuck in Capeside and her life would end up a big, empty nothing.

She didn't want to think about Dawson.

She *especially* didn't want to think about Dawson.

The song ended. Danny stopped moving. He reached for the rose in her hair and pulled off a petal. He ran the petal over her face.

He's going to kiss me, she thought. I'm going to let him. I want him to. Outside she could hear the rain begin.

"Joelle." Danny brought his mouth down to hers.

"Stay the hell away from me, Barry!" a girl screamed, as she ran out of the club, careening against the walls in the hallway. "I hate your guts!"

Joey and Danny broke apart. "You okay?" Joey called to the running girl.

The girl whirled around, breathing hard. Tracks of mascara-blackened tears ran down her cheeks. "Keep him away from me!"

A skinny guy with long black hair stood behind

them. "Get back here, Audrey. I mean it. I'll kick your butt!"

He started after her. Danny stepped in his way. "Hey, chill out, okay?" Danny put his hand on the skinny guy's chest.

"Get outta my face, man!" the skinny guy yelled, pushing Danny's chest. It got him nowhere. "I'll kill you, Audrey! You're dead!" He stabbed the air in her direction.

"You're wasted, Barry," the girl yelled. "I hate you when you get like this!"

Barry tried to get around Danny again, but Danny stopped him. "Why don't you go back in there and get some coffee? Leave the girl alone."

The guy reeled backward drunkenly. "Who the hell are you, butthole, the morals squad?"

"Sure," Danny said. He spun the guy around. "Head back in there and get yourself together, man."

The guy swore under his breath and staggered away.

"Thanks," the girl said. "He only gets like that when he's toasted. Otherwise he's great. Really. We're engaged." She wandered out the door and into the rain.

Joey was not into the macho thing, but she couldn't help but be impressed with how Danny had handled things.

"There is nothing lower than a guy hurting a girl," Danny said, shaking his head.

Joey leaned against the wall. "How about a girl hurting a guy?"

"Don't you ever listen to Alice Cooper?" Danny asked. " 'Only women bleed.' "

Joey feigned shock. "Future stockbroker listens to Alice Cooper? How retro!"

Inside the club, a guy began a poetry rant into the mike, something about two-faced girls and broken hearts.

Danny fingered the rose in Joey's hair. "Are you one of those two-faced girls?"

"Yep," Joey said.

He moved even closer. "So in other words, you could be trouble."

"Big time," Joey whispered.

His arms slid around her slender waist. He kissed her. Slowly, sweetly, his lips gently exploring hers. The kiss turned passionate. Her arms went around his neck. Everything fell away—the dark hallway, the poetry rave, the entire world—as Joey kissed him back.

Whoa. The world was spinning. Thunder and lightning. But how could it be, when she didn't even know him?

Stop thinking, she ordered herself. Just feel.

"Joey? Joey!"

She broke away from Danny. Jen was standing in the doorway of the club. Joey smiled at her. Danny's arm was still around her waist.

"Having fun?" Jen said pointedly.

Danny turned to Joey. "Having fun, Joelle?"

"Joelle?" Jen mouthed.

"What Joey is short for," Joey explained quickly.

Jen went along. "Right. I just always forget because no one calls you that."

Danny smiled and pulled Joey close. "I call her that."

"Hey, *Joelle*," Jen said, "come to the ladies' room with me?"

"Why do girls do that?" Danny asked.

Jen grabbed Joey's hand. "We're like wolves, we go in packs."

"I'll be back," Joey told him over her shoulder.

They wormed their way through the crowd to the ladies' room. The walls were covered with graffiti, but it was deliberate—Magic Markers on ropes hung from the walls so people could add their own missives.

There were girls everywhere. One sat crying in the corner while her friend tried to comfort her. Two other girls lolled against the wall, sharing a cigarette. There were six more girls in front of the mirrors, primping.

"Maybe you're not pregnant," a girl with a buzz-cut and a pierced eyebrow said to her friend, as she added blush to her cheeks. "Take the stupid test."

The two girls sharing the cigarette stubbed it out and lit a joint. Joey was shocked, but pretended not to be.

Jen turned to Joey. "So?"

"What?" Joey asked.

"Danny."

"I like him." Joey pulled out her hairbrush and began to brush her Veronica Lake hairdo.

Jen leaned against the wall and watched her. It had been weird seeing Joey with someone besides Dawson. Weird in a good way, Jen had to admit. Maybe Dawson and Joey really were over. The thought did not make her unhappy. Which was also weird, because she didn't want Dawson back. True, she still had feelings for him. But a return to coupledom was not on the horizon. Regardless, she did feel some responsibility to tell Joey the truth about Danny.

"Listen, about Danny Fields," Jen said slowly. "He's a player."

"So?" Joey asked.

"I'm serious. I heard he keeps this chart of every girl he's slept with. He grades them on looks, bod, performance—"

"How do you know it's true?" Joey interrupted.

Jen gave her a look. "Come on, Joey!"

"Let me refresh your memory," Joey said. "People said all kinds of things about you that weren't true. People say all kinds of stuff about *me* that isn't true!"

"It's not the same," Jen insisted. "Look, I'm not trying to tell you what to do, but—"

"Good, don't." Joey touched Jen's hand. "I got it, okay? This is not *Romeo and Juliet.*"

"No, it's *Romeo and Joelle*," Jen said.

Joey put her brush back in her purse. "I'm having fun. That's all." She disappeared into a stall.

Jen picked up a Magic Marker and began to doodle mindlessly on the wall. *I tried to warn her,* she thought. *She's a big girl. She can make her own decisions.*

Joey came out of the stall and washed her hands. "So, how's it going with Billy?"

"Like a moth to a flame, unfortunately."

"You guys getting back together?"

"Maybe," Jen admitted.

They headed back into the club. Jen crossed the room to Billy. He put his arms around her. She smiled up at him. He kissed her.

You can fool yourself, Jen, Joey thought, but you can't fool me. You're not going back to Billy. Because your heart belongs to someone else.

She knew this was true because she had seen what Jen had doodled on the bathroom wall without even realizing she had done it.

A heart. And inside the heart, two initials: J + D. Which is fine, Joey told herself. I'm perfectly okay with it. Dawson and I are much better off as best friends.

So why does the thought of him getting back together with Jen tick me off so much? If I don't want him that way, then why is it that—

"Hey."

Danny. Smiling down at her. Reaching for her hand.

J + D.

"Hey back," she said.

"I missed you, Joelle."

J + D.

A memory of Jen and Dawson, kissing passionately, flew into Joey's mind. She remembered how much it had hurt her, when she wanted Dawson so desperately she thought she'd die if she didn't have him. But he was with Jen.

Now, everything was different. Except the hurt of it was still there. And that was the part of her that didn't want Jen and Dawson to—

"Joelle?"

Joey blinked. "What?"

He touched her cheek. "You were a million miles away."

Just a few hundred. In Capeside.

"I'm right here," Joey said.

"Listen, I know a fantastic after-hours club," Danny said. "They open at midnight. It's private—they don't check ID."

J + D.

Admit it, Joey, she told herself. You don't want Dawson but you don't want Jen to have him, either. You are a small-minded person. You need to do something to get your mind off of them completely. Something radical.

"So, you up for it?" Danny asked. "You'll like the club. It's cozy. Very private."

Something radical. And Danny was so hot. So nice. So . . . hot. Joey reached up and wrapped her arms around Danny's neck. "I have a better idea."

His arms went around her waist. "What's that?"

"Come back to Jen's with me."

Danny's face lit up with pleasure. "Yeah?"

"Yeah," Joey said. "Absolutely."

Chapter 10

"**Y**ou did *what*?" Jen asked Joey.

"I invited him back to your apartment," Joey said. "What's the problem?"

"Invited who back to Jen's apartment?" Billy asked, coming up next to Jen. He was sipping from a glass of fresh-squeezed juice from the juice bar. Jen knew he'd laced it heavily with vodka.

"Danny," Joey said. She cocked her head toward the other side of the club. "He just went to tell his friends."

"Great," Billy said, slipping an arm around Jen's shoulders. "I'll go tell my friends adios, and the four of us can go party."

"Hold it," Jen said. "Do I have any say in this?"

Billy grinned at her. "You have all the say in the world. Your lips already told me."

Jen made a face. "That is so . . . ick."

77

Billy laughed. "I'm kidding." He stroked her hair. "But really, Jen. We need to be alone. We have a lot to talk about."

Danny joined them. "All set." He put his arm around Joey. "It's pouring out, and it's hell getting a taxi around here late at night. I called a limo service."

Limo as in limousine, Joey thought. Those long, fancy cars you see stars getting out of at movie premieres. It is *so* not Capeside.

"I love limos," Joey said, smiling at him.

"Good." Danny ran one finger down her forehead, down her nose, until it landed on her lips. "I want us to do everything that you love."

Red alert, Jen thought. Big red alert.

She grabbed Joey's hand. "Uh, I just realized that I need to . . . go back to the ladies' room."

"We were just there," Joey protested.

"Well, we need to go there again." Jen half-dragged Joey through the crowd.

"Why do I feel like I'm starring in a remake of *Groundhog Day*?" Joey asked, when they got back into the ladies' room.

"Look, Joey, those guys are not coming back to my apartment with us."

"Why not?" Joey leaned against the wall. She knew exactly what it said on the wall, just about at the level where her butt met the wood. J + D.

"Because Danny thinks you're inviting him back to have sex with him," Jen said bluntly.

"He does not."

Jen gave her a jaded look.

"Okay, maybe he does," Joey allowed. "That doesn't mean I have to do it."

"Why put yourself in that position?" Jen asked.

"Because I want to kiss him," Joey admitted. "A lot. And I don't see why I can't kiss him—a lot—and then tell him I don't want to go any further."

Jen shook her head. "You don't know him."

"Neither do you," Joey shot back. "Don't you want to be with Billy? You've been doing the vertical bop with him all night. All you lack is the bed and the horizontal."

Jen sighed. "Look, I didn't come here this weekend to get it on with Billy. When I'm with him, something happens to me. It's like, this is my brain—" she gave an intelligent nod, "—and this is my brain on Billy." She let her tongue loll out of her mouth and crossed her eyes.

Joey laughed. "Attractive illustration."

"I just . . . I need some time to think. And I can't think if those guys come home with us. Not to mention the fact that the ever-vigilant Mrs. Richardson will put it in my report card to my parents."

The door banged open and two drunk girls staggered into the bathroom, retching. "Interesting. Getting wasted is just as obnoxious in New York as it is in Capeside," Joey said, making a face. "Let's go."

They went back into the club. On the stage a longhaired guy wailed something unintelligible into the mike.

"Can you just tell Danny the plans have changed?" Jen asked. "And I'll take care of Billy?"

Joey knew that Jen was right. It was stupid to invite Danny and Billy back to the apartment.

Danny would obviously get the wrong idea. As for Billy, just because Joey wanted it to be J + B and not J + D didn't mean she could make it so.

"Okay," Joey relented.

They found the guys in the entranceway to the club.

"Limo's here," Danny told them. "You ready?"

"I need to talk to Billy," Jen said, taking him aside.

Danny turned to Joey, slipped his arms around her waist and nuzzled her hair. "I can't wait to be alone with you."

Joey stepped out of his embrace. This was not going to be easy. "Listen, I kind of . . . I made a mistake."

"I don't understand."

She fiddled with an earring. "I mean that when I invited you back to Jen's, you got the wrong impression."

Danny looked confused. "I did?"

Joey nodded. "You thought I meant I want to . . ."

He grinned. "Because you *do* want to."

"Look, it was an impetuous offer that I didn't really think through," Joey explained.

"I have a feeling that you're one of those girls who does way too much thinking, Joelle."

Right on the first guess. Maybe they were soul mates. And he was *so* hot. She took his hand. "It's not that I don't want to be with you . . ."

He took his hand back. "So then what's the problem?" There was a new, impatient edge to his voice.

"I'm not ready for what you're ready for."

He gave her a cool look. "You don't want it?"

"No."

"Yeah, right," he laughed sardonically. "Girls like you kill me. You want it. You just don't want to take *responsibility* for wanting it."

Suddenly Joey could not figure out what she was doing with him. It was so bizarre. In one split second everything changed. He was cute, but so what? Guppies were cute, too. But they ate their babies.

"Well, it's been swell deluding myself into thinking that you were someone I might want to know," Joey said, backing away from him. "I'll just be going now."

Danny's jaw fell open. "You're not serious."

"It appears that I am," Joey said.

"I don't believe this!" Danny kicked the wall.

"Believe it." Jen said, joining Joey. "You ready?"

Joey nodded. She noticed that Billy was sipping from his drink, eyeing Jen, cool as ever. "There's still tomorrow night," he reminded her.

"Let's go," Jen said, pulling Joey toward the door.

Danny walked over to Billy. "What's up with them, man?"

"Down, big guy," Billy told him. "You'll live."

Jen looked back and smiled at Billy.

Joey zipped up her leather jacket and eyed the downpour outside. "I wish I had an umbrella."

"Hey, Joelle!" Danny called.

Joey turned around.

"The virgin tease act is real tired, you know?" Danny called nastily.

"Excuse me while I go drive my knee through his gonads," Joey told Jen.

Jen stopped her. "I've got a better idea. Come

on." She dashed out into the freezing rain and jumped into the waiting stretch black limo before the driver could even get out of the car. Joey jumped in next to her.

The short, balding driver turned back to them. "You're the Fields party?"

"That would be us," Jen agreed.

The driver pulled away from the curb.

"The dispatcher said to put this on your father's tab, like usual. Going to the home address?" The driver looked in the rearview mirror at them.

"Change of plans," Jen said. She gave him her address.

"You got it," the driver said. "Help yourself to anything in the fridge back there. Classical music okay?"

"Fine," Jen said.

Mozart wafted through the car.

"We stole Danny's limo," Joey mouthed to Jen.

Jen nodded. "He deserved it."

"You were right about him," Joey admitted. She leaned back against the cool leather. "Why is it that if a guy wants a girl just because she's hot, he's a player, but if a girl wants a guy just because he's hot, she's a slut?"

"Labels created by small people with small minds who have a need to put everyone into little boxes because it feels safer," Jen said. "Want to know my fantasy?"

"Does it involve massage oil and see-through lingerie?"

Jen shook her head no. "My fantasy is to be able

to be best friends with a cute guy. No sex, even though he's hot. Just friends."

"Why?" Joey asked.

"Because sex changes everything," Jen said simply. She reached into the fridge and took out a small bottle of sparkling cider. Then she got two champagne glasses from the small, recessed area under the bar, handed one to Joey, and filled them both with cider. "Here's to . . . what?"

"Friendship?" Joey queried.

"Friendship," Jen said. "Like you had with Dawson."

"*Have*," Joey corrected.

"*Had.* You can't go back to where you were before, Joey. What happened in between is always going to color where you are with him now."

"I guess that means it's always going to color where you are with him now, too," Joey said.

Jen gave her a rueful smile. "Yeah," she admitted. "Let's drink to that."

Chapter 11

Dawson woke up shivering inside his mummy-style sleeping bag. Even though he'd zipped it shut before he'd fallen asleep, it hadn't kept the cold out. Now he saw why—there was a huge rip near his left ear. That is, assuming he still *had* a left ear. It was too numb from the cold to tell.

Rubbing his ear back to life, he stuck his head out of the bag like a turtle, and squinted, bleary eyed, into the early morning light. Next to him in the back of the truck, Pacey was still out, snoring loudly. They were parked in a deserted McDonald's parking lot, somewhere in, of all places, Staten Island.

Dawson burrowed down into his sleeping bag again as he recalled just how they had ended up there. Once the rain had slowed down the night before, Pacey had headed for Manhattan. Without a map. Which was no problem, Pacey insisted. He knew exactly where he was going.

Right. They drove in circles—bridges leading to highways leading to tunnels leading to new highways, all of them requiring the payment of tolls, until neither of them had a clue where they were. Dawson finally convinced Pacey to stop and ask for directions, but the only place they found open was a biker bar with a fight in progress in the parking lot. It seemed like a good idea to move on.

They'd traveled on for another half hour when Pacey pointed to the large green sign that led to Manhattan. Ha! Hadn't he said he knew what he was doing? He crossed a bridge, got on something called the FDR Drive, went through something called the Battery Tunnel, all the while bragging about his excellent skills at a navigator.

Then Dawson saw a new sign. A sign that did not fill his heart with joy. Somehow they had crossed the Verrazano Narrows Bridge, which put them on the delightful island borough of—tada!—Staten Island.

Dawson had considered killing Pacey and had only refrained because he didn't know how to drive the truck. It was past four o'clock in the morning and both of them were wiped out. So they'd simply pulled into the parking lot of this McDonald's, and, under the benevolent gaze of a giant plastic Ronald, they'd crawled into their sleeping bags and passed out in the back of the truck.

Dawson stuck his hand and his head out of the sleeping bag so he could see his watch. Six-thirty. He'd gotten a big two and a half hours of sleep.

Gee, what a swell adventure this was turning out to be.

He climbed out of his sleeping bag and nudged Pacey with his foot. Pacey just snored louder. Dawson nudged him again, harder this time.

"I'm sick I can't go to school let me sleep," Pacey mumbled, turning over.

Great.

The lights went on inside the McDonald's. Dawson's stomach rumbled hungrily. He picked up his video camera and scrambled out of the truck, his breath coming in puffs from the cold.

"Good-morning-welcome-to-McDonald's-can-I-take-your-order-please," a short girl with big hair behind the counter asked in a bored monotone. She clicked her gum and waited.

Dawson ordered coffee and two muffins, ate the muffins quickly, and went back outside with the coffee. Maybe the cold air combined with the coffee would wake him up.

Cars pulled into the parking lot. People went inside the restaurant for breakfast. A line of cars quickly formed at the drive-through. An old blue Mustang convertible pulled in and caught his attention. For one thing, cold as it was, the top was down. And for another, the girl behind the wheel was sensational-looking.

She had straight blond hair tied back with a ribbon. With her was a little boy with red hair and freckles. She parked and they got out of the car. Now he saw what she was wearing—black leggings and an oversized sweater. Even though she walked with her toes kind of turned out, there was an awesome grace about her.

"I want a milk shake!" the little boy yelled, jumping around with excitement.

"It's breakfast, Tommy," the girl said. Her voice had a soft, southern twang to it. "Don't you want a muffin or some eggs?"

"You said everything I wanted I could have! The top down, a milk shake, and an ice cream cone for dessert!"

I wonder if she's his au pair, Dawson thought. He'd already been down that road the previous summer, when he'd met Sheila. But this girl was light-years more beautiful than Sheila. Not only that, but every time she moved, it was as if she was floating. Poetry in motion.

"I know I did, but your momma will kill me if I—"

"Milk shake! Milk shake! Milk shake!" Tommy chanted at the top of his lungs.

"Dang, quit yelling!" the girl said. "If you promise to hush, you can have ten milk shakes."

"Yeaaaaaahhhh!" Tommy cheered.

Dawson was mesmerized. He loved everything about her, from her soft accent to the funny, graceful way she walked, to promising the kid he could have the top down on the car.

She knelt down to the little boy and zipped up his jacket. Then she tied his shoe. Impetuously, Dawson lifted the camera and aimed it at her. She turned and looked at him, cocking her head to one side on her long, slender neck. Then she took Tommy's hand and walked over to him.

87

"What are you doin'?" she asked softly.

"Filming you," Dawson said. "You just looked so . . . you're very graceful. I hope you don't mind." He lowered the camera and looked at her.

"No," the girl said. "And thanks for the compliment. Sayin' that I'm graceful, I mean."

"Let's go, Dixie!" the little boy yelled. "Milk shake!"

"Hush," she told him. She looked at Dawson again. "So, do you live around here?"

"No." He lifted the camera again and began to film her as he spoke. "I live quite a ways from here. My friend and I—he's in the truck over there—drove in last night to visit some friends."

"I'm Dixie," the girl said, sticking her hand out.

Dawson switched the camera to his left hand and shook with her. Her hand was small and soft, and, in spite of the cold, warm. "Dawson," he said.

She gave him a shy smile. "Dawson. I like that."

"Weren't you cold with the top down?" Dawson asked her.

She laughed. "It was Tommy's idea. Today is his birthday—"

"I'm six," Tommy piped up.

"—and I told him he got to pick everything he wanted," she finished. "So, top down."

"It was fun," Tommy said. "I wasn't cold."

She smiled at the kid. "Me, neither."

Tommy pulled on Dixie's hand. "Let's go now!"

"Thomas Joseph, you be a gentleman," she chided him.

"Yuck." But he stopped tugging.

Dixie smiled at Dawson again. "My nephew. I'm just here visiting from Mississippi. Ever been?"

Dawson shook his head no.

"I came up for an audition with the City Ballet. I've been studying forever."

"Did you get in?" Dawson asked.

She shook her head no sadly. "Shot down. But I guess I'll try again next year." She got a faraway look in her eyes. "All I ever wanted to be is a dancer." She focused on him again. "Want to see me dance?"

Before Dawson could say anything, the girl—Dixie—had dropped Tommy's arm and gracefully raised her hands over her head. Then she began to dance. She swirled and swayed, leaped and twirled to music only she could hear. Dawson got it all on camera. Finally her hands fluttered back to her sides, and she stopped.

"That was beyond incredible," Dawson said. He put the camera down.

Her face lit up. "Really?"

"Really."

"Thanks. Bein' the best dancer in Jackson, Mississippi isn't—well, what you said means a lot to me. After gettin' shot down and all."

"You're going to be so famous one day," Dawson said fervently. "I know it."

She scuffed one sneaker into the cement of the parking lot. "Sometimes it feels stupid to have a dream."

Something gave way in Dawson's heart. "It isn't. A dream is . . . it's everything. No one can take it away from you. All great people began with nothing more than a dream."

She gave him a radiant smile. "Yeah. I like that."

"Now can we go, Dixie?" Tommy said, reaching for her hand again.

"Yeah, sweetie," she told him. "You were a real gentleman too, Tommy Joseph." She turned back to Dawson. "Well, it was nice to meet you." She turned away.

"Wait!" Dawson cried. He couldn't just let her go. "Are you—I mean—what are you doing later?" he blurted out.

"Taking dance class," Dixie said.

"After that?" Dawson persisted. He didn't know where the nerve came from.

"After that is Tommy's birthday party. And after that, well, I'm going back to Mississippi tomorrow."

Dawson didn't know what to say. But it just felt so tragic to think that he'd never see her again.

"I guess we're just ships that pass in the night. Well, the day, anyway," she amended, giving him that golden smile again. She reached for his hand. "Goodbye, Dawson. Thanks for—well, just thanks."

He watched her walk her funny duckwalk into McDonald's, too upset to even lift the camera to film her.

"Hey." Pacey stood there, blinking sleepily.

"How is it that you can meet someone, purely by chance, and in the briefest of encounters they can touch you so deeply that you feel a profound loss at the thought of never seeing them again?" Dawson asked.

"Okay, I'm filling in the blanks here," Pacey said.

"My guess is—call me crazy—you met a girl. A babe. And said babe has already passed in and out of your life."

"She's in there," Dawson said, cocking his head toward the restaurant.

"Cool," Pacey said. "Let's go in and do the breakfast thing, you can hook up with the babe while I look up Jen's address in a Manhattan directory."

"No," Dawson said sadly. "If I see her again and then lose her again, I'll feel even worse."

"Well, I'm gonna go in and use the john, get some food, and get Jen's address," Pacey said, yawning. "You coming or not?"

"Not. I'll wait in the truck."

"Dawson, cheer up and try to follow my logic. You met a babe. There are an infinite number of babes in this world. The best one could be around the very next corner. This babe is but one in an infinite series of babe possibilities." Pacey clapped Dawson on the shoulder, then went into the restaurant.

Dawson went back to the truck. He hoped they would leave before Dixie left the restaurant. He'd rather have a perfect memory of her than have to watch her walk away again. At least he'd recorded her forever on videotape.

With a start, he realized something. He had completely forgotten about Joey. And Joey was the reason he was sitting in a parking lot in Staten Island. Which meant if it hadn't been for Joey, he never would have met Dixie.

Which was way too weird to figure out on two and a half hours of sleep.

Chapter 12

"This is dee-lish," Joey said, as she buttered her third slice of the thick, yellow bread and took a huge bite. "What's it called again? Challah?"

Jen laughed. "Not chah-lah, like chew. Challah, like you're clearing your throat. It's a New York thing. Try it."

"Challah." It came out exactly the same way.

"You can take the girl out of Capeside," Jen joked, "but you can't take—"

"Yeah, yeah." Joey grinned, taking another huge bite. "It's awesome. In fact, all this food is to die for. Of course, I would basically feel that way about any cuisine that did not involve me serving it."

They were having lunch at Kiev, a funky Ukrainian restaurant in the funky East Village. So far Joey had tried borscht, a cold beet soup; pierogis, moon-shaped dumplings with mashed potatoes inside; and a delicious dish made up of bow-tie noodles with some kind of nutty grain, all covered in brown sauce. And of course, the incredible bread with the unpronounceable name. They were on their second basketful.

The night before they'd fallen asleep quickly—it was after two by the time they got back to Jen's. Joey had woken up early, full of energy. She wanted to make the most of every single minute she had in New York. Even the evil eye of Mrs. Richardson couldn't dampen her mood. So what if Danny had turned out to be an idiot? She had loved the adventure of it anyway. So just bring on some more, was her motto for the rest of her weekend.

They ordered up breakfast from the coffee shop across the street from Jen's building—Joey had loved that. Then they'd gone to the Statue of Liberty and climbed to the top, and then Joey had wanted to go to the Empire State Building. Jen had tried to convince Joey that they should go to the World Trade Center instead, since it was newer and higher, but Joey was adamant. She'd wanted to go to the Empire State Building ever since she'd seen *Sleepless in Seattle* and *An Affair to Remember*.

It had been freezing on the observation deck, but Joey had just stood there, her hair blowing around her face, tourists from all over the world bustling past her, tingling with happiness. She was Meg Ryan waiting for Tom Hanks. Anything could happen. Anything at all.

"So, what do Ukrainians eat for dessert?" Joey asked Jen, as she swallowed the last of the challah.

"You really have room?" Jen asked, incredulous.

"Sure," Joey said cheerfully. "Besides, when will I ever get to eat Ukrainian again?"

"Actually, they're famous here for the rice pudding."

Joey's face changed. "I haven't had that since . . ."

"Since when?"

"My mom used to make it," she said quietly. "Maybe I don't have room for dessert after all. So, what's next?"

"We hop in a cab and go down to lower Broadway," Jen said, whipping out her credit card to pay the check. "And then we shop till we drop." The plump Ukrainian waitress took away the card and the check.

"My funds range between extremely limited and nonexistent," Joey said self-consciously. Each time Jen paid for something, she felt a little more embarrassed. And Jen paid for everything.

"We can just walk around and look," Jen said.

They got a taxi quickly, but the driver barely spoke English, and even though Jen kept yelling that he was going the wrong way, he took them crosstown to run up the meter before he took them downtown.

"They love to pull that scam. No tip for him," Jen said when they got out of the taxi.

The wind had died down, the sun now shone brightly, it had warmed up a lot. It was as if the storm of the night before had never happened. Joey wore Jen's leather motorcycle jacket over a long-sleeved thermal T-shirt and jeans. Jen wore an old flannel shirt with a ripped collar under a cropped cotton sweater, jeans, and a New York Yankees baseball cap.

Joey couldn't help wondering if Jen had dressed down to make her feel more comfortable. Well, if she did, it's working, Joey thought, as they crossed the street and turned onto Broadway.

"You ladies are as fine as wine," a skinny street guy in filthy clothes said, bowing to them elegantly. They kept walking, and the guy walked with them. "Could you ladies perhaps spare a dime, a quarter, or whatever to help out a hungry man in his time of need?"

Joey reached into her purse and felt around for change. She handed him whatever she came up with.

"God bless you, sweet thing," he said, bowing. He began to hit up the couple walking behind them.

The street scene was fantastic and crowded, mostly young, and oh-so-hip. There were people of every color, most of them were wearing black clothes.

Vendors lined the sidewalk close to the busy street, selling sunglasses, socks, incense and jewelry. There were art galleries and used clothing stores. And boutiques so exclusive they only had two or three items in their pristine window displays.

"Come and look, pretty girls," a vendor called to them. He had smooth, dark skin and spoke with a lilting singsong. "I give you very good price."

They just smiled and walked by.

Joey stopped in front of a display of silver jewelry that looked different from the others. She picked up a delicate silver ring with a moon, a sun, and a star in the center. She tried it on and waggled her fingers.

"Pretty," Jen said.

"It suits you," the handsome vendor told her. "All my jewelry is one of a kind. I don't make any two alike."

Joey was surprised. "You're the artist? I thought you just sold the stuff."

He smiled. "I do both. That's the first ring I made after my girlfriend gave birth to our daughter last month, so I have a soft spot for it. I call it a dream ring."

Joey looked at the tiny white tag with the price on it. Twenty-two dollars. It was almost all the money she had with her. I'm not going to go home empty-handed, she told herself. When I wear this ring, I'll always remember my very first trip to New York.

"I'll take it," Joey said. She counted out the money and handed it to him.

He handed Joey her change and smiled. "May all your dreams come true."

"Thanks," Joey said, smiling back at him. "Really." She admired her ring as they walked along.

"Oh, let's go in here," Jen said, "it's a hoot."

The store was called Truly, Madly, Deeply. Loud rock music blasted through the sound system. The first thing Joey saw was a hot pink latex dress with the breasts cut out, trimmed in hot pink feathers.

"Who would wear something like that?" Joey asked.

"Someone who is truly, madly, deeply desperate for attention." Jen held up a tiny transparent plastic skirt covered with handpainted daisies.

"It's so *you*," Joey teased her. She wandered through the store, looking at this and that, almost backing into a nude mannequin draped in nothing but a feather boa. She checked the price tag on a tie-dyed cotton minidress. A hundred and eighty dollars. She dropped it quickly.

"I actually like this," Jen said, holding up a black lace minidress layered over baby-blue chiffon. "What do you think?"

Joey shrugged. "I'm a jeans and T-shirt kind of girl."

"I'm gonna try it on." Jen disappeared into one of the tiny stalls. The door only covered her from midthigh to shoulder level. But it didn't really matter, because the door was entirely transparent.

"Uh, Jen?" Joey called. "Everyone out here can see everything."

"Watch this," Jen said. She flipped the lock. Instantly Joey could no longer see through the door.

"Amazing," Joey marveled. "I mean, I don't see the point, but still, it's amazing."

A gaunt salesman dressed in black approached Joey. He wore eye makeup. Both his ears were pierced, with large gold hoops in them. He looked Joey up and down. "Can I help you?" His voice dripped disdain.

"My friend is in there," Joey said quickly, feeling flustered. "I mean, she's trying something on."

"Just scream for Roberto if you need help," he

said. "I'm not Roberto, of course, but I do like the name." He wafted away.

Jen came out in the dress. "What do you think?" She peered at herself in a three-way mirror.

Joey's confidence took a nosedive.

Because Jen looked, in a word, perfect.

"It looks great," Joey told her.

"You think?" Jen turned her back to the mirror to check out her butt. "I don't look fat?"

"Please Jen, don't turn into one of those girls with a great body who insists that she's fat, I'm begging you."

Jen laughed. "Back in New York for twenty-four hours and I'm already falling back into all the old head games. I think I'll buy this."

Jen handed the dress to the salesman who was not named Roberto. Joey glanced at the amount printed on the credit card slip. Two hundred and sixty-five dollars. Plus tax. And Jen hadn't thought about it twice.

Joey tried not to resent it. It wasn't like Jen threw it in her face or anything. And Jen was being so nice about taking Joey to the touristy places, and treating her to everything.

Because I can't afford to pay for anything, Joey thought glumly. It is just so unfair.

"I think I'll wear this dress tonight," Jen said as they pushed out the door and strolled down lower Broadway. "It will make my aunt insane."

"Why?" Joey asked.

"Because Courtney's sweet sixteen is formal."

Joey looked at her blankly.

"You know. The guys wear black tie and the girls wear long gowns," Jen translated.

"Oh, yeah, right," Joey said, nodding. "I've gone to, like, a million of those." A scary feeling fluttered through her stomach. "Unfortunately, though, I left my formal collection at Buckingham Palace, last time I was hanging with the queen. She's crazed to fix me up with Prince William, by the way."

Jen bumped her hip into Joey playfully. "I've got the perfect dress you can borrow. Don't worry."

"I wasn't," Joey lied. They walked for a while, looking in shop windows. Joey cleared her throat. "This perfect dress would be long, correct?"

"Correct."

"But long on you would be midcalf on me."

"This dress will be long on you," Jen assured her. "Because—"

"Don't tell me," Joey interrupted. "You never got a chance to shorten it."

"Right."

"Why, if it isn't Jen Lindley," a girl getting out of a taxi cooed. She was small and thin, with perfectly streaked brown hair framing her pinched features. Over jeans and black velvet shirt her mink coat, dyed blue, flapped open. "Long time no see and blah, blah, blah."

Jen's face went stony. She'd known Miranda Briarly just about all of her life, and she'd loathed her for an equal amount of time. Miranda lived to spread rumors, the nastier the better, and she'd spread many a rumor about Jen. The problem was, about half of the vicious rumors she told were actually true.

"Hi, Miranda."

Miranda shook her hair off her face. "I heard a nasty little rumor that you were going to show your face at Courtney's party tonight."

"You know how much I love nasty little rumors," Jen said.

Miranda laughed. "That's because they're usually about you. How was rehab?"

"*What?*" Jen asked.

"I heard you were in rehab for . . . well, it doesn't matter, if it isn't true." Her eyes flitted across Joey. "And you would be—?"

"And you would be—?" Joey shot back.

"Miranda Briarly," the girl said. "Jen and I go way back."

"Joelle Potter."

"Potter, Potter, do we know any Potters?" Miranda mused. "What do your people do?"

Joey shrugged. "The usual. Have babies out of wedlock. Go to prison on felony charges. Whatever."

Jen snorted back a laugh.

"Aren't you amusing," Miranda oozed. "Well, must run. I've got to get a manicure and a facial before tonight." She hesitated. "I don't know if I should tell you—"

"Right," Jen said. "You shouldn't. Let's go, Joe—Joelle." They started to walk away.

"I think you'll want to know about this before tonight," Miranda called.

Jen turned around, resigned. "What?" she snapped.

"It's about Billy. And your cousin Courtney."

Jen just stood there waiting.

"Well, in case you haven't heard," Miranda said slowly, "they've been seeing each other for months. In fact, they're practically living together." Her mouth curled into a cold smile. "I knew you'd want to know."

Chapter 13

Dawson ate the last bite of his hot dog and leaned back on the bench, watching the Rangers fans scurrying into Madison Square Garden. Rodents of civilization, he thought. It will never, ever, ever be me. I will become a famous filmmaker, and I will do great, important things.

Or, I will kill Pacey and gladly face the death penalty. Because so far he has managed to screw this trip up every single step of the way.

That morning, at the McDonald's in Staten Island, Pacey had discovered a crucial New York City fact—no one outside of Manhattan had a Manhattan phone book. So they came up with a plan: drive into Manhattan, park the truck, and find a phone book.

Some plan. Dawson got directions into Manhattan, that part came off without a hitch. But getting from lower Manhattan to Times Square—where Pacey wanted to go, since he saw it on television every New Year's Eve—took forever.

It was as if the traffic was reproducing; it just kept getting worse. People crossed the street in front of them and behind them, blithely ignoring the DON'T WALK signs. Kids on in-line skates and skateboards whizzed by.

They kept getting gridlocked. As in not moving at all. A half hour behind a jackknifed tractor-trailer. An hour in a traffic jam caused by a broken water main. Another half hour due to construction.

But finally they made it to Times Square, only to find that parking in a lot near there cost a small fortune. The next hour was spent trying, in vain, to find a parking spot on the street. Finally Pacey maneuvered the truck between a taxi stand and a fire hydrant, on a deserted-looking block so far west it was practically in the Hudson River.

They walked to Times Square, asking in every restaurant and every tourist trap if they had a phone directory. They might as well have been asking for the Holy Grail. Either no one in New York possessed a Manhattan phone book, or else no one was giving said phone book to them.

Finally, Dawson had come up with the brilliant notion that Pennsylvania Station would have phone booths and directories. After all, it was full of travelers from out of town catching trains. They got directions from a cute girl, and hoofed it there, getting caught in an unruly mob heading to the hockey game at Madison Square Garden.

Excellent. Phone booths. Phone directories. Now

all they had to do was find Jen's address and phone number. Lindley. But what was Jen's father's name? And who knew there were dozens of Lindleys in the Manhattan phone book?

Dawson eyed the bank of phone booths across from him, where Pacey was trying yet another Lindley on the list. They had hit answering machines, no answers, busy signals, disconnected numbers, little kids, and adults. What they had not hit was one single soul who had ever heard of Jennifer Lindley, currently residing in Capeside.

Just as Dawson was debating the purchase of another hot dog, Pacey came over to him. "No luck. We need more change."

Dawson pointed in the direction of the newsstand.

"Have a heart," Pacey whined. "He hates me. Last time I asked for change he cursed my mother in Hindi."

"How do you know?" Dawson asked.

"He translated." Pacey thrust a ten-dollar bill at Dawson. "My last tenspot, so guard it with your life."

Dawson went to the newsstand and smiled at the Indian vendor, who eyed him and his video camera suspiciously.

"A roll of these mints, and could I have all the change in quarters, please?" Dawson asked, handing over the ten.

A stream of Hindi flew from the vendor's lips. "I am not a bank, young man!" he added in lilting English.

"Right," Dawson agreed. "But if you could just

spare as many quarters as you can, I would be very grateful."

The vendor humphed his anger, but he turned to his cash box and began to count out quarters. Dawson lifted his camera to film the crowd in the train station while he waited. A little girl and her mother in matching dresses, both carrying red balloons. A couple kissing. A businessman surreptitiously picking his nose. Ugh—zoom off of that. A beautiful blond girl who walked with her toes turned out—

Dixie! He was sure it was her. She had just gotten on the escalator, which led up to the street. He wanted to run after her. But they were so low on funds, he couldn't leave the ten dollars with the vendor.

"Can I have that change quickly?" Dawson asked, eyeing the escalator.

"You should be patient, young man," the vendor said, cracking open a fresh roll of quarters. "I am only doing this for you out of the goodness of my heart."

"I'll just take the ten back, then." Dawson held out his hand, craning his neck to try and see Dixie on the escalator. Come on, come on, come on!

The vendor eyed him. "You are a sorry excuse for a human being. You must buy more than mints for my trouble. And then I will give you change. But not," he added, folding his arms, "in quarters."

A beat, as Dawson's eyes slid from the vendor to the escalator. To the ten-dollar bill. Without allowing himself to think, he grabbed the money and ran for the escalator. From behind him, Dawson heard the vendor yelling in Hindi, and Pacey yelling in English.

Dawson ran up the escalator and looked both ways. No sign of Dixie. He ran outside, onto Seventh Avenue. There were so many people, all hurrying somewhere or other.

Pacey ran up to him. "What was that about?"

Dawson's spirits sagged. "She's gone."

"Who's gone?"

"Her. Dixie. The girl from this morning. I saw her, but I lost her."

"Mirage," Pacey said. "Your mind playing tricks on you. Also known as wishful thinking."

"No," Dawson said. "It was her."

"If you say so, *compadre*." Pacey grabbed the ten-dollar bill from Dawson's hand. "This is about to translate into more hot dogs—love those push-carts. You?"

Dawson shook his head no. They walked over to the hot dog vendor. Dawson's mind was still on Dixie. "I can't believe I let her get away again."

Pacey paid the vendor and took a huge bite out of his onion-topped hot dog. "You seem to have already forgotten Pacey's Theory of Babe Relativity." Mustard dribbled down his chin.

"What if you're wrong?" Dawson asked him. "What if in fact there is only one perfect soul mate out there for each of us? And if we get lucky enough to meet that soul mate, we have a responsibility to make a true connection, or risk spending our entire lives yearning for something we didn't even realize we had?"

Pacey cocked an eye at him. "And what if there's another babe around the corner?"

Dawson sighed. "Wipe your chin."

Pacey complied. "Let Doctor P. give you a little lesson in human nature, Dawson. You want Joey. Joey does not want you. You feel rejected. You meet Dixie, a babe. You project onto said babe characteristics that make you think she is your soul mate. This you do out of your massive insecurity due to rejection by said Joey."

"And I suppose it's your wealth of experience with women that leads you to this conclusion," Dawson said.

"I have a sensational love life," Pacey replied. "Unfortunately, the vast majority of it takes place with paper partners."

"You realize that we're not going to find Jen's address."

Pacey popped the last bite of hot dog into his mouth. "That thought had crossed my mind. However, I have already come up with plan B."

"Plan B," Dawson repeated. "So far your plan A has been a one hundred percent failure."

"Which is why plan B will look so excellent in comparison," Pacey said. "Can you spell 'crash,' boys and girls?"

Dawson looked at him blankly.

"This much we know: the sweet sixteen is at the Plaza Hotel," Pacey said. "There can't be more than one sweet sixteen there tonight for a girl named Courtney."

"Probably true," Dawson allowed.

"Definitely true. And what sweet sixteen wouldn't

welcome two manly men such as ourselves?" He clapped Dawson on the back. "I know a few things have gone wrong. But from now on it's going to be smooth sailing. Just let Captain Pacey set the course. Tonight, my man, we cruise into party mode, full steam ahead."

"Somehow that does not fill me with confidence."

"Trust me, Dawson. We have reached a dead end on the ol' problem highway. Of that I am sure."

Doug Witter parked his police car in a no-parking zone in front of the Ice House—one advantage of being a cop was that you never got a ticket—and went inside. The place was hopping, but then, it usually was on a Saturday afternoon.

"Hi, Bessie," Doug said, taking a seat at the counter. "Just a quick coffee and a couple of those doughnuts."

Across the room, Abby Morgan sat with Nellie Olson, flirting with some cute guys from the University of Massachusetts who were sitting at the next table.

"So, what do you do for fun in this town?" one guy asked.

"It's so provincial here," Nellie said, shaking her curls. "But we're up for anything. Right, Abby?"

Abby wasn't paying any attention. Her eyes were glued to Doug Witter's back. She distinctly remembered Pacey saying that his brother and his father would be at some police convention thing all weekend, which was how Pacey was able to steal their truck. So why was Doug sitting in the Ice House on Saturday afternoon?

"Ab?" Nellie called. "Yoo-hoo!"

"Be right back." Abby got up and crossed the room. She took a seat at the counter next to Doug, pretending to look nonchalant. Then she pretended to notice him. "Say, aren't you Pacey Witter's brother?"

Doug nodded.

"I see who got all the looks in the family," Abby said.

"Thanks." Doug smiled and took a bite of his doughnut.

"Oh, I'm so rude," Abby admonished herself. "Where are my manners? I'm Abby Morgan. I go to school with Pacey."

"Doug," Doug said. "Nice to meet you."

"Pacey talks about you all the time," Abby said. "Really. You must be his idol or something."

"I doubt that," Doug said, polishing off his doughnut.

"No, really!" Abby insisted. "Like just yesterday at school, he told me how proud he was that you and your dad were going to some police convention this weekend."

"Dad's there," Doug said. "I came back early—just got back, in fact. I haven't even been home yet. Two officers here went down with the flu. Had to come back and take over their shift. Can't have Capeside unprotected from the criminal elements."

"See, that's just the way Pacey described you," Abby gushed. "So concerned for everyone else. Like how you talked your dad into letting Pacey borrow the truck for the weekend—"

"Come again?" Doug asked.

"Pacey told me how you talked your dad into letting him take the truck this weekend," Abby explained. "You know. So that he and Dawson could go to the Nightshade concert in Albany."

Doug's face began to turn an angry red.

"Is something wrong?" Abby asked innocently.

"Why that little . . ." Doug threw some money on the counter. "Excuse me." He hurried out of the Ice House.

Bessie picked up his check and his money, and watched Doug practically run out of the restaurant. "He rushing to the scene of a crime or something?"

Abby smiled. "Oh, you might say that." She looked down at Doug's plate. He'd left one doughnut untouched. She picked it up and took a dainty bite.

No sense letting it go to waste.

Chapter 14

Gale Leery paced with the portable phone in her hand. Her head was spinning. She and Mitch had been having such a great Saturday, just lying around the house. Mitch had left just a few minutes ago to pick up a pizza for dinner. And then the phone had rung.

It was Doug Witter, Pacey's older brother. Dawson was not at Pacey's house for the weekend. Pacey wasn't even at Pacey's house. In fact, Pacey and Dawson had stolen Mr. Witter's truck and driven it to Albany, New York, of all places. To a rock concert.

"But . . . are you sure, Doug?" Gale asked. "Dawson is the most honest, trustworthy—"

"I'm sorry to say that my little brother is a terrible influence on your son, Mrs. Leery," Doug said.

"Oh, Pacey's a good kid," Gale insisted.

"I guess you just don't know him very well then, ma'am," Doug said.

Gale winced at the "ma'am" thing. It made her sound so *old*. "You can call me Gale."

"This is official police business, so I'm afraid I have to respect the formalities," Doug said.

"Official police . . . what are you talking about?"

"Stolen property," Doug said. "Actually, crossing state lines with stolen property, I might add, which could add a federal count to the charges."

"You mean because they took your dad's truck?" Gale asked, incredulous. "Is that what you're talking about?"

"Yes, ma'am. I'll be calling my father as soon as I get off the phone with you. He may want to swear out a warrant—"

"Oh, come on, Doug, that's ridiculous—"

"No, ma'am, it is not. I have a feeling that Pacey is never going to change unless he gets good and scared. It's called tough love."

Gale felt desperate, she had to do something, say something, to stop this. "How did you find out about this, Doug?"

"A witness."

"Who? Maybe the person isn't reliable."

"The witness had no reason to lie, Mrs. Leery. She's a friend of Pacey's."

"What are you planning to do now?" Gale asked.

"Call my father. Then we'll see if there's a way to track them down. I'm sorry to be the bearer of bad tidings, ma'am. I'll call you as soon as I know anything at all."

He hung up and took a piece of paper from his

back pocket. The phone number of the hotel where the law enforcement convention was being held. Quickly he dialed the number.

A good son had to do what a good son had to do.

As for Dawson's mom, she just stood there in the family room in a state of shock, the dead phone in her hand.

"I'm telling you, it's not true," Jen told Joey for maybe the twentieth time. "Billy is not involved with Courtney."

During the entire taxi ride uptown from lower Broadway, Jen had done a monologue about how Billy couldn't stand Courtney, and how Miranda was the kind of witch who knew exactly what lie to tell to freak you out.

"What I don't understand is why it would freak you out if you don't want to be with Billy anyway," Joey said.

"I don't want to be with him . . . not like I was with him before," Jen said, struggling to explain.

"You mean you want to be friends? Like me and Dawson?"

"Maybe."

Joey shrugged. "You're the one who told me that Dawson and I couldn't go from friendship to romance and then back to friendship."

Jen peered out the cab's side window. "The difference is, Billy and I were never friends in the first place."

The knowledge of that made her sad. But that was what happened when you lusted for someone so much that you never really got to know them. And they never really got to know you, either.

The driver pulled over in front of Jen's apartment building, and the doorman opened the door for them even as Jen paid the fare.

"How come we never take the subway?" Joey asked, as Jen stuffed her change carelessly into her purse.

Jen shrugged. "Habit."

"Good afternoon, Miss Lindley," the other doorman said, nodding politely, as they strode through the lobby toward the elevators.

"Someday I'm going to live in New York," Joey said. "I'll eat Chinese food every day. And Ukrainian. I'll buy my clothes at Truly, Madly, Deeply. I'll go to that bar where all the movie stars go— what's the name of it?—the one where the girls dance on the bar and leave their bras behind?"

"Heifers, I think. I went there with Billy once," Jen said. They got on the elevator. "It was wild."

"So, did you do it?" Joey asked.

"Dance on the bar and leave my bra behind?" Joey nodded.

"I don't remember."

Because you were drinking back then, Joey realized. And you don't remember because you were wasted.

Jen unlocked the apartment door, took two steps in, and stood there in shock. Because the entire living room was full of flowers.

They were everywhere. Vases of brilliantly hued blossoms sat on every available surface. More tall vases holding long-stemmed blossoms sat on the floor. And there were rose petals all over the gleaming wood floor surrounding the tapestry white-on-white area rug.

"Wow," Joey said. "Somebody robbed a florist."

"Or spent a fortune," Jen said. "This is amazing."

"They have to be from Billy. Which means you were right about Miranda, and he wants you back truly, deeply, and might I add, madly."

On the white marble side table sat a small white card, propped up against a crystal vase of red and pink roses.

"You really should go back to him," Joey said, sniffing some exotic-looking blossoms in a black vase as Jen read the card. "This sort of extravagance should be rewarded."

"They're not from Billy," Jen said.

Joey stared at her. And then she realized. They had to be from Dawson. To make me jealous? she wondered. Or because he really wants Jen back?

"And they're not for me," Jen added.

Oh my god. Dawson had sent *her* flowers.

He must have gotten Jen's New York address from her grandmother, Joey realized. And these flowers must have cost him every penny he ever made at Screenplay.

She thought back to last year, when she had wanted him so desperately that she hurt inside all the time, because Jen had him and she didn't. And now. Now that they weren't together, he did this. It was so . . . so Dawson. To do the most incredibly sensitive right thing at the most incredibly wrong time.

"I'm beginning to think that there is something to

the theory that men lust for the chase," Joey said. "Dawson never did anything remotely like this when we were a couple. But now that we're not a couple, he—"

"Joey," Jen interrupted, "they're not from Dawson." She held out the card.

Joey read it. "Dear Joelle," she read aloud. "The only thing greater than my stupidity is your beauty. I was an idiot last night. Can I make it up to you? Danny."

She looked up at Jen. "This has to be a joke, right?"

"I have no idea," Jen said, shrugging.

"But, but . . . I hated him," Joey sputtered, looking at the card again. "And he hated me. And . . . this is extremely weird."

"Hello, girls," Mrs. Richardson said in a nasal voice. She stood in the hallway rubbing her red-rimmed eyes. She blew her nose into a lace hankie. "I see you got the delivery."

"Who could miss it?" Jen asked.

Mrs. Richardson sneezed. "I'm terribly allergic to most flowers," she said, blowing her nose again. "This is torture for me."

"You could leave," Jen suggested innocently.

"So that you can have young people up here against the wishes of your parents?" Mrs. Richardson asked.

"Well, basically, yeah," Jen replied.

Mrs. Richardson ignored that. "By the way, your parents called while you were out. They said Courtney's birthday present is in the blue box in the china cabinet. And I was to remind you to give Courtney's parents their regrets for their not having attended."

"Present. Regrets. Got it." Jen turned to Joey. "This is so perfectly my parents. Why put yourself out when simply buying something extravagant will suffice?"

"They also asked how you were conducting yourself," Mrs. Richardson added.

"You didn't tell them about the orgy, did you?" Jen asked.

"I told them the truth," the older woman said. "Other than being extremely rude to me, you hadn't done anything untoward at all." She sneezed again. "I'll be in my room. And you can be as rude as you like, Miss Lindley, I'm not leaving." She strode down the hall.

"Hey, hang in there, fight the good fight!" Jen called after her. She turned to Joey. "This is crazy. I'm actually kind of starting to like her."

The antique phone on the coffee table rang, she picked it up. "Hello?"

"Hi, Jen? Danny Fields."

"Somehow I don't think you called to talk to me. Hold on." She held out the phone to Joey.

"Who?" Joey asked, taking the phone. She put it to her ear. "Hello?"

"Joelle."

Danny. He had said her name—well, the name she had invented, anyway—like it was a prayer.

She had no idea what to say to him. "Hi." She winced. Hi. How sophisticated.

"Did you get my little present?" Danny asked.

117

"Jen's living room looks like the Rose Bowl parade."

He laughed. "I figured you'd gotten flowers from guys so many times that I needed to make a grand gesture to stand out from the crowd."

"How very *Pretty Woman*," Joey quipped sarcastically.

"Pardon me?"

"Julia Roberts? Richard Gere? He spends significant money on her, and in return she gives him—"

"That's not why I did it," Danny said into the phone.

"No?"

"No. And besides, Julia Roberts was poor. A prostitute. You're rich. And you had the class to both turn me down *and* tell me off last night."

Joey paced with the phone. "So, I abused you and you liked it, is that it?"

Danny laughed. "You'd be surprised how many girls don't respect themselves, Joelle. I just really wanted to apologize, and to make it up to you. I was wondering if I could take you to dinner before Courtney's party?"

"No," Joey said bluntly. "Look—"

"Wait, wait, don't hang up," Danny said quickly. "Can I at least escort you to the party? I've got the limo."

Right. Like a big car was going to make her change her mind. "Gee, let me think about it. Okay, I've thought about it. No."

"I'm not giving up, Joelle."

"Hey, may the force be with you." She hung up the phone.

"What did he do, offer to buy you the Hope Diamond?" Jen asked.

"Just dinner and a ride to the party in Dad's limo."

Jen grinned. "You were exceedingly great with him just now."

Joey flushed at the compliment. It wasn't like she had so much experience with guys that she knew what she was doing, because she definitely did not. "Jen he . . . for some reason, he thinks I'm rich."

"Because he met you with me, I guess," Jen said. "All those kids are. Well, none of their parents are hurting for money. Does it bother you?"

"No. I just wish it was true."

"Money isn't everything, Joey."

Joey flushed with anger. "Do you have any idea how obnoxious it is when rich people say that? Do you have any idea how it makes someone like me feel?"

Jen thought a minute. "You're right."

"I am?"

Jen nodded. "I take money for granted. It's not fair."

Joey folded her arms. "How am I supposed to get all self-righteous and indignant if you give in that easily?"

"You're not," Jen said. "Now, can we get back to the subject at hand, namely Danny I-Want-You-So-Desperately-I-Could-Die Fields? I say we make sure that you look so incredible tonight that he is drooling for you."

"So that I can stomp on his shallow, self-involved, conquest-driven, tiny little whatever-organ-I-choose?"

"Exactly." Jen reached for Joey's hand and pulled her toward the bedroom. "Let's go play makeover. Cinderella is going to the ball!"

Chapter 15

Jen and Joey stood side by side, checking out their reflections in the floor-length mirror on the double doors of Jen's closet.

"I have to hand it to you, Cinderella," Jen told Joey's reflection, "you clean up nice. Just like for the beauty contest."

Joey nodded thoughtfully. "It's amazing what two hours of intense primping—not to mention a small fortune's worth of clothes, cosmetics, and accessories—can accomplish."

Joey wore a long, formfitting, Asian-inspired red satin gown with a tiny Mandarin collar and a slit up one leg, courtesy of Jen's closet. Her hair was up, courtesy of Jen's styling, with just a few sexy tendrils hanging down around her face. Her ears sparkled with ruby studs, courtesy of Jen's jewelry box. Her eyes were lined with smoky black eyeliner. Her lipstick was as red as her dress.

Next to her, Jen had on the dress she'd bought that afternoon. Her hair was piled on her head, stayed by rhinestone butterfly hairpins. Her lipstick was as pale as Joey's was dark.

"I ask you, are we hot or are we hot?" Jen queried.

"The former," Joey agreed. "As well as the latter. Lucky for me you don't remember to shorten your clothes. Just one thing, though. What do we wear over this so we don't freeze?"

"I've got a fake fur jacket you can wear." Jen rummaged through her closet and brought it out.

"You're sure it's fake?" Joey asked, as she tried on the black fur jacket. "It looks so real."

"I don't do fur, trust me," Jen said. "I might as well wear the motorcycle jacket. After all, I'll be the only girl there who isn't wearing a floor-length dress. And I do have a certain bad-girl rep to maintain."

In the elevator, Joey started to feel nervous. "There aren't any royal curtsies involved at this thing, are there?"

Jen laughed. "Courtney would like to think so, but trust me, her royalty is only in her mind."

They swept through the lobby, the doorman nodding to them appreciatively. When he rushed to open the door for them, Joey didn't feel funny at all.

"Actually, Jen, I could get used to—"

"Uh, Joey?" Jen cocked her head toward the street.

Joey looked. There at the curb was a white and gold horse-drawn carriage. The driver wore white tails and a gold top hat. And, leaning against the carriage, clad in perfect black tuxedos, were Danny and Billy.

The girls walked over to them, dumbfounded.

Danny kissed Joey's hand. "You are so hot."

"Wh . . . what is this?" Joey stammered, dazzled in spite of herself. "I mean, you said a limo. And I said no. Didn't I?"

"You did," Danny admitted.

"We were hoping we'd impress you ladies so much that you'd relent," Billy said, smiling that way-too-sexy smile at Jen. "And by the way, you look fantastic."

"So do you," Jen admitted. Why did he have to be so handsome? How did he manage to retain that rebel look in a tux? Why did she fall for it?

"Uh, excuse us." Jen pulled Joey a few feet away. "What do you want to do?"

"I don't know," Joey admitted. "I mean, I don't trust Danny. I don't want to be his date or anything, but . . ." She looked wistfully behind her. "It's just so fairy tale."

They went back over to the guys. "We'll go with you," Jen said, "on one condition."

"Which would be?" Danny asked.

"No strings," Jen said. "Understood?"

"Understood, Madame Warden," Danny said, bowing.

The driver helped them all into the carriage, covering their laps with a warm blanket. Joey couldn't help it; when the horse began to trot, she felt as if she was starring in some fantastic movie. She looked over at Danny. If only she was in love with the leading man.

"Having fun?" Danny reached for her hand.

She smiled at him; she couldn't help it. He was so gorgeous. And rich. And he was so into her. Maybe he'd just had an off night the night before. Maybe he wasn't really such a player after all.

"Yeah," Joey admitted. "This is fantastic."

"No, *you're* fantastic, Joelle." He put his arm around her. She let him. Across from them, Billy was kissing Jen. And Jen was kissing him back.

Joey felt something cold sting her forehead. She looked up. "It's snowing! Too cool!" She threw her head back, stuck out her tongue and let the snowflakes dissolve on her tongue.

"Do you have any idea how adorable you are?" Danny asked her.

"Oh, I have some idea," Joey replied. "On a one to ten adorable scale, I'm an eleven point five, easy."

"Joelle, let's pretend last night never happened," Danny said, gazing into her eyes.

"I suppose we could hire a hypnotist to erase it from our memories," Joey teased.

Danny laughed. "He can name his price. I'll do it." Gently he tipped her face to his.

"Forget last night?" Joey whispered.

He nodded, and waited. The snow danced in her hair. She was in a horse-drawn carriage in New York City, on her way to a fantastic party at a fancy hotel, where everyone would be young and rich and beautiful. And for the first time in Joey's life, she *felt* rich and beautiful. Carefree. It just felt so perfect, and she never wanted it to end.

"Joelle?" His question hung in the air.

Her kiss was all the answer he needed.

The Rose Room of the Plaza Hotel took Joey's breath away. It was huge, with crystal chandeliers and a dance floor surrounded by tables covered with snowy linen and set for ten. Along one wall there was a buffet table, in the center of the table was a huge ice sculpture. COURTNEY'S SWEET 16 was carved into the ice, surrounded by a halo of white orchids and pink roses. Next to that was a bar. An orchestra played on a raised stage. Waiters moved silently among the guests, offering champagne or soft drinks.

On one wall a continuous slide show was being presented—slide after slide of Courtney. She was a little girl playing in the snow. She was Mary in the Christmas pageant at church. She danced with her father. She posed on a beach someplace tropical.

"This is . . . amazing," Joey whispered to Jen.

"No, *that's* amazing," Jen said.

She was facing the opposite wall. Joey turned around. There was a huge oil painting—it had to be more than ten feet high—a copy of the famous *Mona Lisa*.

Only instead of Mona Lisa's face, there was Courtney's.

Joey was flabbergasted. "Is this, like, normal?" she asked Jen. "I mean, I have no basis for comparison."

"Trust me," Jen said. "Normal does not enter into it."

"Cousin Jen!" a tall, slender girl with perfectly

125

streaked straight blond hair headed for them, her arms opened wide. She wore a stunningly beautiful long, white lace dress with a pink underlayer, and a single strand of pearls around her graceful neck.

Has to be Courtney-the-Perfect, Joey thought, as the tall girl leaned over to air-kiss Jen in the vicinity of first one cheek, and then, as if she had been raised in France, the other.

"Hi, Courtney," Jen said. "Happy birthday."

A table in the corner piled high with brightly wrapped presents caught her eye. Oops. She'd forgotten to bring Courtney's present. "I'm having your birthday present delivered because it's . . . special."

"You're just so sweet," Courtney cooed. She looked at Joey. "And you must be Jen's little friend she said she was bringing."

"Joey," Joey told her. "Thanks for inviting me. Your dress is really beautiful," she added shyly.

"Thanks," Courtney said. "It's a Vera Wang. I had such a fight with Mother over the pink silk under the lace! She said wearing a long white gown for your sweet sixteen is a sign of breeding and purity, can you imagine?" Her eyes flitted over Jen's dress. "And you're wearing black! And it's short! But you always were daring, Jen. I'd never have the nerve!"

"Oh well, you know nervy me," Jen said.

Courtney frowned slightly. "It's a tad low-cut, Cuz. I just don't want people to get the idea that . . . well, that you haven't mended your ways."

"Actually, Courtney, I don't even have on underwear," Jen pretended to confess. "I was thinking of dancing on the buffet table. High kicks. Very Rockettes."

Courtney paled.

"It's a joke, Courtney," Jen explained. "And before you ask, I'm totally sober. Twenty-four-seven."

"I wasn't going to ask," Courtney protested.

"Sparkling cider?" Billy asked, coming up next to her. "Evidently the powers that be gave strict orders not to serve liquor to anyone underage, or I'd be offering you champagne."

"Oh, you know how my parents are," Courtney said, rolling her eyes. "But you came prepared, right, Billy?"

Billy feigned hurt. "See, this is how rumors get started."

"You're just so *bad*, Billy," Courtney slapped playfully at his arm. "What did you bring?"

Billy held out his hands. "Empty-handed."

"Oh, poo," Courtney pouted. "Well, when you score something—*anything*—come and find me, okay? My mother is driving me *insane*."

"Sure," Billy said easily.

Courtney gazed up into Billy's eyes. "You're going to dance with me later, right?"

"I wouldn't miss it, birthday girl."

"Can't wait." She kissed him lightly on the lips, then gave Jen a smug look. "Well, excuse me. I have to mingle. Have fun!" She hurried off to greet some other guests.

Jen reached for Billy's hand. "Hey, thanks for not bringing any liquor. Really."

He put his arms around her. "No prob. But you don't mind if I go score some for Courtney, do you?"

Jen gave him a scathing look. "Oh, poo."

"She still gets to you, huh?"

"The question is, Billy, does she get to *you?*" Jen asked pointedly.

"Courtney?" He made the idea sound crazy. "You know better." He sipped his cider and turned to Joey. "Where's Danny?"

"He went to see some old friend named Jack D., I think he said."

Billy thought a beat, then he laughed. "Yeah, Jack's a buddy of mine, too. Excuse me. I shall return."

Joey scratched her chin. "At the risk of sounding like I'm from Capeside, did he just go somewhere to get whiskey?"

Jen nodded. "Jack D. is Jack Daniels. And here I thought Billy came without a bottle to make me happy." Something caught Jen's eye. "Uh-oh. See that woman making a beeline for us? Courtney's mom, my Aunt Grace. Better known as the aunt from hell."

"Jennifer!" Aunt Grace grabbed Jen and did the same affected air-kiss thing. Her hair was up in a classic French twist. Diamonds sparkled on her ear-lobes. Her exquisite evening gown was dove-gray silk, trimmed in a deeper gray velvet.

"Hi, Aunt Grace," Jen said.

The older woman held her at arm's length. "Let me look at you." She frowned. "Have you put on weight?"

"Don't think so, Aunt Grace."

Grace wagged her finger at Jen. "You have to be constantly vigilant, young lady. Where are your parents?"

"Didn't they tell you they'd be out of town?"

"My secretary keeps track of all that," Grace said dismissively. "You'd think their niece's sweet sixteen would be important enough for them to make the effort. Or is your mother in one of her snits with me again?"

"I have no idea," Jen said, quite honestly.

Grace sighed. "Your mother has never spent a day of her life thinking of anyone but herself. Just look at the way she's neglected you over the years."

"Well, not everyone can be the wonderful mother that you are to Courtney," Jen said sarcastically.

Her jibe went right over her aunt's head. "Thank you, dear. Now, tell me why you felt you just had to wear that utterly inappropriate cocktail dress when you knew Courtney's party was formal."

"It's what I wanted to wear, Aunt Grace."

"Oh, Jennifer." Her aunt sighed. "I would have thought you'd outgrown it by now, but you still have this need to try and upstage my Courtney, you always have."

"No, Grace, I really don't. And I don't want to fight with you, either." She turned to Joey. "This is my friend, Joey Potter. Joey, this is my Aunt Grace."

"How nice of you to come," the older woman said.

"Thank you for having me," Joey replied.

"Can you excuse Jen for a little bit?" Grace asked, taking her niece's hand. "Her Uncle William is in the next room having cigars with his cronies, and he'll never forgive me if I don't bring in his favorite niece for a kiss."

"Sure," Joey said.

"Are you sure you're okay?" Jen asked.

"I'm fine," Joey assured her. "Go." Jen handed Joey her cider before she left with her aunt. Joey sipped it and watched them walk away, Jen's hand captive in her aunt's.

God, what a family, Joey thought, shuddering. And I thought *my* family was bad!

She looked around the room, recognizing some faces from the night before at The Cellar. The girl with the long red hair, Carson, waved to Joey from the dance floor. Joey waved back. Standing near the bar was the girl with the curly dark hair, what was her name? Amy something. She wore a long blue gown cut low in the back, and she was talking to Miranda the gossip queen.

Miranda and Amy looked over at Joey and caught her eye. Joey waved. They didn't wave back. Instead, Miranda leaned over and whispered something to Amy, then they both looked at Joey again.

Swell, Joey thought. Just like Capeside.

"Hi! Joey, isn't it?" A short, handsome guy stood next to her, grinning. "We met at The Cellar last night?"

"Right!" Joey said. She scrambled to try and come up with his name. "Chuck?"

"Tuck," he corrected her. "Tucker, actually. But everyone calls me Tuck."

"Sorry."

"Hey, it's fine," he said easily. "You got closer than most people. You look really beautiful."

"Thanks."

"This party is over the top, huh? Did you see that oil painting?"

130

"Who could miss it?" Joey asked.

Tuck laughed. So did Joey. "Great smile. It lights up your face. Would you like to dance?"

Joey hesitated. He was shorter than she was. Wouldn't it be kind of . . . awkward?

"I'm not great, but I think I can manage not to step on your feet."

He was just so sweet. "Sure," Joey said.

The orchestra was playing something slow and dreamy. Joey stood there self-consciously. Tuck put his arms around her. He didn't pull her close, the way Danny had. But he wasn't stiff, either. Actually, it was just fine. No fireworks. But fine.

She relaxed, as they moved to the music.

"Jen and I were in some classes together before she moved," Tuck said. "I always liked her. She's smart."

"She *is*," Joey agreed. "Everyone talks about how pretty she is, but they never talk about how smart she is."

"You guys are good friends, huh?"

Joey considered that for a moment. "We're . . . friends," she said cautiously. It was way too complicated to explain.

"Yo, Friar Tuck!" the tall guy dancing with Carson called from across the dance floor. "You're dancing! Psych!" His fist pumped the air.

"Friar Tuck?" Joey asked.

Tucker groaned. "I was an altar boy when I was a kid. And I do volunteer work at a Boy's Club. My friends think I live like a monk. I don't. But I want to hear about you."

"Like what?"

"Like I don't know. What's your dream?"

Joey looked at the dream ring on her finger. "My dream is to go to college. Ivy League, maybe, if I can ever get in. And to do something incredible with my life."

He smiled at her. "You will."

The music ended. As they applauded the orchestra, Miranda and Amy came over to them.

"Hey you two," Miranda chirped.

"Hi," Tuck said. He didn't sound thrilled to see her.

"Having fun, Joelle?" Amy asked.

"Sure," Joey replied.

"I just love your dress, Joelle," Miranda gushed. "It's so wonderfully tacky. Where did you get it, Chinatown?"

"Excuse me, was that supposed to be an insult?" Joey asked. "The reason I'm not sure is that it wasn't really clever enough to qualify."

"Oooh, dissed you, Miranda!" Amy hooted.

Miranda's eyes narrowed. "Very amusing."

"You ladies will excuse us, won't you?" Tuck asked. "We were just going to dance."

"Get over yourself, Tucker," Amy said, laughing. "You sound like your father!"

"We really only came over to ask you one question, Joelle," Miranda said.

Joey gave her a hard look. "Go for it."

"All right-y, then," Miranda said. "Is it true that you had sex with Danny Fields one hour after you met him?"

Chapter 16

Dawson and Pacey climbed up the subway stairs and began to walk toward the Plaza Hotel through the gently falling snow. They had dined on fast food, then cleaned up and changed clothes in the men's room back at Penn Station, being careful not to go anywhere near the newsstand run by the irate money-changer.

Under his ski parka, Dawson had on clean jeans, a denim shirt, and a tie. He carried his video camera under his arm. Pacey wore an old army fatigue jacket, the same jeans he'd worn since they'd left Capeside, and a clean, albeit extremely wrinkled, shirt.

"You really ought to lose the tie, dude," Pacey said, as they walked west toward Fifth Avenue. "Trying too hard is the kiss of death."

"I have other, more pressing concerns at the moment."

"Such as?" Pacey asked.

"Such as how can we just walk into a sweet sixteen party to which we were not invited? Such as what if Joey and Jen are not overjoyed at our uninvited and unannounced presence?"

"See, Dawson, one of your many problems is that you worry too much. Go with the flow."

"That can be problematic if the flow is not flowing in the direction of your choice." The wind gusted, and Dawson zipped up his parka. "It occurs to me that I might be the dork of all time for chasing Joey to this party. I may need to rethink this."

"Fine," Pacey said, nodding. "Spend your life in your room, endlessly analyzing events and emotions that you are too weenie to actually live. Prove Joey right."

Dawson edged closer to the buildings to his right, trying to get out of the gusting wind. "Is that your attempt at reverse psychology, Pacey? In other words, am I supposed to want to crash this party because deep down I'm afraid that Joey was right, ergo, now I have this intense need to prove her wrong?"

"Basically, yeah," Pacey replied. "It's working beautifully, I might add."

They reached the Plaza Hotel, walked through the side entrance and entered the lavish lobby. The ceiling was high, the room lit by dangling crystal chandeliers. The carpet under their feet was a rich tapestry, the furniture elegant. A string quartet played in an area to their left, where well-dressed couples sat having drinks. Everyone looked like they belonged to some exclusive club to which Pacey and Dawson would never be admitted.

"My stomach is registering somewhere between acute anxiety and overwhelming panic," Dawson managed, "and my mind is not far behind."

"Breathe, Dawson," Pacey instructed. "Follow my lead."

Pacey strolled over to the concierge's desk. "Good evening," he said, smiling unctuously at the gray-haired, uniformed gentleman.

"May I help you?" the concierge asked politely.

"Yes, you can," Pacey said. "We're the deejays from Bauhaus O'Funk."

The concierge looked at him blankly.

"Our equipment is out in the truck," Pacey continued. "We're doin' a little hamma-jamma thang at the sweet sixteen here this evening?"

"There's a sweet sixteen party in the Rose Room, one flight up," the concierge said. "But they have an orchestra, so I doubt that—"

"Hey, after midnight these things get wild and crazy," Pacey told him, winking. "Thanks. Stop on by later, when you get off. We'll throw a few Sinatra tunes on for you." He grabbed Dawson's arm and they headed for the elevator.

"Deejays from *Bauhaus O'Funk*?" Dawson's voice was withering.

"It's a sideline we should consider, actually," Pacey said. "Better pay than Screenplay. We wouldn't have to put up with Nellie. And deejays score all the hottest babes."

"Do you have any idea how demeaning to women it is when you talk like that?" Dawson asked.

135

"No," Pacey replied.

They got off the elevator and followed the brass sign directing them to the Rose Room.

And then, there they were. Staring in through the open doors.

It looked like a movie set. Everything female was in an evening gown, and everything male, including the orchestra and the waiters, was in a tux. It was beyond opulent. And way beyond them.

"Jack. Rose. *Titanic*. Ring any bells?" Pacey asked Dawson nervously.

"And you thought my *tie* was trying too hard," Dawson hissed at him. "We can't go in there!"

Pacey spied a pair of sunglasses someone had left on a white-clothed side table outside the Rose Room. He slid them on. "Dawson, we have not yet begun to party. Follow my lead."

"Pacey, no—"

Too late. Pacey bopped into the Rose Room, his eyes hidden behind the dark sunglasses.

Dawson caught up with him. "This is not *American Gigolo*. Lose the shades!"

"But—"

"I mean it, Pacey. Or I'm outta here."

Pacey reluctantly took off the sunglasses and stuck them in his back pocket. "You are soul-free, Dawson."

"Now go put the glasses back where you found them."

Pacey pointed at Dawson. "That sounded suspiciously like Deputy Doug. Not a good thing."

"Just do it," Dawson insisted.

Pacey sighed. "I shall return."

Dawson looked around. No sign of Joey or Jen. People stared at him, whispered, pointed. I look like a total goober, Dawson thought. He smiled and nodded to people.

A pretty girl with long red hair came up to him. "Hi."

"Hi."

"Are you sure you're at the right party?" she asked.

"I believe I am," Dawson said. Sweat began to pop out on his forehead, and he felt his armpits begin to drip sweat down his sides. He took off his ski parka.

"I'm Carson Finchworth. And you're—?"

"Dawson. Dawson Leery." She was staring at him as if she needed further explanation. "Deejay!" Dawson blurted out. "Bauhaus O'Funk!"

Carson laughed. "No way did Courtney's mom hire a deejay for this gig. She won't even let the orchestra play songs written in this decade. So who are you, really?"

"Really I'm . . ." Dawson looked down at the video camera in his hand. And it came to him. "I'm the videographer."

"Oh, cool!" Carson said. "So, you're gonna video the party? But didn't Grace tell you it was formal?"

"Grace?"

"Courtney's mom," Carson said. "Isn't she the one who hired you?"

"Screenplay Videos is a huge company," Dawson invented. "So they just send one of us videographers out."

"Mission accomplished," Pacey reported, as he

137

walked back over to Dawson. Then he noticed the cute redhead. "Hi there! I'm—"

"The other videographer," Dawson filled in. "I know I said they send one of us out. But in this case, they sent *two* of us. Because it's such a big party."

Carson gave Pacey a dubious look. "Where's your camera, hotshot?"

"I'm his boss," Pacey explained. "I direct. He does the actual grunt work."

"Uh-huh." She sounded highly dubious.

"Dawson, get some footage on this beauty," Pacey directed. He smiled at Carson. "Just look into the camera and tell Courtney whatever you want to tell her on her special day."

When this is all over, I really will kill Pacey, Dawson thought, as he aimed the camera at Carson. No jury of my peers would convict me, either.

"Why does every party hire you video guys?" Carson asked. "I look so fat on video. And I hate my voice!"

"You look great," Dawson insisted. "And your voice is cute. Just be yourself."

"Okay," Carson said. She looked into the camera self-consciously. "Happy sweet sixteen, Courtney. Your party is fantastic."

"See, you're a natural," Pacey told her. "I see Hollywood in your future, no lie."

Carson laughed. "Right. You are so full of it that I know why your eyes are brown."

"Hi, I'm Miranda," a small girl with pinched features said, coming over to them. "What are you guys doing?"

"They're the videographers," Carson said. "Say something for Courtney."

"Are Courtney's parents going to see this?" Miranda asked Dawson.

"Yes," Dawson said. "They hired me. I mean us. Our company. Screenplay Videos."

"Oh, too bad," Miranda said. "Then I don't dare say anything about how Courtney got so wrecked last weekend that she jumped in the hot tub naked with three guys."

"Is that true?" Carson asked, her jaw dropping open slightly.

"That's what I heard," Miranda said innocently. "Hey, you guys, come here!" she called to a group nearby. "We're making a tape for Courtney."

"Can you get all of us together?" one girl asked.

Dawson aimed the camera at them—three girls and two guys. They put their arms around each other.

"Happy birthday, Courtney," a tall guy said. "The party's rad, but kind of sedate. We'll have to do the alternate experience next weekend."

"No parents allowed!" a short girl added.

They all laughed, talking into the camera, fooling around, telling Courtney how much they loved her.

"You're groovin'!" Pacey whispered in Dawson's ear.

"Go see if you can find Joey and Jen," Dawson whispered back. "I didn't come here to make home videos."

"Excuse me." Someone tapped Dawson on the shoulder.

He turned around. A beautiful older woman in a dove-gray evening gown stood there.

Next to her was a middle-aged man in a tuxedo holding a video camera. On the man's left lapel was a plastic-enclosed badge that read "Sarrat Video Services, Joseph Sarrat, videographer."

"Hi," Dawson squeaked. His life passed before his eyes.

"I am the hostess of this party," the woman said. She pointed to the man next to her. "This gentleman is Joseph Sarrat, the videographer I engaged for this event. Now, you two have exactly twenty seconds to explain yourselves before I call hotel security."

Chapter 17

Joey checked the smoking room again. No Danny, just middle-aged men and a few women who thought it was cool, puffing on expensive cigars. She'd spent the past half hour looking for Danny. When she found him, she was going to force him to tell them all the truth. Or die trying.

But, after three trips around the massive ballroom and into the adjoining two suites, and even having checked out the other ballrooms on the hotel's second floor, she hadn't found him. Or Billy. Or even Jen, for that matter.

Joey plopped down on a buttery leather couch just outside of the ballroom. She felt that ache at the back of her throat that comes before tears, but willed them back.

This sucks, she thought. This really, really bites

it. All of Courtney's friends think I had sex with Danny. And Jen just deserted me.

"You okay, Joelle?" It was Tucker with two friends.

"Sure," Joey lied. Never let 'em see you sweat.

"Catch you later." Tucker went back into the Rose Room with his friends.

He doesn't want to know me anymore because he thinks I had sex with Danny, Joey thought. *Everyone* thinks I had sex with Danny.

She jumped up from the couch and made her way through the Rose Room to the coat check, where she'd left Jen's faux fur jacket. Forget it. She was not going to sit there and have a pity party for one. She'd just get a taxi back to Jen's apartment. Mrs. Richardson would let her in.

And then she remembered. She had spent her money on the dream ring. She didn't have enough left for a taxi.

The coat-check girl handed Joey the fur jacket. There was a small silver tray on the counter in front of her. Tips, Joey figured. She knew about people who lived on tips. She put one of her last two dollar bills on the tray. She'd be walking back to Jen's apartment anyway. It didn't make any difference.

"Joelle!"

She turned around. There was Danny, coming toward her in all his glory.

"I missed you," he said, his gait unsteady. Clearly he'd been either drinking or smoking pot or both. "I've been looking for you everywhere."

"And I've been looking for you, too," Joey said sweetly. "Want to hear something really weird? A lot of people at this party think I had sex with you last night."

"No kidding?" Danny asked, trying to laugh.

"No kidding. Miranda says you showed her some kind of chart where you rated my performance."

"Forget her. She's just jealous 'cuz she looks like a troll," Danny slurred. He reached for Joey but she stepped out of the way.

"You lied about me, didn't you." It was a statement, not a question. *"Didn't* you?"

He gave her a winsome little boy look that had clearly worked for him in the past. "Okay, Joelle, you busted me. But you wouldn't want me to ruin my rep by telling everyone you walked out on me, would you? Anyway, I made up for it tonight, right? And don't worry, I plan to keep on making up for it."

Joey grabbed the lapel of his tuxedo and yanked him to her. "You are a scum-sucking, bottom-feeding pile of puke. Your brain is in your pants, and it's a rice brain at that. Don't you ever, *ever* even breathe my name again as long as you live. If you see me on TV winning the Nobel Peace Prize, refer to me as 'that girl.' Because if I ever find out that my name has been uttered by your mouth— Joelle, Joey, Joe, take your pick—if I find out, and I *will* find out, I will make you so sorry."

She let go of him. He stumbled. She turned on her heel and headed for the door.

There was some commotion under way not far from the entrance to the Rose Room. A crowd of people was gathering to look at someone or something. Joey had zero interest. She was just about to walk by when she heard the ruckus.

"It's a perfectly innocent mistake! We were hired to video a different sweet sixteen!"

Joey jerked to a stop. No. It couldn't be.

That voice had sounded exactly like Pacey's.

"Right," another voice said. "We were hired to video . . . Courtney Giuliani's sweet sixteen."

Joey closed her eyes. She felt sick. Because there was absolutely, positively no mistaking that voice.

Dawson's voice. "This isn't happening," Joey moaned.

"We'll just wait for hotel security to straighten this all out, shall we?" Jen's aunt said frostily.

Joey worked her way through the crowd. There they were. Dawson and Pacey. In jeans. The eyes of the storm.

Dawson's gaze met hers. Then he looked quickly away. He was going to pretend he didn't know her, so he wouldn't risk getting her in trouble, too.

"Raymond, could you call security, please?" Courtney's mother asked one of Courtney's friends. She had one arm draped proprietarily around her daughter's shoulders.

"Don't do that," Joey said quickly.

Everyone turned to look at her. "I know these guys. I invited them."

"Wait, I don't understand," Courtney said. "You invited *your* friends to *my* sweet sixteen? I mean, I don't even know you."

"Danny knows her," someone smirked. There were a few muffled laughs.

"I guess you know lots of guys, huh, Joelle?" Miranda asked nastily.

"Shut up, Miranda," Carson said. "You're such a witch. No one can stand you!"

"Mother, my party is getting ruined!" Courtney wailed.

"Excuse me, excuse me," Jen said, muscling her way through the crowd. She desperately hoped she was wrong, but she could have sworn she'd heard the voices of Pacey and Dawson.

She reached the center of the commotion. She had been right. She was furious. Beyond furious. Her eyes met Dawson's. He looked like a deer caught in someone's headlights.

Attitude adjustment. Jen forced herself to smile. "Hi! You guys finally made it, huh?" She threw her arms around Dawson and hugged him, then she hugged Pacey.

"Jennifer?" her aunt asked in an icy voice.

"Oh, you know me, Aunt Grace," Jen said. "I invited these guys and forgot to tell you."

"You did this to ruin my party!" Courtney screeched.

"Honestly, Courtney, I—" Jen began.

"You haven't changed at all," Courtney accused, cutting her off. "Why don't you just get drunk and tear off your clothes, Jen, like old times?"

A few people gasped audibly. Jen flinched as if Courtney had hit her.

Dawson stepped forward and reached for Jen's hand. "I take full responsibility for this," he said. "Don't blame Jen or Joey. They didn't know we were coming. That's the truth. So I apologize,

145

Courtney. My friend and I will be leaving so that you can all get back to your party. That is, Courtney, just as soon as you apologize to Jen."

"You must be on drugs," Courtney spat. "I don't have to listen to you, and I certainly don't have to apologize to *her*. Mother, tell them!"

"Leave now or I am calling security," her mother said.

Pacey touched Dawson lightly on the shoulder. "Let's just go, pal."

"Not until she apologizes to Jen," Dawson insisted. He wouldn't move.

Someone else pushed through the crowd. Hotel security? No. It was Danny. His eyes lit up when he saw Joey and he reeled over to her. "Baby! You couldn't tear yourself away from me after all, huh, Joelle?"

"I told you never to say my name again," Joey told him. She pulled her fist back and let fly with a right cross that landed squarely on the left side of his nose. Hard. He lost his balance and fell over backward.

Everyone began to yell at once. Courtney's mother screamed for hotel security.

Joey looked at Jen, Dawson, and Pacey. "I think we know how this movie ends. Shall we?"

"We shall," Jen said.

The four of them walked out the door.

Chapter 18

By unspoken agreement they hurried out of the hotel and jumped into one of the taxis waiting at the curb, the guys and Joey in back, Jen in front.

The driver took off, heading down Fifth Avenue. There was a beat of silence, then everyone but the driver started yelling.

Jen and Joey both screamed at the guys for showing up without an invitation. The guys shouted back their loud, if conflicting, explanations. Then Joey turned her wrath on Jen, screaming at her for having deserted her at the party.

"Time out, time out!" Jen yelled over the fray. They didn't listen. She put two fingers in her mouth and whistled shrilly. They stopped. The cabdriver just kept his eyes on the road, as if screaming matches in his taxicab were an everyday occurence.

"Thank you." She twisted around in her seat so

she could see them. "Now, if we speak one at a time, maybe we can make some sense of this. First let's deal with you and me, Joey, and then we can both deal with Dumb and Dumber."

"I resent that remark," Pacey said.

Jen shot him a disdainful glance. "If you value your life, Pacey, shut up." He mimed zipping his lips together.

Jen looked at Joey. "I know you think I abandoned you, but I didn't. After a few minutes of playing the dutiful niece to my Uncle William while he blew cigar smoke in my face, I went looking for Billy. When I found him, he and Jack D. had already gotten up close and personal. I got mad. We had a fight. I came back to look for you and you were gone. The end."

"I went looking for Danny," Joey said. "He told everyone that he . . ." Her gaze slid over to Dawson.

"He what?" Dawson demanded. Joey didn't reply.

"Is Danny the guy you punched?" Dawson asked, his voice tight. "Well? Is he?"

"None of your business," Joey snapped.

"As your best friend, it behooves me—"

"*Best friend?*" Joey echoed. Her eyes shot daggers at him. "You dare call me your *best friend?* Did it ever occur to that excuse for a brain you carry around between your ears that showing up at that particular party without an invitation was not exactly a *best friend* thing to do, Dawson? Because I'm just curious."

"You're the one who said I would spend my life in my room analyzing things to death instead of taking any chances," Dawson reminded her. "I believe your exact taunt to me was, 'Be bold, Dawson.' Well, I took a chance. I was bold. You just don't like the chance I took."

"That is just your verbose and exceedingly lame excuse for showing up at that party, Dawson! And that is not exactly what I would put under the heading, 'bold.' "

"Were you with that guy Danny?" Dawson asked doggedly.

"Yes, Dawson," Joey said sarcastically. "You see, I deliberately punched out my own date. I *was* planning to run away with him after the party, but the instant I saw you, I decided I just had to break his nose instead."

"All right, I asked a stupid question," Dawson allowed.

"The word 'pathetic' doesn't even begin to cover you right now," Joey said, fuming.

"I just don't get it," Jen told Dawson and Pacey. "I mean, what were you two thinking?"

"Road trip," Pacey said lamely.

Dawson could not let it go. "But if you *weren't* on a date," Dawson continued, "then why did he call you 'baby' and why did he—"

"I swear, Dawson, if you don't shut up I will hit you a lot harder than I hit him!" Joey yelled.

"Please! No violence in my cab," the driver said, looking at Joey in his rearview mirror.

"Fine," Joey said. "I'll wait until we get out."

The taxi pulled up in front of Jen's apartment building. "You pay him," she told the guys. "Joey and I will meet you in the lobby."

The two girls got out of the cab; Joey strode angrily into the building.

"I can't believe Dawson and Pacey," Joey said, pacing the lobby. "This is the lowest. Truly the lowest thing he has ever done to me." Then a vision of Danny lying on the ballroom floor filled her mind. Oh, god.

"And I can't believe I punched Danny out at your cousin's sweet sixteen," she added. She turned to Jen. Outside she could see the guys getting out of the taxicab. "Do you hate me?"

"Frankly, watching your fist connect with Danny Fields's face was one of the more satisfying moments of my life."

"But you wanted to change your rep with everyone, and then I . . . well, it couldn't have helped."

"I don't care what they think anymore, Joey," Jen said, "so forget it."

"Are you going to let Dawson and Pacey stay over?"

"Maybe they have a hotel room," Jen thought aloud.

"Dawson and Pacey? Hel-lo? What bank would they have robbed?" The guys came into the lobby. "How did you two even get to New York?" Joey asked them.

"My father's truck," Pacey said.

"We slept in it last night," Dawson added. "We had a detailed plan that involved calling you this morning, as opposed to springing our presence on you at the party. But do you know how many Lindleys there are in the Manhattan phone book?"

"Lots, none of them my parents. They're unlisted." Jen said. "So?"

"So we called them all!" Pacey held up his pointer finger. "I've got bursitis from punching numbers into the friggin' pay phone. Show a little pity."

Jen sighed. "I already regret what I'm about to do."

"You're about to offer us room at the inn, sustenance and shelter, I love you!" Pacey cried.

"Well, I don't love you," Jen stated matter-of-factly. "At the moment, I don't even like you. Either one of you."

They took the elevator to the penthouse floor.

"What about Mrs. Richardson?" Joey asked.

"What about her?" Jen let them into the dark apartment and turned on a light. Which was when the guys saw the abundance of flowers.

"Jen, you should be thinking float in the Tournament of Roses Parade," Pacey said, looking around.

Dawson nodded. "Quite the floral tribute."

"It so happens the flowers weren't for Jen," Joey said.

Dawson looked incredulous. "*You?*"

"What, is that so hard for you to believe?" Joey asked defiantly.

"No," Dawson said sadly. "I only wish I had sent them."

"What is going on here?" Mrs. Richardson was standing in the hallway. She held her modest flannel robe closed at the neck. Her hair stuck out in all directions.

"Some friends came back with us," Jen explained.

"Miss Lindley," the older woman began, "your

parents specifically forbid you to have male company here while they are away."

Jen walked over to her. "Look, these guys are from Capeside, and they don't have a place to sleep tonight."

"Capeside?" Mrs. Richardson asked dubiously.

"Where I live now," Jen replied. "So Joey and I are going to sleep in my bedroom. And my friends Dawson and Pacey are going to sleep in the guest room. That's the whole story. Nothing else. You can tell my parents I had two guys up here if that's what you need to do, Mrs. Richardson. They will have a fit and assume the worst about me, but what they assume won't be true. Now, even if all that happens, my friends are still going to spend the night. Because I don't turn away friends in need. So what's it going to be?"

The older woman fiddled with the collar of her robe. "I'm going to bed now, Miss Lindley," she finally said. "It's a pity I never woke up when you came in from your party this evening, but you see I took some allergy medicine and slept deeply through the night. Which means this conversation could not have even taken place. Good night."

She turned and left.

Jen smiled. "I knew I liked her."

"So, your parents are out of town, huh?" Pacey asked.

"I can see visions of strip poker dancing in your head, Pacey, but it's not gonna happen. You should be thrilled that I'm letting you stay at all." Jen looked over at Joey. "I'm beat."

"Me, too," Joey said.

"The guest room is second on the left," Jen told the guys. "Towels are in the guest bathroom. We can hash all this out tomorrow."

The girls headed out of the room.

"Joey, wait!" Dawson said. "We really need to talk—"

"No, Dawson. We really don't." She walked away.

A half hour later, the girls had changed into over-sized T-shirts, shut the door, and climbed into Jen's huge bed. An old-fashioned orange night-light provided the only illumination.

"My right hand hurts," Joey confessed. "Do you think I might have busted his nose?"

"I hope so." Jen stared up at the ceiling. "I'm such an idiot. I never should have come back here. Did I really think my parents would magically be here to greet me with open arms? Or that my so-called friends would have changed? Or that Billy would be the answer to my problems?"

"What problems?" Joey asked softly.

"The usual adolescent angst of the overprivileged and underloved," Jen said. "I'm such a cliché that it's funny. All I want is someone to love me."

"I thought you told me you want friendship with a guy, not romance," Joey reminded her.

"I do. But my neediness ends up getting in the way of the friendship," Jen admitted. "So then I call it love—I even believe it's love!—because I want it to be true so badly. But I haven't ever had it, really. Not like you and Dawson."

"Dawson? We're *friends*," Joey insisted. "Not

that a friend would do what he just did. I am so ticked at him."

Jen got up on one elbow and peered at Joey. "How can you be so blind, Joey? You and Dawson are never going to be just friends again. He's in love with you and he always has been. And you're in love with him, too."

Joey sat up. "You're so full of it! I saw what you wrote on the wall in the girl's john at The Cellar. J + D. Jen and Dawson. You want him back. Why don't you just admit it?"

Jen laughed.

"What's so funny?" Joey asked crossly.

"You. J + D stood for Dawson and you!"

"I'm so sure."

"It did," Jen insisted. "You can't see what's right in front of your face. I don't want Dawson back, Joey. And I couldn't get him even if I did want him. He's your leading man, not mine."

"But I don't *want* him to be my leading man anymore!"

"What if we don't get endless chances at love, Joey?" Jen asked. "You wanted Dawson so badly. And then you got him. And then . . . then you just threw it away."

"You don't understand," Joey said, her voice low. "You're this sophisticated New Yorker. You've dated lots of guys. But I'm from Capeside and Dawson Leery is the only guy I've ever known. How am I supposed to know if he's the one for me when I haven't even lived yet?"

"Maybe you aren't," Jen allowed. "But don't fault

him for loving you, Joey. Love is too precious and rare to throw away. Trust me, I know."

After a while, Joey heard Jen's breathing deepen, and she knew Jen was asleep. She just lay there with her eyes closed, watching the geometric patterns and lights playing on the insides of her eyelids. But she couldn't sleep. She was thinking. Finally she got up and padded down the hall to the room where Dawson and Pacey were asleep.

She opened the door slowly, so that a shaft of light fell on Dawson's bed.

His wide-open eyes met hers. As if he could read her mind, he got out of bed and followed her, wordlessly, into the living room.

"I couldn't sleep," she said finally, as she stood by the living room window facing Dawson, the lights of Manhattan silhouetting her from behind.

"Me, neither."

They sat down together on the couch, in the dark. He had on gym shorts and a T-shirt. Joey pulled the hem of her long T-shirt even longer, and tried to find the words she wanted to say.

"Remember last fall, Dawson? We had one of our revoltingly intense, pseudo-mature conversations about honesty. And I told you it was time for you to grow up and be honest with me. Remember?"

Dawson nodded.

"Well, I wasn't exactly honest with you tonight. The truth is . . . I was on a date with Danny. That is, I agreed to go to the party with him. I met him Friday night with Jen. It was all very Julie Delpy and Ethan Hawke, you know, strangers who see each other and feel this intense spark—"

Like I felt with Dixie, Dawson thought. No. That was different. That was real.

"—And this intense spark feels so awesome, so special—"

"I don't want to hear about your sparks with another guy, Joey."

"You have no choice, Dawson. So, this girl and this guy have this intense spark," she went on. "Only it turns out that, beyond the hormonal, the spark was an illusion. Because all he was interested in was sex. And when he didn't get it, he lied and told everyone that he had."

Dawson's throat ached. "I don't know what to say to that, Joey. I don't know what role to play now. The avenging boyfriend? The distant ex-boyfriend? The understanding friend?"

Joey got up and went to the window again. The lights of New York beckoned seductively. Was it just the night before that the skyline had called to her so sweetly? Jen had been right. Everything that glittered was not gold.

"I can't tell you what role to play," she said, still staring out at the glittering lights. "All I know is that I wanted to tell you the truth."

She slowly turned to him. "Dawson, I don't know if you can understand because I don't even understand it myself. When it comes to guys I'm still in the infant stage. I have a lot of learning to do, and I'll probably make a lot of mistakes along the way."

She waited. He was silent. Impassive.

"So I can't tell you that I want more than your friendship right now," she continued, "because it would be a lie. But I can tell you that even though

I'm incredibly ticked at you for following me to New York, I value your love and your friendship more than anything in the world. If I lost it, I don't know what I would do. So I just wanted you to know."

Silence.

She went back to the couch and sat down. She looked into his eyes. "Dawson? Could you please say something?"

Their faces were so close that he could smell the mint of her toothpaste. And something else, something uniquely and sweetly Joey. He longed to kiss her. And knew he couldn't. Shouldn't. Wouldn't.

"Dawson?"

He stood up. Avoid temptation. Don't think. Don't feel. "Thanks for being honest with me."

She stood up, too. "Is that *it*?"

"What do you want me to say? That I understand? That in the future you can feel free to come to me to expound on your burgeoning love life? Because I can't say that." He walked to the door. Then he turned back to her.

"For once you don't get the stinging exit line, Joey. I do. But for the life of me, I can't remember what it is."

Chapter 19

Jen rested her head on the truck passenger window, her mood as gloomy as the gathering clouds. She'd been awakened that morning by a phone call. Aunt Grace. Her aunt yelled at her hysterically for ten minutes. The party had been ruined. Danny had spent hours in the emergency room—yes, his nose was broken—and it was all Jen's fault for bringing that white-trash girl with her.

"Jennifer Lindley, you'll be a pregnant, alcoholic drug addict before you're a senior in high school," her aunt had predicted. "And you won't even know who the baby's father is."

"Aunt Grace?" Jen had finally interrupted.

"What?" her aunt asked.

"Go to hell." Jen hung up on her. Click.

Almost instantly, the phone had rung again. Billy. Everything that had gone wrong had been his fault.

He loved her. He wanted her back. Couldn't he see her before she went back to Capeside? In fact, why did she have to go back to Capeside at all?

She didn't hang up on him, as she had on her aunt. All she'd said was "I have to go, Billy. I need some time alone. I'll call you when I call you." Click. Disconnect. From him, from her entire life in New York.

"According to my calculations," Pacey said, as he switched lanes to pass a Taurus, "I will have this truck back in the Chief of Police's parking spot exactly one hour before he hits Capeside. He'll never know it was gone."

"Maybe I'll tell him," Joey said. "You deserve it."

"There are things that I believe you would do to me, Joey," Pacey said, "many of them most unpleasant. But ratting me out to my father is not one of them. Besides, you're going home in the lap of luxury."

Joey was squished between Pacey and Dawson on the cab's single seat. Jen was curled up behind them.

"Very amusing," Joey retorted. "On the big scorecard of life, you and Dawson are batting zero for this little stunt. No. *Sub*-zero. You will have to do something amazing, like, say, cure cancer, to *rise* to zero. A free ride home in a stolen truck does not qualify."

"Okay, you're still mad," Pacey allowed, as he switched back to the right-hand lane.

Joey stretched and almost elbowed Dawson in the nose. "Aren't you the mental giant, Pacey. How could I have missed such burning intellect?" Ragging on Pacey was so much easier than thinking about Dawson. Or even *looking* at Dawson. It was bad enough sitting pressed against him like this, even if he was studiously ignoring her.

"Consider adopting Jen's approach to anger," Pacey suggested, looking at Jen in the mirror. "Sure, she's not altogether happy. Yet her deep affection for us is untarnished. Plus, her pensive silence is much easier on the eardrums."

"Think again, Pacey," Jen said. "Joey's the bad cop and I'm the good cop. Don't be fooled into thinking we aren't on the same side."

"Meaning that your deep affection for us *is* tarnished?" Pacey asked, sounding surprisingly vulnerable.

"What do you think?" Jen asked. "In some parallel universe you might do something this idiotic and your friends would still give you the unconditional love that your family seems incapable of giving, but you don't live in that universe, Pacey. And neither do I."

It began to rain, which seemed fitting. For a long time, no one said anything.

"Your father will know about the truck," Jen finally said. "The odometer."

"He and my brother are oblivious to that stuff," Pacey said. "Too busy combatting Capeside's many serial killers. I had a new run-in with Deputy Doug last week. He waited up for me when I came in late just so he could tell me one more time what a loser I am."

"Fast-forward," Joey snapped. "Been-there-done-that."

Pacey nodded. "Okay, one whine over the pity

line. But you know what? Even if I woke up tomorrow as Deputy Doug the second, in everyone's eyes I'd still be Pacey-the-loser. Because once people think they have you pegged, they never change their opinion of you. Right, Jen?"

Jen didn't answer.

"Right," Pacey said. "But someday I'll escape from Capeside, just like you escaped from New York. And when I do, I too will reinvent myself. But in the meantime, a road trip to New York was as close as I'm gonna get."

Joey looked back at Jen. "This is where we gain the insight that elicits newfound sympathy for a previously unsympathetic character."

Pacey just shook his head. "Thanks, Joe. Your compassion runneth over."

"Just a word of advice," Joey said. "Resist the temptation to have your character tell us how he feels, instead of allowing us to discover it for ourselves."

"Forget it," Pacey mumbled with disgust. He turned the radio on, loud.

Dawson cut his eyes at Joey. He knew her too well—her inverse relationship between happiness and verbosity. Meaning that if she was on a verbal roll, she was probably miserable.

But not over me, he realized. What kind of mental meltdown made me think she'd welcome my presence in New York? She wants to see other guys. And no brilliant turn of phrase or impetuous, romantic trip to New York is going to get her to change her mind.

A movie moment in his head: a graceful girl, with

long blond hair, dancing in the parking lot of Mc-
Donald's. Dixie. If he was with Dixie, she'd appreciate him. She'd—

"Look at the poor woman!" Jen said.

Off in the distance, on the shoulder of the road,
a small elderly woman stood in the downpour, looking helplessly at her blown left tire. Cars whizzed
by her.

Pacey quickly checked his watch. Time to spare
without risking the wrath of the Long Arm of the
Law. He slowed down and pulled the truck off the
highway, right behind the woman's Lexus.

"This is where you get out of the truck and actually go *help* her," Jen pointed out.

"I'm going, I'm going," Pacey said. He watched
the highway hopefully. "That is, if some other Good
Samaritan with an *umbrella* doesn't pull off to help
her first."

Jen nudged him in the back. "You won't melt."

"Oh, *that's* original," Pacey said.

Dawson unlocked his door. "Come on."

Dawson and Pacey ran to the woman, the rain
soaking them. "Hi!" Dawson said. "Can we help
you?"

"Bless you for stopping," the woman said. "I'm
such a ninny. I forgot my cell phone and I'm hopeless about cars."

Pacey knelt down to look at the left rear tire of
her Lexus. "Your basic blown tire."

"Yes, I can see that," the woman said. "I have a
spare and a jack." She unlocked the trunk and
Dawson and Pacey lifted out the tire and the jack.

"We can put the spare on for you," Pacey offered.

"You're a lifesaver," she said gratefully. "My name is Phyllis Hanover, by the way."

The boys introduced themselves to her.

"Wait in our truck if you'd like," Dawson suggested. "No sense in your standing in the rain."

"I will," Mrs. Hanover said. "I simply can't thank you enough for this." She made her way to the truck and got in.

Dawson stared at Pacey, the rain pelting down on him. "Now what?"

"What do you mean 'now what?' " Pacey asked. "Don't you know how to change a tire, Dawson?"

"I'm sure I will learn how to change a tire in the near future," Dawson said, "but—"

"Get Joey," Pacey said, shaking his head. "Go! I'm in a time crunch, here!"

Dawson went back to the truck. Joey came out. Wordlessly she grabbed the jack and wedged it in place while Pacey got down and loosened the lug nuts and bolts. Then, she jacked the car up.

"Thanks for your help," Pacey said.

"I'm not helping *you*," Joey said. "I'm helping *her*. Where's the spare?"

"Here."

Inside the truck, the older woman dried her curly gray hair with some paper towels Jen had found in the cargo space. "I just don't know what I would have done if you young people hadn't stopped."

"We're glad we could help," Jen said.

"It's amazing how rarely people help each other anymore. It's a pity. The world is a poorer place for it. What did that young man say his name was again?"

"Pacey Witter," Dawson told her.

"Unusual name, Pacey," Mrs. Hanover said. "Where do you children live?"

"Capeside," Jen said. "Actually, Pacey's dad is the Chief of Police there."

"Capeside, Capeside," the woman mused. "I don't believe I've heard of it. We summer in Martha's Vineyard. Is it near there?"

Jen laughed. "It's light-years from there."

The door opened. Joey got into the driver's seat as Pacey stood in the downpour.

"Listen, Mrs. Hanover, your spare tire is flat," Joey said.

"Oh, no!"

"Oh, yes," Joey said, shivering as the water dripped off of her. Wordlessly Dawson helped her off with her jacket. Then he took off his ski parka and put it around her shoulders.

"We'll have to find a service station that can bring you out a tire or get one of yours fixed," Pacey said. He looked around. "We're not near anything. It's Sunday. It could take a while."

"No, wait," Jen said. "There are emergency call boxes on this highway every mile. We've been passing them."

"I'll go see if I can find one," Pacey said.

"I hate to trouble you," Mrs. Hanover replied.

Pacey quickly glanced at his watch. If he cut loose from this little mission of mercy within the next thirty minutes, they were still home-free.

"Well, it's not exactly a *cure for cancer*," he intoned, looking at Joey pointedly, "but it's no trouble."

"Look Pacey," Joey shivered slightly as she talked. "Why don't you throw Mrs. Hanover's spare in the back of the truck and go see if you can get some help. Go to the call box, or maybe there's a gas station that's open."

"Good idea," Pacey said, glancing at his watch again.

"I'll go too," Jen said suddenly.

"But why?" Dawson asked. "You can wait in Mrs. Hanover's car with Joey and me."

"Frankly, Dawson, I don't think you want Joey and me both with you right now. That much anger aimed in your direction might be too much anger for you to deal with."

Dawson nodded. He and Joey got out of the truck and went to Mrs. Hanover's car. Pacey threw the spare tire in the back of the truck. Then, he, Jen, and Mrs. Hanover headed down the road.

In the front seat of Mrs. Hanover's car, Joey shivered and watched Pacey's truck disappear down the highway.

"They'll be back soon," Dawson said.

Joey started the car so she could turn on the heater. Warm air blew from the vents.

Dawson's eyes slid over to Joey. "You're still shivering," he noted.

"That might be because I'm still freezing."

"What I'm about to do is meaningless beyond a human desire to raise your body temperature." Dawson put his arm around her. "In a nonsexual way, I should add," he said hastily.

"Got that, Dawson. Thanks."

They sat in silence.

"Who said 'Timing is everything'?" Dawson asked.

Joey shrugged. "Fred Astaire? The Unabomber?"

Dawson stared straight ahead, watching rain pelt the windshield. "I'm sitting here with you, my best friend, and what I want to do is tell you all about this magical girl I can't stop thinking about. How her hair curls up around her face when it gets wet. How her eyes change with every emotion she feels. How no one could possibly understand her the way that I can. But I can't tell you about her, Joey, because you *are* her. So that's what I mean about timing. Ours is decidedly off. And I just don't know what to do about it or how to fix it."

"It's not a movie, Dawson. You can't fix it."

They sat in silence again. Minutes passed. A half hour. They both fell asleep. When they woke up, they realized they had been there more than an hour.

"Pacey's schedule has been drastically altered," Dawson said, stretching. "He must be going crazy."

Joey shrugged. "Here's what happened. They found a call box and called the state police. The state police said that with this weather and it being Sunday, all the wreckers were busy. But if they'd drive three exits north, they'd find a service station that could help them. And that's where they are now."

"Do you run a psychic service you neglected to mention to me?" Dawson asked.

"When you ride with Bessie in her bomber, you know everything that can go wrong in a car," Jen said. "And you know where every service station in this part of Massachusetts is located."

"Pacey's father is going to kill him," Dawson said.

"Amazing," Joey said. "Pacey Witter refused to leave Grandma Moses deserted by the side of the road. This is like discovering the eighth wonder of the world."

Dawson nodded. "Just when you think you can trust someone to always do the wrong thing, Pacey goes and does the right thing. It's a little off-putting."

"A miracle on the road to Capeside. An amazing moment. Pacey transcends self-involved stupidity." She gave Dawson a dry look. "Who knows, Dawson, maybe it'll be contagious."

Chapter 20

"Jennifer? Is that you?" Jen's grandmother came out of the kitchen, wiping her hands on her apron.

"Hi, Grams." Jen put down her suitcase and hung her sopping-wet leather jacket in the hall closet.

"I thought you were going to call me from the train station, Jennifer."

"We got a ride."

"I see. Well. It's funny. I found myself rather missing your company. I know you find that hard to believe."

"I do," Jen agreed. "Because most of the time I'm not very good company to you, and we both know it."

"Did you have a good time?"

"Swell," Jen said. "Any calls for me?"

"Just one from Clifford Elliot," Grams said. "I left his number by the phone. How was Courtney's sweet sixteen?"

"The word 'unforgettable' comes to mind."

"Really?" Grams asked, her face lighting up. "I'd love to hear about it."

"Some other time," Jen said. "I've got a splitting headache."

Grams' face fell. "I see."

Jen picked up her suitcase. "I'm beat. I'm going to bed." She headed upstairs.

"What about dinner?" Grams called after her. "I prepared some of your favorite things."

"Thanks, I'm not hungry."

She went up to her room, changed into her favorite nightgown, and crawled into bed.

A terrible loneliness swept over her. It was time to face the truth. She didn't belong in New York anymore. Everyone back there thought they knew her, but they really didn't know her at all. And even worse, they didn't care about her. Not really.

Pretend affection is the worst, Jen thought. I would rather have no affection at all. Except that no affection is just so lonely.

A single tear slid down her cheek and she fisted it away. The odor of roast chicken wafted up the stairs. Her stomach growled hungrily. It was sweet of Grams to make roast chicken and to say she missed me. But I can't talk to her. If only Gramps was still alive. . . .

"But he isn't," she said aloud, as if it would help her to accept it. "He isn't, and she is. And that is just the way it is."

From downstairs, Jen heard her grandmother singing a church hymn. They came from two different planets. There were all kinds of things about her life that she could never tell Grams, because she'd never understand. But at least Grams was there for her, which was more than she could say for her parents. And her friends in Capeside were there for her, too, which was more than she could say for her so-called friends in New York.

Jen got out of bed, padded downstairs, and went into the kitchen. Her grandmother was in the process of taking away one table setting.

"Can I join you?" Jen asked.

Grams turned around. She took in Jen's long nightgown. "Not unless you dress properly for the table."

"Do you think just this once we could dispense with the rules, Grams? I thought we could have a nice dinner together. And I could tell you about the sweet sixteen."

Grams pressed her lips together, but put the second plate back on the table. "All right. Yes."

They sat down, and Grams said grace. Jen put a napkin on her lap and reached for the mashed potatoes. "Well, Grams, you wanted to hear about the party. It was fantastic," she began. "It was held in the most exquisite ballroom. There was an orchestra. And dancing."

"How lovely," Grams said happily, and passed the platter of chicken to Jen. "Ballroom dancing."

"And let me tell you about this oil painting of Courtney her mother had done . . ."

Jen went on and on, painting a beautiful picture of a fantasy party. As for the tawdry truth, *that* she could hash over with Joey. What a weird thought.

Were they going to be, well, friends?

* * *

Dawson walked in the house. His parents were watching television. They clicked it off immediately.

"Hi," he said.

"How was your weekend *at Pacey's*?" his father asked.

Dawson could tell from the tone of his father's voice that he was in major trouble. Chief Witter must have already called them.

Dawson sat down. "Mom, Dad, I lied to you. You know I wasn't at Pacey's for the weekend."

"You were in Albany at some rock concert," his mother said. "We've known that since yesterday when Doug Witter called us. He said the police were going to press charges against Pacey for stealing the truck."

Dawson shook his head as if to clear it. *"What?"*

"Someone told Doug where you guys were," Mitch said. "We've been frantic, Dawson. We had no way to track you down, no way to get—"

"Dad, we weren't anywhere near Albany."

"You weren't?" Gale asked. "Where were you then?"

"New York."

"City?" his mother asked incredulously.

Dawson nodded. "Joey went there with Jen for the weekend. We sort of . . . we decided to . . . join them."

"Follow them, you mean?" his father asked. "You took Witter's truck and followed Jen and Joey to New York? Have you completely taken leave of your senses?"

"That's one possible explanation," Dawson agreed.

Gale shook her head. "I just don't know what to

say to you, Dawson. Can you even imagine how worried we've been?"

"Now I can. But I didn't know that you knew. And what you knew wasn't the truth." He looked from his mom to his dad. They had never looked at him like that before. Like he had disappointed them. Let them down.

"I used poor judgment," Dawson added.

"This is much bigger than 'poor judgment,' " his father said. "Poor judgment is coming in a half hour after curfew. Poor judgment is a beer at a party. Dawson, we've always trusted you. And until now, you've never given us a reason not to."

"I'm sorry," Dawson said. "If I could do a total rewrite on this past weekend, believe me, I would."

Mitch sighed. "Well, your mom and I agree that we have to punish you for this. Grounding you is pointless. Everything you love is up in your room."

Not quite everything, Dawson thought.

"So we've decided to take away your VCR and your video camera for two weeks," his mother said.

"But I need my camera for film class!" Dawson cried.

"You should have thought of that before you pulled this stupid stunt," Mitch said. He turned to his wife. "Oh my god, I sounded exactly like my father just now. Scary."

Dawson got up. "All right. I accept my punishment. And while I could tell you that I'll never do anything this stupid again, the odds are that, as a teenager on the brink of adulthood, I will."

"I imagine that's so, Dawson," his father said.

"And your mom and I will be right here to kick your butt for it."

Dawson nodded. For some bizarre reason, the idea didn't upset him all that much. In fact, it didn't really upset him at all.

Even walking up to the house, Joey could hear the baby's colicky howls. She briefly considered turning around and rowing back over to Dawson's house. But she knew she couldn't do that. So she went inside.

Man, that kid has a set of lungs. Joey dropped her backpack in the living room. It was a mess. A bottle leaking milk lay on the battered coffee table. There was a pile of Pampers next to a mucky-looking teething ring. The carpet was littered with zwieback crumbs.

Home, sweet home.

Bessie came into the living room, the baby wailing in her arms. "Shhhhh," she crooned to him. "Poor little guy. Please stop crying." She looked up and saw Joey. "Thank God you're back." She made a beeline for her sister and dumped the baby into her arms.

"I have had to pee for the past hour but I didn't want to put him down." She hurried to the bathroom.

Alexander upped his decibel level. He was wet. He smelled like sour milk. "What's wrong with him?" Joey yelled to her sister.

"Teething!" Bessie called back. "The doctor told me it's normal. What the hell do I know?"

Joey sat on the couch with the infant. Something

stuck into her butt. She pulled it out. A rattle. She shook it at the baby. He swatted it away and kept crying.

This will never, ever be my life, she vowed, rocking the screaming baby in her arms. I will never get stuck with a baby and no money and no way out. And I will never get stuck in Capeside.

Bessie came back from the bathroom and sat next to Joey. The baby cried frantically and grabbed for her. She took him, rocked him, but it was futile. "I'm losing my mind here, Joey."

"Well, you picked it," Joey snapped before she could stop herself.

"What's that supposed to mean?"

"It means who told you to have a baby if you weren't ready to take care of a baby?" Joey asked.

"Some things just happen, Joey," Bessie said, an edge to her voice. "Look, can you take him for five minutes? Maybe change him? I need to call the restaurant." She didn't wait for an answer, and thrust Alexander at Joey.

"No!" Joey jumped up, ignoring Bessie's outstretched arms. "I don't want to take him. He's your responsibility, not mine. You had him, not me. So just deal with it!" Joey picked up her backpack and headed for her room.

"You give new meaning to the word 'selfish,' Joey!"

Joey wheeled around. "Me? How about a 'Welcome home, Joey.' Or 'Did you have fun, Joey?' But no. I walk right back into the same crap that was here when I left."

"Because I covered for your absent butt so you

could leave!" Bessie exclaimed. "I didn't mind, Joey. I was happy, because it was actually something that I could do for you. But forgive me if the world didn't stop while you were away. Contrary to what you think, it does not revolve around you."

"Nice, Bessie. Very Joan Crawford. I understand her kids screamed a lot, too." Joey stomped out of the room, went into her bedroom, and slammed the door so hard the whole house shook.

Pacey sat in the living room facing his father. He'd been shocked to find out that Deputy Doug had come home from the convention early and somehow had heard that Pacey and Dawson had gone to the Nightshade concert in Albany.

Not that it made any sense, but it did mean that all the time he'd been sweating it, playing Dudley Do-right to Mrs. Hanover, waiting for the service station to repair her spare tire, he was already in doo-doo of the deepest sort.

There was a certain irony to it that, if his father hadn't been about to kill him, Pacey might have even appreciated.

"If you and Dawson were not in Albany, Pacey," his father asked in measured tones, "then where were you?"

"New York City," Pacey replied. "To see friends."

"You stole my truck and went to New York to see friends," his father repeated.

"I don't supposed you'd consider plea-bargaining it down to 'borrowed'?" Pacey ventured.

His father leaned forward on the couch. "You

have no idea how close you came to spending tonight in my jail."

Pacey smiled. "You wouldn't do that."

"Damn straight I'd do that," his father said. "I probably should have. You're out of control, Pacey. The sad thing is, you think it's funny. It's all a big joke to you. I'm ashamed to call you my son."

There it was. That swift, lethal pain as the knife went in.

"Look, I messed up," Pacey admitted. "Can we just move on to the sentencing phase?"

His father's face mottled with anger. "Look at you. You've never done a decent thing in your life. You don't care about anyone but yourself. You made your own bed, Pacey. Now you can damn well lie in it. You know, there's a program for juvenile offenders in Utah—"

"Wait, wait," Pacey interrupted. "You can't be serious."

"As a heart attack. You're still subject to arrest for stealing my truck. And that's exactly what I intend to do."

"This scene would benefit from rewrites," Pacey said. His heart was hammering in his chest.

"I have nothing to say to you anymore, Pacey. I wash my hands of you."

Mr. Witter got up and went to the phone. But before he could place a call, it rang. He picked it up. "Chief Witter speaking," he said.

"Chief Witter," a cultured female voice said. "You don't know me. My name is Phyllis Hanover. I'm a retired county clerk. I live in Andover. I must speak with you about your son, Pacey."

Mr. Witter shook his head. "What did he do now, ma'am?"

"Well, he was wonderful, Chief Witter," the woman said. "My tire blew on the interstate this afternoon. Not only did your son stop to help me, he insisted on taking me to a service station that would repair it, and he didn't leave me until I was back on the road."

"Are you sure you're talking about my son?" Mr. Witter asked. "Pacey Witter?"

"I'm absolutely certain," the woman said. "I offered him a reward but he refused to take anything from me. So I just felt I had to look up your number and call you, to let you know what a truly remarkable son you have raised. You should be very proud of him, Mr. Witter."

"Yes, ma'am," Mr. Witter said. "Thanks for calling." He hung up and turned to Pacey. "That was a woman by the name of Phyllis Hanover. She met you this afternoon?"

"She did."

"She says you spent hours today helping her after she lost a tire."

"I was there," Pacey agreed.

"Why didn't you tell me about it?" Mr. Witter asked.

Pacey looked confused. "When? When you said you were ashamed I was your son? Or when you told me you were having me arrested?"

His father shook his head sadly and walked heavily from the room.

Pacey hurried after him. "Might I assume that my arrest is not imminent?"

177

His father didn't turn around. "No arrest, Pacey."

"And no Utah boot camp thing?"

"No Utah," his father said. Now he turned to his son. "I'll ground you just like I always ground you. You'll stay home for a while and then you'll weasel out of it until the next time. For the life of me, Pacey, I will never understand what makes you tick."

"That makes two of us, Dad," Pacey said. "That makes two of us."

Joey took the pillow off her head. She listened carefully. Could it be true? Yes! Alexander had finally stopped crying! She tiptoed into the living room, knowing from experience that any noise would wake the kid up again.

Her sister and the baby were asleep on the couch, the baby in Bessie's arms. Bessie looked like a wreck. Tired. Old. Worn out. It tore at Joey's heart. What had happened to her cool sister? When had she given up on her dreams?

When Mom died, Joey thought. She thought she had to be my mom. And her own mom. And now Alexander's mom, too.

Joey began to clean up some of the mess on the coffee table. At least when Bessie woke up it would be a little neater. The ring she'd bought in New York, now on her forefinger, caught her eye. The sun, the moon, and the stars. A dream ring, the artist had called it.

Joey pulled it off. Then she slowly, carefully, slipped it into Bessie's right hand. "I brought you something back from New York, Bessie," she whispered. "Sweet dreams."

She took the phone to her bedroom and punched in Dawson's number.

"Hello?" he answered.

"I see your parents allowed you to live," she said.

"They implied it might be temporary," Dawson replied.

"Isn't everything?" Joey asked. "I just called to say good night, Dawson. No clever exit lines. I know I should have one for every occasion and I'm a little disappointed in myself for being so unprepared but there you are. I won't be climbing in your window tonight. But I did want to hear the sound of your voice."

"Joey?"

"What?"

"Nothing. Just Joey."

"I haven't changed my mind about anything, Dawson. You need to know that."

"I know that. Joey?"

"What?"

"There's something I didn't tell you about this weekend," Dawson said. "I met a girl. A ballet dancer named Dixie. And even though I only knew her for the briefest time, something about her touched me."

"Why are you telling me this, Dawson?"

"You asked me to be honest," Dawson told her. "You were honest with me."

"Are you going to see this girl again?"

"I don't even know her last name," Dawson admitted. "And I realize that if I did get to know her, the reality of her might be nothing at all like my fantasy. I suppose I could simply be making her into what I want her to be. A new romantic heroine for Dawson. But for five minutes there, I felt like anything was possible."

A tenderness clutched Joey's heart. "Dawson?" she whispered.

"What?"

"Nothing," Joey said, smiling. "Just Dawson."

About the Creator/Executive Producer

Born in New Bern, North Carolina, Kevin Williamson studied theater and film at East Carolina University before moving to New York to pursue an acting career. He relocated to Los Angeles and took a job as an assistant to a music video director. Eventually deciding to explore his gift for storytelling, Williamson took an extension course in screenwriting at UCLA (University of California, Los Angeles).

Kevin Williamson has experienced incredible success in the film medium. His first feature film was *Scream,* directed by Wes Craven and starring Drew Barrymore, Courteney Cox, and Neve Campbell. He has also written other feature films including the psychological thriller *I Know What You Did Last Summer,* based on the Lois Duncan novel, and directed by Jim Gillespie. His first foray into television, *Dawson's Creek*™, has already received high praise from television critics for its honest portrayal of teen life.

About the Author

C. J. Anders is the pseudonym for a well-known young-adult fiction-writing couple.

A selected list of Dawson's Creek books available from Channel 4 Books

The prices shown below are correct at time of going to press. However, Channel 4 Books reserve the right to show new retail prices on covers which may differ from those previously advertised.

The Beginning of Everything Else	Jennifer Baker	£3.99
Long Hot Summer	K. S. Rodriguez	£3.99
Shifting Into Overdrive	C. J. Anders	£3.99
Major Meltdown	K. S. Rodriguez	£3.99
Double Exposure	C. J. Anders	£3.99
Trouble in Paradise	C. J. Anders	£3.99
Calm Before the Storm	Jennifer Baker	£3.99
Don't Scream	C. J. Anders	£3.99
Too Hot To Handle	C. J. Anders	£3.99
Dawson's Creek Omnibus 1	Baker/Rodriguez/Anders	£5.99*
Dawson's Creek Official Postcard Book		£6.99*

* Coming Soon

All Dawson's Creek titles can be ordered from your local bookshop or simply by ringing our 24 hour hotline on 01624 844444, email *bookshop@enterprise.net*, fax 01624 837033 or fill in this form and post it to B.S.B.P. Limited, PO Box 29, Douglas, Isle of Man IM99 1BQ.
Please make all cheques payable to Channel 4 Books.

Name ————————————————————————

Address ————————————————————————

————————————————————————————

————————————————————————————

Card Name: Visa ☐   American Express ☐   Mastercard ☐   Switch ☐ please tick one

Expiry date ——/——/——

POSTAGE AND PACKAGING FREE FOR ALL ADDRESSES IN THE UK

www.panmacmillan.com   www.channel4.com